She'd thought she could trust him, but now she wasn't so sure...

"Joel!" an angry voice sounded from across the room.

Every head turned in the direction Jackson came from as he strode across the room.

"Oh, shit," Josh mumbled, causing Jackson to throw a heavy scowl in his direction.

Joel didn't respond. He looked at Jackson with a curious expression but remained silent. He was on the defensive, Mia realised. She knew then that a media-based interrogation was about to come his way.

"What the hell is this?" Jackson demanded as he unfurled a newspaper in Joel's face.

Joel still remained silent. She noticed Charlie's mouth fall open and she heard Josh mutter, "Oh shit," again.

"Well?" Jackson demanded.

"Well, what?" Joel snapped.

"What the hell happened? What the hell do you think you're playing at?"

Joel didn't answer. He wasn't looking at Jackson, he was staring at Mia. Her eyes were riveted on the morning newspaper that Jackson was brandishing in Joel's face. She could feel anger and humiliation quickly beginning to rise in her chest.

Joel Coben in Wild After Show Party with Five Girls. Singer seen leaving show with mystery brunette.

The newspaper's front-page story boldly screamed out at her from Jackson's hand. She didn't need to read the rest of the story. There was a blazing photograph next to the headline and sub line that showed Joel clustered around numerous women.

"We're trying to get an album together. You're not on tour yet!" Jackson snapped at him.

Still he said nothing, just continued staring at Mia.

She felt humiliated.

Not only had Joel made a fool out of her, he had done it spectacularly in front of the entire studio. And her manager. And her friend.

"Bastard," she snapped at him before angrily storming away across the room and fumbling with her key card to swipe herself out of the building.

When struggling barmaid Mia Ryan is scouted from behind the beer taps of Dublin's Temple Bar and placed on a flight to Los Angeles, she can hardly believe her luck. Years of struggling to become a musician have seemingly paid off. When she's picked by lucrative Sixth String Studios to write songs for their biggest stars, she finally begins to feel at home among like-minded musicians, despite her haunted past. Then she meets Joel Coben. One of the biggest stars in the world and Sixth String Studios' prized possession, Joel's as famous as they come. He's also one of the rudest people Mia's ever met. Music eventually connects Mia and Joel, and slowly she begins to see behind the media-reluctant star to the man beneath. But can she trust her troubled past to someone who lives his life under the spotlight?

KUDOS for *Chasing Shadows*

In *Chasing Shadows* by Melissa Speight, Mia Ryan is a singer in an Irish pub in Dublin. Her dream is to break into the big time and record her music for the world to hear. She gets her chance when two Americans come to the pub to hear her sing. They offer her a three-month contract to come to Los Angeles to work as a song-writer. Not exactly what she had hoped for, but it's a foot in the door to the music recording world. Once in Los Angeles, Mia meets Joel Coben, the studio's mega superstar recording artist. To Mia, he seems rude and self-centered, and she doesn't understand why he spies on her every time she plays. As they get to know each other, Mia discovers the lost little boy behind the façade, and the two fall in love. But life soon gets very complicated for Joel and Mia as his past comes back to haunt them. This book is a great read for anyone who ever wondered what it's like to be rich and famous. Speight does an excellent job of describing the mixed-up crazy world of a superstar, combining a suspenseful plot with a sweet romance. ~ *Taylor Jones, Reviewer*

Chasing Shadows by Melissa Speight is the story of a young woman who dreams of becoming a star. Our heroine, Mia Ryan, lives in Dublin, Ireland, where she works as a waitress and part-time entertainer in a local tavern. One night, two Americans are in the audience and hear Mia perform. The result of that is a three-month contract for Mia to come to California and work at Sixth String Studios as a songwriter. Mia is ecstatic, thinking her dreams are coming true at last. But life in LA isn't exactly what she was expecting…Still, things aren't all bad. Mia falls in love with none other than the studio's top star Joel Coben, so life should be great, right? Well, not so much. Joel is a troubled soul whose past has been hard and whose life seems to go from one crisis to another, dragging Mia along with him. *Chasing Shadows* gives us a glimpse into a world that so many people dream about, but very few really understand. With a strong plot that is full of surprises and a heart-warming romance, it's a book that will strike a chord with readers of all *ages*. ~ *Regan Murphy, Reviewer*

CHASING SHADOWS

Melissa Speight

A Black Opal Books Publication

Black Opal Books

BECAUSE SOME STORIES JUST HAVE TO BE TOLD

GENRE: CONTEMPORARY ROMANCE/ROMANTIC SUSPENSE

CHASING SHADOWS
Copyright © 2016 by Melissa Speight
Cover Design by Matt Cheetham
All cover art copyright © 2015
All Rights Reserved
Print ISBN: 978-1-626943-94-0

First Publication: JANUARY 2016

Published by Black Opal Books **http://www.blackopalbooks.com**

for my mum

CHAPTER 1

Placing the last box carefully into the back of the hired car, Mia turned to say her goodbyes.

Sharon's eyes began to tear the instant Mia faced her.

It wasn't that she was leaving forever, although Sharon had made her feel as though she were immigrating to Australia.

"Promise you'll call us as soon as you get there?" Sharon asked while dabbing the corners of her eyes.

Mia rolled her eyes before laughing. "I promise."

Mike's eyes wandered over the boxes piled high in the car. "Drive carefully, and not too fast either, remember all the luggage you've got in the back here."

"I know, I know," she said, offering a smile, "I'll be fine, honest."

An awkward silence then lingered in the air. Throwing her hands into the pockets of her jeans, Mia began to thumb the waistband. Only knowing the pain it would cause Sharon and Mike was making her sad to be leaving. She loved them, and she was eternally grateful to them for everything they had done for her, but there would always be that one thing missing in their relationship. It would never have the one thing she needed it to have. The nagging, empty feeling that had hovered in the corners of her heart, from her infancy, would always taint their relationship.

That feeling had always been there. Though she hadn't been old enough to understand, Mia knew. And despite her upbringing with Mike and Sharon, she knew ultimately what their relationship was. She looked at them both hesitantly. "Right, I guess I'll be going then."

They both stared back at her. Sharon wasn't bothering to hide her tears anymore and Mia even noticed Mike's eyes were glistening. Realising she had never seen him cry made her understand the impact her leaving was having on their lives.

But her time had come, and what had to be done, would be done.

Sharon put her hand on Mia's arm. "Are you sure about this?"

Mia squeezed her arm. "One hundred per cent. I have to try."

"You'll do great, sweetheart. I know you're gonna make it big," Mike said.

Pride glowed in his face and forced her to swallow the rising lump in her throat. She hoped he was right.

Mike was a tall, strong, and gentle type of man. He didn't believe in speaking unless he had something decent to say, so Mia admired his honesty.

"Thank you," she stepped forward and gave him a hug. He wrapped his strong arms around her and squeezed her tightly, before quickly letting her go again.

"Come here you." Sharon dashed toward Mia and pulled her close. Immediately, she felt all the air in her lungs being forced from them as her body was held in a vice-like clamp. Tears began to soak through the shoulder of her T-shirt, as Sharon held her close, and she knew then how much the moment was hurting her. After all these years, she finally had to let Mia go.

Saying her final goodbyes, Mia then climbed into the car. She started the engine and wound down the window as she pulled out of the driveway of the little house on the coast. Inhaling deeply, she allowed the fresh ocean air to fill her lungs. She could smell brine in the air from the ocean and the fishing port farther along the coast. Where the rolling green hills and fields sloped toward the sea, and the rocky coastline finally met the water's edge, she took one final look at the gentle, yet rugged, coastline. The town populated the coast and houses were dotted snugly between trees as they came farther inland. Mia smiled to herself, committing the image to her memory, hoping it wouldn't be too long until she saw the picturesque little town that she called home again.

She watched them waving at the end of the driveway in her rear-view mirror and thrust her hand out of the open window into the fresh, crisp air billowing past the car to wave back. The sea rolled gently in toward the land in the distance and, as the picturesque coastline began to fade in her view, so did Mike and Sharon.

Sighing heavily, Mia knew the inevitable lay ahead. Her heart was torn in two—although not in equal halves.

The smaller half of her heart longed to stay in the sleepy little coastal town of Kinsale, with Michael and Sharon, where everything was familiar and safe. Where she could work her shifts in the local pub every week and, once she finished early on a weekend, step from behind the bar to behind the microphone. She could stay in her hometown, comfortable and content, playing to her crowd of regular patrons every week or she could pack up and leave.

She had opted to follow the larger half.

The larger half of her heart longed for a life she envisioned in her mind each and every second of the day. Those seconds she spent longing to while away her days in a recording studio, strumming away at her guitar for hours and hours and writing endless songs behind studio doors to be played out in the arena by her idols.

Mia shook her head. She had to follow her heart. Her life was for living and she had to live it her way. There was no way she could stay in Kinsale for the rest of her life. She wasn't a dreamer, she was a doer. She had to take her chances and make a shot at what she believed in. The rest of her life couldn't be spent feeling relatively content and yet always wondering.

Life hadn't had the easiest of beginnings for Mia, not that she remembered it very much. She hadn't had the most conventional of starts, but she was grateful for the chance Mike and Sharon had given her. She was grateful for them taking her in when she needed someone most. They had given her a lifetime of love and support and she knew that they would always be there for her. No matter what the origins of their relationship, they would be behind her one hundred per cent.

But Mia knew. She still felt the emptiness eating away at her. She knew her time would come and, although it was two years later than it should have been, it was time for her to leave. Mike and Sharon had allowed her to stay with them long after they shouldn't have, but her conscience and her ambition had won out in the end. Their goodwill was endless and Mia knew they would have allowed her to stay with them forever.

But Mia was an orphan.

Mike and Sharon were her adoptive parents.

The agency had insisted that she move out and find her own way in life as soon as she turned eighteen, but Mike and Sharon had allowed her to stay. Two years on, Mia had decided to follow her heart and make the move she longed for. Leaving her job and her adoptive parents behind to chase her dreams of song writing and making music, Mia was moving to the city of Dublin.

CHAPTER 2

Three years later:

Laughing to herself, Mia opened her card. She hadn't looked forward to turning twenty-three. In her head, it sounded just that little bit older than she liked.

Although she told herself she was being stupid, she couldn't help it, and Sharon had taken full advantage of how she felt. The birthday card told a joke about the recipient's age, along with a not-so flattering picture of the birthday girl after one too many drinks. If her colleagues had anything to do with it, Mia knew there was a strong possibility she would end up resembling that image later that night. Placing the card on the kitchen counter, she made a mental note to call them both later that evening after her show.

Mia shrugged on her jacket before picking up her bag. She rummaged around inside to find her phone, quickly sending Sharon a thank you text and promising to call later. She grabbed her beloved guitar from the sofa and packed it into its case before she headed out of the door and into the cool March air.

The streets were busier than usual, and more tourists were heading to the city in the onset of St. Patricks Day. Although it wasn't for a week or so yet, the streets were packed with swarming crowds that stared glassy eyed at the numerous bars and pubs they passed in the city.

Mia always took delight in watching them. It never ceased to amaze people that they couldn't walk far in Dublin without encountering a pub where the sounds of a live musician were resonating from within onto the street outside.

Three years had passed since she packed up her things into the boot of a car and had made the life-changing decision to move from the other end of Ireland to Dublin. Thinking of the card on her worktop, she smiled wistfully as she remembered Sharon's words to her when she announced her decision.

"If you're brave enough to say goodbye, life will reward you with a new hello," Sharon had enthusiastically told her through tear-brimmed eyes.

Mia sighed as she thought back to those words, wondering when life was going to finally reward her with the promised new hello.

While she enjoyed living in Dublin—in fact she adored the city—she was still struggling along as she chased her dreams.

She had settled into her small flat that was a stone's throw away from the shops and bars, and she had quickly found work in Glen's Tavern in the heart of the city's thriving Temple Bar. Her job had allowed her to make friends quickly, most of whom were aspiring musicians like her who took to the streets and stages of Temple Bar each night in the hopes of being spotted for their talent. Some were simply happy to share their gifts with the throes of tourists who swarmed that particular area of the city each evening and after dark.

While Mia loved being around like-minded people, having others who saw and thought of life the same way she did—through music—she still wondered if anything more would come of her talent.

Every tourist, local, musician, and colleague told her how much her songs touched their hearts, how her words echoed the unspoken thoughts of everyday troubles, and how she poured her heart and soul onto the stage. Mia was indifferent to performing. She did it for the love of her music, and it was the only way her songs would be heard. Song writing was where her heart lay, in the ability to pour her every feeling onto a piece of paper and bring those unspoken words to life. She felt at home when she was writing, as if she could write anything to anyone. She could express exactly how she felt.

Most of her music, despite the beliefs of her friends, was about her heartache. Anyone who heard Mia's songs assumed she was singing about a broken relationship. They wondered who could cause such pain and desperation to someone so young, what kind of man left a girl feeling so alone? After she finished her sets, they would always ask her the same questions as she stood at the bar.

"Who is he?"

"Does your ex-boyfriend know you sing about him like that?"

"What did he do to you that was so bad?"

"I'd never do those things to you. Can I buy you a drink?"'

"How on earth do you write songs like that? I felt like you were singing every thought I've ever had."

As always, Mia simply smiled in return.

ⓔⓢⓔⓢ

Pushing open the door to the bar, Mia made her way through the swarms of people clustered around the place. She lifted up the hatchet to the bar and slid underneath.

"Hey, Mia, happy birthday," Ben called from across the bar as he poured a pint.

"Thanks," she called back over the hum of noise.

Ben was a sweetheart. He was a charmer with the ladies and the typical Irish boy the tourists loved to watch pour their pint of Guinness. Though he wasn't much taller than Mia, his blond hair, blue eyes, and dimpled smile made up for his lack of height. She couldn't help noticing three young girls gathered at the other end of the bar, who were eagerly watching Ben work.

"Mia! Why are you working on your birthday?" the loud, thick accent of Niamh's voice called over the kitchen galley as she bustled toward Mia.

As always, Mia heard her before she saw her. "Girl's gotta eat, gotta pay the rent, y'know?"

Mia laughed as Niamh shook her head at her before embracing her warmly.

Niamh's messy dark ponytail bobbed as she cocked her head to one side. "Sweetie, it's your birthday, you are allowed a night off."

"And where else would I want to be tonight?" Mia mimicked her actions before dashing away to store her jacket, bag, and guitar upstairs.

"Can't say I'd disagree with you," she heard Niamh call upstairs after her.

e/ɔe/ɔ

Smoothing her ponytail one final time in the mirror before pulling the strings of her apron tighter over her jeans, she was ready for work in minutes. It was only a short apron and Mia was grateful she didn't have to wear a hideous uniform to work. All Glen asked was that they wore clean, neat jeans and a white or black T-shirt with the bar's name on the back.

Glen was her boss and he had owned Glen's Tavern for several years. Mia still had no idea how he had acquired the place. Rumours ran rife around the bar that Glen was a lottery winner, a dealer in various things—or substances in the worst rumours—or had inherited riches. Her own theory was simply that he was a hard worker who had invested his savings in his dream of running a bar in Dublin. Many tried and failed. There was simply too much competition in the city, but those who succeeded often made a profitable living from the tourists lapping up the Irish music scene.

He was a quiet, private sort of man, and Mia understood why Glen kept to himself. Sometimes silence was the best answer. *Say nothing and they'll know nothing*, she thought. He was a tall, slim man with a shaved head and had tattoos across his upper arms. Glen was the type of boss who only said what needed to be said and, in doing so, he had made her feel at home straight away. He reminded her of a younger Mike. She had never seen him raise his voice at anyone and, when he knew the place was being run well, he left his staff to it. Mia couldn't ask for a better boss. He had given her a job when she had desperately needed one, and he had given her a stage to perform on. After hearing her play, he immediately gave her a prime slot every Friday and Saturday evening on his stage and paid her wages each week, never asking any questions about her music, her lyrics, or her past. Mia was grateful for the silent, understanding, mind-your-own-business qualities in her boss.

Unlike Niamh.

Niamh's face appeared around the corner of the doorway as Mia prepared to step behind the bar. "What are you playing tonight?"

"A few crowd pleasers, maybe a couple of covers, and I'm going to try a new song I've been working on for a while, too."

"Sounds great. Did you hear anything from that company?"

"No." Mia sighed.

Niamh was referring to another record label Mia had tried to pitch her music to a few weeks ago. There was no word from them yet.

"Keep your chin up, sweetie, I got a feeling something big is right around the corner for you." She winked before dashing away to clear some glasses from a nearby table.

Mia rolled her eyes and grinned to herself.

Niamh was a force to be reckoned with. Twenty-five years old, tiny in height and body but with eyes and vocal chords larger than many twice her size, Niamh was Mia's best friend. Mia loved her to pieces and admired her eccentricity and confidence. With that natural confidence that Mia secretly envied, Niamh carried on with her shift, sashaying around the bar chatting to patrons between clearing tables, ducking, and weaving her tiny self through the crowds.

Glen had agreed it made sense to have Niamh work the floor. She was too tiny to see much over the bar taps and she easily squeezed between the crowds to clear the tables faster than anyone else could.

Ben was the clean-cut charmer behind the bar. Dylan was the other bartender who personified the moody, troubled rock star image. Niamh kept up everyone's spirits, and Mia filled the space in between. Along with his wife Leah, Glen often helped out during the busier periods, but at present they were alternating between supervising and drinking with their friends at a nearby table. Either Glen or Leah would step in when Mia's shift ended in a few hours.

"Happy birthday, beautiful." Dylan gave Mia a kiss on the cheek as she joined him and Ben behind the bar.

"Thank you and thanks, you guys, for the present," she said.

All the staff had clubbed together to buy her a silver necklace with an artistic silver guitar pendant hanging from the chain.

Dylan raised a dark eyebrow at her. "Not too clichéd?"

"No, not at all, it's perfect." She glanced up from the pendant to see Dylan eyeing her sceptically.

"If you say so." He looked at the nape of her neck where the chain hung. "It looks good on you, though."

"Thanks, Dylan, you're always such a charmer," she teased.

Dylan usually tried not to show his emotions. Mia was sure he thought it helped him with his rock star persona. She knew deep down that he was a kind soul. He just had a habit of allowing his music, and the accompanying lifestyle, to get in the way of that. Sometimes he would allow his true personality to show through and Mia preferred the Dylan she saw underneath the image. When he wasn't acting the rock star in front of a harem of women, he could be funny and charming.

Tonight, however, Dylan had an audience and so the image was firmly in place. He wore the same outfit to work he usually did—a pair of dark blue jeans tucked into his boots and a tight white T-shirt that contrasted with his dark hair and eyes. Dylan would saunter up and down the bar, serving customers and keeping his eyes averted, perfecting his troubled soul image. But he never left the place alone. His dedication paid off and by the end of his shift, he always left with a girl on his arm, one who fell for his image hook, line and sinker.

Mia shook her head at Ben as she noticed Dylan begin serving the three girls who had previously been admiring Ben. Looking across at them, he simply laughed before shrugging his shoulders in a *what-you-gonna-do* way.

Taking one final glance at Dylan, working his magic on the trio of girls, Mia laughed again before beginning to serve the crowd in front of her.

She began to pour the first pint of beer. Through the crowds, she didn't notice the two men walk through the door and wait to be served a few places down the bar.

❦❦❦

Stacking yet more empty beer glasses into the dishwasher, Mia looked over her shoulder as another customer appeared at the bar. She hurriedly filled the rack and slammed the door shut before flipping the switch and hearing the loud sloshing noises as the dishwasher whirred to life. Wiping her hands across her apron, she took a swift glance at her watch. Ten more minutes until her shift was up and then she could pick up her guitar and get up on the stage, where another local band was currently butchering Poison's "Nothing But A Good Time."

As she flipped the tap to pour the customer's beer, Mia

laughed to herself as she watched the lead singer belting out the words and leaning over the stage into the crowd. The band wasn't particularly good, but Glen still booked them time and time again. The lead singer had stage presence and never failed to get the crowd warmed up. It was a shame they couldn't sing and play a little better. Despite those thoughts, she still tapped her foot along to the beat and murmured the words of the classic song as she waited for the glass to fill.

"Are all the band's that play here this bad?"

The customer whose drink Mia was pouring snapped her out of her thoughts.

She laughed again. "No," and shook her head. "No, they're not. These guys are kind of a warm up act."

He arched an eyebrow at her, a quizzical smile on his face.

"They're not, I promise. I'm playing next," she added.

"You are?" The man's quizzical smile then turned into genuine curiosity.

Mia noticed the American accent in his voice. *More tourists*, she thought.

"Being a barmaid isn't my lifelong ambition, you know."

He laughed again. "No, that's not what I meant. You're just a little different from Poison tribute acts."

"Yeah." Mia smirked. "I should hope so."

"Can you make that two?" The man nodded to the beer glass as Mia placed it on the bar in front of him and handed her a twenty Euro note.

"Sure."

She noticed another man join him at his side. Both were smartly dressed in clothes that looked too expensive to fit in with the usual tourist crowd that Glen's Tavern pulled in. Overhearing the second man's accent as he spoke to his friend, Mia noticed he was also American.

Not that American accents were unusual in the capital city, but the well-dressed business-like types were an unusual sight in Glen's. It just wasn't the type of place they came to after a long day at the office.

Glen's Tavern had a tendency to attract more tourists and aspiring musicians than suited professionals.

He turned to smile at Mia as she attempted to hand him the coins. "Keep the change."

"Thanks." She shrugged and placed the generous amount of change in the tips jar on the bar.

He nodded at her as he raised his beer to his lips. "I think we're going to stick around to hear your set."

"Thanks," Mia repeated, eyeing him with suspicion, "I hope you like it."

She turned to leave, untying the strings on her apron as she left, still feeling the man's eyes on her back as she exited from behind the bar.

As she picked up her guitar case from beside the lockers, Mia heard the cheers of the crowd as the tribute band left the stage downstairs. She knew their loud cheers were more for the band's enthusiasm than their musical ability but she still hoped the crowd cheered as loudly for her when her set was over.

Mia never failed to receive a rapturous applause from the crowd, but as the audience was a varying mix of regular customers and ever-changing tourists, she was always nervous about the reception her music would receive each time she took to the stage.

She made her way through the crowds, receiving hugs and pats on the back from the band as they passed her on her way to the stage. The crowd began to hush their cheering as Mia prepared the stage and the usual quiet murmur of conversation once again filled the bar as they waited for her to begin.

After plugging in her guitar, adjusting the strings, and sound checking the microphones and amplifiers, Mia took a seat on the stool in front of the microphone and nodded to Glen who was waiting at the side of the stage.

"And now, ladies and gentlemen, would you please put your hands together and give a huge round of applause for our very own barmaid, the very talented, Mia Ryan."

She placed her hand on the guitar neck and her fingers effortlessly moved into place over the strings as she waited for the crowd to quiet again.

As the applause hushed, she began her song. Her fingers gracefully switched across the strings as she changed chords, the pick in her right hand gently strumming away at the guitar. She reached the first verse and began to sing. The moment she began to sing, Mia felt as though she were alone in the room.

Music was her solace and, despite being on a stage in front of a few hundred people, she felt as though no one else were in the room the moment she became enveloped in her song.

In her music, she poured out her heart and soul. Despite singing about her darkest moments and deepest thoughts in front of a bar full of people, she felt as though only she alone knew what those words meant.

Because she did.

Each night that she took to the stage, the crowd would lap up her songs, whispering to each other at how heart breaking the lyrics were, or the regulars would sing along to the words they had heard before. Only Mia knew who and what she was truly singing about.

Despite knowing that the place had quieted to hear her perform, that Ben and Dylan had stopped serving customers at the bar to stand and watch her, she saw none of them. Niamh was standing to the side of the stage, her eyes glued to Mia as she quietly sang along to the familiar songs she had heard before.

Glen was also standing close to the stage, his arms wrapped around Leah as they both watched her sing, but she saw none of them. The gentle spotlight was pointed directly at her in the center of the stage and the rest of the bar was in soft darkness, but Mia could have been anywhere in the world, for as she came to the end of her first song, the bar and everyone around her had drifted away with the sound of her music.

CHAPTER 3

Groggily opening her eyes, Mia frowned at the shrill ringing that was piercing through her slumber.

Squinting around the room for the source of the noise that had so rudely awoken her, she noticed her mobile phone illuminated and ringing on the bedside table.

Squinting even harder at the caller ID, Mia groaned.

"Hi, Sharon," she mumbled, running a hand over her eyes.

"Someone sounds happy this morning." Sharon's voiced chirped a little too loudly down the phone. "Did you have a good birthday?"

"Fantastic," Mia grumbled. Truthfully, she had. After her set, she had stayed in the bar with her colleagues and friends until closing time. Once Glen had shooed the last of the customers out of the door, he reopened the bar for the staff to celebrate her birthday. Needless to say, Mia had stayed longer than she had intended and had forgotten to call Sharon that night as promised.

"How did the show go?" Sharon shrilled through her thoughts again.

"Yeah, it went great, same old, you know?"

"Don't worry, Mia, it will happen for you, just be patient."

"I hope you're right."

"I am, trust me. Why don't you audition for that television show?"

Mia groaned. Sharon had tried for years to persuade her to audition for a television talent show and she flat out refused every time.

"Sharon—" she said, beginning the same speech she had already given time and time again.

"You never know if you don't try, love."

"It's just not how I want to start my career. Those singers never last more than five minutes anyway."

"It's a foot in the door of the industry?" Sharon would never give up.

"Sorry, it's just not for me. It's not my kind of thing."

Though Mia loved singing and playing guitar, she would feel ridiculously out of her comfort zone performing on one of those shows. The huge stage productions and covers of cheesy songs left her cringing. She was only happy singing her own music and music that she loved. She didn't want to be played like a puppet on national television. Truthfully, Mia could live without the limelight. The music was all that mattered to her.

Sharon exhaled in defeat. "So what else happened last night?"

Mia stayed on the phone with her for another twenty minutes, relaying everything that had happened on her birthday, the present that her colleagues had bought her, and that she still hadn't heard from the recording company.

After twenty minutes, Mia hung up the phone and rolled over in bed, burying herself among the covers. As she began to drift back to sleep, nestled in her covers and still feeling a little worse for wear, the shrill ringing noise started again.

Pulling the pillow over her head, she groaned louder than before but the ringing continued.

Praying that it wasn't Glen calling her in to work at lunchtime, she reached out and grabbed the phone. When she saw Niamh's face on the screen, she managed a sigh of relief.

"Hey," she mumbled.

Niamh made an incoherent noise down the other end of the phone. "Do you feel half as bad as I do right now?"

"Yeah, it sounds like it."

"Whose idea was it to bring out the whiskey?"

"Umm…yours I think," Mia struggled through blurred memories in her mind.

"Ugh." Niamh sighed down the phone. "I need coffee."

"That sounds pretty good right now," Mia agreed, but she resented the need to get out of bed to find coffee as her head pounded with every move she made.

"I'll be round in half an hour."

Mia smiled to herself as she hung up the phone. Niamh really was a good friend. Mia still wondered how she had been so lucky to find her. No matter what she did, Niamh would be there for her. Mia could rely on her for anything. *Even for those dreadful, feeling and looking like death moments,* she thought as she stumbled to the bathroom and looked at her reflection.

Instantly regretting thinking the "looking like death moments" metaphor as a pair of bloodshot green eyes stared back at her, Mia ran her hand through her long brown hair and turned on the shower to freshen up. Feeling the hot water run across her face and down her body, she instantly began to feel more awake. Although running water lacked the power to dispel the still pounding sensation in her head, Mia managed to feel fresher and less groggy than before. After standing under the shower for much longer than usual, she realised Niamh would be arriving soon. Not wanting the pounding on her front door to add to the pounding in her head, Mia hopped out of the shower and wrapped a warm towel around herself as she went in search of clothes.

Throwing on a pair of jeans and a faded AC/DC T-shirt, Mia rubbed her still damp hair with the towel before scraping it back into a damp, messy ponytail. She was ready just in time for the knock on her front door.

"Damn, how do you manage to look so good without make up?" Niamh rolled her eyes as she swept past Mia and into the flat, shoving a Styrofoam take-out coffee cup into her hand as she passed.

"Good morning to you too," Mia replied as she sipped her coffee, shutting the door behind Niamh.

"It's true, I look absolutely horrendous. I swear the guy in the café actually *recoiled* from the till when I walked up to the counter."

Mia laughed. "I doubt that."

Niamh did look a little tired but she was still as beautiful as ever. She looked up at Mia under her eyebrows in a *you-weren't-there-so-you-didn't-see-it* expression.

Mia held up her hands in surrender and laughed again. "Fine."

"Anyway, I've brought food." Niamh held up a bag in her hand and Mia instantly noticed the smell of bacon sandwiches filling the kitchen.

"Oh, you're an angel." Mia sighed, knowing that combined with coffee, the sandwiches would instantly make her feel better.

"I know." Niamh shrugged, she turned around and began opening cupboard doors, "I'm sure you have some aspirin in here somewhere."

"Third one along." Mia shook her head and grabbed the delicious smelling bag from the counter. "I'll be in the living room."

℘↶℘↶

A day curled up on the sofa, watching films and drinking coffee with Niamh, was exactly what Mia had needed.

They had lounged around her flat all day, watching girlie romcoms and feeling sorry for themselves. Relaxing with Niamh had eventually allowed Mia's head to return to feeling normal. At first, even laughing at the films made their sore heads hurt, but eventually the effects of food and caffeine kicked in and, reluctantly, they knew they would have to face the inevitable.

Mia nudged her friend with her foot. "Come on, time to move."

Niamh, who was curled up at the other end of the sofa, grumbled in reply.

"*Come on*, we need to go," Mia tried again, nudging harder.

"No," came a muffled reply as Niamh pulled the blanket over her head.

Laughing as she got up from the sofa and knowing exactly how Niamh felt, Mia inevitably knew they would be late for work if Niamh didn't get up soon.

Reaching under the blanket, she grabbed her by her ankles and pulled her away from the sofa. Niamh screamed out in shock and then burst into fits of giggles before trying to crawl back into the corner of the sofa, "No, you can't make me, get off!"

Mia doubled over laughing as she tried to hang on to Niamh's ankles and pull harder.

"Get up!"

"No!" Niamh tried to pull away but Mia was holding on too tight.

Giving another tug, Mia pulled Niamh away from the sofa and onto the floor with a loud bump. Despite pretending she was in pain, both girls collapsed into hysterical giggles as Niamh landed on the floor. "Okay, all right, I'm up," Niamh managed breathlessly through her laughter.

Heaving herself up off the floor before offering her hand to Niamh to help her up, Mia then reluctantly began clearing away the evidence of their lazy afternoon from her living room.

Folding up the blanket, Niamh asked, "Are you playing again tonight?"

"Yeah, I am," she answered as she pulled her hair from its ponytail and began combing through her thick hair in the mirror on the living room wall.

Niamh winked at her. "Good job we didn't get you too drunk last night then."

Mia shook her head at the memories. "I think you guys did pretty well to be honest."

At first, her birthday celebrations had been blurred and indistinguishable when she woke, but as the day had worn on, piece by piece, the night had come back to her. She remembered playing a drinking game with Ben and Dylan, involving far too many shots of whiskey. Then she remembered Glen turning up the music system, to a deafeningly loud level, followed by jumping on the bar with Niamh and Leah as they danced away to the pounding rock music.

Yes, she had drunk far too much, but she had had one hell of a birthday. It had been perfect. Just her friends and colleagues in their own private party inside Glen's Tavern, with loud music, dancing, and good times.

The morning-after-feeling has been worth it, after all, Mia thought.

Niamh winked again with a devilish smile on her face. "There's always tonight."

٤/ى٤/ى

Glen's Tavern was equally as crowded as the night before when Mia walked through the door after Niamh. Friday's and Saturday's always pulled in a good crowd, which gave her even more reason to be grateful to Glen for giving her the biggest crowds of the week to perform to. He could have easily let her make do with a Monday or any other week night. Mia was grateful he appreciated her music enough to give her two of the best slots of the week.

Ben grinned at both girls as he held open the hatchet to the bar for them. Glen had chosen to keep the old-fashioned hatchet on the bar to prevent over-boisterous customers from wandering behind it and helping themselves.

"How are we feeling today, ladies?" Ben asked, still grinning.

Niamh playfully slapped him on the arm as she sauntered past. "Exactly how you feel, I suppose."

"Always a pleasure, Niamh," Ben retorted as she threw him a wicked smile that made her huge eyes sparkle. "And you too, Mia," he added as he put down the hatchet, his other arm gently touching hers as she passed.

Mia returned the gesture, grateful that she had friends like them both. And, of course, it helped that Ben was ridiculously cute. Not that she would ever consider her friendship with Ben extending beyond that, but it helped when your friends were so easy on the eyes.

Even easier on the eyes was Dylan, who was too busy talking to the female customers he was serving to notice Mia and Niamh arrive. She saw him tensing his arm as his fingers curled around the beer tap in front of him, and one of the women was openly staring at his upper arm. *Subtle*, Mia thought.

Quickly dropping their stuff in their lockers and Mia's guitar in the upstairs staff room, they hurried back down to the bar, as the evening rush was underway. As always, Mia took a sneaky glance at her watch and mentally began counting down the hours until she would be back on stage where she belonged.

ℰᔕℰᔕ

"Heads up, Mia!" Ben called from one side of the bar.

"What the—" Mia looked up just in time to see a pint glass twirling through the air toward Dylan, who was casually waiting to catch it at the other side.

She squealed in shock and ducked out of the way, just in the nick of time.

Dylan artfully caught the glass in one hand, gave it another twirl in his fingers, before placing it under the beer tap in front of a group of giggling girls.

A cheer erupted around the bar as waiting customers had watched the two of them perform. Mia slapped Ben on his arm as she reached past him to grab a glass.

He grinned as he filled a glass with coke from a handheld plastic tap. "Y'know, I could have passed you one?"

"I don't like your methods, thank you very much." She tried to stifle a smile. Though working behind the bar with Ben and Dylan was sometimes risky, Mia always wound up laughing until her stomach muscles hurt.

"I've no idea what you're talking about?" His eyes sparkled as he taunted her by twirling another glass in front of her with one hand, the other hand palm upturned in questioning.

"Oh, I think you do." She chuckled, giving him a gentle nudge on the shoulder as she moved around him, easily navigating her way to the drinks she needed for her customers.

Ben quickly grabbed the glass before it fell, spinning it once more before throwing it to Dylan's casually waiting hand.

They made it look effortless. Dylan didn't even watch the glass fly across the bar. He caught it one handed while continuing his conversation with his admiring crowd.

Mia rolled her eyes. There would be no glasses left in Glen's if she joined in their act.

They switched sides. Dylan, moving across to the other side of the bar, flipped a glass behind his back for Ben to catch as they crossed each other. A customer whooped while several others cheered and clapped.

Their act could sometimes pull in more of a crowd than the musician onstage could, depending on who was playing. Mia laughed as she watched Dylan move to her side.

"Having fun?" he asked. A playful grin danced across his dark features as he leaned in a little too close.

Mia put a finger on his chest and pushed him back into his own personal space. "Of course," she replied.

"You're gonna miss us when you hit the big time, superstar." His top lip curled up in the corner as he smiled a suggestive smile—a look that Dylan had spent years mastering.

She laughed. "As if I could forget about you two."

He raised his eyebrows as he leaned in too close again. "Baby, I can make sure you never forget about me,"

Mia raised her own back at him, in a non-suggestive manner. "Does that line actually work for you?"

Dylan scowled and feigned being hurt. "Yeah, usually."

Giggling as she shoved him out of her way to serve the waiting customers, Mia noticed one customer had been watching her conversation with Dylan.

The well-dressed American man from the night before was casually rolling a twenty-euro note between his fingers as he waited to be served.

If Mia had had to guess his age, she would have placed him in his mid-thirties. He rested on the bar on his forearms as he stood and Mia wondered if the sleeves of his suit jacket would end up covered in stale beer. *More than likely*, she thought.

His blond hair was cut short and neatly styled, but gave the impression of an expensive haircut that someone had paid a few hundred dollars for. What little skin she could see was fairly tanned and complemented the color of his dark blue suit. Mia had to admit, he would have been fairly attractive, if it wasn't for the standoffish behavior. The man's companion from the night before was also standing beside him, dressed equally as smart. Though the African-American man he was with always eyed Mia with a look that seemed to be evaluating her every move. Taking a deep breath, she walked over to where he was leaning on the bar.

"What can I get you?" she asked.

"Two beers, please," he asked as he quickly looked up from rolling the note in his fingers.

She felt both pairs of eyes follow her as she reached above her head for glasses and began to fill them.

"That was a great set you did last night," the blond man said.

Despite the beer tap partially obstructing her view, Mia could have sworn she saw the other man elbow him.

"Thank you." She tried to sneak a glance around the glass in front of her vision.

"Do you play here every Friday?" he continued.

"Yeah, every Friday and Saturday." She set down the first glass and realised the African American man was glowering at his friend.

"Awesome." He nodded. "So you're playing tonight?"

Mia raised her eyebrows sarcastically at him over the beer tap. "As tonight is Saturday, yeah I am."

His smile met his pale blue eyes, as he laughed. "Just checking."

He handed her the note and once again left an overly generous tip with his change. Leaving the bar, he followed his companion as he made his way through the crowd to find a table. One that was fairly close to the stage, Mia noticed.

"Who's that?" Dylan's voice sounded at her ear and Mia felt his breath on her skin.

"I have no idea," she said, noticing how close he was standing as always.

"Hmm…" Dylan mused. "There's something about those two."

She looked up at Dylan's brooding face. For once, the brooding wasn't being staged for an admiring female audience. Mia knew what he meant. There was something about the two Americans that put her on her guard.

"I know what you mean," she replied, taking a subtle step to one side as Dylan was invading her personal space yet again.

❧❧❧

Strumming the final note on her guitar, Mia heard the sound echo around the room for a brief moment before the whole bar erupted in applause. Pushing away the surging emotions that were toiling away behind her eyes, she stood up from her stool and gave a small bow to the crowd. Desperately willing the tears not to surface, she tried to focus on the overwhelming response she was receiving.

As they always did whenever she played, images and fading memories flashed in front of her eyes, shutting out the crowd completely, as if she were playing to those memories alone, the sound of the music keeping them alive before her. Each time she sang the words, she felt the rising surge of emotion that threatened to come pouring forth, and each time she had to force it away as she rose from her seat, pushing her feet onto the stage as she pushed them away. It never got any easier.

Some of the lights began to come up and she saw people cheering and clapping in front of her. Niamh was jumping up and down in applause close to the stage. Glen and Leah were clapping too and she could see Ben and Dylan standing on the bar as they cheered and whooped their support at her from across the room.

People standing in front of the stage were cheering and those seated at the tables around the dance floor were on their feet clapping. Mia took a moment before she descended from the stage to appreciate that the whole place was on their feet cheering for her. She felt elated. So many people were clapping for her and her music. Making people feel that good through her songs was the energy Mia lived for. There was no other buzz like it.

She waved to the crowd as she stepped down from the stage, still taking in the entire cheering crowd as she went.

There was one table in particular that Mia noticed. Situated close to the stage again, the two American men were also on their feet politely clapping and staring intensely at her.

CHAPTER 4

The following day passed Mia by in a blur. Dazed after her overwhelming applause on Saturday night, she passed through Sunday on a blissful high.

She always received a great response from the crowd, but that one had somehow seemed different. It had felt momentous, bigger, and stronger—almost. The happiness that had followed had been an emotional surge that Mia had been riding for the following day, wondering when the wave would reach its crescendo and crash to the shore.

Sundays were a day she never usually worked. They were often too quiet to warrant a full team of staff on shift but somehow she almost always ended up back at Glen's Tavern, even if only to talk to her friends.

After spending the day rehearsing some of her songs and penning down some new material, Mia had needed to escape the four walls of her small flat and breathe some fresh air. In hindsight, she realised Glen's wasn't the best place to seek un-breathed air and serenity but she felt at home among her friends. And the constant hum of music and conversation that was Glen's Tavern's was its own unique brand of oxygen for her.

Glen had Ben and Niamh working on Sunday evenings and Keith, a quiet middle-aged man who often worked shifts during the week. Keith didn't like to work Friday's and Saturday's as he didn't like to deal with the crowds. He quietly pottered around the bar and Mia barely noticed he was there as she perched on her barstool and chatted to Glen and Leah. Niamh tried to join in the conversation as often as she could before someone needed serving or tables needed clearing.

Midway through the evening, Leah announced she had paper-work that she needed to finish before Monday morning, and as Glen was behind the bar helping serve a sudden influx of custom-ers. Mia was left to entertain herself for the moment. Just as she considered calling it an early night, Dylan strode in through the door.

"Do you come here often, sweetheart?" He wrapped his arm around her shoulder and leaned in close, despite saying the words loud enough for most of the bar to hear.

Mia laughed and quickly returned his hug before shoving him away. Dylan plonked himself down on the recently vacated chair next to her and ordered a beer. He politely asked if she wanted another but Mia shook her head and pointed to her still full glass.

He smiled up at her before taking a deep swig from his drink. "How's it going?"

"Good, in all of the twenty four hours since I last saw you," she said sarcastically.

He winked. "I know, it feels like forever. I've missed you too."

His eyes had a cheeky sparkle to them when he wasn't putting on a show, Mia noticed.

She shook her head at him, laughing. "Don't flatter yourself, Dyl. What are you doing here anyway?"

"Can't a guy enjoy a beer with his friends?" he teased, gestur-ing at her and the other staff. Glen rolled his eyes and said noth-ing, smiling to himself.

"Dylan, this is you we're talking about."

"And?" he questioned, his eyes still dancing.

She stared pointedly at him. "You know what I mean."

Dylan didn't usually come into Glen's unless he was working. There was the odd night when he would come in for a drink, but usually he would be elsewhere entertaining a new acquaintance. That was the nicest, least crude way Mia could describe Dylan's recreational activities.

He just had a knack for attracting women. Some men had it and some took a bit more work. Dylan had something in his aura, which meant he only had to smile at women, and they would fol-low him home like a herd of sheep following a shepherd. But Mia preferred Dylan the way he was right now—honest, cheeky, and good fun. When he was trying to make a new *acquaintance*—she mentally rolled her eyes at the expression—he put on his dark and brooding rock star persona. It worked for him and the women lapped it up. They were intrigued by the handsome, deeply mysterious man, with the come-to-bed eyes. Not that he needed an alter ego. Dylan was charming enough without it. He just seemed to shut himself off when it came to picking up women.

Mia wondered if he'd had a bad experience. Maybe that was why he was one way with his friends and another around women. He hadn't had a steady girlfriend in a long time. Or perhaps she was reading far too much into it entirely and Dylan simply knew what made women tick and used it to his advantage.

"I'm performing." He jerked his head toward the stage, his voice bringing her back to the conversation.

"Glen finally caved then?" Mia asked, raising her voice so that Glen could hear her.

He had been reluctant to let Dylan perform in the bar, dubious as to how good he would actually be. While his talents at pouring drinks, flipping glasses, and picking up women were extraordinary, Glen had always been dubious to let Dylan onto his stage.

Glen looked at Mia with a defeated look on his face and shrugged. "He beat me down eventually."

Mia giggled. "So you gave him the Sunday night slot?"

"Hey, I could have given him a week night," he argued.

Weeknights were hit and miss, sometimes the bar had performers, and sometimes they didn't. But Fridays and Saturdays were the biggies. The crowd pullers. And Glen's Tavern pulled in huge crowds. Glen didn't take lightly to letting anyone on his stage on those nights. Sunday night was almost a go-between, not quite good enough for the big nights but better than a weeknight.

With a disgruntled face, Dylan huffed, "Just you wait and see."

Just then, the teenager with shoulder-length dark hair and long baggy jeans finished his set on stage and the light crowd gave their applause. Despite his age, Mia looked forward to hearing him play every Sunday night. He didn't sing but he played some incredible blues rhythms on the guitar and his fingers nimbly swept up and down the fret board as he riffed through his set.

Dylan got up from his seat and picked up the guitar case at his side. He pointed at her with his cheeky grin back in place. "Just you wait and see," he repeated and strode off to the stage.

Glen sighed as he stacked the last of the freshly washed glasses back on the shelf and went to introduce him. Mia gave him an encouraging smile as he passed.

Glen gave a hesitant glace at the crowd gathered in front of the stage. His eyes were full of reluctance. She caught his eye again from beside the bar and he looked back from her to Dylan before shaking his head. He turned to the stage and his voice soon echoed through the room. "Guys and girls, please give it up for Glen's Tavern's very own Dylan O'Connor."

The crowd clapped and Mia heard a few girls near the stage squeal as Dylan stepped up to the microphone.

After adjusting his guitar, he began playing and Mia's eyes flitted between watching Dylan and watching Glen's reaction. Much to their surprise, Dylan was quite impressive. His guitar playing wasn't advanced, but it was pretty good and his soft, husky voice glided silkily over words he sang along to the chords of the guitar.

It was clear Glen hadn't been expecting much. His eyebrows rose higher as Dylan's song progressed. Noticing movement from the corner of her eye, Mia saw Leah poke her head out from the back of the bar and give her a big thumbs up. Mia smiled and returned one back. Farther along Ben was nodding his head in time to the music, swaying his body with the melody, as he poured drinks. She could see Niamh in her usual spot close to the stage, gazing up at Dylan.

How long it would take him to notice Niamh was crazy about him? Mia wondered. For him to notice the beautiful, intelligent girl who was right under his nose?

Probably not for a long time, she realised. Dylan would continue enjoying the effect that he had on women, which was guaranteed to increase tenfold if Glen continued to allow him to perform on the stage regularly. But Mia was also happy for Dylan. He deserved recognition. His music was soulful and heartfelt, and his voice was so wonderfully easy to listen to. If he was passionate about his music, then Mia could empathise with him. She would always feel akin to those who connected with music as deeply as she did.

As she swayed along to the music in her seat, watching her friends do the same across the room, she had never felt more at home.

ഇൗൗ

Mia's week passed by the same as any other. In between working her shifts at Glen's and spending her free time with her guitar practising and writing and, occasionally, visiting the gym, the week soon began to whittle away.

Awaking early on Thursday morning and unable to sleep, she decided to go for a run. Feeling restless and unable to either concentrate or go back to sleep, she was in a mood to release some energy. She threw on her clothes and trainers and headed out into the crisp morning air.

It was only 6.30 a.m. so there were a few early morning commuters heading through the streets but, for the most, the city was quiet. Soon enough, the streets would be crowded with tourists as St. Patrick's Day was approaching on Sunday. The tourists had been slowly descending on the city all week and, as the weekend neared, the crowds were coming thicker and faster.

She knew she was in for a ridiculously busy weekend at work. It was the one weekend each year when Glen asked them all to work all day, every day. Mia didn't mind. It kept her busy and the extra money always came in handy, despite how tiring the shifts would be. Beginning to wonder if running had been a good idea, she thought perhaps she should have been storing her energy for the hectic three days that would be coming. As she rounded the corner, St. Stephen's Green lay in front of her. Crossing the tram tracks, Mia headed into the park to do a lap around the duck ponds and pathways that lay inside.

There were a few other early morning runners inside the park, but she found the quiet of the almost-empty park comforting and calming. Despite the blaring music in her ears from her headphones, running seemed to help clear her mind of thoughts and worries. It was also a time when she found that inspiration and ideas for her own music seemed to enter her clearing head.

As she made her way around the final edge of the park, she listened to the lyrics her mind was beginning to form. She had been toying with the idea for the opening of a new song for a while, but for a long time she hadn't been able to find the right words to fit the chorus. Even though the melodies and lyrics of other musicians were blasting through her headphones, she could hear her own lyrics forming as though they were the only ones there. Words to the song sounded perfectly in her head and her mind formulated the rest of the lyrics. She began to up her pace as the streets close to her home grew nearer, desperate to reach her flat and find a pen and a piece of paper to write down the words before they disappeared forever.

Feeling refreshed from running and full of eagerness and creativity to begin working on her new song, Mia hastily unlocked her front door and charged into her flat to write down the words that had entered her head during her run. She scribbled them down frantically on the back of an electricity bill on the kitchen worktop, feeling relieved that she had remembered them until she got home. In a bid to remember them, she had switched off her iPod and had been mentally singing them to herself as she ran through the streets back to her flat.

Overcome by the rush to begin working on the music to accompany her song, Mia kicked off her running shoes and pulled off her clothes on her way to the bathroom. She turned the dial on the shower and hastily stepped under the flowing hot water.

She began to relax momentarily as the hot water flowed across her skin, erasing the traces of her exertion.

Interlaced with the hot water from the shower, her tears trickled silently over her face. Reminiscing on the faint memories that were behind the song, Mia allowed her tears to fall even faster. Hugging her arms tightly to her body and feeling completely alone, she begged her memory to hold on to the visions that became fainter as the years wore on.

The one photograph she had in her drawer entered her mind as clear as the image itself, but the real memories she had faded in and out of her mind, as if never coming fully into focus. She tipped her head down toward the floor and cried as the water poured over her head, her tears invisible in the fast flow of water, almost as if they were never there.

Her tears fell even harder at the thought, as she choked back a sob for, as with her tears, the memories seemed as if they too were never there.

CHAPTER 5

Another shoulder barged into Mia's as she pushed her way through the swarming crowds in a bid to arrive at work on time. It was only Friday lunchtime but already the weekend crowds were descending, thick and fast, on the city. As much as she enjoyed St. Patrick's Day, working in Dublin city center on the holiday weekend had its downsides. Bustling through tens of thousands of drunken celebrators was one of those downsides. Being almost deaf for the following three days after was another. Mia couldn't begin to describe the noise that would fill Glen's Tavern on Sunday evening as the celebrations reached their pinnacle.

"All right, darling, you coming in for a drink?" a leering voice called toward her as she made her way down Temple Bar.

Mia pulled the strap of her guitar case higher, as it slipped down her shoulder. She was bumped into once again and tried to ignore the wolf whistles and cat calls that followed her down the street.

"Here, love, I've got an instrument you can play!" came a slurry British voice from the doorstep of a nearby pub as she walked past.

Rolling her eyes at the all too familiar slurs of the holiday weekend, she breathed a sigh of relief as she pushed open the door of Glen's. She knew only too well that more would be in store for the remainder of the weekend, but once inside she felt safer. Glen wouldn't tolerate customers speaking to her or Niamh in that way and, as always, he hired a couple of bouncers for the St. Patrick's Day weekend.

Usually, Glen's Tavern wasn't the type of place to need security or a doorman. Glen was as laid back with that as he was with most things, but for one particular weekend out of the year, it was essential. They never knew what they were going to get and sometimes it was just too much for one person to deal with. Reluctantly, Glen knew it was the best for his bar and his staff to have back up on the rowdiest weekend of the year.

Seeing Glen, Dylan, and Ben already frantically serving the four-deep queue at the bar, Mia rushed through the hatchet and up the stairs to drop her things off and get to work. In her haste, she almost ran smack into Niamh on the staircase.

"Oh hey, sweetie." Niamh sounded as breathless as Mia was. "It's already so crazy down there."

"I know, here we go again," Mia said, reminiscing.

Niamh nudged her in the ribs as she passed. "We're in for an interesting weekend."

"See you down there." Mia ran the rest of the way up the stairs. She quickly shoved her coat and bag into her locker and propped her guitar against the wall before grabbing an apron from the pile of freshly laundered ones on the table.

Checking her reflection one last time, she smoothed down a few flyaway hairs from her ponytail—not that it mattered. She would look more than a little dishevelled by the end of her shift.

"Nice of you to join us." Ben winked as he dashed past her en route to prepare another drink.

"Quit complaining," she teased as she was immediately given an order for four beers by the closest customer.

"Hey, Mia." Dylan's hand rested on her shoulder in the briefest of greetings as he too dashed past to grab more glasses.

She somehow managed to respond before the next impatiently waiting patron grabbed her attention.

"Hey, you doing okay?" Glen's gentle voice was as calm as ever, despite the mayhem going on around him.

Mia wondered what his secret was to staying so calm. Nothing ever fazed the man.

"Yeah, I'm okay. You?" She laughed breathlessly as she grabbed the twenty-euro note out of the customer's hand.

St. Patrick's weekend wasn't the time for pleasantries or customer service. It was a case of get serving as fast as you can possibly move.

"Same old." He shrugged as he poured the beer from the tap

with all the tranquillity of having only one customer to serve, despite the dozens of waving hands demanding attention up and down the bar. Mia shook her head and laughed. "Any news yet?" he asked as he followed her to the till.

She smiled wryly, her mood disheartening for a moment. "Nope, nothing yet."

"It'll happen, kid, don't worry." He nodded at her with certainty and Mia wished she could believe him.

"Three Guinness's please, love," asked an already swaying man wearing an over-sized bright green felt top hat.

She couldn't help but smile as she looked out at the sea of green. The familiar pride, she always felt for being Irish every time St. Patrick's Day came around, swelled in her chest. Some of the outfits were imaginative, whereas others had opted simply for a green T-shirt or novelty hats like the man in front of her.

She began pouring the thick, dark liquid from one of the six taps that were ready for the busy weekend. Glen soon materialised at her side as she waited for the drink to settle before she could pour the remainder. He began filling several of his own glasses and gave Mia a knowing smile, which suggested this was only one of many Guinness moments to come that day. As delicious as the drink was, it was time consuming waiting for it to settle in order to be poured correctly, something they tried to do each time it was made. However, St. Patrick's Day weekend didn't always allow them to be as arduous with their task as the weekend wore on. Knowing it was only Friday lunchtime, Mia knew a long, long weekend lay ahead.

"That reminds me." Glen tipped his head toward her, his deep accent curling wonderfully around the words as he spoke. "A couple o' guys were in here earlier asking if you were playing tonight."

"Oh?" she wondered. Most regular customers knew that she played every weekend so it would have been odd for them to ask. "Who was it?"

"Dunno." Glen shrugged. "Some American guys, dressed fancy n' all that."

Mia knew instantly who Glen meant. She wondered who on earth these suited Americans were and why they had returned a week later to ask for her. She didn't even know their names. It wasn't as if the man was interested in Mia. He was too much older than her for that. She didn't have long to ponder on the Americans as another waiting customer grabbed her attention. The rest of her afternoon passed by in a blur of glasses, swirling with beer and Guinness, and an endless sea of money-waving, green-colored patrons.

c/se/o

Before Mia knew what had happened, her alarm clock was signalling to her that Saturday had already begun. After what had felt like only an hour's sleep, her eyes cracked open, feeling like sandpaper, and she lifted an exhausted arm out of the duvet to switch off the incessant ringing.

Sitting up and rubbing her eyes, she felt vaguely aware that her arms and legs ached considerably after standing up and darting to and fro across the bar for more than twelve hours. And in just over an hour, she would have to do it all again. Stumbling in a half-drunken state of tiredness, she made her way to the bathroom and switched on the shower. As her senses returned to a state of near-wakefulness under the hot water, she remembered Glen's words to her in the early part of the afternoon.

She had worked non-stop throughout the afternoon and well into the evening before Glen had forced her to take to the stage and perform, despite the unrelenting wave of people at the bar still going strong. Though she didn't remember serving the two American men, she had seen so many faces they had all blurred into one. Somehow, she knew that she would have recognized those two had she been the one to serve them.

Still pondering over them asking about her performance yesterday, she dressed and got ready for work in a painfully tired haze.

With only several minutes left before she needed to leave the house to make it across to Glen's in time, Mia grabbed her keys and guitar and headed out of the door. She hated how feeling so tired made her usual routine take twice as long as normal, forcing her to grab something to eat en route to work.

She walked through the streets of Dublin, on her usual route, not needing to look up to the faces of the passing crowds as she made her way along the familiar streets. Shouts, singing, cheering and music could be heard from every street Mia passed.

Rounding the corner, she pushed open the door of one of her favorite places in the city and the warm, comforting aroma of coffee instantly filled her senses. Thankfully, not too many tourists knew the place existed and so it was much quieter than the many Starbucks and chains on the main streets.

"Morning." The girl behind the counter smiled in recognition as Mia approached the counter. "The usual?"

"Yes please." Mia returned her smile gratefully as she rummaged in her leather jacket pocket for some of the generous share of tips she had received at the end of her shift the night before.

"Here, allow me." An American-accented man appeared at her side and handed the barista a ten-euro note.

Looking up, Mia was startled. The blond American man from Glen's was standing in front of her, smiling politely. She spotted his friend seated at a nearby table watching them.

"No, you don't have to do that," she said in a firm voice.

"I insist." His smile remained in place. He appeared professional, as if this were a regular occurrence for him.

"Thank you," she managed. She noticed he wasn't wearing a suit as he had been on the times she had seen him before. He was still dressed impeccably—his jeans were clearly designer, as were the dark sunglasses hanging from his shirt that was unbuttoned at the neck and rolled up at the sleeves.

"I'm Jackson." He held out his hand to her. "Jackson Miller."

Shaking his hand, she eyed him suspiciously. "Mia Ryan," she said.

"I know." He smiled, releasing his strong no-nonsense handshake. "Listen, Mia, do you have a minute?"

"Erm…" She looked at her watch, realising she genuinely didn't. "I'm sorry, I don't. I'm going to be late for work."

Jackson's smile turned understanding. "No problem. May we speak to you after your performance tonight?" he asked, motioning to his friend sitting nearby.

Mia paused as the barista handed her order over the counter. "Thank you," she said, realising the girl was slyly listening to their conversation. Mia frowned curiously at him. "Yeah, I guess so."

"I understand this may seem a little odd," he added, "but I assure you it's strictly professional."

The word professional, Mia thought, *can cover a broad range of subjects.* "Okay, I'll see you after the show." She turned to leave and he held out his hand to her again.

"Thank you, Mia." He gripped her hand and shook it again before she finally turned to leave the coffee shop.

Frowning as she sipped her coffee and resumed her route to work through the crowds, Mia wondered how on earth she managed to bump into the man named Jackson. Of all the coffee shops in the large city, he just happened to be in the one she frequented. And what on earth he could consider "professional" managed to consume her thoughts for the rest of the walk, before her day was once again consumed with a beer drinking, green ocean of tourists.

ഛ൦ഛ

"Mia, get your arse up on that stage now!" Glen's voice called out over the noise of the surrounding crowd.

"But we're too busy!" she called back. If she had thought Friday had been busy, Saturday was even worse. She dreaded to think what the next day would bring.

"We also have people who want to hear you sing." He came over and playfully snatched the glass out of her hand. "Now move it."

"You sure you're going to be okay?" She looked dubiously at the sea of waiting faces, feeling guilty at bailing on her colleagues when the place was so busy.

"They're thirsty, so they'll wait." He winked. "Now go!"

Mia giggled and untied her apron before running up the stairs to grab her guitar.

Pausing as she picked up the case in the staff room, her eyes lingered on her bag that was hastily shoved inside her locker.

Inside her bag was a notebook full of songs that were still in progress. Mia didn't usually bring it with her. She knew the songs she performed by heart but the one that had entered her mind, while she had been running on Thursday, had turned out to be a lot better than she had expected. After playing around with the melody on Thursday afternoon, she had grown to really like the song.

There was something special about it. She just had a gut feeling that there was something different about it.

Despite having only played the song to herself a few times, Mia grabbed the notebook and headed downstairs.

୧୰୨

After the last song ended and the green-colored crowd cheered more raucously than usual, Mia reached down and picked up the notebook on the stage beside her.

Finding the page she needed, she propped it open on the music stand beside her. She had a feeling she wouldn't need it, but it was there as a backup. The last thing she needed was to forget her words or music in front of the biggest crowd of the year. Not that the size of the crowd fazed her. They could have increased ten-fold—and yet every single one of them would still have disappeared the moment she started to play.

This time in particular they would disappear faster than ever. She just knew there was something about this song.

Taking a deep breath and adjusting her fingers on the fret-board, she began her song.

Almost instantly, the bar fell eerily silent. She knew, even as she stared upward into the blinding spotlight, that no one in the room was speaking. Every pair of eyes and ears in the place were riveted on her.

Her song began to near the end and Mia struggled to keep hold of the rolling wave of emotions that were crashing inside her. She could feel her stomach tensing and her voice quivered slightly on the final notes. She knew her eyes were watery, but she couldn't help herself.

The song ended and for the briefest of moments, an agonising silence followed. Mia stayed rooted to her seat, wondering if she had made a huge mistake in playing a song that perhaps wasn't quite ready yet.

As the house lights began to come up and the spotlight was lifted from her face, she looked down to see almost every face in the crowd was wearing teary eyes like her own. Some women were openly crying. She could see Niamh standing nearby with an armful of collected dirty glasses with tears streaming down her face.

And one by one, they began to clap.

As she rose from her seat, the applause for her intensified. The crowd clapped harder and began to cheer. Once again, the place was on its feet cheering, but almost every face staring back at her was a tear-stained one.

Wiping her own eyes with her hand, she made her way down from the stage and just managed to put her guitar down before a tiny body was wrapped around her own.

"Mia, that was incredible," Niamh gushed through her tears, her voice sounding watery. "Well, you always are, but wow! That last song was really something else."

"Thanks, Niamh, I wasn't sure if it was ready yet." Mia returned her embrace, grateful for someone being there when she needed them.

"It really was…" Niamh's sentence trailed off as swarms of people began to surround Mia at the side of the stage, patting her on the back and congratulating her on her performance.

Eventually, the swarms of Guinness-smelling well-wishers filtered away and she was able to return her guitar to its case and pack up her things.

As she snapped shut the case and turned around, slinging it over her shoulder, there he was.

"Wow, Mia." Jackson's relaxed American accent was immediately in front of her. "That was incredible, congratulations."

"Thank you," she smiled, noticing his friend was standing behind him as silent as always.

She wondered if his accomplice was a bodyguard. *Just who is this man?*

"Are you free for a moment?" he asked, cautiously glancing back at the bar.

Mia eyed him suspiciously. Still full of toiling emotions from the sadness of projecting her song to the crowd and from the high of the response afterward, she blurted out, "What is it you want with me?"

Jackson paused, looking taking aback. He cocked an eyebrow at her, before glancing around to his friend who nodded. "We're from Sixth String Studios in Los Angeles. We wondered if we could have a chat with you about your music."

৩৩৩

Mia sat across the table from Jackson and his colleague,

whom she now knew to be Cole Johnson, with her mouth still agape.

The constant hum of the noise in the bar and the hustle of moving bodies around their table disappeared as she tried to process the words she had just heard.

After hearing her set, Jackson had taken her to a nearby table in the corner of the bar, where they could just about hear one another speak above the noise of the crowds.

Cole had remained almost silent throughout their conversation. Jackson, however, had explained they were interested in her music. They had been intrigued, after happening upon the bar last week, and had extended their business trip in Dublin by an extra week in order to hear her perform again. They had been in Glen's Tavern last night and had returned tonight to express their interest in her as an artist, hearing her perform her new song and seeing the reaction of the crowd had only affirmed their decision in staying. "*Mia?*" Jackson sat across from her with his hands clasped in front of him on the table.

"I'm sorry," she mumbled. "This is kind of overwhelming."

"Don't worry, I understand." He smiled a sympathetic smile of a man who had seen the same situation a hundred times before. "So, Mia now that you understand how interested Sixth String Studio's is in you, we have a question for you."

She hesitated, unsure of what was coming next. "Okay..."

"We wondered if you would be interested in working with us." Jackson's expression remained neutral.

Mia's, however, crumbled. "You what?" she gasped.

Jackson repeated his statement and Mia could have sworn she saw Cole almost crack a smile.

"We want you to work with us, with the studio," he continued.

"B—but—" she stammered. "You're from Los Angeles."

A moment of silence hovered over the table before Jackson tried to stifle a chuckle.

"Come on, man." Cole's voice finally sounded across the table as he nudged him.

Jackson laughed as he looked down at his clasped hands before holding Mia's gaze firmly. "Mia, we want you to come to Los Angeles to work for us."

e/ᴈe/ᴈ

Making her way through the crowds silently, Mia reached the hatchet of the bar and slid underneath. She slipped through the back of the bar and slowly climbed the stairs to the staff room. Her stuff was dropped in its usual places. She turned from the room numbly and descended the stairs at the same slow pace.

Although knowing she should be moving faster to return to help with the crowds at the bar, Mia couldn't seem to focus on anything other than what she had just heard. Her mind didn't seem to be processing anything. She could still see Jackson and Cole's faces across the table. She could still see Jackson's lips moving in a polite smile, as he spoke, but her brain wouldn't register the words she had just heard. Her emotions felt all out of sync. She had been on her feet all day and was exhausted. She had then played what was possibly the most emotional set she had ever poured her heart into and had almost cried onstage. That was something she had never done before. She had then received an equally emotional response from the crowd, all followed by the conversation, she had waited the majority of her life just to hear, uttered in a matter of seconds. *Phew.*

Exhaling, she dropped her weight onto the stairs beneath her. She rested her arms on her knees and put her head on her arms, staring at the empty wall in front of her. Her mind still repeated her conversation with Jackson and the words that had followed. His business card felt like it was burning its way through the pocket of her jeans and onto her skin.

She buried her head in her arms and tried to shut out the confusing thoughts that were rolling around in her mind.

"You look like you need a drink," came a familiar voice as an arm slipped comfortingly around her shoulders.

Looking up from her arms, she came face to face with a generous measure of bourbon. Taking hold of the glass, she immediately threw the contents down her throat, feeling it sear its way down her insides. She closed her eyes, allowing the sensation to take over the rest of her senses, momentarily. Opening her eyes, she saw dark brown ones staring back at her. "Thanks, Dylan."

"You look like you needed that?" he asked.

"I did."

"You want to talk about it?"

"I don't know."

"Is it those American guys you were talking to?"

Mia nodded.

"Everything all right?"

She nodded again.

"Your set was awesome, by the way."

For once, she was glad for Dylan's lack of regard for personal space as she leaned into him. "Thanks, Dyl."

His arm tightened around her shoulder. "You sure you're okay?"

Mia nodded a third time. Tipping her head back against his arm and staring at the ceiling, she sighed. "I'm going to Los Angeles."

"Holy shit."

♥♥♥

The clinking of the glass on the metal beer tap made Mia jump out of her reverie.

She had been running on autopilot for the last couple of hours, still trying to come to terms with the thought that a recording company wanted to work with her. *And not just any recording company.*

Sixth String Studios was one of the biggest recording companies in the world, the front-runners in the rock music industry. If you played guitar, Sixth String Studios was where you wanted to be. The best in the industry wanted to work with her. Some of her greatest idols signed with Sixth String Studios. And the music that had guided her through her life, the songs that had been the soundtrack to her greatest and darkest moments in her life, were all recorded in that building.

Needless to say, it was taking some time for the realisation to hit home.

"Give us a smile, darlin'." The punter in front of her waved his money just out of her reach as he taunted her.

Mia picked up his pint glass and held it out of his reach in return, holding her other hand outstretched, waiting for him to place the money in her palm.

"Oh come on," he leered.

Mia cocked her head to one side, still waiting. She raised pint glass even farther out of reach.

"Fine," he grumbled, shoving the money into her hand.

She could hear Ben chuckling beside her as he watched her taunting the customer.

He grinned. "Depriving a man of his beer on Paddy's Day, Mia?"

"It gets results." She returned his smile and heard the man complaining on the other side of the bar about her smiling for Ben.

"You all right?" Ben asked.

"Yeah, fine, just a bit overwhelmed," she answered honestly.

She knew he would think she was talking about the customers. She had made Dylan promise to keep quiet about what Jackson and Cole had offered her. The last thing she wanted was for Glen or Leah to hear the news from anyone else but her. They had been the ones to offer her the stage to perform on every weekend and had supported her, and her music, for the years she had lived in Dublin. Both of them had believed in her music from the word go, and Mia didn't want them to hear that she was leaving from idle gossip from someone else. She owed them more respect than that. She wouldn't have been noticed in the first place if it wasn't for them.

She knew she had to tell them. She had to talk to them as soon as possible. But finding a free moment with them both, in the middle of the busiest weekend of the year, was going to be difficult.

And Jackson wanted her to fly out to Los Angeles in just over a week.

♥◇♥

The smell of coffee overwhelmed Mia as she stared down at the cup full of black liquid on the table in front of her. She had forced her aching and tired body out of bed early on Monday morning for the conversation she knew she had to have. Her body ached tremendously, every muscle in her legs felt like lead and her arms were sore and heavy. And she could still hear the ringing in her ears from listening to the sounds of several hundred rowdy punters for an entire weekend.

Yet, she was awake at 9 a.m. on Monday morning, trying to force down a second cup of coffee, for she knew she had arrangements to make with more than one person.

Jackson had promised to call her on Monday after he flew home on Sunday.

Allowing for the time difference in Los Angeles meant he wouldn't be calling until late in the afternoon.

In the meantime, Mia had decided to get up and catch her boss at the quietest time of the week to tell him the news she had.

In many ways, she was looking forward to the conversation. She knew Glen and Leah would both be thrilled for her, as would everyone at Glen's Tavern. They all knew how much this meant to her. It was all she had ever wanted. It was the reason she had packed up her life in Kinsale and left her adoptive parents to move to the other end of the country. It was the reason she worked every single hour she could manage to afford to live in Dublin. It was the reason she practised at every spare hour she had to herself. It was also the reason she spent weeks waiting for phone calls, emails, and letters from recording companies that never came. Until now. Except this one happened to be on the other side of the world.

After making one big move, Mia wasn't afraid to be leaving for Los Angeles.

Jackson had offered her the opportunity to work with Sixth String Studios for three months, as a kind of probation period. A period that would allow her to settle in and see if the studio was right for her and her music, and vice versa.

What worried her was leaving behind the life she had created for herself in Dublin. Although a career in the music industry was what she wanted, she knew she would miss her life in Dublin. She had found genuine, life-long friends in the city and she was happy. Though she had been content living in Kinsale, it was a quiet little seaside town that Mia would have lived merely content in until the day she died had she not made the decision to leave.

Leaving Mike and Sharon had been difficult, but she knew she needed it do it. She missed them terribly, and they had done so much for her over the years, but Mia always felt their connection had something missing. The genuine bond between parent and child would never be there. They felt more like an aunt and uncle to her. Despite their unwavering love and support for her, she knew deep in her heart that she wasn't theirs. And they weren't hers. Despite having barely any recollection of her birth parents, Mia always knew they were once hers. Mike and Sharon had tried to fill that void ever since, but there was always a space that could never fully be filled.

Thinking back to her birth parents, Mia looked over at the guitar case that lay on the sofa. The guitar had been her fathers. She had carried it around with her ever since he and her mother died. Although she could barely remember her father playing to her when she was little, the one faint memory she had inspired her to continue playing in his legacy. It helped her to feel closer to her parents. She could always picture them standing in the crowd watching her perform each time she took to the stage. She knew that, although they may not have been there in body, their spirits would always be with her when she performed, silently cheering her on louder than anyone else in the crowd.

Mia also knew that they would have been ecstatic about her to be going to Los Angeles, her father particularly, for she was being given the opportunity he never had. He would have been thrilled for her to be living out her dreams as well as his.

Thinking of her parents reminded her she had another phone call to make. She knew it was a little too early to head down to Glen's just yet, so she picked up her mobile phone and called Sharon.

"Hello?"

"Hey, Sharon, it's me."

"Mia, love, how are you?"

"I'm great. How are you both?"

"Fine, just the usual, you know?"

"Yeah."

Picturing the quaint little town on the seafront, and Mike and Sharon going about their usual routines, made Mia smile to herself. Her life now seemed a million miles away from what she had left behind. And it was about to change again.

"How's things? Have you heard from that record company yet?"

"No, nothing yet—" Mia's sentence was cut short.

"Well, don't worry, love. It'll all work out soon enough."

Mia grinned to herself at the irony, hearing their usual route of conversation beginning to form.

"That's kind of why I'm calling you." She hesitated. "I have some news."

"Oh?"

"I've been offered a job—In Los Angeles."

Mia had to hold the phone away from her ear as Sharon screamed with delight.

"That's fantastic news! Oh that's brilliant, Mia! I knew all your hard work would pay off!"

Laughed at hearing her excitement, Mia continued. "It's only for three months though, just to see how things go, first."

"But still? Los Angeles!" Sharon squealed again.

"That's not the best part."

"There's more?"

"Yes, it's for Sixth String Studios."

Again, she had to hold the phone away from her ear as Sharon screamed. Mia had often talked to her about the industry, artists, and studios she had always wanted to work with. Sharon knew how big this opportunity was for her.

"Oh, Mia, I'm so happy for you. You deserve this, you really do."

"Thank you."

"I just know this will be the start of something big for you."

"I hope so."

"It will. Have faith, love."

"It's only a job as a song writer—it's not a recording contract."

"It doesn't matter, it's a step in the best possible direction and who knows where this could lead for you."

"I know." Mia sounded wistful. She, herself, had barely dared to hope where the opportunity could lead. She would only allow herself to focus on the present.

"When do you leave?"

"That's why I'm calling, well, besides to tell you the news. They want me to fly out next week."

"Fecking hell, Mia. Have you told Glen?"

"No, not yet. I'm going to head over there in a minute."

"He will understand. He will be happy for you, I know it."

"I know that too. I just feel so bad to be leaving them on such short notice."

"Mia, love, Glen of all people would want you to go running for this at full speed."

Though she knew Sharon was right, Mia just couldn't feel excited until she had spoken to Glen.

Getting through work yesterday without saying anything had been difficult. She had wanted to jump up and down and scream her news to the entire bar, but that had hardly been the right time or place.

"Listen, you go and talk to Glen. Tell him the fantastic news. I'm sure he will be over the moon for you. I'll call Mike at work and let him know. He'll be so happy for you. We'll call you later on this evening, okay?"

"Yeah, okay, I'll speak to you later."

Mia hung up the phone and swirled down the remnants of her coffee before zipping up her jacket and heading out the door.

Noticing how much faster the walk to work was now that St. Patrick's Day was over, she reached Glen's Tavern before she knew it. With all the tourists either heading home or sleeping off one hell of a hangover, it was no surprise that the streets were quiet on Monday morning.

Anticipating that the delivery lorry would be parked around the back of the bar, Mia headed for the back entrance. The bar was still closed and she knew she could slip unobtrusively into the back if the beer delivery had arrived.

She smiled a hello to the drivers as they offloaded the huge wooden barrels into the cellar with ease as if they weighed the same as a bag of sugar. Both her own experience, and the loud bangs they were currently making, told her those barrels were incredibly heavy.

Silently, she walked through the stockroom and past the corridor to the bar, which remained in eerie darkness—the outlines of the furniture and beer taps just visible in the darkness.

The light was on in Glen's office and she knocked gently on the door.

"Come on in," came his deep voice from inside.

She pushed open the door and saw Glen seated at the desk, buried among a mountain of paperwork from the holiday weekend. His eyes looked tired when he looked up to the door.

"Mia, what are you doing here this early?" he asked, standing up from his seat as he glanced at the clock on the wall.

"I—umm—I came to talk to you," she said in a quiet voice, glancing down at the floor.

"Is everything okay?" Glen's voice sounded concerned and he perched on the front of the desk. "Have a seat, love."

She sat in the leather office chair and began to twirl her fingers in her lap.

"Mia?"

Glen rested a hand on her shoulder and she looked up to meet his gaze. His face showed he was genuinely concerned there was something wrong. She took a deep breath.

"I've been offered a job," she began.

His hand instantly fell away and all concern was wiped from his face. "Oh," was all he said.

"Wait, it's not like that," she added hastily.

Glen raised his eyebrows at her. Sometimes, just sometimes, she wished her boss could be a little more vocal.

"It's in Los Angeles, for a recording company."

A small smile began to creep across his features. "Those guys who were in here the other night?" he asked, "Those Americans?"

"Yeah, they're from Sixth String Studios."

Glen was as big of a rock music fan as Mia, so he instantly understood. "Jesus, Mia." He exhaled and began to laugh. "You really had me going for a minute there."

She laughed along with him.

"I mean, bloody hell, woman, that's fantastic news!"

"I know." She grinned, finally able to appreciate the incredible opportunity now that she knew Glen was happy for her.

"So what is it? Is it a recording deal?"

"It's just as a songwriter. They want me to head over there for three months to write some material for their artists, just to see how it goes."

"To *write* for their *artists*? Sixth String Studios wants you to write for their artists?"

Mia nodded.

"Bloody hell, Mia! I always knew you were too talented to be a barmaid. This is incredible!"

"Thanks, Glen," Her smile now stretched from ear to ear. She had never seen her boss so animated before.

He jumped up from the desk, clasping her shoulder tightly as he passed. Mia spun in her chair to see where he was going.

He stuck his head around the office door and yelled, "Leah, come in here, quick!"

Mia giggled as she heard Leah curse at Glen before stomping through the corridor.

"Glen, I'm busy with—Oh hey, Mia," she breezed as he turned to allow her to see who was sitting at the desk.

Glen grinned. "Mia has some news."

Leah looked from her husband's enthusiastic smile to Mia's matching one. "What's that?"

After relating the information she had just told Glen, Mia received another response like Sharon's. Mia winced as Leah screamed in delight and clapped her hands.

"Oh that's amazing news! I'm so happy for you!" She strode over to the chair and gave her a tight hug.

"When do you go?" Leah asked, still smiling.

"That's the other thing—" Mia paused, her good mood temporarily suspended as she awaited their response to her next piece of information. "They want me to fly out on Monday."

She needn't have worried. Neither Glen nor Leah showed one ounce of disappointment at her abandoning her job so soon. As Sharon had promised, they were enthusiastic and supportive.

"This is your dream, love." Glen patted her on the shoulder. "You'd be crazy to worry about leaving us behind."

"We'll still be here when you get back." Leah smiled. "We're not going anywhere. We'll be cheering you on all the way."

"There's one condition though?" Glen's faced looked serious.

"Okay?" Mia asked, not imagining what his condition could be if he wanted her to take the opportunity.

"You have to let us know everything that happens over there." He grinned again. "And possibly get me a few autographs."

She burst into giggles from the suspense. "I think I'll be able to manage that."

"This is the start of something big for you, Mia, I can just feel it." Leah clasped her hands together. "And you deserve every moment of it."

Mia looked at them gratefully. "Thanks, guys, I really appreciate everything you've both done for me."

Glen shrugged her off. "Ah, stop it now."

"No, I mean it. I wouldn't be where I am now, and I wouldn't have been given this opportunity, if it wasn't for the two of you."

Leah began to look tearful at her words, "Nonsense. We did what anyone would have done. You're a talented, beautiful young woman, Mia."

Mia looked at them both and bit her lip. "I feel bad for leaving you guys on such short notice after everything you've done for me."

"Don't be ridiculous, you go for this with everything you've got," Leah said.

"Take all the time you need, Mia." Glen smiled encouragingly. "Your job will still be here for you when you get back. Not that you're gonna need it, though."

"Don't be replacing me just yet." She laughed as he clapped her on the shoulder once again.

CHAPTER 6

I f Mia had thought Sharon and Leah had screamed loudly upon hearing her news, she had been wrong.

Niamh's reaction blew the roof off anyone else's.

Glen had assembled his team together before their evening shift on Tuesday night, giving Mia the opportunity to announce her news to everyone officially. Even though everyone but two of those gathered already knew.

He'd assembled everyone behind the bar with Leah to one side and the team in front of him, waiting expectantly. Although Mia had already told Dylan her news and had made him promise to keep quiet, she hadn't told him the specifics. He had no idea she would be leaving so soon.

After running over the usual business details and announcing the phenomenal takings for the holiday weekend, Glen nodded to her. "And I think Mia has some news she would like to share with you all."

Mia swallowed. *Thanks, Glen*, she thought. *Nothing like being put on the spot.*

"So—I—I'm going to Los Angeles," she said, stumbling over the words, not knowing how to announce to her friends that she would be leaving them so soon, "to work with a recording com-pany."

Niamh screamed at the top of her lungs in excitement and be-gan jumping up and down, still screaming. "Mia, this is incredi-ble! Oh my God! Los Angeles!" She clapped her hands together, ran forward, and embraced Mia so tightly, Mia could have sworn her spine met the front of her ribcage inside her chest.

"Niamh," she gasped.

"I just—I just can't believe it, this is amazing!" she continued, screaming in Mia's ear.

"*Niamh.*" Mia tried again and looked round at the smirking faces standing in front of her.

Niamh continued her praise, unaware of Mia's breathlessness. Rolling her eyes, Mia smiled as she hugged her enthusiastic friend back. She didn't want to think how much she would miss Niamh's presence once she was gone.

"I'm so pleased for you, Mia." Ben grinned from ear to ear as he prised a reluctant Niamh away from Mia in order to embrace her.

"Thanks, Ben, I'm really going to miss you guys," she said as she wrapped her arms around the slender physique of her friend.

He pulled back and stared at her confused. "Why?" he asked. "When do you leave?"

Out of the corner of her eyes, she noticed Niamh's face fall beside her. "On Monday."

"*Monday?*" Niamh whispered beside her.

Mia nodded.

"For how long?" Niamh's huge eyes looked saddened, her enthusiasm momentarily lost.

"Three months," Mia told her. "They want me to work as a songwriter."

"And then they will see how fabulous you are and want to keep you forever." Niamh laughed as she perked up.

Neither of them had to say anything. Mia knew how much they would miss each other. They didn't need to say anything to cement those feelings further.

Dylan broke his usual silence from the corner of their group. "Well, you know what that means."

Everyone turned to look at him. "What?" Ben asked.

"We need to give you one hell of a send-off this weekend," Dylan said with his signature smirk.

⌒⌒⌒

Mia shook her head furiously. "*No!*" she shouted above the noise of the crowd.

Still, Dylan grinned mischievously, the crowd egging him on. "Come on, Mia," he cooed over the microphone.

He waved the guitar in his free hand in her direction, teasing her with the upturned smirk on his face. It wasn't often Dylan dropped his guard in front of such a big audience and he was doing it for her. She had to smile to herself.

Suddenly, a small pair of hands were pressed against her lower back, pushing her toward the stage. Niamh giggled from behind her. "Come on, it's your last night."

Mia turned to face her, matching her amused expression. "Don't tell me you're in on this, too?"

Niamh offered a devilish smile. "I wouldn't dream of it."

Throwing up her hands in surrender, she laughed. "Fine!" she said and made her way through the parting crowd that was allowing her passage to the stage.

Dylan's face said it all as she approached. His grin spread even wider, knowing she had caved in.

She pointed a finger at him as she stepped on the stage. "You—" She tried to feign being serious. "—are in serious trouble."

He tried to stifle a laugh. "You know you really want to," he teased. He held out the guitar to her and patted the stool he had conveniently placed beside his.

Mia rolled her eyes and laughed. Looking down at the crowd, she could see they were as amused as he was.

She dared not look over at Ben and Niamh. Or Glen for that matter. She could possibly be destroying her reputation at Glen's Tavern on the night before she left for Los Angeles by agreeing to duet with Dylan.

How, she questioned, *did I allow myself to agree to this?*

Shaking her head, she adjusted her guitar as she waited for Dylan to begin. He had promised to give her "one hell of a send-off." This, however, was not what she had imagined.

"Ladies and gentlemen, as most of you know, our lovely Mia, here, is leaving us tomorrow for the bright lights of Los Angeles—" He paused as the crowd cheered loudly. "Now how about her and me giving you one heck of a final performance?" The crowd cheered again as they agreed. "You all know the words to this one so sing along, guys. Let's give Mia a show to remember," he added before the lights went down and the crowd cheered in agreement.

Dylan turned to the backing band and gave them a nod, signalling their cue to begin. He turned and gave Mia one final smirk before he began to play. Holding her breath, she wondered what he had in store for her.

Hearing the familiar notes of the music begin, Mia giggled to herself.

Only Dylan, she thought.

She positioned her fingers and on the next chord change, she joined in with him and the band.

The crowd began to cheer as they recognized the familiar lyrics to Red Hot Chilli Peppers', "Dani California."

As they reached the chorus, Mia heard the crowd singing along as loud as she had ever heard them before. She smiled as she sang along to the song, her and Dylan's voices lost into the mix of the crowd. Looking over at the bar, she saw Niamh and Ben with their arms around each other's shoulders as they sang along loudly, with their free hands in the air. Glen was standing nearby, his head bouncing along to the beat of the song and he, too, was singing along.

Reaching the crescendo of the song Mia could feel the energy and enthusiasm radiating from the crowd. It was a euphoric feeling, knowing she and Dylan had created such an atmosphere in the bar that night.

The final verses of the song resonated around the bar so loud they must have been heard from halfway down Temple Bar.

"California rest in peace,
Simultaneous release,
California show your teeth.
She's my priestess, I'm your priest, yeah, yeah."

Rapturous applause burst out across the room as the song ended. The crowd was jumping up and down cheering and a thunderous amount of clapping deafened the room.

Dylan grabbed Mia's hand, pulled her from her stool, and held her hand with his aloft in celebration. The crowd cheered even louder. She laughed at their incredulous applause and began to turn from the stage, figuring Dylan had gotten what he wanted.

"Ah, ah, ah," came his smug voice over the microphone, his hand still firmly grasped around hers.

She saw him and the eager waiting crowd.

"I think she can do a couple more songs, don't you, guys?" he asked the crowd and they cheered loudly in agreement.

Mia laughed and gave him a look that firmly said, *You're in serious trouble later*.

She sat back down on her stool and adjusted her guitar, waiting for Dylan to continue.

Giving her a smug grin, he nodded. *He is enjoying this far too much*, Mia thought. He signalled to the band and her that he was about to start the next song.

She heard the first few notes of the song and rolled her eyes as she laughed again. She had a feeling she could guess Dylan's theme of music for the night.

She waited a beat before joining in with "Hotel California" by the Eagles.

> "Welcome to the Hotel California,
> Such a lovely place, Such a lovely place,
> Such a lovely face.
> Plenty of room at the Hotel California,
> Any time of year, Any time of year,
> You can find it here."

The crowd was once again singing loudly, joining their arms together, and swaying along to the music as they sang.

Strumming her guitar enthusiastically, Mia admitted to herself she loved Dylan's choice of music and the enthusiasm of her final crowd at Glen's Tavern. The whole room was still on their feet, singing along and moving with the music. Every one of them was joining in with the song choices. She smiled as she looked across at Dylan singing in time with her. He threw her another wicked grin out of the corner of his mouth. Mia knew she was in for a long night. This really was going to be one hell of a send-off, after all.

ᘓᓍᘓ

Turning the key in the lock and tugging on the handle once more to be sure, Mia turned to pick up her suitcase beside her. The finality of locking up her flat and leaving with her suitcase was an overwhelming sensation. Knowing she wouldn't see it again for three months was also a strange feeling. Also realizing she wouldn't be seeing Glen's Tavern for three months was weird. The place was part of her daily life. If she wasn't working there, she was performing, and if she wasn't performing there, she was socialising. She wondered how her temporary life in Los Angeles would fill the gaping void that Glen's would leave.

Her head still pounded from the number of drinks her friends and the crowd had bought her after she had left the stage. Ringing noise still played in her ears and she could still hear the crowd singing along to their performance. Mia knew everyone at Glen's had given her the best possible send off.

Dylan had given her a show-stopping last performance. The well-known Californian-themed songs had the crowd singing along all night, and the atmosphere was truly electric. The after party with her friends had only continued the high Mia was riding after her performance. She knew she would have to sleep on the flight for the late night they had given her. She really was going to miss the place—her friends especially. Niamh had cried endlessly at the end of the night and had promised to call Mia every day. And Mia knew she would. She was already looking forward to hearing Niamh's voice on the phone, filling her in on everything that was happening at Glen's Tavern in her absence.

On the other hand, Mia could have run the length of the corridor and down the stairs to the waiting taxi as fast as her legs would carry her and scream at the top of her lungs with giddiness and glee.

She was finally on her way to realising her dreams. All the endless hours and days of practising until her fingertips were numb and engraved with the shape of the guitar strings and her voice was raspy from singing, all the hours of dedicatedly pouring her heart and soul onto reams of notepaper was finally paying off. The hundreds of nights she had performed at Glen's over the last three years had been worthwhile. Someone had finally noticed her.

Or at least she hoped. Jackson had seen something in her to warrant flying her out to Los Angeles with a week's notice to work with the best recording company in the rock music industry.

That, Mia mused, *is an overwhelming thought.*

The taxi was waiting patiently at the side of the curb as she exited her building and the driver immediately got out to take her suitcase as he saw her approach the car. She handed him her suitcase first and then her beloved guitar case before she slid herself in the back seat of the car.

As the car began its journey through the streets of Dublin toward the airport, Mia leaned her head against the glass as she stared at the passing streets. Thousands of memories came flooding back as the bars, shops, and streets she had grown to know so well began to zip past the taxi. Knowing she wouldn't be seeing them for a while made her feel nostalgic as she watched them fly past the window. She thought back to the journey that had brought her to Dublin and the one she was yet to take. The new life she would form in Los Angeles and the people she was yet to meet, the friendships waiting to be formed, and the possible career waiting to be developed.

ℰ∽ℰ∽

"Flight 259 to Los Angeles is now boarding."

The announcement Mia had waited three painstaking hours for finally sounded across the airport. She unplugged her headphones, peeled herself off the uncomfortable plastic seat in the waiting lounge, and gathered her belongings together, tightly clutching the boarding pass and her passport in her hand.

As she made her way through the crowds toward her departure gate, she couldn't help but wonder about the people around her in the airport. *Where are they all going? Why are they going to those places?* She wondered if their journeys were as exciting or as hopeful as hers was.

She wondered what lay ahead for the people around her once they stepped off the plane at their destinations.

Gazing up at the departures board as she made her way toward the gate, she read the outbound destinations. New York, Dallas, Florida, Dubai, London, Amsterdam, Paris, Cancun…so many places were flashing their imminent departure, taking their passengers across the globe for whatever fate awaited them. There was one departure that appeared to Mia to flash brighter than the others did.

Los Angeles: Flight 259
Gate 14: BOARDING

Those letters somehow seemed to glow a little brighter than all the others, their text was a little bolder, the letters flashed a little faster. The sight filled her stomach with butterflies. Some butterflies danced around her insides with excited little flutters while others flapped their wings frantically in anticipation.

Mia knew which butterflies she favored.

Nerves were only natural, she told herself as her place in the queue came closer to the desk. This was everything she had ever wanted in life and yet she had absolutely no idea what to expect. She had no idea what would happen when she arrived or where this would lead when her time was up. Filled with nerves, excitement, and great expectations, she walked the seemingly endless corridor to the plane doors.

"Hi, welcome aboard," said a woman wearing too much make up and a false smile.

Mia handed her the boarding card in her hand.

"The aisle on the left, head toward the back." The woman pointed in the direction of Mia's seat.

"Thank you." Mia took back her ticket and began to shuffle between the rows of seats in the direction the hostess had indicated.

She removed her iPod and notebook from the font pocket before she stowed her bag in the overhead locker. She noticed gratefully that she had been assigned a window seat and she sat idly staring out of the window at the green fields on either side of the runway as the seats around her slowly began to fill with their occupants.

Eventually, after the last-minute passengers had found their seats, the plane prepared to leave.

Mia heard and felt the propellers of the engine on the wing beside her begin whirring to life. The plane began to move, slowly easing out of the gate before gradually turning to taxi down the runway. Engines whirred even louder as they built up speed and, suddenly, the plane was heading down the runway and lifting away into the sky.

She stared out of the window beside her, down at the green landscape of her beloved Ireland disappearing beneath her. The city of Dublin was barely visible in the distance as the plane rose even higher into the sky.

Watching her world descend away from beneath her, Mia

thought back on how drastically her life had changed over the years.

Orphaned at five years old, she had only the vaguest memories of her parents. Her life in Kinsale with Sharon and Mike had been quiet and stable, the kind any child would wish for. But an endless yearning for something more had forced her to pack up her sheltered life and move to Dublin, in search of the food of her soul—music.

Dublin lived, breathed, and thrived on the stuff and so had Mia. Living in the ever-chord-strumming city had fuelled her love for music more than she could have ever imagined. She had developed not only her love for music but also her talent and her skill.

The city had given her opportunities that she never would have found if she had remained in Kinsale. And that beloved city had also provided her with the seat she was now sitting in, the one that was once again taking her away from everything she knew and into the unknown, in search of that ever-playing music beating in her heart.

CHAPTER 7

Mentally picturing the map in her mind, Mia navigated the streets of downtown Los Angeles. The recording studio was only a few streets away from her hotel so the directions weren't difficult to remember and she hadn't wanted to look like a lost tourist, wandering the streets with a guidebook. A hotel receptionist had told her it was only a ten-minute walk away, and she had been right. As Mia rounded the corner of the block, Sixth String Studios was right in front of her.

Situated on the corner of the next block, the four-storey building had a sleek, modern look that oozed its rock and roll reputation with its virtually all black glass exterior.

Mia thought it looked perfectly at home, nestled between the other buildings and the palm-tree-laden sidewalks, in the LA sunshine. The dark glass exterior glistened as it reflected the already-bright morning sunshine.

As she crossed the road, she couldn't help but notice the impressive collection of cars that were parked in the parking lot in front of the building. In between the huge Escalades and pickups, there were a few Audi's; a Hummer; and a couple of muscle cars, such as Chevrolets and Fords. She even noticed a Lamborghini Murchielago parked next to the entrance. Mia walked through the car park with an impressive smirk plastered across her face, knowing she had been hand-picked by the finest in the business and, as she strolled among their cars, she couldn't help but picture pulling up to the building in one of those cars herself. She was beginning to feel at home at Sixth String Studios and she hadn't even opened the front door yet.

Looking at the unmoving glass doors in front of her, she then noticed the keypad and speaker next to the door. She pressed the buzzer and immediately a chirpy Californian accent answered. "Sixth String Studios, how can I help?"

"My name's Mia Ryan. I'm here to see Jackson Miller."

"Oh hey, Mia," the woman answered as if they were friends. "Come on in."

An audible beep sounded and the glass doors slid open.

Inside the spacious foyer, the décor matched the building's exterior. Black ceramic tiles lined the floor and black leather sofas and a glass coffee table furnished the waiting area. Photographs of some of their prized artists, on stage mid-performance, collecting awards, or posing for the camera, decorated the white walls.

Directly in front of Mia was a black glass reception desk and perched on the chair behind it, like a colorful exotic bird, was a young woman Mia couldn't take her eyes off.

She had cocoa brown hair that was shaved at the sides and the top was styled into an elegant quiff with blonde streaks running through one side. Her skin was pale velvet brown and her features were emphasised by her mixed Caucasian and oriental heritage. The young woman's huge brown eyes looked even bigger with her make-up. Several earrings on each ear glinted in the light. Underneath a pristine black blazer jacket, the woman wore a Guns and Roses T-shirt. Mia admired her quirky style, wondering if she could pull off a similar look. This woman was beautiful and, yet, fashionably different. She was riveting.

"Hi there, Mia," she piped up as Mia approached he desk. The sound of her heels clacked against the tiles as she rose from her seat to greet her. "Welcome to Sixth String Studios. I'm Charlie." She held out her hand. Her voice and her expression greeted Mia as if they were long-time friends. Mia liked her already.

"Hi," she said as friendly as she could and returned the handshake.

Charlie handed Mia a clipboard and a pen. "If I can just get you to fill out a couple of forms for me and then I'll get you a security pass sorted too."

"Sure." Looking down at the paper in front of her, mandatory questions stared back at Mia—name, date of birth, address, contact number, email address, followed by bank details.

"Bank details?" she raised an eyebrow at Charlie.

She grinned. "Sure, you want to get paid don't you?"

"I just didn't think—"

"What? That'd we'd fly you all the way out here for three months and not pay you?" Charlie smiled empathetically. "Don't be dumb."

"Oh," Mia said.

Jackson hadn't mentioned anything about being paid. Mia had simply been grateful for the experience at the company, finding out she was getting paid was an added bonus.

"Jackson will go through your contract with you in a moment," Charlie explained. "If you just want to look into the camera here for me." She pointed a manicured cobalt blue fingernail at the webcam on top of her computer.

Mia smiled at the camera.

"Beautiful," Charlie said to the screen as she looked at Mia's image. A machine by the side of the computer whirred loudly before spitting something out with a clatter. "Here we go," Charlie said a moment later, holding up an ID card attached to a lanyard.

Mia's own face stared back at her on a shiny plastic ID card with *Sixth String Studios: Staff* printed alongside it. Mia felt the butterflies rise up in her stomach in excitement.

Seeing her face on a staff ID card was a surreal feeling. It was slowly beginning to dawn on her where she was.

"Mia, good to see you again," came a professional, clipped voice with the trademark Californian accent approaching from the corridor.

She knew who was striding toward her across the foyer. "Hi, Jackson," she answered politely and extended her hand to him.

He shook it as firmly as she remembered before clasping his hand on her shoulder. "Are we done, Charlie? Can I borrow her now?"

"Sure you can," she responded as chirpily as before. "Have fun, Mia."

Jackson then led Mia down a long corridor to the left of the reception desk. "How was your flight? Is your hotel okay too?" he asked.

"Yes," she replied, "both were great, thank you."

"All right, now what's going to happen today is that we'll go through your contract, explain a bit about Sixth String Studios, and then we'll get you in a studio with two of our producers, TJ and Chad, so you can see how things work. How does that sound?"

"That sounds fantastic," she answered honestly.

⌒⌒⌒

Mia headed back into the reception foyer as she and Jackson broke for lunch.

After a long morning talking about her contract and what she would be doing at the studios, she just finished listening to an hour and a half presentation from Jackson about the company and their artists. She was blown away by the artists who were signed to the studios—some of her biggest musical inspirations worked under the same roof where she would now be employed.

There was a lot of information to take in over the morning, and Mia was silently relieved when Jackson said she could break for lunch. He had gone to answer emails in his office and left her to her own devices.

Remembering she had noticed a deli around the block from the studios that morning, she intended to head there.

"Hey, Mia," called a chirpy voice from across the room, "you going for lunch?"

"Yeah," Mia spun on her heel to see Charlie rising from her desk.

"Mind if I join you?" she asked as she grabbed her phone and purse.

"No, not at all," Mia replied. She really was beginning to like Charlie already.

⌒⌒⌒

Lunch with Charlie was an entertaining affair. Mia laughed almost constantly for an hour as Charlie recalled countless stories of artists at Sixth String Studios who she had seen over the years she had worked there.

This beautiful woman had a knack for making Mia feel completely at ease, and as if they had known each other for years. With all the information she had to remember and good first impressions to make, Mia was grateful for a friendly face by way of Charlie on her first day.

Seven years after starting as an intern straight out of high school, Charlie had worked at Sixth String Studios ever since then. At the ripe old age of twenty-five, she had seen things and befriended more rock stars than many double her age could ever dream of. Before Mia knew it, her hour was up and it was time to meet back with Jackson at the studio.

"You're gonna love TJ and Chad," Charlie assured her. "They're the nicest guys in there. Jackson couldn't have put you with anyone better."

"I hope so," Mia replied.

She was nervous about working with, or watching, two of the producers. She had no idea what to expect and desperately wanted to make a good first impression. It was crucial she worked hard enough to impress these guys.

"They really are," Charlie continued as they crossed the street. "They're so sweet. And they totally know what they're doing. They're some of the best we've got."

"Wow." Mia raised her eyebrows. Jackson really must believe in her to put her with two of his best producers on her first day.

"Yeah, that's a big honor." Charlie looked impressed. "You must have something special girl. I gotta hear you play sometime soon."

"You will, I promise," Mia agreed. Charlie had been more than kind to her. It was the least Mia could do.

"Now don't worry," Charlie assured her as she walked her down the corridor, "these guys are great." She knocked on a door marked *Studio Two* and waited for a reply.

A faint male voice told them to come in.

"Hey, guys." Charlie smiled sweetly as she walked into the room. "This is Mia."

The two men seated at the large mixing desk in the studio spun in their chairs to look at her.

"Hi, I'm TJ," a man with a mop of dirty blond, curly hair answered as he stood up to greet Mia. She shook his hand readily.

"And I'm Chad," said the second man, whose long, un-styled brown hair fell around his face.

Both men couldn't have been older than thirty and were dressed in T-shirts, jeans, and trainers. They both had the same laid-back Californian attitude that Charlie had and Mia instantly felt at ease.

"You guys be nice now." Charlie winked as she closed the door.

Mia could hear her high heels clacking away down the corridor as she returned to the reception desk.

"So, Mia." TJ's twinkling blue eyes smiled up at her through his curls as he sat back down. "Ready to get to work?"

"Absolutely."

 excess

Working with TJ and Chad, Mia instantly felt as though she was back at Glen's Tavern on a shift with Ben and Dylan.

They chatted and joked with her, like they were old friends, as they showed her how the studio worked and allowed her to help with the editing and buffing of a nearly ready album. The album was by one of Mia's favorite bands. She was dumbfounded at being able to assist with the final production of their latest album and wondered when reality would finally begin to hit her. So far, everything about Los Angeles had been a dream.

She could understand why so many people traveled here to find their fame and fortune. It really was the city of dreams. Or it was for her, anyway.

After spending the afternoon listening to the band's album several times over as they made various slight edits and changes, TJ and Chad said it was almost time to call it a day. Her first day at the studio had been surreal. She had seen the building where some of the most iconic modern rock music had been recorded and produced and she had even had a hand in the process herself.

She also felt as though she had made several friends already.

"Right, come on then, Mia." Chad grinned at her as he spun in his seat at the desk. "Let's hear what we're working with tomorrow."

She glanced at him, puzzled. "Huh?"

"Your music," TJ answered. "Hasn't Jackson told you? We're going to have a go at some song writing together tomorrow."

"Yeah, so come on, give us a demo," Chad teased with an impish grin on his face.

"Okay, hang on." Mia got up to grab her guitar.

Right on cue, Charlie poked her head around the door to the studio as Mia sat back down with her guitar.

"Ooh, are you going to play?" she asked.

"Looks like it," Chad joked.

Charlie playfully slapped him around the back of the head as she perched on the edge of the desk.

No pressure then, Mia thought.

Deciding to play her most recent song—the one that had had such a rapturous response when she had played it at Glen's Tavern as it was the one that was also the most emotional to her, she took a quiet, deep breath. She needed to make a good impression. She knew this one would do the trick.

Feeling felt the atmosphere in the room fall silent and grow tense as she began to play, she wondered what reaction two of the greatest producers in the building would have after hearing her music.

Pouring her heart and soul out into a song in front of three strangers in such an intimate setting felt strange. She was normally on stage, performing to hundreds, where she could shut out the crowd. Seeing their faces so closely was intimidating.

She reached the end of her song and the final note faded away into the room.

Holding her breath, she waited for the reaction.

She looked up to see Charlie wiping away tears from her eyes.

"Wow," was all TJ said.

"Shit, Mia," Chad said, looking flabbergasted, "that's incredible. You sure we only signed you up as a songwriter?"

She giggled in relief. "Yeah, you did."

"I think we may need to have a word about that," TJ smirked as he ran his hands through his floppy curls, his face still riveted on her in amazement.

Charlie shook her head in awe and wiped away another tear. "I haven't heard a song like that in a long, long time," she whispered.

ᘐᘐ

Californian sun shone brightly in the early morning sky as Mia walked the short walk to the studios from her hotel. The heat from the sun was already beginning to prickle her bare arms, despite the early hour of the day.

Stopping at the Starbucks on the corner of the block before the studios, she grabbed a coffee, as she always found that a caffeine fix helped her brain along with the creative process.

She had been working at Sixth String Studios for over three weeks now and felt like part of the family. Already she had progressed from editing albums with TJ and Chad to being given her own studio to work in with them both on her music. The studio wanted Mia to write songs for some of their artists who didn't write their own music and, from there, they were going to see how the fans reacted to her songs.

The thought was mind-blowing. Mia had been plucked right out of Glen's Tavern and dropped into the LA sunshine to work in the best rock music studio and write songs for some of her favorite artists—artists who performed across the globe to sell-out arenas and tours and who won Grammy awards and headlined festivals.

Jackson really believed she had talent in order to put her in such an esteemed position straight away. As Charlie told her, "Some of the best artists started out writing songs here," she would say with a wink of her long eyelashes.

TJ often praised Mia's abilities on a daily basis after hearing her perform. He was insistent she should be in the booth, rather than behind it. Chad was the more brazen of the two and repeatedly asked Jackson to sign her up whenever he walked past the studio door.

"Have you written Mia's contract yet?" he called out as he leaned over the edge of his chair as Jackson strode past the open studio door.

Feeling her cheeks flame with embarrassment, she saw TJ smile and shake his head at Chad.

"Not yet, Chad," Jackson would always call over his shoulder as he carried on his way.

Mia was grateful for their praise but sometimes she silently wished Chad would keep quiet. She didn't want Jackson thinking she was expecting more from this opportunity. She had only been there a little over three weeks.

As she crossed the street toward the studio, she could see a large group of people clustered just outside the parking lot. To get a better view of what was happening, she lifted her sunglasses as she approached. Drawing nearer, she dropped her sunglasses again, realising who the people were.

A large group of paparazzi were clustered around the entrance to the parking lot. Two security guards stood on the other side of the entrance, ensuring they stayed off the studio grounds.

The paparazzi nervously fidgeted with their cameras as they glanced up and down the street at the passing cars and approaching pedestrians. They looked up as Mia approached their cluster. A few looked her up and down before disinterestedly glancing away while others continued their scanning of the passers-by.

As she approached the security guards and showed her security pass, several of the paparazzi began to take photographs of her as they realised she was entering the building.

From behind her sunglasses, she frowned as she looked over her shoulder at the paparazzi taking her picture. That was part of working at Sixth String Studios that she hadn't expected to experience while in Los Angeles. She knew the studio had numerous A-list artists signed to their books, but somehow Mia hadn't expected the paparazzi to be waiting outside the door every morning for them.

She swiped her security card on the side of the door and strode through the sliding glass doors, which made their now familiar swoosh sound. Several expectant faces looked up at her as she entered the building. Seeing who had come through the doors, like the paparazzi, they returned to their tasks.

Honing in on the reception desk, Mia dashed to Charlie who was typing furiously at her computer as she approached.

"Oh, hey, Mia." Charlie smiled. "You here to see Chad and TJ?" she asked as she typed the entry into the computer. Sixth String Studios required everyone entering the building to sign in with her.

Charlie was wearing a printed black and white T-shirt with a sleeveless leather jacket that morning. Stacks of jewellery clinked up each of her wrists and various hoops and studs glinted from up and down her ears. Mia envied Charlie's outlandish sense of style. Her effortless rock and roll look fitted in perfectly with the face of the studios.

"Yeah," she answered as she placed her coffee on the counter and signed into the building.

"Oh God, that smells good." Charlie nodded at the cup on the counter. "Right, you're good to go. You're in studio four today."

"Okay, thanks." Mia wondered why they had been moved and

realised the answer was probably why the paparazzi were waiting outside. "What's going on today?" she asked, jerking her thumb in the direction of the security guards and paparazzi waiting outside.

A devilish smile crossed Charlie's face, full of knowing. "Have you not heard who's coming?"

Mia shook her head. Working at Sixth String Studios meant any of her musical idols could come walking through the door at any moment. "Nope," she answered.

Charlie's grin widened and curved up one side of her face in a wicked, lop-sided smile. "Joel Coben is back from his world tour. He's coming back in the studio today to start working on his new album."

Instantly Mia's mouth fell open in shock. "Joel Coben?" she repeated.

Charlie nodded. "I know, right?"

"Wow." Mia knew Joel Coben was signed to Sixth String Studios, but she hadn't expected to see him. Joel was a megastar. He was Sixth String Studio's biggest selling artist and was an incredible guitarist and singer. Not only had he won several Grammy awards and numerous other accolades, he was returning to the studio from his latest sell-out worldwide tour. The man was a musical phenomenon.

He was also extremely reclusive. The media had preyed on him for years, trying to uncover his secrets. It was no secret Joel hated the media and avoided being seen in public at all costs. There were numerous stories in the media about his supposed secret social life and many wannabe models sold their stories, claiming to have bedded him. Joel made no comment on any of those stories. And like most rock stars, he was also ridiculously beautiful. Mia mentally thanked herself for choosing one of her better outfits that morning in her hotel room.

"Keep your eyes peeled," Charlie hinted to her as she headed down the corridor.

৫৩৫৩

Several days passed since Mia had seen the paparazzi outside the studios and, despite endless rumours, she hadn't seen Joel Coben in the building.

Charlie had enthusiastically told her repeatedly, every time they had lunch, how beautiful he had looked that particular morning. Though Mia feigned rolling her eyes at her over the table in the deli, secretly she was envious that Charlie got to see so many of her idols every single day.

"He was so pissed about the paps waiting outside," Charlie mumbled through a mouthful of salad.

"I'm not surprised." Curious, Mia added, "Is he a bit of a diva?"

Charlie began to laugh before coughing on her salad. After taking a sip of her drink, she managed, "Oh God, no. He barely ever speaks. He's so quiet. But you could just tell, you know?"

Mia nodded as she ate her own lunch. She had been desperate to catch a glimpse of one of her favorite singers all week—but still nothing.

Her beautiful, quirky friend told her that Joel varied the hours he arrived in order to throw off the waiting paparazzi, who were still camped outside the studio. Joel would often stay, working late into the night. It was no wonder Mia hadn't seen him yet.

"I mean, it must be difficult for him, trying to keep his privacy," Charlie continued, "but he just gets followed everywhere."

"Yeah, I can only imagine." Mia tried to picture being chased down the street by several men with cameras everywhere she went.

"But don't believe everything you read about him, though." Charlie gave her a knowing look. "Ninety per cent of that stuff is total bullshit."

"I figured." Some of the stories Mia read in the media, not just about Joel, she couldn't begin to fathom were true. The lengths the media would go to in order to have stories was baffling.

"He is strange, though," Charlie continued. "He's been there longer than I have and he still barely speaks to anyone. Apparently the only person he really talks to in there is his producer."

"Who's that?" Mia knew it wasn't TJ or Chad as she had been working with them most of the week.

"A guy named Ruben. You'll see him from time to time, but they mainly keep him for Joel. The best for the best, you know?"

Mia shrugged. "Sure."

"Ooh, have you seen his brother yet?" Charlie's face immediately lit up as she spoke.

"No," Mia answered.

She knew Joel had a brother and she remembered seeing him in a magazine article once but, in general, she didn't tend to read gossip magazines unless she couldn't avoid it. Niamh had a habit of buying the trashy magazines and leaving them on the staff room table at Glen's. Mia sometimes flicked through them on her break if she had nothing else to do.

"Josh is lovely." Charlie's face became almost swooning as she spoke. "He's not quite as hot as Joel, but he's so much nicer. He's a whole lot of fun."

Mia had a sneaking suspicion that Charlie was rather fond of Josh.

"You're bound to see him soon enough. He always shows up when Joel's in the studio, except he actually speaks to everyone."

Charlie flashed a smile and Mia immediately pictured a Joel look-a-like lounging against the reception desk while Charlie batted her long eyelashes at him.

"Come on, you." Mia laughed at a still-swooning Charlie as she stood up from the table. "Time to head back to work."

Sighing loudly, Charlie quipped, "There goes the fastest hour of the day."

"Speak for yourself," Mia teased.

As much as she enjoyed her lunch hours with Charlie, she really was enjoying working at Sixth String Studios. Being locked away in a recording studio writing songs with two like-minded producers for hours on end was her idea of bliss. She finally felt like one of those few, fortunate people who truly enjoyed their jobs. Going to work wasn't going to work for her anymore. She was being paid to spend her days doing what she loved most. And, for Mia, nothing about that was work.

CHAPTER 8

Twirling her pen between her fingers, Mia stared blankly at the words etched across the paper on the table in front of her. She had been staring at those words, willing the rest of the verse to come to her, for the last hour.

Picking up her guitar that was propped against her chair, she began to strum the chords she imagined the lyrics flowing to—well, the lyrics that she had so far, anyway.

She strummed the first few notes, feeling the strings vibrate underneath her fingertips and instantly feeling her inner-self calm. Music was her sanctuary. The moment she laid her fingers to the fret board, she immediately felt at home. Her mind switched off everything and focussed on the forthcoming notes of music and the lyrics etched into her mind.

All the confusion, the hurt, the pain, everything calmed as soon as she began to play.

First, she strummed softly, getting a feel for the new melody, forcing the rhythm to commit to her memory and willing her mind to better the melody she had created, allowing the lyrics to flow along with it.

Singing the first few lines of the song, she let her voice match the guitar in pitch and volume, easily coordinating the strumming of her fingers. As she reached the chorus, she allowed the song to take over her mind fully, letting herself to relax and fall completely into the music.

She raised her voice as she pushed down her fingers harder onto the strings. Neither singing nor playing too loud for the small room, she allowed the intensity she felt to be expressed in her music.

The second verse followed. Her uncertainty over the lyrics never showed in her face or her voice as she sang and she slipped easily into the second chorus.

On she continued, strumming the melody, willing her brain to create the lyrics for the final verse. She could feel the words at the back of her mind, but somehow her brain wouldn't allow her to process them fully and let them to appear on the paper before her. She felt frustrated with herself, knowing the answer was there but her own mind wouldn't let her to create the lyrics she so desperately needed.

Switching some of the chords of the introduction, she started from the beginning to see if a change in chord progression was what the song needed to feel complete.

As she reached the end of the first chorus, she was startled by a voice in the doorway.

"I prefer the way you had it the first time round."

Mia jumped in her seat, her fingers instantly stopping their rhythm on the guitar. She spun in her seat to see who had been both watching and listening to her performance.

In the quiet and solace of the small studio at the end of the corridor, Chad had promised Mia she would be free from prying eyes and ears to focus on her song writing. He and TJ had left early for the afternoon and Mia thought she was alone in the studio.

She hadn't realised the door was not fully closed when they left.

That door was now wide open.

Frozen in her seat, she faced the door with the guitar still in her lap, her mouth still open as if it waited to sing the lyrics that were ready to come before she had been interrupted.

Joel Coben was standing in the open doorway.

He had been listening to her music. Listening to her singing. Listening to her playing.

Mia remained frozen, embarrassed to her core that one of the greatest musicians she had ever admired had been listening to her practise her work-in-progress.

And not only was Joel Coben an incredible musician, he could work rhythms out of a guitar that she could only dream of. His voice was a deep, sultry, husking sound, and he was also breathtakingly beautiful.

Magazine pictures and Charlie's ramblings had all failed to do justice to the man standing before her.

And he was staring at her.

His intense dark brown eyes bored straight into her, giving the impression of consuming her entirely with his gaze.

Mia shifted uncomfortably in her seat, readjusting the guitar on her lap. "Umm, thanks. It's not finished quiet yet." Her voice sounded as weak as she felt in the shadow of her idol.

Joel shrugged, his eyes still not leaving hers. "It sounds pretty good to me, and those lyrics are quite intense." His voice was soft and deep, the laid-back Californian accent rolling the words effortlessly off his tongue.

Mia stared. One of her most idolised lyricists was giving her a compliment on her song writing. "Thanks," she managed again. "It still needs a third verse though."

"I'm sure you'll figure it out." He glanced down at the paper on the table in front of her. The loss of his gaze reminded Mia she was holding her breath.

In the seconds that he glanced at the table, Mia stole a moment to appreciate the man in front of her.

Joel Coben, one of rock music's most notoriously reclusive men, was tall, ridiculously lean, and muscular in just the right way, and had thick, dark hair that was usually an unruly mess on top of his head. Naturally, that unruly mess made him even more exquisitely handsome. He had a seductively rugged appeal. His cheekbones had a light stubble across them and his dark brows and eyelashes framed those intensely dark eyes that were so brown, they were almost black.

He wore a hooded sweatshirt, zipped almost to the top, which covered the tattoos on his arms that Mia knew all too well were underneath. She had seen them in the media before. All his inkings were either song lyrics or beautifully intricate black and white designs. She could see the edge of one from where his T-shirt met his neck underneath the sweatshirt.

His jeans were tucked into his boots and Mia couldn't help but remember Dylan wore his exactly the same way, most probably copying his idol, who now stood before her.

Joel, however, pulled off the look naturally and effortlessly, as did Dylan, but the image seemed perfected on him.

The dark colors of his clothing emphasised the intensity of his stare, which Mia now noticed was fully honed back on her. *Shit*, she thought. How long had he noticed her staring?

"Well, good luck with that." He nodded his head toward the notebook on the table and impassively glanced over her before turning and leaving the room.

That smouldering, dark stare of his had, in a second, made her feel completely non-existent. He had the strange ability of making her feel completely overwhelmed in one moment and as if she never existed in another.

CHAPTER 9

That brief encounter seemed to have acted as a trigger as, from then on, Mia couldn't seem to go anywhere in the studio without seeing Joel Coben. She wondered how she had gone from several days of him being in the same building and not seeing him to bumping into him every time she left the room.

Naturally, Charlie found her frustration amusing. "He's freaking hot. How can you be so mad at bumping into this guy so much?" she whined at Mia over the reception desk one afternoon.

"Because he's weird," Mia muttered under her breath.

Everyone in the building practically fell over their own feet and all but bowed down before Joel whenever he entered the room. Mia however, found him weird.

Charlie scowled and threw up her hands in frustration. "What? Why?"

Mia raised her eyebrows at Charlie's scowling. "Because he spied on me practising, said a few words to me, he looked at me as though I never existed, and left the room."

"Yeah, he does that." Charlie shrugged nonchalantly, as if it were the most natural behavior in the world.

"Well, it's rude." Mia frowned back at her and snatched a pen from the every growing collection on Charlie's desk, as hers had gone missing.

"So are you!" shouted a sarcastic voice across the foyer as Mia stalked back to her studio.

She didn't turn around to let Charlie see she was trying not to laugh.

❧❧❧

Over the next few days, Mia continued to see Joel more around the studios.

Trying to fathom him out was impossible. His behavior began to both intrigue and irritate her. He would pass her in the corridor or the foyer without a second glance. Other times, he would pass her with his head down before briefly looking up at her underneath his eyebrows—his intense dark eyes staring into her own as she hurried by.

She noticed his frame loitering in the doorway of her own recording studio several times. He was always standing in the corridor, watching and listening. No matter how many times Mia passed Joel or caught his eye as he disappeared from the doorway, not once would he say anything. Not even a smile in passing or a hello.

Charlie couldn't understand her confusion. To her that was simply the way Joel acted. He always did that.

"I feel like he's spying on me." Mia sighed exasperated as she leaned against the reception desk. She was trying to vent her frustrations at Charlie, who wasn't lending a sympathetic ear.

Charlie raised her eyebrows over the computer screen at her. "Don't flatter yourself."

Mia sighed again and threw her hands up at her in frustration. "I'm serious," she tried again, but Charlie continued to stare at the email she was reading on the screen. "He's just weird. Who talks to someone one minute and acts as if they don't exist in the next?"

Charlie raised a perfectly styled eyebrow at Mia. "He does," was all she said.

Her face was surrounded in the glow from the monitor in front of her, her eyes glued to the screen in concentration.

"But it's not normal. I wouldn't be allowed to stand in the doorway of his studio all the time, listening to him."

That eyebrow arched even higher. "Sure, you wouldn't. Why do you think it's always locked?" Charlie casually sipped the iced drink that Mia had fetched for her.

"I might have to try that one," Mia mumbled.

Charlie chuckled to herself as she returned her gaze from the screen to Mia's face. "I'm sure Chad and TJ would love that."

Mia rolled her eyes. TJ and Chad were so relaxed, she doubted they even locked their cars in the car park in front of the studio, let alone the recording studio itself. She was really beginning to bond with TJ and Chad. She felt like she connected with them deeply on a musical level. Jackson couldn't have picked a better pair of producers for her to work with. It was as if he had known who would understand her before he even knew her himself.

She had connected with them as if they were her brothers. They almost filled the void in her life that had been made by leaving Ben and Dylan behind in Dublin. And Charlie was certainly doing her best at filling Niamh's void, although Mia was sure no one could ever take Niamh's place. She smiled inwardly to herself at the thought of Niamh and Charlie meeting. Despite being oceans apart, the two really were cut from the same cloth. Mia wondered how she had been lucky enough to land two such friends in her lifetime. Despite her losses, fate had a funny way of dealing with replacing the missing values in her life. *Fate has a funny way of dealing with most things*, Mia thought.

She sighed over the desk at an unsympathetic Charlie. "Anyway, I'm heading back to work,"

Charlie winked and plastered a hugely mocking smile on her face as Mia turned to leave. "Have fun,"

Mia resisted the urge to give her the finger as she strode down the corridor back to her studio, knowing Charlie was still watching and enjoying Mia's discomfort. Charlie was used to Joel's standoffish behavior. Over the years, she had seen him come in and out of the studio and he had always been the same.

But, for Mia, somehow, it seemed different. There was something in his mannerisms that she didn't like, something that bothered her. Something was different about the way he treated her from everyone else.

Sure, he disregarded most people at the studio who he didn't need to converse with, but for her there seemed to be an extra dose of rudeness. An added spice of resentment.

She wondered what caused Joel to be so different with her. Though she had only spoken to him once and seen him on a number of occasions afterward, yet the resentment was clear in his eyes. Something distinguished her from the rest of those Joel deemed beneath him. Mia couldn't understand what or why, but there was something different about the way he treated her.

She pushed open the studio door and set down the cardboard tray of drinks on the coffee table behind the soundboard and mixing desks. No way had Mia ever dared to put anything spillable on those. It was doubtful she would even earn enough in her entire three months' paycheck to cover the amount of the equipment in the room.

Chad pushed his swivel chair backward from the desk and pedalled himself along the floor with his feet in order to reach the drinks.

TJ shook his head at his co-worker. "Man, it would have been easier if you just got up."

Picking up his drink with a satisfied smile on his face, Chad shrugged. "I didn't wanna get out of my chair."

"We figured." TJ sighed and stood up to collect his own drink. "Thanks, Mia. Listen, about that track we started last night, I wondered if we could run through it again?"

"Sure." Mia grabbed her guitar from the sofa and set her drink down. She prepared herself to begin playing as TJ advised on the minor details he had been considering changing within the song.

She nodded and listened attentively before beginning playing to her frappuccino slurping audience.

As she worked her way through the song, she made the adjustments that TJ had suggested as she went. Somehow, he had a way of connecting with Mia musically that allowed her to focus on the music without relying on the rising tide of emotion that threatened every time she strummed a note. Singing her own lyrics that were modified by someone else had a lesser effect on her emotions. They were still there. There was no doubt about that. They just seemed more in check. TJ had helped Mia to hone in on her music while finding a mute button for the uncontrollable feelings she often found her songs brought out in her.

When the song ended, both her colleagues clapped softly against one hand that was still clasping the plastic cup filled with blended ice. Mia grinned at them both. In some ways, they were more switched on than men double their age and sometimes they released their inner five year old. *An inner five year old who seems to lurk somewhere beneath the surface of most adult males*, she thought.

At once, she could feel Joel's eyes on her again as she spoke to TJ about the song. He simply stood a few feet behind them in the room, observing their conversation without joining in. Mia wondered again if conversing with the staff was below his standards. Since watching her practise, Joel had started appearing at the doorway every now and then to hear what was going on in the room. Sometimes she never noticed him appear and leave. Chad would tell her after she had finished. Other times she could feel his eyes burning into her skin as he watched.

Today, however, he had entered the room as she had been practising and remained watching from a distance. She'd heard the door softly click behind him as she was midway through her song. She wondered how he knew she was practising when he was locked away inside his own studio.

"You're Irish," he commented suddenly, nodding at Mia as if she were an object on the desk.

"You're observant," she quipped back in an instant.

TJ did a sharp intake of breath at her remark to their most precious talent. Chad snorted in a mouthful of frappuccino and tried to stifle a giggle.

Mia, however, didn't see their faces.

She curiously watched Joel's reaction. His mouth fell open in shock, as if in wonder at how she had spoken to him. He quickly closed his mouth again. The reaction was so quick that Mia would have missed it had she turned to look at TJ and Chad.

Joel, however, looked at none of them. After closing his mouth, he quickly turned and stalked from the room as if no one had been there in the first place.

☙❧

As she sat with her headphones on listening to the new edit of a track, Mia was surprised to look up and see Chad and TJ chuckling to themselves.

She lifted the headphones off her head and realised what they had been laughing at. Her phone was vibrating loudly in the pocket of her bag on the floor nearby.

Rolling her eyes at them before reaching down to grab it out of the pocket, she asked, "Why didn't you tell me?" She shook her head at them both still chuckling to themselves.

Honestly, Mia thought, *they are so laid back it's a wonder they aren't both stuck in reverse.*

Catching the phone call before it cut off to her voicemail, she answered, "Hello?"

"Hey, sweetie," a familiar Irish accent said over the phone line.

"Niamh? Oh my God, hi." Mia immediately recognized the musical accent of her best friend. She hadn't looked at the caller ID in her attempt to grab the phone before it stopped ringing.

"How are things in the City of Angels?" Niamh's voice sounded as distant as she really was over the line, reminding Mia of the vast space between her and her friend.

"Yeah, it's fantastic. I'm learning so much every day. I still can't believe I'm here. And I've met some great people." She mentally kicked herself for saying those words in front of TJ and Chad who mockingly wiped tears from their eyes and mimicked thanks at hearing her words.

"I'm so happy for you, finally living the dream." Niamh giggled softly down the line. "I miss you, though. Things aren't the same around here with you gone."

Mia sighed. "I miss you too."

She missed having her friend to talk to everyday. The time difference and expense of long distance calls were making keeping in touch difficult. "How's everyone at Glen's?" she asked wistfully, missing her old workplace. Although she was thriving in her new environment, Mia still missed her friends and the routine she had back in Dublin.

"Yeah we're good, same old. Nothing ever changes around here." Niamh giggled again and the sound made Mia smile. "Everyone misses you, though."

"I miss them all too."

"Ben and Dylan say hi and Glen says you owe him a phone call. He's dying to know who you've met so far."

Laughing as she told Niamh to return the message to Ben and Dylan, she heard the shouts of her friends in the background and, quickly adding on to the time displayed on her watch, Mia realised they would be finishing up for the night at Glen's Tavern.

As they were pretty much done for the day, TJ and Chad got up to leave, waving to Mia as they collected their things and left the studio.

"See you tomorrow," she called after them.

"Who's that?" Niamh asked.

"Just the producers I've been working with." she waved as TJ closed the door behind him.

"Are they cute?" Niamh's tone turned more curious.

"Umm...yeah, I guess they are." Mia cocked her head to one side as she thought. She had only looked at TJ and Chad as colleagues who she admired and was keen to impress in a professional manner. Not wanting to jeopardise her chances with the company if she came across as flirting, she hadn't thought of either of them in that way.

"Are they single?" Niamh asked.

Mia laughed. She knew Niamh was in full Detective Chief Inspector mode now. "I think TJ is." Mia frowned as she thought. She remembered Chad talking about his girlfriend but she hadn't heard TJ mention one, unless he was being coy.

Niamh squealed down the phone in delight but Mia cut her off. "No!" she cried, "don't even think about it."

"Why?"

Mia could already picture her pouting as she spoke. "Because I'm here to work, that's it."

"Speaking of work." Niamh suddenly changed direction. "Guess who Glen gave your slots to?"

Hearing her familiar slots at Glen's taken sounded strange and made Mia hesitate. It gave her leaving a sense of finality. "Who?" she asked.

"Dylan."

Mia giggled with Niamh at the news, relieved it was someone she knew and someone who equally deserved it. Dylan was surely reveling in the extra crowd attention that came with Friday and Saturday night's performances.

"I'm pleased for him," she said. "He deserves it."

"Yeah he does." Niamh sighed and Mia recognized the admiring tone in her voice. She wondered how long it would take Dylan to realise. "So come on," Niamh continue. "Glen's dying to know, who have you met so far?"

Laughter filled her end of the line as Mia heard Glen muttering to Niamh on the other end of the phone, vying for information. She knew how much he would love to see the studios and where some of his favorite songs were recorded.

"Umm—"

Mia paused again. She had seen a couple of familiar faces by then, which she related to her, and she could hear Glen sigh with jealousy.

"Anyone else?" Niamh asked.

Wondering whether to tell them, Mia hesitated again. She decided to, figuring if their roles had been reversed, she would want to know herself, if only out of curiosity. "I've met Joel Coben a couple of times," she mumbled.

Niamh screamed deafeningly, like a teenage fan, on the other end of the phone. Her scream was so loud, Mia wondered if she could have heard it across the Atlantic Ocean. She held the phone away from her ear momentarily and, once her fan-girl delight had returned to a bearable level, put the phone back to her ear. She could hear the shouts and questions on the phone from Glen, Dylan, and Ben as Niamh told them why she was so excited.

Naturally, they wanted to know everything. *What was he like? Was he nice? Was he as good looking in person?* To which Mia begrudgingly answered, "Yes, very." *Had she heard him play yet? Did she have his autograph?* That one was Glen.

She answered all the questions as much as she could, knowing how in awe her friends were of her meeting one of the biggest stars in the world. She would have done the same—in fact, she would have still been asking questions if she were on the receiving end of such news.

"Yeah, well…he's kind of odd," she muttered quietly.

"What do you mean?" Niamh's voice sounded confused at the thought.

"I don't know…he's just…rude I guess."

"Hello? Details?" Niamh wasn't the most patient of people at times.

Mia sighed and related the events of the past few days to her friend, hoping she would hear confirmation that she wasn't the only one who thought so.

"Oh." The excitement had drained from Niamh's voice. "I guess that's pretty weird. Hey, there was this article about him the other day…"

Out of politeness, Mia listened as Niamh related the story from a gossip magazine about how Joel Coben had supposedly been an adult-movie star.

The story made Mia rolled her eyes again, grateful Niamh couldn't see her do so. She wondered how magazines still existed when they made up such garbage on a regular basis. It was a wonder they weren't sued on a daily basis, too.

"Hmm, I'll ask him about that one if I get the chance," she mumbled once Niamh had finished telling her the specifics of the story. Mia smiled to herself at the reaction she could picture on Joel's face if she did ask.

"Oh my God, I mean I'm sure he already knows about the article," Niamh continued to ramble. "But they haven't released the tapes yet. I wonder if they even have any. I mean, do you think he seems the type?"

Mia giggled at her friend who seemed to think she was on well-acquainted terms with Joel already. They sat talking to each other for several more minutes as Niamh walked her way home through the early morning streets of Dublin. Once Mia had heard her shut the door of her flat, they wrapped up their conversation.

"I'll give you a call on the weekend, okay?" Mia wondered what time would suit them both best with the time differences and Niamh's shifts at Glen's.

"Okay, sweetie, speak to you then."

Hanging up the phone, Mia felt much brighter now that she had reconnected with her best friend after a few days with no contact. She also felt relieved to have vented her frustrations about Joel's behavior to someone unbiased and to have her thoughts confirmed.

A heavy sigh of relief exhaled as she realised she wasn't the only one unfazed by Joel's charms. Mia grabbed her bag, collected her things, shut down the computer, and switched off all the equipment. She turned off the lights as she swung open the door into the corridor.

And she instantly wished she hadn't.

She immediately wished she had left the lights on and could disappear to feign remembering something forgotten in the studio.

Joel Coben was standing in the corridor opposite her studio door.

He was busy texting on his phone, as she opened the door, casually leaning against the wall opposite her. Mia took another deep breath, as quietly as she could, at the sight of him.

He had on dark jeans and a white, long-sleeved T-shirt with the sleeves rolled up to his elbows. The tattoos on his arms clearly snaked down his forearms from underneath the rolled up sleeves of his T-shirt. And of course, she mentally sighed, his shirt was perfectly tight. Tight white cotton fabric clung to every inch of his beautifully defined torso. Every single muscle was visible underneath the fabric.

The sound of a throat clearing made her jump. Snapped from her rather obvious ogling, Mia looked up into an equally beautiful pair of inquisitive eyes.

Looking up at her from the phone still illuminated in his hand, Joel's eyes curiously stared at her underneath his thick, dark brows.

Mia could feel her cheeks flame with heat at being caught in the act. She hadn't realised she had been staring for so long.

Joel still eyed her with an air of expectancy. His eyes still twinkled with light humor.

Crap, she thought. Predictably now was the time for him to have a personality transplant. Any other time, he would have left the corridor and stormed into his studio as if she were never there. Now he decided to remain in the same space as her for more than thirty seconds.

Mia quickly mumbled something resembling an apology as she turned around to shut the studio door. She pulled the handle on the keypad lock several times, ensuring it was locked.

"I think it's locked," came a surprisingly cheerful voice opposite her.

"Just checking," she mumbled again, feeling her cheeks flame red as she heard his voice.

His deep voice curled delicately around the words, as if they fell gently of the tip of his tongue.

Reluctantly, she turned back to face him. Joel was still leaning against the wall with his phone in his hand, looking so casually propped there he could have been posing for the pages of a fashion magazine. He ran a hand through the mop of thick, dark hair on his head, and allowed his hand to fall on his thigh. On anyone else, doing so would have made their already bedhead hair turn into a dishevelled mess. On Joel, simply running his hand through it gave the effortless look of being tousled for hours by a stylist. Mia swallowed. Why did he have the knack of making everything look so effortless?

He continued to stare at her through his eyebrows, his illuminated phone still awaiting his attention in his upturned palm.

"How's it going?" he asked, casually jerking his hand that held his phone in the direction of the studio door.

"Great, thanks," she answered, surprised. She eyed him with an air of caution, due his sudden change in temperament.

"You like it here?" His eyes never left hers.

The unwavering gaze was rather unnerving. Mia shifted her guitar case on her shoulder and nodded. "I do."

Joel's lips pulled inward as he nodded in return. She wondered what he meant by his reaction. He took a step away from the wall, heading back in the direction of his own studio door.

As he passed Mia, he simply held up his phone toward her and nodded. He left the corridor, closing the door behind him with a soft click.

Crap, Mia thought again. He had heard her conversation. She wondered how much, if not all, of it he had heard.

CHAPTER 10

The studio's practise room was quiet and, for a change, empty.

Late on a Friday evening, most of the staff had already left for the weekend and Mia had stayed behind to finish a song she had begun writing with TJ earlier that afternoon. She knew the song was almost finished but she had wanted an amplifier and microphone to hear the sounds blend together as she performed. Although she was confident about her writing abilities, she took a different perspective when writing for an artist who would be performing the song live to thousands of adoring fans. The microphone and amplifier would give her a better sense of how the song sounded live. Their song was set to be used for a solo artist at the studios who was fairly well known. Mia still hadn't gotten over the idea of editing one of her favorite band's new albums, let alone writing songs for them.

She closed the door behind her, knowing the studios were all but empty. She still wanted privacy and respected the other artists and staff who may still have been working.

The room was fairly large—large enough to hold a drum kit, a piano, keyboard, a small DJ set, several guitar racks, and numerous amplifiers and microphones. A large carpet was situated in the middle of the floor for the performance space. A few sofas, which looked as though they had been collected over the years, were placed against the wall facing where the band would perform.

Mia propped her guitar against a stool on the edge of the carpet while she set her notes on a music stand nearby. After finding a jack cable and plugging her guitar into the amplifier and positioning the microphone in front of her stool, she sat down and got comfortable to play.

The song was co-written by her and TJ and somehow having his input into the song made it more bearable on her emotions. Singing the foreign mix of someone else's lyrics intertwined with her own gave the song an alien feeling. It somehow enabled her emotions to find an off switch, as if the mixture of TJ's lyrics with hers made the song someone else's altogether. She still found the ability to connect with the song and give it the work it needed, but having the other lyrics there gave her more focus than usual. Now she was able to concentrate on what she was doing rather than trying to quash the rising onslaught of emotions that were a constant threat on the horizon.

Although she wished she could always have this off switch, some days she wondered how the sun rose and set without a barrage of tears falling down her face as she crumpled to her knees. Some days were easier than others were. On those darker days, Mia often wished there was a way to silence her mind completely—a way to just switch everything off.

After several times over and a few key changes here and there, she felt that the song was pretty much ready. She knew TJ would be pleased when he came in on Monday morning and no more work needed to be done on the song. She was still keen to earn extra brownie points and staying late on a Friday evening to finish working was sure to do that.

She pondered for a moment over the finished song, still picturing the artist who would be soon performing it to his fans. Her eyes drifted across the room to a guitar rack nearby and she began to wonder.

Hesitating only for a moment before sliding off her stool and propping her own guitar against the rack, she then lifted out another guitar. The electric guitar felt cool and smooth in her hands as she slid it out of its fixture. Adjusting the strap, she lifted the guitar and placed the strap over her shoulder. She returned to her stool and looked down at the music in front of her, wondering if she should play the song the way it would soon be played to an audience.

Deciding to go for it, she began to play.

She imagined TJ's face when she told him not only was the song finished but she knew it sounded great on an electric guitar, as she had tried it. TJ and Chad had only ever heard Mia play her acoustic guitar. She favored her acoustic, as it was what her father had taught her to play. Always she preferred the raw, authentic sound of the notes as they strummed through the instrument, resonating through the body of the guitar.

The notes of the music pierced through the amplifier as she began to play the song over again on the electric guitar. Enjoying her moment of solitude as she got into the rhythm of the electric, she didn't hear the noise of a door opening and closing down the corridor over the sound of the amplifier.

Again the song came to its end and Mia smiled down at the instrument in her lap, marveling at it and thinking that she should get into the habit of playing it more often. She had no idea who the guitar belonged to but, as it was left in the practise room, she assumed they wouldn't mind it being borrowed.

Once the jack was unplugged, she slid off her stool again. She gathered up her notes from the music stand and shoved them into the front of her guitar case. After returning the electric guitar to its rack and stowing her own away in her case, she turned off the equipment and turned to leave the room.

As she reached the door, she noticed it was now open, only by a fraction.

Hesitantly pushing the door open with her hand, Mia waited as it swung open into the adjoining studio. Knowing she should have guessed who would be on the other side, she let out an exasperated sigh as the image of Joel Coben came into view from the shadows beyond.

He stood in the darkness of the doorway with his arms folded, his eyes firmly fixed on her. She knew he had been watching her perform, again. But for how long?

"What are you doing?" she asked rather sharply.

"What's it to you?" he quipped back.

"Well, to me, it looks like you're spying," she snapped.

Joel scowled and said nothing. His face was his usual mask of closure.

His features appeared even darker in the shadows—his face almost hidden in darkness. Mia could still make out the outline of his strong jaw, his near black eyes, and the dark brows that framed them. Those dark brows were now scowling right at her.

"Well?"

Still, Joel said nothing.

Mia sighed again, "You're really rude. Do you know that?"

She thought she saw Joel raise an eyebrow in the shadows.

"Excuse me?" His deep, yet lazy Californian accent sounded faintly amused.

"You heard me. I said you're rude."

His top lip curled in a smile as he watched her becoming agitated. "Why's that?"

"Because you swan about the place, acting like royalty, and yet you look and speak to everyone as if they are nothing more than dirt on the bottom of your boots."

Joel stared at her, as if aghast that she had dared to speak to him so.

"What? You're not even going to answer me now?" She could feel herself getting more irate. Her pulse pounded loudly as the blood pumped furiously through her body. She was tired of seeing people falling over themselves for someone so arrogant. Not long ago she had idolised Joel's music, but after meeting the man in person and seeing how he treated others around him with such disregard, Mia was beginning to lose any respect she had for him. Musical or otherwise.

"The people who you give those looks, they idolise you. I used to idolise you. I loved your music, your lyrics, everything. But now I see what an arrogant idiot you really are, I'm beginning to see your music in a different light completely." She spat the words at him before she had realised they had left her mouth, her thoughts working directly in time with her mouth.

However, despite her temporary contract with the company, Mia didn't regret the words she said to Joel. She doubted he would even mention them to anyone—that would involve initiating a conversation.

Joel's face had returned to an unreadable expression. No words left his firmly tight lips, no emotion marred his blank face. His eyes simply swallowed her in their endless voids, their darkness unending.

He continued to stare as the tension built in the confined space of the doorway. She could feel herself getting even more frustrated. Joel had shut down. There was no way he was going to answer her.

The tension had by then wound to its breaking point. Mia

stepped closer to Joel, her face inches away from his. She wanted to reach up, grab those shoulders, and shake them until he moved, said something, anything.

"You think you're something special because you're some big shot rock star? You think you're better than me because you're famous?" Her voice remained calm and strong as she spoke the words so resolutely and yet only inches away from a man she had once idolised. He frustrated her by being so ridiculously handsome.

Standing so close to him in the doorway, Mia was inches away from his achingly beautiful face. Part of her wanted to reach up and touch the tanned skin with the gentle stubble running down the side of his jawline.

The other half of her wanted to reach up and slap her hand across his defined cheek in frustration. Partly to reassure herself that this too-beautiful creature was still a human whose skin turned bright pink in reaction.

It would have been so much easier to be angry with him if he wasn't so good looking.

Joel's face remained impassive.

"You think you can treat me like shit because no one knows my name? Screw you, Joel. You're nothing special. I thought you were, but I see now that you're not. You're the exact stereotype of a musician I hoped you weren't."

Still he said nothing, he simply stared his almost-black eyes at her with a mildly wondrous look on his face, as if wondering why the fly on the wall was speaking to him.

His nonchalance angered Mia even further. He was beginning to stare at her with an almost bemused smile on his face. Furious at his arrogance to everyone who he deemed below him, Mia took one final look at him and shook her head in disgust. Making a frustrated sigh of exasperation, she stormed past him and out of the studio.

Joel still said nothing as he watched her leave.

જ્જ

For Mia, the weekend that followed her confrontation was painfully long. She spent hours, wondering if, indeed, Joel would say something to someone at the studio about the way she had spoken to him. Although she didn't regret saying what she did. She knew Joel needed to hear those words and she assumed no one had dared to say them to him yet.

She fretfully wondered if she had put her opportunity with Sixth String Studios in jeopardy by insulting their most prized artist. To ease her mind she made phone calls home to both Sharon and Niamh and reassured them both that everything was going great, although Mia was beginning to wonder if she was assuring herself more than them.

After what had felt like weeks of agonising waiting, her alarm finally began to announce the arrival of Monday morning. She sat up in bed and stared out of her hotel window with the sheets wrapped around herself. The curtains of her room hadn't closed yet during her stay. She preferred to watch the changing night and day over the Los Angeles skyline. Presently the sun was just beginning to peek between the skyscrapers, the soft rays of orange light filtering through in varying angles between the buildings. Mia could hear the soft hum of activity from the city below her window, the traffic on the highway, and the hustle and bustle of the morning commute beginning again for the week.

She rose from her bed and left the sheets behind, knowing she would have to face what lay ahead. Either way, she would soon discover if Joel had ended her temporary career at Sixth String Studios and made it even shorter than it already was.

છ૭છ૭છ૭

As Mia crossed the street opposite Sixth String Studios with her morning coffee in hand, the still-waiting paparazzi gave her nothing more than a cursory glance as she passed.

By now they had realised she was a member of staff and not an upcoming megastar they could gain a few hundred dollars from selling a picture of. She wondered if they were ever going to give up waiting to get a picture of Joel, who had managed to outsmart them every day. Mia wondered if there was a back exit to the studios that he used.

After swiping her pass on the door, she took a deep breath as she crossed the threshold into the foyer. Her breath escaped her faster than it should have, for standing next to the reception desk was Joel.

Mia mentally rolled her eyes. Of course, he was. Out of all the days she would have liked him to disappear, today he was there practically waiting for her when she walked through the door.

But as she approached the reception desk she did a double take.

She briefly wondered if she had drunk from the mini bar in her hotel room last night, for she seemed to be seeing double. As she drew closer to the desk, she noticed Charlie's expectant face honed in on her approaching one. Mia then realised who was standing before her.

Joel's almost identical younger brother Josh was lounging against the reception desk, just as she had imagined, unashamedly flirting with Charlie.

Joel himself, however, was standing a little farther behind the desk with his usual masked expression in place. That expression faltered as Mia approached and, for a moment, she wondered if he was about to tell her to leave.

"Mia, I've heard so much about you." Josh stepped forward into her line of vision and held out his hand to her. His accent sounded brighter than Joel's and reminded her of Charlie's sense of familiarity.

"Thank you, I…" Her sentence trailed off as Josh shook her hand and kissed her on the cheek.

"Charlie here's been telling me how incredible your music is." He flashed a cheeky smile that lit up his face and winked. "I have to hear you play. And soon."

"You will," Charlie piped up, leaning over the desk. "We'll get her to play for you later on."

Josh flashed a dazzling white-teeth smile at Mia. "Sounds great."

She found herself letting out a small giggle at Josh and understood immediately why Charlie preferred him to Joel. He was friendlier, happier, and had a cheeky side to his personality. It was infectious. Mia realised she was grinning herself as she listened to Josh talk.

Charlie had been right about him. Josh Coben was almost the spitting image of his brother Joel. It was like looking at Joel but on an eighteen-month delay. Again Charlie had been right as Mia noticed there was something "not quite as hot as Joel" about him, but he was still well above the average calibre. But whatever was missing from his appearance, Josh more than made up for in his personality. Mia could sense he and Charlie would make a great match. They both had an infectious air of confidence and happiness.

Josh stepped from her side to lean on the reception desk and be close to Charlie again, so Joel was once again in her sight. He still hadn't spoken and Mia waited with baited breath for the moment he mentioned their encounter on Friday evening. She wondered if he would have the nerve to say such a thing in front of so many people, especially his brother.

His expression remained unchanged. His eyes remained observing and consuming.

Mia knew he was watching and taking in everything that was happening before him, but he still wouldn't interact.

It still made her pulse race in anger to think that he refused to speak to those he deemed below him. She would have given anything to be the fly on the wall that Joel regarded her as, to witness him off guard in his own studio. Idly, she wondered what the man behind the impassive mask was really like.

"Well, I better get to work. Nice meeting you Josh." She gave him a smile as she turned to leave.

"You too, Mia. I'll swing by later to hear you play." He winked at her and, in the briefest of moments, she thought she saw a frown flash across Joel's face.

"That'll be great," she said, knowing she was riling Joel. "I'll look forward to it."

eɔeɔ

True to his word, Josh's face appeared around the studio door late in the afternoon. "Hey." He flashed his grin again as he poked his head around the door, making Mia jump in her seat. "You ready to play for us yet?"

She glanced at TJ and Chad, who were lounging in their chairs. They nodded lazily. Despite their laid-back Californian attitude, they somehow always managed to get things done.

"Awesome." Josh strode through the door with Charlie in tow who, to Mia's surprise, held the door open after her. And through it walked Joel.

Again? Mia thought. She could have enjoyed playing for Josh and Charlie without his ominous presence looming over the room. The man seemed to be showing up everywhere lately.

Josh and Charlie took a seat nearby while Joel remained in his usual spot, standing in the doorway. Mia picked up her guitar that was leaning against the decks and placed it in her lap, the feeling all so familiar as she did.

She turned in her chair to face her audience of four, ignoring the image in her peripheral vision as she did. He would stand and stare and say nothing, as he always did, so she faced away to shut him out. As she began to play, her fingers ran down the familiar fret board of her guitar and the familiar notes filled her eardrums. She reached the first verse and the familiar words sounded around the small room, her gentle voice resonating through the space.

Her song progressed and she could see Josh's face spreading with glee and Charlie nudging him as if to say, "I told you so." Mia tried to hide her own smile as she sang her way through the song.

When she finished, Josh jumped up from his seat, let out a loud whooping cheer, and began clapping loudly. Charlie quickly followed suit, although not as loud.

"Wow, Mia, that was really something," he praised as he continued clapping.

Charlie looked up at him, her face enamoured. "I told you she was amazing."

TJ and Chad were also clapping and whispering quietly to one another, which was nothing unusual.

Placing her guitar back on the floor, she shrugged, all the while still aware that Joel was watching from one side. Mia didn't even look at him. She couldn't read his immovable expressions anyway.

Being intimidated by someone she once, and still in some ways did, consider an idol was a strange feeling.

Josh walked over to Mia's side and clapped a hand on her shoulder, his enthusiastic grin still spread across his face. "I mean, really, that was something else."

"Thanks, Josh, that really means a lot." She beamed at Charlie standing by his side.

"It was. You really weren't kidding when you said how talented she was, bro," Josh said, cocking his head toward Joel standing near the doorway.

It took all of Mia's self-control not to allow her jaw to hit the floor.

ℰↃℰↃ

She turned on her heel to face Joel, who was still leaning against the doorframe. He looked at her with a bemused expression before nodding to his brother. "I told you."

Mia fixed Joel with her own stare. His endless one was once again rooted on her face. She couldn't figure him out. He was the most puzzling man she had ever come across.

He spied on her, he was rude to her, he treated her as if she didn't exist, and then here he was telling his brother how amazing she was. *Men*, Mia thought.

Charlie was trying to contain her excitement as she stood beside Josh. Mia could see her hands twitching by her sides and her eyes crinkled in excitement as she held back words she was desperate to say to her.

Mia gave her a glare that was immediately readable. Charlie knew Mia was saying *Don't you dare*. Joel did not need to hear what Charlie was so desperate to squeal aloud in front of him and his brother.

This was Mia's turn to say nothing, her turn to fix Joel with an endless stare. His once unexplainable behaviour had now been turned back on him. Mia knew he wanted a reaction. His own gaze bored into her face. He seemed to be almost taunting her, waiting for a reaction. She wasn't going to take the bait. That was exactly what Joel wanted. *Time for a dose of his own medicine*, she thought.

The color of his eyes almost matched his black T-shirt. His haunting stare was still waiting for a reaction. Mia wondered how that conversation had happened with Josh. She simply couldn't picture Joel and his brother alone together and him casually bringing up the subject of a talented young songwriter at the studios.

His eyes began to narrow and Mia knew he was getting impatient. That stare that had once appeared to hold the capability to stare into an eternity was growing frustrated.

He hadn't gotten the reaction he had expected. She wondered what Joel had expected her to do. He couldn't go from spying on her and ignoring her one minute to singing her praises in the next. She then realised the room had become awkwardly silent.

"Umm, I think I'm gonna head back to work." Charlie's voice was now void of excitement. It had a strange air of curiosity to it.

Instantly snapped from her reverie, Mia turned to see Charlie's curious expression. She was clearly trying to decipher the situation happening in front of her. Everyone in the room had watched their stare-off.

Josh, on the other hand, was grinning from ear to ear.

Men, Mia thought again as she refrained from rolling her eyes. They were far more complicated than women.

"Josh?" Charlie held the studio door open after her and waited for him to leave the room.

Josh stood between Mia and Joel and clapped a hand on Mia's shoulder. "That was awesome." He continued grinning from ear to ear. "Thanks for letting us watch." He turned to Joel and for a moment, she wondered if he meant her performance or the scene afterward. "Bro, you coming?" He grabbed Joel's shoulder and pulled him toward the door.

As usual, Joel said nothing. He gave her one final stare before he turned to leave.

But Mia saw a changed expression behind those nearly black eyes. For a brief moment they looked sad. Disappointment flickered across his eyes as he shoved his hands into the pockets of his jeans and stalked from the room.

Joel's sculpted shoulders rounded the doorway and into the corridor before disappearing from her view. The door softly clicked shut after him and Mia turned to the almost empty room.

TJ and Chad, meanwhile, had the lazily entertained faces of two spectators idly watching a scene from their favourite soap opera.

☙❧☙

Charlie slid down into the seat next to Mia at the table in the deli. Today her lithe body was dressed in a long leopard print vest that she was wearing as a dress with tights and biker boots. She took a long sip of her soda before fixing Mia with her gaze.

Mia looked up at her eyes, which today were framed with gold and brown eye shadow to compliment her attire, colors that also accentuated her mixed Caucasian and oriental coloring. They began to eat their lunches while Charlie continued to stare at her with an amused expression on her face. The look she was giving implied she knew something but was waiting for Mia to broach the subject.

"What?" Mia asked finally.

"Nothing." Charlie turned her attention to her food but Mia could still see the look lingering on her face.

The silence continued for several more minutes and her amusement never faltered. Though she tried to ignore it eventually, her curiosity won out. "Come on, spill. What is it?"

Charlie's eyes sparkled in her amusement as she twirled her lunch idly on a fork and studied Mia's expression. "You—" She paused mid-sentence as she crunched some salad. "—and Joel."

"What about us?" Mia frowned, confused.

"When were you going to tell me that you like him?"

"What?" Mia's response came out much louder than she had anticipated.

"Sssh." Charlie giggled and waved a hand in front of her in attempt to calm her. She rested her bare, tanned arms on the table before continuing. "I've seen the way you two look at each other." She raised her eyebrows at Mia's open mouthed expression. "And yesterday, what was that about?"

Thinking back to her stare-off with Joel in the studio, Mia realised how it must have appeared to those watching. She shrugged. "I was giving him a taste of his own medicine."

Charlie's eyebrows rose even higher. "That's not what it looked like to me."

"How did it look?" Mia asked.

One of those eyebrows then arched suggestively in response.

Despite the warm humid afternoon air, Mia felt her cheeks flame. "That's not how it was."

Charlie said nothing as she waited for an explanation.

Putting down her fork, Mia began to tell her what had happened with Joel over the last few days, particularly on Friday evening when she had been alone in the practice room. She told Charlie how Joel had been appearing at the studio doorway almost every time she had been practising alone and yet he still didn't speak more than a few words to her. He just stared at her like that—every time. And then yesterday she heard he'd been telling his brother how fantastic her talent was. It just didn't add up.

"Oh it adds up perfectly." Charlie's voice sounded sarcastic and Mia frowned. "Honey, are you really that blind?" Charlie asked.

Mia scowled even more as Charlie's expression turned to amusement again. A smile danced about her lips and her eyes sparkled in excitement as she drummed her long blue fingernails on the table and waited for Mia to realise what Charlie already knew.

Mia sighed in exasperation. "What?"

Charlie's manicured blue fingernails reached across the table and took hold of Mia's hand. She could not contain her smile any longer and her face looked as if it would burst with excitement. Her grin creased from ear to ear and she began to giggle like a young girl. "Joel Coben likes you, Mia."

CHAPTER 11

The furious knocking on her hotel room door made Mia jump. She had been quietly flicking through the channels on her television in the early evening when the usually silent corridor outside her room announced she had a visitor.

Getting up from the small sofa that was part of the uniform hotel room furniture, she went to unlock the door. A cocoa brown quiff with blonde highlights on one side greeted Mia the moment she opened the door.

"Hey." Charlie's voice was as perky as usual and, tonight, she was wearing an electric blue T-shirt with her black skinny jeans and a pair of incredibly high black heels with studs running down the heels. Mia wondered if Charlie would mind her wardrobe being raided one day. Then again, Mia doubted she could pull off the looks as easily as Charlie did.

"Hi, what's up?" It was perfectly like Charlie to turn up at her hotel room unannounced but tonight she looked overly dressed, even for her, for such an occasion.

"Can't we pay our friend a visit?" a deeper, yet still chirpy Californian accent came from the other side of the doorway.

Mia jumped again. Tonight was full of surprises.

She poked her head out of her doorway to see Josh Coben leaning against the wall near her door. He flashed Mia his devilish cheeky smile as she did.

Suspicious she glanced between the two of them. "What are you up to?"

Instantly she could tell from their faces that there was more to their arrival than simply paying her a visit.

Josh's smile curved up one side of his face in guilty amusement and Charlie dodged past Mia through the doorway into her room.

"What are you doing?" Mia couldn't help but laugh, despite wondering why they had come.

Charlie dashed quickly across the room in her extremely high heels and grabbed the guitar case leaning against the sofa. "Got it," she called out into the hallway.

Mia turned to Josh but before she could say a word, he grabbed hold of her around her waist, hauled her over his shoulder out of the doorway, and began to walk down the corridor.

"Josh!" she squealed out as he effortlessly threw her over his shoulder.

He only laughed and Mia caught a glimpse of his face. It was sparkling with amusement at their attempted heist.

Josh was trying desperately not to burst with laughter at their success.

She turned her head as much as she could to see Charlie locking her hotel room door, before slinging the strap of the case over her shoulder and trotting lightly in her heels to catch up with them.

How she managed to move so deftly in such high heels, Mia would never know.

"Josh! I can walk, you know?" she squealed again as he carried her into the arriving elevator while Charlie's laughter cackled loudly in the foyer behind them.

He threw her a wicked grin as he set her down in the small, enclosed space. "But you wouldn't have. That's the point."

"Where are we going?" she cried once Josh had set her down and she was happy there was enough distance between them so he couldn't throw her over his shoulder without warning again.

Like his brother, he didn't answer and Mia knew he had been given orders by the woman in the electric blue T-shirt in front of her. His playful smile still spread across his cheeks as he quietly chuckled with glee at their success.

Mia turned and raised her eyebrows at Charlie. "Well?"

"We're taking you to an 'open mic' night."

❧❦❧

The taxi cruised along the boulevard and Mia realised they

were leaving downtown Los Angeles. As the long streets she recognized became less and less familiar, she realised they were heading in the direction of West Hollywood and Beverly Hills.

"Will you guys just tell me where we're going?"

Charlie simply clamped her lips together and shook her head, her hair unmoving.

All they would tell Mia was that they were headed to an open mic night.

That was all.

Mia had no idea where in LA they were taking her. But as she stared out of the taxi window at the passing shops and apartments that were becoming more and more luxurious, she realised the direction the taxi was headed. As the studios were situated in downtown Los Angeles, Mia hadn't really been in this area of the city much.

On a couple of Saturdays, Charlie had taken her into Beverly Hills to show her around. They walked the famous boulevards together and window shopped in the designer boutiques. They had sipped iced tea and eaten frozen yoghurt outside a café in Hollywood and, for the afternoon, imagined they were the rich and famous enjoying a leisurely weekend in the sun.

Charlie had even suggested they take the infamous Homes of the Stars tour, in her attempt to show Mia more of Los Angeles. Mia had been a little sceptical about the tour but by the end of it, she had to confess she had enjoyed spying on the luxurious mansions of the super-rich and famous actors and singers.

The tour even pointed out Joel's house, which was surrounded by a ridiculously high fence and electronic gates. There hadn't been much Mia could see from the tour bus but she could see the rooftops of an enormous house and the tops of the trees in its well-groomed surrounding gardens. She had wondered what the house looked like inside. Just how did a world-famous rock star, with a hatred for his fame and the media, decorate his mansion?

She wondered if his interior design taste matched his taste in clothing and was mostly black. Any other singer who dressed mostly in black would have been labelled gothic or alternative but, somehow, for Joel it worked, and he had thousands of adoring female fans.

Mia shook her head as too many thoughts of Joel filled her mind. It didn't help being one seat away in the taxi from someone who was almost his double. That person was currently texting on his phone. Automatically, she wondered what Joel would write in his text messages. Maybe he was more forthcoming with his use of words when he could write them down.

After several more minutes, the taxi's indicator began signalling and it slowed to a stop at the side of the curb. Mia looked at the building where they had pulled up outside the front door. She turned to look at Charlie beside her who had an eager, yet hesitant look on her face as she awaited Mia's reaction.

The taxi had stopped right on the doorstep of the Kibitz Room.

A deli by day and a cocktail bar by night, the Kibitz Room was famous for hosting one of Los Angeles's many open mic nights and reportedly harbored some of the best in unsigned talent.

And Charlie had brought her to perform there.

Mia reached over and hugged her friend. "The Kibitz Room? I can't believe it," she gushed as she threw her arms around Charlie.

Charlie let out a relieved giggle beside her.

"Aw, can I get in on the love, too?" Josh threw his arms around them both before a giggling Charlie pushed him away.

"Girl time, get off." She laughed before pushing him out of the taxi door.

Mia laughed too as she scrambled out of the taxi after her friends.

As they made their way through the already packed bar, Mia noticed several heads turning and whispering as Josh passed through the crowds.

She knew she should have expected the public's attention when out with Josh Coben. Heads were bound to turn when he was the spitting image of his rock-star brother, especially female heads.

Despite their slight age difference, the two could almost have passed for twins. Mia began wondering how the reactions would have differed if Joel had been with their group. She doubted their route to the bar would have been as easy if the world-famous megastar had joined them.

Idly, she wondered if he was still at the studio. She couldn't picture him walking into a bar with Josh, sitting down, and enjoying a quiet drink. He would attract too much attention. Just what did a rock star do with his time off? No wonder the media pried so much when he was so reclusive. *It is easy to let your mind wander astray*, Mia thought.

Josh was already chatting to a cluster of girls who had grabbed his attention as he had ordered drinks at the bar.

"You're Josh Coben?" a young blonde girl asked with a look that peeked suggestively up at him through her eyelashes.

"Last time I checked." He winked and the group burst into excited giggles.

"Is Joel not with you tonight?" another pouted at him over-enthusiastically.

Mia gave a sly glance at Charlie, who rolled her eyes.

"Sorry, girls, not tonight. He's busy working on his new album," Josh answered, just as Mia had guessed he would be.

"Can we have a few pictures with you?" the blonde girl asked.

Mia wondered if she was their nominated spokesperson. None of the others dared to speak. They all stared wide-eyed and shot goofy smiles up at Josh.

"Sure." He took their camera and turned to Charlie. "Do you mind?" he asked and gave an adorable smile that Mia could tell was just for Charlie.

After several photographs, Josh politely escaped the clutches of his female fans and wrapped his arm around Charlie's waist, much to the disappointment of the girls who stalked away with hugely pouting faces. Mia felt her own lips curl into a smirk as she watched them.

Not that she could blame them for trying. He was beautiful, but he and Charlie made a perfect match. Mia wondered if it was official or just flirting. She made a mental note to ask Charlie.

"Excuse me, are you Mia Ryan?" asked a middle-aged man wearing a Kibitz Room Café T-shirt and holding a clipboard.

"I am," she replied.

He didn't look the type of camera wielding fan seeking a photograph.

"You're up next." He nodded toward the stage and scribbled a note on his clipboard before disappearing into the crowd.

Mia nodded and, leaving Charlie in Josh's arms at the bar, made her way toward the stage. Getting to the stage wasn't an easy feat when the crowd was packed into the place like sardines.

Jostling her way through, she kept a tight grip on her guitar case as she shoved her way toward the stage. A young man with a Canadian accent on stage was thanking the crowd and Mia spotted the man with the clipboard by the side of the stage.

The performer gathered up his things and left the stage, vacating it for Mia. She went through the familiar motions of unpacking her guitar and setting up the equipment around her as she prepared to begin her set.

"You get up to five songs, okay?" the clipboard bearer quipped in her ear. "We're pretty quiet tonight."

"Quiet?" Mia repeated.

She looked around the bar at the crowd in front of the stage. *How jammed is this place on a busy night?*

"Yeah, that's what I said. No more than five, you hear me?"

"Yeah, sure."

She nodded in agreement, guessing some artists had a habit of overstaying their welcome on the stage. Mia mentally prepared just three songs in her head. She didn't want to exceed the limit. If the crowd didn't like her music, the last thing they would want to do is hear five songs' worth of it.

"Ladies and gentlemen, give it up for Mia Ryan, all the way from Ireland," the man announced in a not-so-enthusiastic tone of voice.

Monday nights clearly weren't his best performance.

Mia stepped forward into the spotlight and took the man's place in front of the microphone. Immediately she felt at home. Closing her eyes for a brief moment, she savoured the familiar feeling. She hadn't played live music since she had left Dublin over a month ago and she had been craving the feeling ever since. For Mia, performing live was her adrenaline rush. If music was her oxygen, performing live was her water. She needed it for her existence. While working at Glen's Tavern, she had assumed she could take or leave the performing live side of music, happy enough to accept the song-writing position Sixth String Studios had offered her. For music was where her heart lay entirely. But her lack of twice weekly performances had her feeling strong withdrawal symptoms. She had been yearning to get back on stage and hear her music amplifying through the speakers and into the crowd around her.

She opened her eyes on the first note of the song and the crowds welcoming applause died away as they began to listen to the music offered them. Mia effortlessly played her way through the familiar song, feeling the familiar wave of emotions come rushing back to her as she sang her own lyrics. Never had she imagined she would miss the onslaught of feelings that threatened to rain over her every performance whenever she sang the words behind her story. But relishing the feelings coming back to her, she knew it was part of the complete package with her music. Without those emotions, her music wouldn't come alive and, without her music, neither would Mia. She realised then that they needed one another to come full circle.

The feeling was euphoric as she relished the realisation that such heady emotions, she had so long struggled with, were what her music needed to come alive. In front of her, the crowd began clapping and cheering as Mia reached the end of the song.

"Thank you very much," she whispered softly into the microphone before launching into her next song. She could see Josh and Charlie in front of the stage. They had untangled themselves from one another and had made their way to the front of the crowd to cheer her on. Despite his arm around Charlie's waist, Mia could almost imagine that he was Joel standing, before her watching her performance, and cheering her on.

That thought did strange things to her emotions, emotions that she wasn't quite sure how to deal with. As she lost herself in the second song, she pictured her conversation with Charlie in the deli earlier that day.

What if Joel did like her? Did she like him?

Sure, she was attracted to him. But she had no idea about the man beneath the emotional mask, and that was where her issue lay.

The crowd erupted once again and Mia began the notes of her final song. She lapped up the attention of the cheering crowd as she began her most emotional song. She had played the same song before Jackson had asked her to work for the studios. Hearing the familiar silence descend over the crowd, she knew they were listening to the words of her song.

> "Do you remember me?
> When you lay awake at night,
> Do you remember me?
> Clutching your pillow tight..."

The silence in the bar was overwhelming. She could feel the attention of every ear in the room zoned in on her song. Tension and atmosphere radiated throughout the room. Mia could feel every bone in her body absorbing the emotions that only came from performing. There was nothing else on earth that compared to this. She knew she had every soul in the room hooked on every word she was singing.

> "I still wake up
> In the dead of the night,
> Calling out your name,
> I wonder, do you do the same?
>
> Do you remember me?
> Like I remember you..."

As the song reached its end, Mia felt a tear escape the corner of her eye, which she quickly wiped away as she stepped out of the spotlight. The crowd erupted into applause and, as her sight returned to her fully once out of the spotlight, she saw a similar sight to what she had seen after her final performance at Glen's.

The crowd was simultaneously wiping their eyes and cheering at the tops of their lungs. Mia kissed her hand and offered it to the crowd as she waved and went to leave the stage. She took one final look at the crowd, who were chanting for more and she saw Charlie and Josh chanting with them. Smiling as she looked out across the crowd, her eyes came to rest on a figure standing in the corner of the room.

Despite wearing a hooded sweatshirt zipped to the top and a baseball cap pulled low over his almost black eyes, Mia knew who she was seeing. Although he had gone unnoticed in the bar, she knew she would recognize that disguised face anywhere.

Joel Coben was standing in the corner of the bar.

He had come to watch her performance.

೧ఌ೧

The final note echoed around the empty room and as Mia closed her eyes. For the briefest of moments, she could picture herself standing back on the stage at the Kibitz Room. In the quiet of the empty studio, she smiled to herself in disbelief that she had performed there and that she had received such a rapturous applause from the LA crowd. She then remembered who had been quietly standing unnoticed in the corner of the Kibitz Room that night. How Joel Coben had gone completely unnoticed in such a place was both fascinating and infuriating to her. He was one of the world's biggest stars and yet he was standing completely incognito in the middle of a Los Angeles open mic night.

Only that morning, Mia had seen one of his music videos on the screen of her hotel television as she got ready for work. The song was still riding high in the charts, despite his tour finishing weeks ago. She replayed the images of the music video over in her mind, the scenes of Joel sitting alone on the floor in an empty room as he strummed away on his guitar. Light from one window shone on the side of his face, casting half of his features in darkness. The angling of the light highlighted the curve of his cheekbone, the arch of his eyebrows, and their frame around those near-black eyes. Eyes that, when hidden in shadow, appeared even more dark and troubled, an image that the camera picked up on incredibly well. Mia could see why thousands of women across the world threw themselves at Joel, desperate to be noticed by those eyes, wanting to lift the troubled darkness from their aching beauty.

She remembered the way he glanced up from his guitar and into the camera, the camera capturing the longing need from those eyes looking up from under their long eyelashes. Mia shook her head. Those eyelashes were too long to be wasted on a man. At least she tried to convince herself of that, anyway.

"Are you going to play another one?"

Damn. She should have known by now that he would have been standing in the doorway. Mia still hadn't gotten used to him creeping around the place and loitering in the shadows while she played. She reminded herself to face the doorway when she next practised as she spun the swivel chair around to face the owner of those wasted eyelashes who was standing in the doorway.

In his usual position, Joel was propped against the door with a casual air of a fashion model as he idly stood watching her. She also reminded herself not to frown as she took in his appearance. How on earth was it possible for one person to eternally look so good? Mia was still waiting for the time she would see Joel with one strand of his mussed up hair out of place on his head or for him to pick an unstylish T-shirt for the day. She knew that Joel would look good whatever he was wearing. He could even make the Ronald McDonald outfit look sexy.

He had his arms folded across his chest. She tried not to stare at the outlines of the muscles in his arms or his chest that they were resting on. Joel was dressed in a simple gray T-shirt and a pair of blue jeans. Surprised, she noticed he was wearing trainers. She had gotten used to seeing him in boots. Of course, the trainers that Joel was wearing fitted his rock-star image perfectly. She knew she wouldn't catch him wearing any old pair of Nikes.

Joel raised an eyebrow at her. Mia realised she hadn't answered in time again.

Damn, she thought again. If he wasn't so good looking, she might have been able to focus her brain into working at a normal speed.

"Umm, sure, if you want," she mumbled and turned her chair back to face the table where her notebook lay open.

She turned the page to another song and adjusted her fingers on the guitar as she prepared to play. To her complete surprise, she heard Joel shift his weight from the doorframe and came to sit on the chair opposite her.

That made her pause. Her fingers hovered on the fretboard as the beautiful form of one of her musical idols seated himself in the chair opposite her and looked expectantly up at her, waiting for her to play.

No pressure then. She took a deep breath to steady her nerves. Though she usually wasn't nervous about the size of her audience—two or two hundred people, the difference usually didn't faze her. But somehow, having Joel Coben sitting opposite her, waiting for his own personal performance, gave her the jitters. Butterflies danced in her stomach and she swallowed the lump in her throat as she attempted to steady her breathing.

Mia was sure he could hear the loudness of her breathing. The sharp intake and the deep exhale sounded incredibly loud in the small room. Feeling her cheeks begin to flame, she took her eyes away from him and focussed on the notebook before her.

Although she knew her songs by heart, she felt she would need the reminder in front of her with Joel sitting so closely.

Adjusting her fingers into the correct positions, she began to play. As her song went on, Mia was aware, more than ever, of the sound of her own voice in the small room. She could hear every move her fingers made on the fretboard, every single squeak as her fingers moved up and down the strings of the instrument. Every time her pick connected with the strings and every word her tongue curled around, she heard them both. Never before had she been so conscious of her own performance. Sitting across from Joel was nerve-racking.

She looked down at the notebook in front of her, her eyes not leaving the page, refusing to look up and meet those eternally unreadable eyes of his.

As she strummed out the final notes of the song, she gripped the neck of her guitar, hanging on to her solace for those final few precious moments.

> "I still wake up
> In the dead of night,
> Calling out your name.
> I wonder, do you do the same?
>
> Do you remember me?
> Like I remember you..."

The guitar faded out its last note again, the sound echoing from within the instrument and into the room around them. This time she was aware of her audience.

Joel leaned forward in his seat, resting his elbows on his knees and placing his head on his fists. He stared at the floor, allowing the words of the song to settle in his mind for a moment before he spoke.

Minutes passed in silence. Mia felt their every second tick by with agonising patience.

Eventually, Joel looked up into her eyes. Those disturbingly dark eyes locked hold of hers. That soul-reading stare bore into her eyes, appearing to read her every thought.

"You're not singing about a lover, are you?" he said calmly.

Mia swallowed. No one had ever asked her that question.

"You're singing about someone who's gone."

CHAPTER 12

Mia glared back at Joel, furiously staring into his eyes, trying to understand how he had worked it out.

Feeling her emotions rising from deep inside her, she desperately tried to swallow away the lump that was growing in her throat. The onslaught of a wave of tears threatened behind her eyes. Ones she furiously tried to blink away. She hadn't cried very much since her parents died, very few events in her life warranted the necessity of tears after the depth of emotions she'd had when she was younger.

Only one event in her life since then had brought about so many tears—an event that Joel had no way of knowing about.

And yet he did.

His gaze still remained on her face, awaiting an answer.

"How do you know that?" she asked, still blinking away tears that were now forming in her eyes.

Joel looked away from her, suddenly averting his gaze. He was thrown by her question, Mia noticed.

It was common knowledge that Joel had lost his mother when he was a teenager. The media loved prying into his past, trying to uncover the secrets behind the media elusive rock star.

"Because I know how it feels." He sighed, his voice sounding low and soft. "I hear those lyrics the way they were meant to be heard—" His words caught in his throat momentarily before he continued. "I know you're singing about the pain of losing someone."

On his final words, he returned his gaze to Mia. Those unreadable eyes were back to analysing her face again, but somehow they seemed softer—understanding, almost.

But, as always, they never let anyone in. They were as closed as could be, a locked-down vault that was hiding endless thoughts and feelings.

Mia sighed, allowing a tear to escape the corner of her eye. "I am."

"It's never been about a lover, has it? None of them have?"

"No," she said as the tear fell down her cheek and dropped over the strings of the guitar, causing them to vibrate slightly. The sound and their voices were almost a whisper in the small room.

"They're not about your parents either, are they?"

છબ

"I was fifteen when they told me." She looked down at the notebook as she spoke, as if she were finally telling the story so many notebooks before already had. "I can barely remember him—" She paused in the silence. "It's almost like I can still feel him." She sighed again, knowing how crazy she must sound.

Joel looked at her, his expression unreadable yet, somehow, allowing her to go on.

"I don't feel like I had closure. I don't ever think I'll get closure either. I can't explain it, I just…I still feel like he's here." Mia knew she was beginning to ramble. She had told Joel what no one but Mike and Sharon knew, that her music was entirely about her brother.

"Mia, you're chasing shadows." Joel's voice softened. "He's gone."

"I don't know that for certain, though. He could still be here."

He frowned. "How?"

Thinking back to the one photograph she still had of a dark-haired young boy sitting on a worn sofa with his arms wrapped around the shoulders of his toddler sister, her mind wandered. It was the only picture Mia had of him. Time had faded the image and her memories were faded even more so.

Luke could look nothing like that image now. It was taken so long ago. Mia wondered if she would even recognize him if she were ever to see him again.

She looked up at Joel and blinked back the tears that were still threatening to fall. "We were separated in care after our parents died, when they couldn't find anyone willing to take us both. We were sent to opposite ends of the country. I was in Kinsale. He was in Galway, or so I heard. I guess the family he was sent to thought it would be better if we didn't keep in touch. They thought it would be hard for us, being so young, to understand the different families, the distance, and everything," She paused as she prepared for the final part of her story.

Joel, surprisingly, offered her his hand. She placed her hand on his and felt his long fingers curling around her small ones. The heat of their skin against each other's, and the sudden intimacy from someone usually so distant, made Mia pause for longer than she had intended.

Looking up at Joel, she saw his near-black eyes staring down at their clasped hands then eventually meeting her eyes. He squeezed her hand in reassurance and she returned to her story.

Overwhelmed with the heady mix of emotions brought about from recalling her most private memories and the beautiful rock star in front of her taking her hand in his and listening intently, Mia took a deep breath as she continued. "I was so young. I suppose I just accepted the change more readily than someone older would have. I'm told I asked about him a lot, but Sharon and Mike weren't able to contact his foster parents. Eventually, Luke was moved to another family, whereas I stayed with mine. When I was fifteen, I asked the agency what happened to my brother. All they could tell me was that he was no longer with the first set of foster parents he had been placed with. I was distraught. I needed answers. I needed to know what had happened to my brother, but I was too young, I was still in care and Luke was an adult by then. He would have been out of the system and could have contacted me if he wanted to. When I turned sixteen, I was allowed to ask more questions, to do some more digging by myself. I was no longer in the care system, but Mike and Sharon allowed me to continue living with them. They helped me where they could, but I could find nothing. I tried searching everywhere, but it was as if he had just disappeared." Mia's voice began to waver as she said the final words. Pausing for a moment, she looked at Joel. He was still staring intensely at her, his expression unmoving for the whole time she had been speaking.

He confused Mia to no end. There he was, sitting and holding her hand in comfort, but yet he said nothing. His face said nothing. His expression wore that eternally unreadable mask that was always in place, hiding his emotions. Gripping her hand with his was the only form of expression that showed he cared.

"I eventually got some answers from the agency. I guess they were sick of hearing from me." She smiled a wry smile at the memory of endlessly hounding the foster agency. "They told me that—" Her voice cracked, a single tear escaped down each cheek, as she tried to say the words that had haunted her ever since that phone call. Without an ounce of compassion, the woman on the other end of the phone had reluctantly told Mia all she knew about her brother.

In a voice that was as caring as if she were reading the headlines from the morning newspaper, she had read out the final notes in his file. Mia saw a change in Joel's expression, his features softened momentarily and he reached up his other hand to wipe away her tears. Her skin tingled at the sensation, the feeling of his skin on hers lingering after he had removed his hand. He squeezed her hand again. "Go on," he whispered softly.

"They told me that after Luke left his foster parents, they had been unable to trace him. They had tried to contact him many times but to no avail. It was as if he had disappeared. A missing person's report was filed and still exists to this day, but no one has seen or heard anything from him in years. The police told both me and the agency that—" She exhaled sharply. "—that we should presume the worst. That he's dead."

She tried to bite her lip as it quivered uncontrollably, her tears falling faster as she had poured out her secrets, which she had kept hidden for so long from everyone, to an almost stranger. A stranger who was as dark and mysterious as they came. One who barely spoke a word unless necessary.

Mia had no idea what he thought of her, or why she had just told him all that. She had no idea why she had poured forth everything to Joel. He could turn and leave the room at that moment and might never utter a word to her again. Or he could even write another Grammy-award-winning song about the tragic story she had just told him, and the entire world would hear her pain on his next album.

Unable to look him in the eyes, she immediately resented herself for telling Joel so much. He had only guessed the meaning behind her lyrics, from his own experience, and she had blurted out everything to this global superstar.

As she continued to stare down at the notebook, her tears freely ran down her face, and yet the silence lingered in the air.

She waited for Joel to let go of her hand, get up, and silently leave the room, as he always did. But his grip on her hand remained the same. His eyes still bore into her face, analysing everything she had just said and her every expression. Feeling his gaze upon her, she waited agonising seconds in the silence after ending her story, seconds that felt like hours while Joel continued to stare at her.

Then, without a word, he released her hand.

Mia sighed quietly, knowing she shouldn't have said so much.

Before she knew what had happened, Joel stood up, leaned over her, and wrapped his arms around her body.

She reached up and placed her own arms around his back. Her face nestled into his shoulder and the enticing scent of him filled her senses. She could smell the subtle yet enticing scent of his cologne, which smelled deliciously like vanilla. Forgetting she was enveloped in the arms of one of the world's biggest rock stars, Mia continued to let her tears fall, feeling them soak into Joel's T-shirt beneath her. His head was pressed against hers, his arms were tenderly around her body, and, somehow, despite his usual distance, their closeness seemed to feel right.

Still, he said nothing in the silence. He held her and allowed her to cry, seeming to know what she was feeling, and Mia then understood that he did know what she was feeling.

Although she still didn't have closure, Joel understood the pain of losing someone close to him. And, as if reading her thoughts in the silence, he whispered so quietly against her ear that she almost didn't hear him, "It's okay, I understand."

CHAPTER 13

"So what about this latest fling you're supposed to be involved in?" Mia asked.

Joel's face hardened at her question. Somehow she had dared herself to ask what thousands of journalists already had. Why he should give her an answer any different from theirs, she didn't know.

"You shouldn't believe everything you read." He sighed and brought his hand up to rub his forehead as if he were tired. *Tired of hearing the same questions*, Mia thought. "They make most of that stuff up."

"So why don't you sue them?" she asked.

Every celebrity in America seemed to sue the press.

"Why? Because I'd be forever spending all my time dealing with lawsuits." He sighed again, the frustration evident in his voice. "There's too many of them. And to be honest, I simply don't care. They can write what they want. It's of no interest to me."

His tone of voice gave a resounding sense of finality and Mia presumed their conversation was over. Joel was so hit and miss, sometimes he would open up to her, if only briefly, and then other times he would shut himself down in an instant and not utter another word. Recently, he began changing his routine from standing silently in the doorway every time she played to sitting with her every time she practised a song.

Strangely, the change in routine didn't feel strange at all. Mia had readily adjusted to having the superstar silently open and close the door before coming to sit opposite her every time she picked up her guitar.

To Mia, Joel was simply Joel. She was trying to see him for who he really was, not the person she saw on television and in magazines.

Following the afternoon where she had bared her soul to him after he confessed to knowing the meaning behind her songs, they had found themselves opening up to one another little by little. Mia more so than Joel. He could still be his guarded, locked down fortress self at the push of a button.

There was a moment's silence in the room. Mia daren't converse more with him for fearing she had already agitated him by asking about the press. Treading on eggshells was an understatement when it came to Joel. One moment they could be happily chatting away, then in the blink of an eye, the silence would descend and his emotions would sweep from his face as swiftly as if a delete button had been pressed.

She wondered what made him tick, what made him switch off so quickly. It was difficult trying to keep up with what mood he was in. He was still proving difficult to read.

He stared at her with a puzzling curiosity and then, surprising her again, he continued. "Anyway the press makes me sound far more interesting than I really am." His voice sounded lighthearted and, then to Mia's complete surprise, his face softened and he relaxed into a soft smile. "I'm actually pretty boring, really."

Unable to help herself she let out a giggle. Joel glanced up at her and appeared as if he were about to laugh himself.

"I don't believe that." She tried to hold in her giggles. The sudden change in his mannerism had let go of all the tension in the room. "Not for one minute."

He cocked his head to one side and eyed her with a bemused expression. "Why's that?"

"Because—" She paused, treading on eggshells again. "You're a global superstar. I can't imagine you having the time for a boring life."

Joel looked at her for a moment. The amusement left his face, replaced with sadness. Mia instantly understood and wished she could rewind the last few seconds.

He must have spent his whole adult life with people presuming they knew the man behind the guitar. A world-famous rock star who spent his days writing music and his nights taking to the stage, followed by wild after parties with dozens of girls. Though she knew she shouldn't have made the assumption, looking at Joel, hardly anyone could blame her. Joel was the textbook perfect image of a rock star and he had the troubled persona to match. Or so the press would have everyone believe. And that, Mia realised, was exactly what the press had intended. To paint the portrait of a sleazy, rock and roll life of the beautiful man in front of her, when perhaps, in reality ,all he wanted was some privacy away from the spotlight offstage.

"I—I didn't mean that," she mumbled quickly. "I was just kidding."

"No, you're right," he said quietly, his gaze leaving her face and falling to the floor at his feet.

A moment's silence passed between them again. She watched Joel's hunched shoulders as he continued to stare at his feet.

This time she could read his emotions. The sadness could be felt in the air, the resounding defeat in Joel for the way the world pictured him. Mia had a gut feeling the press couldn't be farther from the truth. Perhaps he really was boring off the stage and they invented this rock and roll life to add to the allure of this beautiful creature. She resisted the urge to put down her guitar, lean over and embrace Joel, the way he had done days earlier with her.

"Perhaps Josh would have made a better rock star?" She tried to add humour to her voice.

This time he couldn't suppress his laughter. She watched his shoulders move up and down as he began to chuckle. He raised his head and looked at her and, although she laughed with him, inside she felt the world stop.

A face that was usually so dark and brooding, so mysterious and troubled, was now animated with laughter. His once dark features were now glowing with life as he laughed. Mia felt saddened. *Joel should laugh more often*, she thought. Such an unimaginable beauty shouldn't have been brooding in the dark for so long. She wondered if his brother and producer saw this side of him. Did Joel let his guard down for the endless hours he was locked away in his own studio?

☙☙☙

Los Angeles never failed to disappoint with its weather. As

Mia strolled along the street on her way to the studios, she basked in the early morning sunshine. The sun was already high in the sky and the pavement before her was hot underfoot. She squinted as the sun's reflection glared at her from the windscreens of passing cars and the shop windows across the street, making viewing the inside contents impossible.

With twenty minutes to spare before she was due in the studio, she made a detour to her favourite coffee shop two blocks away from Sixth String Studios. The Starbucks coffee shop she used to frequent on her way to work wasn't half as good as the little haunt she had discovered one afternoon as she had left the studios. After ordering an iced coffee, she headed back out into the morning sun and leisurely made her way to work.

I could quite easily get used to this, she thought as she sipped her drink and the sun soaked into her skin. Although she loved Ireland dearly, and it would always be her home, Los Angeles had been eye opening for Mia. Finally, she felt as though she belonged somewhere, that she had found her calling in life. She could picture herself working at Sixth String Studios permanently. Writing music for a living in the greatest rock music studios on the planet and living in the Californian sunshine sounded heavenly to Mia.

The thought of living in Los Angeles reminded her of Joel. She remembered his house, or rather *mansion*, which she had seen on her Homes of the Stars tour she had taken with Charlie. She wondered if he really enjoyed living in Los Angeles as much as she imagined herself doing.

As she passed a newsstand with the morning papers and gossip magazines, something caught Mia's attention. She usually glanced at the headlines as she passed, taking in the world events at a glance, but this time it wasn't the cover of the morning newspaper that caught her eye.

Normally, she chose to ignore the glossy covers of the gossip magazines, not wanting to fill her mind with idle gossip and ludicrous stories, but one particular front cover stopped her in her tracks that morning.

She stopped in the middle of the sidewalk and walked over to the newsstand. Picking up the cover of the most popular trashy magazine, she looked down at the familiar face of Joel Coben staring back at her from the shiny cover.

The picture on the front page was of him sitting in the back of a taxi with several other people while the headline proclaimed, *My wild night of passion with Joel Coben.*

However, Mia found herself staring at the other photograph superimposed next to the main one of Joel in the taxi.

A young blonde woman with generous assets was posing suggestively while wearing only her underwear. Her long blonde hair was styled in loose curls that fell over her chest. She posed kneeling down with one hand running through her hair and the other on her toned stomach. Mia couldn't help but look at the woman's toned, tanned Californian body with a mixture of envy and self-conscious doubt.

Never would she have the confidence to pose like that and bare herself for millions to read on the cover of a magazine. She wondered how Joel felt about millions of people reading his few and far between interviews and seeing his face across the world in a magazine.

Looking again at the photograph of Joel, Mia noticed his facial expression. He was frowning in a way that she already recognized well. He was clearly annoyed at being photographed. His expression had a way of saying that he was uncomfortable with the paparazzi.

She knew his mask was in place. He wasn't giving anything away to the media. He had just been in the wrong place at the wrong time. The paparazzi were vultures. They scavenged everywhere, constantly hunting and hovering over the lives of others, while they waited for a photograph they could use to create a story.

Then she noticed the people sitting in the taxi beside him. One was clearly his brother Josh, the other his producer Ruben, whom Mia had only seen twice, and a few other people she didn't recognize. Of those, one was the young blonde woman who was professing her night of wild passion with Joel to the magazine.

Intrigued, she opened the cover page.

"Excuse me, miss?"

Mia looked up to see the owner of the newsstand frowning at her. He crossed his arms over his chest and scowled at her.

"Yes?" she asked, confused.

"Can't you read?" He pointed at a handmade sign above the magazine stand that read: *THIS IS NOT A LIBRARY.*

Mia rolled her eyes. "Sorry." She pulled some change out of her pocket and handed it to him before walking away with the magazine. As she strolled down the street, making her way onto her familiar route to work, she flipped through the first few pages of the magazine to get to the main scoop.

Inside, the pictures from the front cover were larger and accompanied with several others. A large photograph showed Joel leaving a bar with Josh and Ruben. The woman could be seen following the three of them with her friends. Then other photographs showed the group getting into the taxi together and the taxi pulling away. There were other "modelling" shots of the woman, who Mia knew from the opening line to be Lucy who was a twenty-two-year-old college student and "model." Immediately, Mia wondered how much of a professional model Lucy really was. Almost every young woman in Los Angeles was either an actress or a model. Hardly any of those young women worked in those professions on a daily basis.

Mia began to read the rest of the magazine article. *Twenty-two-year-old model Lucy, pictured here leaving a Los Angeles bar with Joel Coben, tells of the pair's wild night of steamy passion.*

After meeting Joel and his friends at the bar, Lucy tells how the pair shared a taxi home after his brother Josh suggested she and her friends shared their ride. Pictured here getting into the taxi with Joel, Lucy tells how things progressed as they left the bar.

"We dropped a couple of my friends off first and Joel's producer, then when the taxi arrived at Joel's house. He asked me if I fancied coming inside for a drink. We had a couple of drinks in the living room and then his brother left. After that, things got a little steamy. Joel couldn't keep his hands off me..."

The next part of the article she skimmed over, as she didn't want to read how Lucy described her encounter with Joel.

"His house is incredible. There's a huge indoor pool and Jacuzzi, the living room has three enormous cream sofas and there's this spiralling staircase..."

Mia scowled at the article. She found herself torn between believing Lucy's story as she was clearly pictured sharing the taxi with Joel, but also wondering if this girl had actually seen the inside of his home. The descriptions could have matched any one of the houses in Beverly Hills. Perhaps Lucy had simply been in the right place at the right time and decided to make a few dollars by cashing in on the picture. Without realising it, Mia let her eyes rove over the blonde's figure again. Her ample chest and toned waist, her tanned body, her flowing long blonde hair—Mia could picture Joel's fingers running through that blonde hair. She forced her eyes away from the images, feeling a strange surge of jealousy creeping through her at the thought of the two of them together. There was no denying that Lucy was a stunning girl. They would have made an impressive couple.

Mia read the final line of the article. *Joel's management declined to comment.*

As she approached the crossing before the studios, she folded the magazine and tossed it into the trashcan beside the traffic lights.

CHAPTER 14

Tap, Tap, Tap.

Mia frowned as she spun in her seat to look at the door. "Come in," she called out to the person whose fist was lightly rapping at her studio door.

She frowned as she saw Joel's face appear around the doorway. With one hand on the handle and the other gripped around the door, he poked his head around it into the studio. She caught the faintest glimmer of a smile as he instantly locked eyes with her before his usual mask was back in place.

"Hey, guys," he called out to TJ and Chad who were frowning as much as she was. They had grown so used to seeing Joel materialise at the door, it was an almost alien sight to see him knocking before entering.

Chad looked up from the screen in front of him with a polite, professional smile in place. "Hey, Joel."

"How's it going?" TJ jerked his thumb in the direction of the studio next door where Joel was often hard at work on his new album.

"Yeah, it's going great." He nodded politely back at them both. He was improving on his conversational skills, she noticed. "Listen," he continued. "I was wondering if I could borrow Mia for a moment?" He looked from TJ to Chad as he spoke, his expression still unreadable.

Mia froze where she sat. What on earth could Joel want with her? In the middle of the working day?

While he was a regular fixture in their studio, she had never once set foot in Joel's studio. Anything could be behind that studio door and Mia would be none the wiser.

TJ and Chad's expressions quickly shifted from polite to puzzled, while she remained frozen in shock.

"Sure." TJ raised an eyebrow questioningly at him, although Mia knew he wouldn't receive an answer.

"Are you sure?" Mia was surprised to hear Joel ask, this time directing the question at Chad.

"Yeah, man, go for it." Chad had that rabbit-caught-in-headlights expression on his face at Joel's request, the look was only enhanced by the radiating glow from the laptop screen in front of him.

"Thanks, guys." Joel nodded politely again, "Mia?" he asked as he jerked his head in the direction of his studio.

Quickly placing her guitar against the chair, she got up from her seat and stepped around the chair toward the door. Joel held the door for her as she looked back to her producers. Chad still wore his startled expression, his mouth agape, while TJ threw his hands up in an *I-have-absolutely-no-idea* way. She shrugged before Joel closed the door after her.

He paused in the corridor with his hand on the door to his own studio. Mia stopped short, only inches away from him as she had expected him to open the door.

In an instant, her was face parallel with his perfectly sculpted chest, which was visible underneath his shirt. She forced her eyes upward, gazing into a pair that were almost the same color as his black cotton shirt that was rolled up to his elbows, showing off his tattooed, muscular forearms.

Joel's gaze danced across her face before settling on her eyes. She noticed the change in his behavior. Usually, he would have riveted her with his unwavering stare but, for a few moments, his eyes roamed her face, seemingly taking in every detail of her features in their swift movements before fixating on her own eyes.

Mia resisted a frown. She wondered what went on behind those eyes, what caused them to behave so. Joel truly was a closed book, but he was a book that she would have liked to read. He was a puzzle, which Mia would like to piece together to see the whole picture, when the world saw only fragments of the jigsaw.

His eyes glimmered as they stared into hers and she felt their connection between her eyes and his as they both stood frozen in their moment together. They seemed to be radiating the communication that his lips would not speak. She understood. For a moment, she felt she understood the strange, beautiful man before her.

"I—" Joel hesitated for a moment. *That was another first*, she thought. "I was wondering if you would listen to something for me?" he continued.

He glanced in the direction of the studio before fixing his eyes back on her. Mia saw something in those eyes that she hadn't seen yet—doubt. Joel was hesitant to ask her, doubtful of what she would say. Not only did he want to know her opinion, he valued it too, Mia realised.

"Of course."

She smiled encouragingly at him. He allowed his lips to curl softly, into the briefest of smiles in return, before opening the studio door and allowing her inside.

၏ၼၔၼ

Inside the room was not dissimilar from the studio Mia was used to working in. The familiar soundboards and mixing desks stared back at her from the same position in the room as the studio next door. The same chairs sat behind them, the same leather sofa was tucked in the corner, and the same equipment littered the room.

Only this room looked slightly bigger. That was the only difference she could discern. A swell of glee rose within her as she realised the studio had given her pretty much the same studio to work in as their biggest-selling artist—an artist who was standing beside Mia, observing her from the corners of his eyes in his usual, quiet, analysing way.

Guitars were propped against the furniture here and there and she could see a guitar rack behind the glass in the booth, holding even more of the instruments. She could see a few that she recognized as being quite expensive and wondered if she knew Joel well enough to ask to borrow a couple of them.

Also inside the room was a producer. One who was also riveting her with a gaze she assumed he had inherited from his artist. He was still seated in his chair and Mia assumed she was looking across the room at the producer known as Ruben.

She had passed this man only a couple of times in the corridor and assumed he was Joel's producer, but they had yet to be formally introduced.

Ruben was a short and slim man. He was wearing a round neck jumper and skinny jeans that only seemed to emphasise how slender he was. His auburn hair was cut short and he wore black rimmed glasses that Mia guessed were more of a fashion accessory than a necessity.

His green eyes studied her as she took in the room, his gaze however, wasn't half as unnerving as Joel's.

"Nice to finally meet you, Mia," he said as he rose from his seat to greet her.

"And you," she replied, shaking his hand.

Joel followed her across the short distance between the door and the mixing desk and stood close behind her as Ruben introduced himself.

"I've heard so much about you recently." Ruben smiled and his entire expression altered.

Mia had simply guessed Ruben was quiet and reserved, but seeing him smile gave her the impression he could be a lot of fun once you got to know him.

The thought made her eye Joel quizzically for a moment. She wondered even more what went on behind closed studio doors. Though she could picture Josh and Ruben as friends, *Joel and Ruben?*

"Thank you, I think." Mia raised her eyebrows at him and laughed, wondering what Joel had said to his producer in order to warrant her opinion as worthy.

"Don't worry." Ruben grinned, flashing her a toothy smile. "It's all good. Everyone in Sixth String has been raving about you. Particularly this guy here." He nodded to Joel.

She looked up at Joel who shrugged in response. "It's all true," he said nonchalantly.

Turning back to Ruben, she asked, "You're not from LA, are you?"

As soon as he had introduced himself to her, she had noticed his accent. She was pretty sure she knew where he originated.

"No," he shook his head, "I'm originally from New York City, and I started out there. I worked for a few recording companies and then I was scouted by Sixth String and I made the move out here."

"I thought I recognized your accent," she noted. "I've always wanted to visit New York."

"You should." Ruben's eyes lit up as he spoke of his home city. "It's the most incredible place on earth. I miss it so bad. I go back whenever I can."

"I'd love to go. It sounds wonderful."

His eyes sparkled as he reminisced. "It is. There's nowhere else quite like it."

In truth, Mia had always wanted to visit the Big Apple. It looked incredible. She'd just never had the opportunity. If things didn't work out in Los Angeles, maybe she could try her luck there.

"Anyway." Ruben shrugged. "Didn't you want Mia to hear the song?"

"Yeah." Joel spoke up again. His presence never left the room, despite his silence. "Take a seat."

He gestured to one of the comfy leather office chairs situated around the mixing desks and sat in the one beside Mia.

Ruben reached over and hit a button on the desk before turning to leave. "I'm just gonna grab some coffee." He winked at Joel before leaving the room.

The door shut quietly behind them and Mia was alone with her idol.

Joel's knee was only millimetres away from hers as they sat side by side, listening to the gentle strumming of guitar that was now filling the room.

Her head was down slightly as she allowed herself to focus on the music she was hearing. Joel, however, was completely riveted on her, as if analysing her every move. His eyes remained unwavering on her face as she listened to the rhythm of the song and the sound of his rich, gravelly voice washing out from the speakers.

The words of the song were achingly haunting. They pulled at Mia's heartstrings as she felt them stoking the fires of her soul. His words felt as though his fingertips were brushing at her heart within her chest. There was something special about Joel's music. It was different from anything else on the planet. He had a way with words that allowed him to sing out the feelings, ones felt by every human heart, in a beautifully poetic and simple way. There was no one else who could write a song like Joel could.

She closed her eyes as the song reached its final verse. The music, reaching its crescendo, crashed around her as his voice sang of the lonely days after a relationship breakdown that were lost and empty, the aching pain of a heart that was longing to be reunited with the one it had lost.

Behind her eyelids, Mia could see Joel's fingers nimbly sliding up and down the fretboard of the guitar as he sang, his long fingers drawing rhythms out of the guitar like no other could. He worked that instrument—nurtured it, soothed it, and caressed it—to make it sing to him in a magical way. The final note of the song ended, the final strum of his fingers on the strings slowly fading away.

Reluctantly, she opened her eyes.

"What do you think?" Joel asked. He was leaning forward resting his elbows on his knees and staring up at her from under his brows. His hands were clasped in front of him, as if pleading with her for the answer to be good.

"It's…" Mia trailed off as she tried to think of a fitting descriptive for what she had just heard.

His hands unclenched and his face fell immediately.

"No, no, wait." In a panic, she waved her hands in front of him. "I was thinking."

Relief spread across his face as he realised she wasn't about to insult his unreleased record. Aside from that, Joel appeared genuinely concerned that she didn't like his song. Her—not just someone—her. As if her opinion was the most crucial one to him.

"It's indescribable," she breathed. "There are no words for it. I have no idea how you do it. Your songs are so beautiful. If you could cut open your heart and record what came out, that's what it would sound like."

Mia cringed. Did she really just say something so cheesy in front of Joel Coben?

"Thank you." He clasped his hands over hers. "I really appreciate that."

In gratitude, she gave him a huge smile. She could feel herself blushing at the touch of Joel's hands against her own. Though part of her couldn't believe she was sitting alone in a recording studio with one of her musical idols with his hands clasped around hers, the other part of her marvelled at how strangely comforting the feeling was.

"You inspired me to write that song." His voice was barely a whisper as he made his admittance so close to her.

She swallowed. "Me?"

Joel nodded. "Your music feels exactly how you just described mine to me. Isn't that strange?"

Mia nodded.

"There's something addictive about the way you play, the sound of your voice, the meaning of your lyrics," he said. "As soon as I hear them coming through the walls or down the corridor, I have to go and see with my own eyes. I've never heard anything like your music, Mia, it's beautiful."

There was something in the way those nearly black eyes stared up at her that made her wonder if Joel was describing only her music.

She tried to inhale but found her breath was barely there. His admittance that he had written such a beautiful song after she inspired him made her head spin on its axis.

Then she realised the closed-book-of-a-man in front of her occasionally flickered open to reveal a few pages of its hidden contents within before it snapped its cover shut once again. She reservedly smiled to herself, knowing that she was slowly beginning to piece the Joel Coben jigsaw together. She was determined to read more than a chapter of the book before her and was confident it was holding an intriguing story among its pages.

"Thanks," Mia gushed and averted her eyes at the floor, unable to hold the intensity of his stare any longer.

"So you think it can make the album?" Joel asked.

Looking up she saw a playful smile dancing on his face. He really did value her opinion, she realised. Mia wondered what he saw in her to value her opinion so highly. Maybe it was a case of kindred musical spirits. Maybe Joel appreciated her music as much as she did his. But she had no recording deal, no singles, no albums, no awards—nothing that put her anywhere close to being on par with someone like Joel.

She winked. "Absolutely."

CHAPTER 15

In her assigned studio at Sixth String Studios, Mia was hunched around one of the computer screens that littered the mixing desks. On either side of her sat Chad and TJ, and they were all listening to the final edit of a song they had spent the last couple of weeks working on.

Her voice filled the room around them as they listened carefully to the acoustics of the heartfelt song. Mia smiled as she heard her own lyrics coming to life inside the room of a recording studio. Hearing her own music filling the air of one of the most famous recording studios in the business made the butterflies in her stomach dance. She felt the teenager within her want to jump up and down and clap her hands with glee at the realisation of what was happening. *If only I was recording my own album.* If she were really to take to the booth one day for a CD with her face on the front cover, she had no idea how she would handle the nerves or the excitement.

"I'm really pleased with that." TJ grinned from ear to ear as he clicked pause at the very end of the song and prepared to set it back to the beginning for a second listen.

"Pleased?" Chad leaned across her to scowl at him. "That, my friend, was epic!"

Mia giggled as the pair began to bicker over TJ's professional opinion and Chad's slightly less professional one.

"Anyway, Jackson loved it," TJ added with air of importance. He slipped Mia a sly grin out of the corner of his mouth and winked. She knew he was enjoying antagonising his co-producer.

"What? You already sent it to him?" Chad asked in disbelief.

"Yeah, man, as soon as we were done. I wanted him to get it out there straight away."

"Get it out there?" Mia questioned.

"Yeah, he'll send it to some of the artists who he thinks may be interested, to see what they think. If they're interested in using it, they'll let him know," TJ explained.

Without thinking, she felt her fingers nervously caress the silver guitar pendant around her neck that her friends had bought for her birthday. The feeling was familiar and comforting as if she were reminding herself of home.

"Wow," she muttered.

It was a terrifying thought to picture some of her favorite artists listening to that track. Her idols would be listening to her voice, her lyrics, and her music. She fidgeted even more in her seat, her fingers twisting the guitar around on its chain.

TJ laughed and clapped a hand on her back. "Relax. They'll love it."

Mia attempted to smile gratefully back at him for his reassurance but failed. She wondered how deranged her smile looked at that moment. The thought of her idols hearing her music and passing judgement terrified her.

"Come on, man, one more time." Chad reached over her lap and clicked the computer's mouse over the play button again before reclining in his chair to listen to the song. As the music played out, he tapped his fingers along to the rhythm of the music on the arms of his chair.

TJ tapped his foot in time to the gentle rhythm and Mia noticed a sadness cross both pairs of eyes as they listened to the haunting words of her song. She hadn't recorded some of her personal favorite tracks, the ones that she performed back in Dublin. She had wanted to save those for herself. From day one in Los Angeles, she had been writing new material with her producers and they were finally listening to the end result of one of those tracks.

As the song finished for the second time, Mia noticed TJ slyly wipe the corner of one of his eyes. She refrained from grinning at her musical success. *To make your producer cry must be a good omen.*

Chad nodded resolutely beside her once the track had finished.

"Incredible. They'd be stupid if they—" Chad stopped mid-sentence as a knock on the studio door interrupted their conversation.

"Come in," TJ called out.

The door opened and Jackson stepped swiftly into the studio before closing the door behind him. Dressed in his usual suit and tie, he was the image of sophistication. Mia could easily imagine him sitting at a board meeting and calling the shots. Jackson was not a man to be trifled with. His manner instantly commanded the room. He was a businessman through and through.

Jackson addressed the room. "Afternoon, guys."

Everyone greeted him in return and Mia noticed he was holding his phone in his hand as if he had just finished a call before entering the room.

"How's it going, Mia? Are you enjoying working with these two idiots?" Jackson asked as he perched himself on the edge of the mixing table.

Looking across at her producers, she laughed. As she gathered her thoughts, she refrained from trying to see if her reflection was visible in his perfectly shined shoes. "It's great. Really, thank you so much for this opportunity. I'm loving every moment. TJ and Chad are fantastic," she gushed with honesty.

"That's wonderful," Jackson gave her a professional smile and dazzled her with his Hollywood white teeth. "Listen, Mia."

His tone of voice changed and she fearfully wondered where the conversation was about to lead. *Please*, she thought, *if you're going to tell me this isn't working out, don't do it in front of TJ and Chad.*

Dozens of scenarios ran through her mind as she imagined, in a few seconds, what could possibly be wrong. Maybe Joel had gone to the man at the top after her run in with him the other week. Perhaps their shining star didn't take so well to hearing the truth. She regretted her outburst, purely on the basis that it may have cost her the dream job she'd worked so hard for. But she and Joel had been getting to know one another since then. They had been getting along, Mia couldn't imagine why Joel would say something now.

"I sent out your track 'Hear Me' to some of our artists to see what they thought and if any of them would be interested in using it," Jackson went on.

He allowed his sentence to hover in the air, while his expression remained neutral. Mia could only manage to nod in the silence. The tension she felt for the words that would follow was unbearable.

She could see TJ and Chad leaning forward on the edge of their seats as they nervously anticipated his next sentence. They were both as eager as she was to hear the verdict for their latest material. The song was only hours old and yet the label's artists had already heard it.

Jackson let out a sigh and she immediately felt her heart sink. On either side of her, she saw her producer deflate with sadness.

"I just wasn't expecting this kind of reaction," he murmured and shook his head.

Mia's head instantly snapped up and she frowned at him. "Huh?" she asked and instantly wished she had asked a little more professionally.

Jackson let out a small chuckle at her reaction and looked at TJ and Chad's confused expressions.

Deciding to put them all out of their misery, he explained. "I sent out the track this morning after you sent it to me. I gotta admit, that's an impressive piece, Mia." He nodded at her and she felt her cheeks blush before he continued. "I loved it straight away. I knew we had to get someone to use this. But you know some of the artists can be a bit funny about using someone else's tracks. They like to keep to their own stuff. Joel, particularly, won't touch anyone else's music. But I sent it out to all the big guys, the best that we have."

He pointed at Mia with his mobile phone for emphasis and she felt the flush returning to her cheeks. With raw nerves, she wrung her fingers together as she waited for him to finish.

"And they loved it."

He winked at her and she let out a relieved exhale. She hadn't realised she had been holding her breath, as she waited for Jackson to deliver the verdict on her track but, as she did, she heard TJ and Chad do the same.

"I had a bit of a fight on my hands for this one," Jackson continued and raised his eyebrows as he spoke. "There were several artists wanting to use your song, Mia."

TJ clapped her on the back and she grinned up at him. She knew the track wouldn't have sounded half as good as it did without the help of her two incredible producers.

"I've spent the last couple of hours listening to them fight it out via email and phone calls to decide who could use the track. I never expected this kind of reaction from your work," he repeated. "I mean, I knew you had something special, but this is incredible."

Jackson stared at her and she instantly felt blown away by the realization. Some of the biggest artists at the label were fighting it out to use her song. Her favorite bands were arguing over her music. The thought made her want to scream at the top of her lungs with happiness, but she refrained from doing so in front of the ever-professional Jackson.

Chad turned to her with an enormous grin covering his face. She gave one back at him and they both turned to Jackson as he finished his sentence, "So after a couple of hours arguing, I decided on who I was going to give the track to."

A moment's silence hung in the air again. Mia felt as though she was on a TV game show or talent show as the host agonisingly lingered over announcing the winner.

"Well?" Chad caved in to his impatience and she resisted the urge to elbow him.

Thankfully, Jackson saw the funny side and laughed as he delivered the eagerly anticipated news. "I gave the song to Glasshearts."

That time she did allow herself to scream. Chad jumped up from his seat beside her and punched the air. TJ grabbed her and hugged her tight with all his enthusiasm. After her initial scream, Mia felt tears prick her eyes as she realised one of the biggest bands on the planet would be delivering her song to a worldwide audience. She knew she had to call her friends and family back home.

"Congratulations." Jackson stood up and shook her hand before leaving the room.

"Wow, holy shit, Mia!" Chad exclaimed.

TJ beamed at her. "This is fantastic."

She could feel her own smile threatening to split the sides of her cheeks as she grinned from ear to ear at the news.

Glasshearts were an internationally successful band signed to Sixth String Studios who had been touring almost nonstop since their career began several years ago. They were a young, attractive rock band plucked from bustling the streets of Atlanta, Georgia, and thrown into the lifestyles of the young and successful. Their careers had been a nonstop whirlwind of successes after being signed to Sixth String Studios. Already under their belt they had multiple number one singles, five number one albums, and several Grammy and MTV awards. If Joel Coben was the studio's prized solo artist, Glasshearts was the band equivalent. Their success was unparalleled and they were going to be releasing her song.

Mia couldn't imagine a band as successful as Glasshearts singing her song to their global army of fans.

"Congratulations Mia." Her ears pricked at hearing the familiar gentle, deep voice at her studio doorway.

She turned along with her producers to see Joel standing in the doorway with a faint smile across his usually tranquil lips.

"Thank you," she replied.

"This is only the beginning for you." He nodded at her before walking away.

Mia heard the familiar sound of his studio door opening and closing again.

TJ beamed at her. "Let's hope he's right."

⌘⌘⌘

"Hey," an all too familiar voice came through the studio door late in the evening.

Mia turned in her chair to see Joel standing in the doorway again.

He was breathtaking. There was no other word for the man. Dressed in a simple white shirt, with the sleeves rolled up to his elbows, and dark blue jeans, Joel had the art of impeccably simplistic taste. His image had no need for fancy clothes—simplicity was all he required to smolder. The contrast between the white cotton of his shirt and the intensity of his dark features was startling. Mia felt herself take a sharp breath as she took in his appearance.

"Hi," she replied a little too breathily. She noticed Joel smirk to himself at her reply and a familiar blush crept across her cheeks, as she realised her body had given her away so easily.

"Are you finished yet?"

He crooked an arm against the doorframe and Mia resisted the urge to gape open-mouthed at the flash of skin showing from beneath the raised shirt at his abdomen.

Focussing her eyes in a more northerly direction, she formulated her answer. "Erm...yeah, I think so?" She turned to look at TJ who was the only other person remaining in the room.

"Sure." He clicked away at the computer as he shut the machine down for the night. Folding away his laptop, he then grabbed a rucksack from underneath the mixing desk and shoved his belongings into it. "See you guys tomorrow." He winked not-so-subtly at Mia before darting from the room.

Feeling as though TJ had made a speedier exit than necessary, she glanced back up at the incredible specimen in her doorway. Running a hand through his impeccable head of dark bedhead hair, Joel fidgeted before returning his eyes to her.

He's nervous, Mia noticed.

He ran his hand down the back of his neck and across his collarbone. The sight was delicious and she tried to hide the fact that she was biting her lip as one of the world's hottest superstars ran his hand down his bare neck in front of her.

"So, I was wondering—" His voice caught in his throat slightly as he hesitated. Clearing his throat he continued, "—if you're not doing anything, do you fancy grabbing a drink with me?"

Mia swallowed.

And again.

Joel Coben—one of the world's hottest superstars—was asking her out.

"Sure," she managed. "I'd love to," she hastily added.

He visibly relaxed as she answered. He let out a breath and a light smile crossed his usually impassive features. She was starting to see another side to the reclusive man.

"I'll just be a second, o—okay?" she stammered and Joel nodded.

Leaving her to finish up in the studio, he closed the door and Mia placed her shaking hands on the mixing desk as she inhaled deeply.

I can do this, she thought. *I can go on an after-work date with an international superstar who just happens to be my musical idol. And who also happens to out-of-this-worldly beautiful.*

Releasing her death-like grip of the mixing desk, she gathered her things before rising from her seat and taking a shaky step toward the door. She turned off the lights and, with a nervous hold on the door handle, twisted the knob, and stepped into the corridor.

There, as wonderfully handsome as always, stood Joel, waiting for her.

When flying out to Los Angeles, Mia had never imagined she would even be lucky enough to meet her idol, let alone be going on a date with him.

He was leaning against the wall with his hands in his pockets. As he heard the door close, he looked up from gazing at the floor and fixed his nearly black eyes on her.

As they looked up at her underneath their frame of long black eyelashes and thick, dark eyebrows, Mia immediately saw the world's fascination with the little-boy-lost. Joel's eyes were the textbook definition of a troubled soul. A troubled soul who a woman instinctively wanted to run to and comfort. It just so happened that this troubled soul was exquisitely beautiful. *That many good genes couldn't belong in one person*, Mia thought. It simply wasn't fair.

"You ready?" the words rolled off his tongue in his luxurious, laid-back accent.

She nodded. The gaze that resonated up through those framing lashes was too intense for her to find words. Her brain couldn't function at that moment. His eyes consumed her—they devoured her completely. They seemed to speak a language all of their own, as if Joel were trying to confess his innermost secrets to her with one look.

Mia got the feeling she understood. Or at least she could possibly, if he gave her the chance.

As she drew closer to Joel, she recognized the delicious scent of his aftershave—or him—she wasn't sure which. It was possibly a combination of both. The clean, fresh scent that had notes of vanilla to it filled her senses as she approached.

Surprisingly, he held out his hand to her to lead her down the corridor. Mia took it unquestioningly and felt the delicate touch of his long fingers entwine with hers and curl around her hand. The warmth of his flesh against hers radiated through her skin and made her fingers tingle. She could feel her inner teenager jumping up and down with glee as she walked hand in hand with him through the studios.

As they approached the foyer, her heart began to race. She prayed that Charlie had gone home for the day. The last thing she needed right now was for Charlie to see them together and shriek giddily at the top of her lungs.

Mia got the impression Joel heard more than enough shrieking from his female fans.

Thankfully the foyer was quiet and deserted when they entered. She and TJ had stayed late into the evening, finishing a piece they had been working on. Chad had left at the usual time and she presumed everyone else had too. Everyone else but the rock star she was currently holding hands with.

"My car's parked out the front," Joel said quietly in the deserted foyer and motioned to the parking lot beyond the sliding glass doors.

Outside the sun was beginning to descend over Los Angeles and the orange glow that accompanied the dusk hours was making its way across the city. The waning sunlight reflected off the windscreens in the parking lot and cast a warm light around everything Mia saw. The tranquil sound of the early evening was peaceful as they strolled toward one of the few remaining cars in the lot.

Tucked into the corner, patiently waiting for its owner to return, was a large black Escalade.

A gentle breeze wafted the palm trees that lined the parking lot, bringing a cool, refreshing air to the remaining humidity from the day.

As Joel strolled across the lot with her, he casually told her about the tracks he had been laying down in the studio earlier that day. Talking about music with him was an easy conversation starter. It was a soul-deep connection, which they both shared and could easily relate to.

Not that conversation with Joel was difficult. It was just that he was so unpredictable.

Mia was never sure if he was in lock-down mode or if he was in his "beginning to open up to her" mode. She then realised that Joel was figuring that out as much as she was.

As he was describing the sound of a particular track he was favoring, a loud piercing shriek broke through the calming tranquillity of their evening.

"THERE! HE'S OVER THERE!" a loud female voice

screamed from the other side of the building and was followed by several more hysterical screams.

The sound of thunderous footsteps could easily be heard as the scores of dedicated female fans, who had been waiting for Joel to appear, caught sight of their idol.

Joel muttered something quietly under his breath as the women quickly approached his car.

He pressed the fob on his key ring and opened the passenger door for Mia.

"Wait in here, I won't be long," he said, before helping her climb into the chunky vehicle which thankfully had heavily tinted windows. "Sorry," he mumbled after her as she climbed into the car.

"No, it's okay. Don't be," she said, still holding his hand before he closed the door after her. She caught a flicker of hope cross his eyes as she told him not to worry about the scene that was now unfolding beside his car.

Within seconds, the hysterical, screaming, and crying female fans surrounded Joel, clamouring for his attention. Several paparazzi had followed the girls and were snapping away at Joel as he obligingly signed autographs and posed for pictures on camera phones.

The paparazzi appeared to have no regard for his personal space. They leaned over the crowd and shoved cameras into his face as he attempted to interact with his fans.

Mia wanted to jump out of the car and shove their cameras away, but knowing she was safer behind the tinted glass than having her image plastered all over the front of every glossy magazine on the newsstand, she stayed put.

Women fawned over him and pawed at his skin as their idol stood before them. Others continued to shriek in hysterics while some openly cried and bawled at the realisation of meeting their beloved rock star. The fans clamoured over one another in a desperate bid to get closer to Joel and have their picture taken with him.

After several minutes, he politely made his excuses to his adoring fans and pushed through the paparazzi to get to the driver's side of the car. Mia leant back in her seat, fearful of the intrusive paparazzi hovering outside the car, as Joel opened his door.

Once he had the door shut and started the engine, he looked

across at her. "I'm sorry about all that." His expression was almost embarrassed as he apologised.

"It's fine, honestly." She chuckled. "Perks of the job."

Joel's lip curled up into a smile at her teasing and he slowly backed the car out of the space as the crowd parted.

The car cruised through the series of traffic lights into the heart of Los Angeles and he visibly relaxed as they drove farther away from the paparazzi.

Mia knew it wasn't the attention of his fans that he minded, it was the intrusive cameras that followed him everywhere that he hated. Joel constantly checked his rear-view mirror as he smoothly navigated the streets.

The sun continued to descend and cast shadows across his already dark features as it continued on its journey.

"Are you hungry?" he asked Mia, his face half shrouded in shadow.

How very apt, she thought. A man so shrouded in mystery, yet so shrouded in publicity was currently half in the light and half in the dark. She nodded. "Yes."

Her stomach had been rumbling and she prayed it remained quiet until she reached the restaurant. She couldn't imagine the embarrassment she would feel if her stomach growled loudly while sitting beside Joel in the car.

The low sounds of a familiar song playing from the cars speakers caught her attention.

Glasshearts' latest single was playing out over the airwaves and Mia couldn't help but smile and softly sing along to the band who would soon be playing her song for the world.

Joel grinned when he realised she was singing and reached over to turn the radio up louder.

"You've no idea how much I love to hear you sing," he said quietly, not wanting to disturb her rhythm with the song on the radio. He then began tapping his thumbs on the steering wheel and singing along with her.

Mia mentally shook herself. She was sitting side by side, en route to a dinner date, and singing along to the radio with one of the world's biggest stars. That sort of thing didn't happen to people like her. It just didn't. Yet there she was with Joel Coben in his car and the pair of them were singing along to the familiar song.

When the song ended, he turned the radio back down again and looked out of the corners of his eyes at her. "You really do have a beautiful voice. It's so unique. I've never heard anything quite like it," he gushed while keeping his eyes on the road.

"Thank you, that means a lot." She nervously twisted the guitar pendant on her neck as her superstar idol paid her a compliment.

"I think our voices sounded pretty amazing together just then." Joel's voice softened as he returned his eyes to the road.

Mia stared at him. "So do I," she whispered.

☙☙☙

The waitress dutifully led them to their table the instant they arrived in the upscale restaurant.

Mia knew from the waitress's disapproving looks that there was no way she would have allowed her into the restaurant on her own if she hadn't been with Joel. Still dressed in jeans and a T-shirt from the day at the studio, she felt significantly underdressed.

With a manicured nail, the impeccably dressed waitress indicated a table in the corner of the room. She held out Mia's chair for her before directing her full attention to Joel.

Staring at the back of her head, Mia listened as the waitress recited the menu explanations to Joel rather than the two of them.

"Can I get you anything else, sir?" she asked after they had ordered drinks.

"No that's okay for now, thank you." His impassive mask was back in place as he spoke to her and she stalked away from the table.

Mia hadn't failed to notice almost every woman in the restaurant turn and gawk at him as he walked through the tables to their almost private spot in the corner of the room.

Joel was aware of how attractive he was to women. There was no doubt about it. He couldn't fail to notice. But she also observed that he never used his sensational looks and appeal to the opposite sex to his advantage. His dark, mysterious air had women falling at his feet as easily as if he were a notorious, womanising, stereotypical rock star. There was just something about him. Something about his mannerisms and the way he carried himself.

It was in his eyes and in his aura. Something about Joel Coben made women forget their decency and throw themselves at him in hysteria. And Mia could see exactly why. Something in those troubled, endless, near-black eyes made a woman want to rescue the darkened soul within. They all wanted to be his saving grace.

The waitress returned with their drinks and set them down on the table. Mia couldn't help but notice the woman graze her fingers against Joel's hand as she set them down.

As always, he remained impassive.

The waitress threw Mia a haughty look before she stalked away again with a distinct pout on her lips at his lack of attention toward her.

With force, Mia stifled her smile at the sight. Joel's eyes were fixed on Mia and she knew that he had taken in every second of what had just occurred. He simply chose not to react.

As soon as the waitress had departed, the soft, familiar smile that she was beginning to see more of materialised on his beautiful face. Mia instantly found her own features mirroring his actions.

"Does that ever get old?" she asked with an arched eyebrow.

Joel laughed. He knew she was teasing from the smile on her face, "Surprisingly, yeah, it does."

"Having women throw themselves at you gets tiring, *really*?" She feigned disbelief and he chuckled again.

"It really does, honestly." He stared right into her eyes. "What's attractive about a woman throwing herself at your feet?"

Taken aback by his answer, all she could do was stare. Of course, the answer was obvious, but what twenty-eight-year-old global superstar wouldn't take advantage of the many opportunities women gave to them. Fame appeared to go straight to most celebrities' heads. She was surprised to earn Joel Coben was an apparent exception.

"It's too easy to get caught up in everything. Pretty much everything is handed to you on a plate in this industry." He raised his eyebrows even though Mia already understood his double meaning.

"I can only imagine."

"You soon won't have to." He gave her a knowing look and she cocked her head at him in question. Eyes almost as black as the night sky stared back at her.

They had an aura of knowingness about them. Mia could imagine feeling her soul laid bare under that gaze, but somehow she didn't seem to. She was beginning to feel comfortable under the intensity of Joel's eyes.

"You're far too good to stay working as a songwriter, Mia," he continued. "The label is being ridiculous by not signing you up."

She shrugged at him. "I can't be that good or they would have."

"They're biding their time. I don't understand why," Joel frowned as he mulled over his thoughts. "Normally, they would snap you up. You'd have an album finished by now. I don't get what they're up to."

Her glass stopped mid-way to her lips as she listened to him. Simply being grateful for the opportunity to work with Sixth String Studios, she had only dreamt of signing to them. She hadn't questioned the company's motives behind their short-term contract.

"I mean, don't get me wrong, they're the best in the industry," he hastened to add when seeing her startled expression. "They would never dream of doing anything below the belt. I wouldn't work for anyone else. They're brilliant. All I'm saying is, it's not like them to not sign you up straight away. Someone with your talent won't go unnoticed in Los Angeles for long."

She could feel her cheeks beginning to blush as Joel paid her compliments. For someone as gifted and successful as he was to be singing her praises was unbelievable. In an attempt to hide her embarrassment, she took a large gulp of her drink.

"I'm serious," he continued. "You're incredible, Mia. Your music is ready made, multi-million copy selling stuff, and I don't understand what they're doing. I think you're amazing."

It was her turn to watch Joel blush at his admission before hastily changing the subject.

"Don't get me wrong, Glasshearts will do great with your song, but it should be you releasing that, not them. No one sings it quite like you do."

"Thank you." She exhaled steadily and tried to quash the conga-dancing butterflies in her stomach.

Naturally, their conversation flowed into music. It was the biggest shared love between them both and made for easy conversation with a rock megastar. Mia had been wondering in the car journey to the restaurant what she would talk about over dinner with a multi-millionaire, Los Angeles mansion dwelling musician. A girl from Kinsale barely had a thing in common with someone like Joel Coben.

How wrong she was quickly proved. Although music was easy conversation between them, long after their dinner plates had been cleared and their refilled glasses emptied, they were still deep in conversation.

"Excuse me."

Halting their discussion about the final scene in the last CSI series, Mia saw the pouty waitress had returned. This time she looked more her usual rude and uppity self.

"I'm very sorry to disturb you, but we closed a while ago." She gave Joel a suggestive pout, hinting that the restaurant had done him a favor.

Rolling her eyes, Mia noticed the waitress's subtle hint for thanks from Joel.

She turned in her chair to see an empty restaurant behind her. Sure enough, the tables were vacant of diners and reset for the following day. The bartender was wiping down the counter, and the only sound was the gentle tinkling of music still playing from the speakers.

"I'm so sorry," Mia said, jumping up from her seat and getting ready to leave. She could see Joel was trying hard not to burst into a grin.

He smiled politely at the waitress and left several bills for the check on the table. "Thank you very much, I appreciate that."

The waitress winked at him as she picked up the cash. "It's not a problem. I hope we see you again soon."

Mia rolled her eyes again, this time not so subtly.

Joel dutifully followed her out of the restaurant and held open the door for her on the way out.

"Why didn't you say anything?" she gasped at him as she passed him in the doorway.

He shrugged. "I was too busy enjoying your company."

"Oh." She stopped in the door and looked up at Joel who smiled softly down at her.

"I'll drive you home," he said as he placed a hand on the small of her back and followed her out of the door.

Mia was grateful to see the paparazzi were no longer outside the restaurant when they left. She had a sneaking suspicion Joel had something to do with that. The paparazzi camped outside the studio for days. A few hours over dinner were nothing to them. Joel's security had to have moved them on.

After opening the door to his Escalade, he held out his hand to Mia to help her into the tank-sized vehicle. She placed her hand in his, feeling him grip it as she lifted herself into the passenger seat.

The touch of his fingers lingered on her skin a moment longer than they should have before he let go and closed the door. She had felt herself wanting to hold onto his hand longer, too, wanting to keep the contact with someone she was beginning to feel a deep, unexplainable connection with.

Joel climbed into the driver's seat and started the engine. As he pulled away from the curb, he glanced across at Mia sitting beside him and she could see the feeling mirrored in his own eyes. Eyes that were the color of the darkness outside the windscreen also looked confused, as if they wanted the same thing she did but were struggling with something else.

Though, she began to wonder, Joel quickly picked up their conversation where they had left off before being interrupted and the feeling was quickly forgotten.

Laughing as he cracked another witty joke, she marvelled at the sharp, quick-witted sense of humor that media knew nothing about. He was incredibly funny when he was acting natural.

Mia felt blessed to be able to see this rare side of him, that Joel felt secure enough with her to let his guard down a little.

All too soon, the blazing light of Mia's hotel sign was glowing in front of the windscreen and the car slowed to a stop right outside the front door.

Joel looked across at her and smiled his adorable, lopsided smile before jumping down from the car and coming around to open her door.

He gripped her hand again as he helped her down from the car and she landed inches away from his body. Joel looked down at her standing so close and his nearly black eyes suddenly seemed to smolder.

Surprising Mia, he loosened his polite hold around her fingers to entwine them with his. He stared at her for a moment longer, as if wondering if she would break their hold. She stared back at him and allowed her fingers to curl around his hand. Joel looked visibly relieved, pulled her way from the car, and closed the door behind her.

He walked her around the car and toward the hotel doors, stopping just before them. "I really enjoyed spending time with you tonight." He smiled again and she noticed the corners of his eyes crinkle as he did so.

"Me too," she replied.

"I mean that, I really did." He squeezed her hand a little tighter. "You really are something special, Mia."

Taken aback be his admittance, she paused. In her moment of disbelief, Joel leaned forward, placing his other hand lightly on her waist and placed a soft, sweet kiss on her lips.

And then he was gone.

Opening her eyes, she saw nothing before her. Her hand still felt as though his fingers should be in the spaces between her own, her other hand searched for his on her waist. But before she knew what had happened, Joel was back in his car and the engine was roaring to life.

She watched the Escalade pull away out of the hotel grounds and into the Los Angeles late night traffic.

Mia ran her finger tips across her lips as if checking that they could still feel. Had she imagined it?

In disbelief, she shook her head.

Did Joel Coben just kiss her?

CHAPTER 16

The slowing of tires in the busy traffic of downtown Los Angeles made Mia's ears prick. Though the car was close by, she continued walking.

Sounds of car horns blaring, as they passed the crawling vehicle filled her ears and she upped her pace and merged into the crowd to be closer to the buildings. It was early evening and the traffic was heavy with the post-work rush hour but the traffic on the sidewalk was thinning. After a long, unusually hot spring day, the air was still heavy and suffocating. The mixture of humid air and the constant smog that hung over Los Angeles felt heavy on her lungs as she tried to walk faster toward her hotel.

"Mia?"

Hearing her own name made her jump. She spun on her heel to face the car that was crawling along the side of the curb. Vehicles were swerving around it in attempt to reach the approaching traffic lights. There was going to be an accident soon if the driver didn't speed up.

To her surprise, the car was a huge black Escalade. Joel was sitting in the driver's seat with the window rolled down, his face on full view to the passing pedestrians.

Some stopped and stared at Mia being slowly pursued by the global rock star, others passed by unawares. *Los Angeles*, Mia thought, *nothing is out of the ordinary.*

"Yes?" she asked, caught off guard.

"Can I borrow you for a minute?" Joel pointed to the vacant passenger seat beside him with a sly grin itching at his lips.

Mia pursed her own. "What for?" Though she tried to hide her tell-tale smile, it threatened to break out any second.

Joel laughed. "Just get in the car!"

Allowing her smile to break, she dashed across the pavement and hopped into the tank-sized car. In an instant, his hand stretched across the seat to help her up as she climbed in.

His hand still lingered over hers once she was seated and the door was closed. She giggled as Joel closed the window and finally gave himself his anonymity back. He pulled out into the traffic just in time for the changing traffic lights.

Mia noticed they were speeding away from downtown Los Angeles. "Where are we going?" she asked, eyeing the passing streets.

Joel shrugged. "To a show."

A conversation flickered in her memory. She remembered Charlie telling her earlier in the week that he was playing the Staples Center in Los Angeles that night. "Don't *you* have a show tonight?"

He nodded, a childish grin was creeping across his cheeks. "I do."

Mia was enjoying seeing the side of Joel the rest of the world did not. He was much more fun than she imagined.

"Then where are we going?"

"To *my* show," he replied with a playful, sarcastic tone to his voice.

Reaching over the seat, she elbowed him in the ribs, causing him to laugh out loud.

Joel's laughter was a beautiful sound. It was a shame that it was silenced too often.

She crossed her arms over her chest and arched her eyebrows. "Don't I get a say in this?"

Joel only laughed and shook his head firmly, "Nope," before adding, "I thought you might like to watch."

That look was back on his face again, Mia noticed. He was still playful, but she could see he was hesitant. He was wondering what she was going to say. He feared the worst.

She grinned, before playfully elbowing him in the ribs again, just for good measure. "I'd love to."

ळ৯৻

Adrenaline and anticipation from the crowd for their eagerly awaited idol filled the arena. The atmosphere in the room crackled with tension and simmering female hormones. From her place in the wings, Mia could see the craning necks of numerous fans as they searched for a glimpse of Joel behind the scenes.

Some were already cheering and shouting while others stamped their feet in thunderous anticipation. The tremors of their stomping made the floor beneath her shake and the noise only added to the anticipation in the air.

This feeling was electric. Mia thrived off the feeling a live performance gave. But even though she wasn't the one taking to the stage tonight, the feeling in the room was sensational. There were no words to describe the addictive buzz she received from the crowd whenever she was given the chance to perform.

She envied the level of Joel's career and the size of the crowd out there waiting so eagerly for him to appear. Joel appeared to take everything in his stride. Mia struggled to understand how he couldn't want to jump up and down along with the crowd in excitement. She could feel herself bouncing up and down on the balls of her feet as she waited for him to appear.

From far across the stage she could see him adjusting his earpiece before going on. Way across the room in the opposite wings of the stage, too far inside for the fans to see, she could see his silhouette as he tweaked the piece in his ear that would block out the sound of the crowd and keep him on track.

Joel looked up to where she stood and gave her a thumbs up. She could see a grin crease his usually masked face when he saw her waiting for him.

In an instant, the room went dark as the lights in the room went down and a spotlight on the stage appeared.

The sound of the crowd was deafening.

Their thunderous applause rose to what Mia was sure was louder than a jet engine. She winced at the noise, suddenly understanding why Joel wore an earpiece.

The spotlight began spinning out into the crowd making them scream even louder. The tension in the room increased tenfold as they became uncontrollably eager for Joel to make his appearance.

Finally, the spotlight settled on the center of the stage and he made his entrance. Mia joined in with the clapping and cheering as she watched him walk into the spotlight.

"Thank you very much."

His low, dulcet voice greeted the crowd and he immediately began strumming at the strings of his guitar.

The crowd erupted louder, than Mia thought possible, at the sound of his voice, before settling down to listen to their beloved musician perform live the songs they had heard time and time again in their cars and on their stereos.

By the side of the stage, she swayed to the familiar sounds of Joel's hit songs. She sang along to the lyrics she knew so well. Despite hearing your favourite songs over and over again, nothing compared to hearing them played live by their creator. There was something about the energy and passion when seeing it played live, the way it was intended to be.

Mia stood, watching him from the shadows, as he played on into his set, the crowd still unrelenting in their enthusiasm and support for him. She marveled at how flawlessly Joel played through his songs, the effortless way he interacted with the crowd, making them feel as if he were performing for them one on one.

And still the crowd continued to scream and clap for their idol. The scale of performing to such a large audience amazed her. She had only played for hundreds of people. Joel played for tens of thousands.

The moment you were placed on that stage, you were placed on a pedestal. Every eye in the room became riveted on you, every ear tuned in to you, every person in the room wanted to be you. In the pace of a few footsteps, in the opening bars of music, you instantly became an idol.

It was an image that Joel worked effortlessly. He moved through his songs, the new and the well-known, all to a rapturous crowd. She could feel the hairs on the back of her neck stand on end as the entire room sang along with Joel to his most loved songs. The sound of one voice and a guitar being accompanied by thousands was soul lifting. The sound was haunting and yet incredibly beautiful. Mia could easily picture herself sitting in the middle of that spotlight with thousands of people singing back her own words to her.

That thought made her shiver. The opportunity was so close, but still so far out of reach.

As soon as it seemed to have started, it was over.

Live shows always came and went too quickly. Mia knew that from experience. Whether she was on stage or in the crowd, the adrenaline from a live show always seemed to speed up the experience.

As he said goodbye to his adoring fans, he waved to those who were glimmers of flashing cell phones in the distance and blew kisses to those on the front row.

Girls cried openly. Tears streamed down their faces as they hysterically pawed after their idol. Thousands of flashing lights signaled cameras and cell phones, desperately trying to capture one final image of their megastar.

Joel reached the edge of the stage. He was only a couple of feet away from her spot in the darkened wings. He took one final bow and blew a kiss to the audience before disappearing from sight. Grabbing his guitar strap, he pulled it over his head before walking directly over to Mia.

His brow was covered in beads of sweat and the edges of his hair were damp with perspiration. He ran his hand through it, ruffling his unruly bedhead style.

She could feel her heart flutter in her chest at the sight of him and immediately knew why thousands of women had been crying and screaming in hysterics for the last ninety minutes.

Joel was undeniably beautiful. He was smoking hot. He was deep. He wrote achingly poetic songs. He could sing like a dulcet-toned angel. He was perfect.

His snug black T-shirt clung to his slender, yet muscular frame and highlighted every sculpted curve of his body. The perspiration from performing made his T-shirt cling to his damp body. Tattoos curved over the arch of the muscles on his forearms, a sight that kept Mia's eyes lingering on his body a second or two longer than she should have.

Joel flashed his teeth in a dazzling smile as he caught her eyeing his body.

"Did you enjoy it?" His grin was the adorable lopsided one that Mia loved to see.

He stopped a few inches away from her. She could smell the perspiration from his body mixing with his usual delicious smell. Somehow, he still smelt incredible. She wanted to step forward and bury her face in his chest, into the middle of his scent.

"Yes," she breathed, her breath coming out heavier than she

realised. She could feel her cheeks flush with embarrassment and Joel let out a chuckle.

"I'm glad." He leaned forward and softly kissed her cheek.

Mia felt his skin brush across hers, his lips tingle against her cheek, and his hand lightly on her waist. She placed her hand on his shoulder and desperately wanted to pull him in closer.

"Come on." His infectious grin was back in place as he took her hand in his own. His skin was still damp, but Mia didn't care. The heat from his body radiated into her from only the touch of his palm pressed into hers.

He led her from the stage wings and through the rigging of backstage, passing many people who stopped to congratulate him on his show. All of who stared at the dark-haired girl holding Joel's hand.

❧❧❧

Click, click, click, click, click.

Dozens of flashbulbs and shutter lenses sounded simultaneously to announce Joel's arrival through the front doors of the studio. The sound they made resembled hundreds of birds all taking flight at once. Mia wondered how celebrities didn't walk around with the noise permanently ringing in their ears.

Whenever they left a building or a car, the sound was immediately there, waiting for them. She made a mental note to ask Joel about it later.

Charlie looked up from her computer to see who had swiped themselves into the building.

Seeing her two favorite brothers—one more preferred by her than the other—walk through the door, her face immediately lit up.

"How's my favorite girl?" Josh asked as he confidently strode across the foyer, leaned over the desk, and, in one swift motion, planted a kiss on her cheek.

She winked at him from behind her computer. "Much better now, thanks."

"And my second favorite?" he turned to ask Mia.

"I'm fine, thanks, though I doubt that." she cocked a quizzical eyebrow at him.

Being almost the spitting image of his megastar brother, Josh wasn't short of admirers and Mia doubted she came second on his list of favorite people.

"Worth a try." He shrugged before turning his attention to Charlie again.

"Hey." Mia smiled at Joel as he patiently waited behind his more outlandish brother to finish making his greetings.

He grinned as he walked up to greet her. "Afternoon."

Joel had arrived at the studio in the early afternoon as he often stayed until early hours of the morning when recording.

She could sympathise as she often found creativity flowed better at night. However, she was contracted to a more scheduled working pattern.

"The press are everywhere today." He frowned. "I think someone tipped them off about the other night."

"Huh?" she asked.

"After the show, someone mentioned to the press that I left with a dark-haired girl. They've been asking everywhere to find out who she is."

Mia could see the frustration on his face. He really hated being hounded by the press at every move he made. With his hands in his pockets, the look he wore on his face suggested he was exasperated and deep in thought.

"Joel!" an angry voice sounded from across the room.

Every head turned in the direction Jackson came from as he strode across the room.

"Oh, shit," Josh mumbled, causing Jackson to throw a heavy scowl in his direction.

Joel didn't respond. He looked at Jackson with a curious expression but remained silent. He was on the defensive, Mia realised.

She knew then that a media-based interrogation was about to come his way.

"What the hell is this?" Jackson demanded as he unfurled a newspaper in Joel's face.

Joel still remained silent. She noticed Charlie's mouth fall open and she heard Josh mutter, "Oh shit," again.

"Well?" Jackson demanded.

"Well, what?" Joel snapped.

"What the hell happened? What the hell do you think you're playing at?"

Joel didn't answer. He wasn't looking at Jackson, he was staring at Mia.

Her eyes were riveted on the morning newspaper that Jackson was brandishing in Joel's face. She could feel anger and humiliation quickly beginning to rise in her chest.

Joel Coben in Wild After Show Party with Five Girls. Singer seen leaving show with mystery brunette.

The newspaper's front-page story boldly screamed out at her from Jackson's hand.

She didn't need to read the rest of the story. There was a blazing photograph next to the headline and sub line that showed Joel clustered around numerous women.

"We're trying to get an album together. You're not on tour yet!" Jackson snapped at him.

Still he said nothing, just continued staring at Mia.

She felt humiliated.

Not only had Joel made a fool out of her, he had done it spectacularly in front of the entire studio. And her manager. And her friend.

"Bastard," she snapped at him before angrily storming away across the room and fumbling with her key card to swipe herself out of the building.

Joel had dropped her off at her hotel after the show. He'd made himself appear the perfect gentleman, driving her to her front door and sweetly kissing her goodnight. He hadn't tried to push his luck with anything more.

And like an idiot, Mia had believed him.

After opening up so much of herself to him, she felt the anger and embarrassment crashing through her body. She wanted to turn around and scream at him, hurl abuse at him, swing at him if she could. But none of that would do any good. Joel Coben had played Mia like he played the media.

The realisation that she was just another game to him hit her hard. *But why?* She wanted to scream across the room to him before she left. When he could so easily land himself several girls, why bother with her?

She heard footsteps behind her and knew she was about to be dragged back into the building. Her key card wouldn't work on the electronic door and in frustration she was fumbling with it even more.

Joel's hand was quickly on her arm, pulling her around to face him.

"Get off me," she spat.

"Mia, just wait," he pleaded. His eyes made her want to stop and listen. He looked pleading and torn—it was the look she thought she knew.

"No," she snapped and fumbled with the door again.

"It's not what you think," he tried and placed his hand on her arm again.

Mia wrenched it out of his grasp. "Oh, really?"

"No." He shook his head. "It's absolute bullshit. They've made the entire thing up."

"Really, Joel?" She spun to face him. "You really think I'm that stupid?"

"No, I don't," he said, his eyes pleaded with her to believe him. "Otherwise, I'd let you go. I know you're not. Please listen to me."

"How the hell have they made that up, Joel?" she snapped again and could hear her voice was rising. The entire studio would soon be out to witness this.

"They heard I was leaving with a girl, *with you*," he emphasised, "so they dredged this old photo out of the archives from some party a few years ago and made the whole thing up."

The key card finally beeped on the door.

She looked at him one last time and could see the pleading in his eyes. He was silently begging her to believe him.

Somehow she couldn't, not right now.

She was angry. She was hurt and embarrassed. She needed space.

Turning away from his pleading eyes, she walked out of the studio doors.

CHAPTER 17

Mia, wait!"

She heard Charlie's voice calling after her as she stormed out of the studio and across the tarmac outside the building. High heels clattered across the tiled flooring as Charlie tried to catch up with her.

Mia picked up her already fast pace, as she strode through the studio car parking lot and across the road. She began to walk as fast as her legs would carry her without breaking into a run. She moved so fast that the muscles in her calves began to burn against the strain. Despite the tearing sensation she felt in her legs, she hurried on until she could no longer hear Charlie's calls behind her or the clattering of heeled shoes dashing to keep up with her.

Car brakes screeched loud in the afternoon air as they slammed to a halt before being followed by several loud blasts from the horns as Mia stormed out across the road before waiting for the signal change.

She didn't care. Let them blast their horns at her, let them shout and curse through the open window and raise their middle fingers as they drove on past.

Several pedestrians stopped and stared at her as she walked out in front of the traffic and continued walking down the road despite almost getting hit by several cars. They stopped in their tracks, their faces agape in shock. They pointed and whispered among one another. Mothers stopped their strollers in their tracks, dog leashes were pulled to a halt, and children's hands were grabbed as Mia walked blindly on past the onlookers who gawked at her apparent suicide bid.

She felt her anger still burning furiously inside her. She

clenched her fists by her sides and could feel her teeth grinding together in her mouth, as she tried to control her raging emotions. She refused to believe what had happened.

Somehow, she had allowed herself to believe Charlie's words—that Joel really did like her. And somehow, despite all the marks against him, Mia had begun allowing herself to like him. Rarely did she let someone into her life with more than an ounce of trust. After a lifetime of disappointments and false expectations, she allowed few people to see past her guard that she held so firmly in place. Somehow, Joel had worked his mysterious charms and crept past her defenses.

She hadn't intended to like him. He was everything she knew she shouldn't fall for in a person. He was notoriously reclusive and mysterious, he was famous for reportedly womanising half of Los Angeles and god knew where else. He came across as rude, as obnoxious. He assumed he had the right to swan into her every studio session and was followed by the media in almost his every move.

But somehow Mia had found herself connecting with him. It was through music that they had found a connection that was different from the norm. She had allowed herself to think that somehow things could be different with him, that despite Joel being a global superstar, they could have a connection that was different from anyone else he had met in his crazy life. They had both suffered great losses and trials from a young age before finding their solace in music. They both wrote their own music, played the guitar religiously, and connected with their music in a way that their emotions had never before found a release for.

Joel had understood her music in the way no one else ever had before. Everyone who listened to her music, initially, and still did, believe she was singing about a lost lover. However, he knew straight away that she was singing about something else entirely. He had heard her music in a way that only she did. Up until then, only she knew how those lyrics were meant to be heard because, to her soul, they meant something else. Joel had seen that straight away and she knew then that there was something different about him. But in one moment, he had thrown away everything she had allowed herself to believe about him.

Mia continued to walk, eventually slowing her pace.

Ignoring the faces that blurred past her, some curiously glancing at her while others strode past obliviously, she continued walking down a nameless street. She had no idea where she was. In her haste to leave the studios, she had dashed across the road and kept walking until her anger had dwindled from a furious pace to a normal step. On the pavement below her, she stared at her feet and concentrated on simply putting one foot in front of the other. Watching her alternating feet step out in front of her body gave her mind something to focus on. She watched her right foot, then her left, then her right, then her left, and so on. It was a meaningless task and it zoned her consciousness into the task in front of her, rather than allowing her mind to analyse what had just happened.

She sidestepped around pedestrians and strode between those who dawdled along the boulevards as they idly gazed into the shops and boutiques they passed. The sounds of friends chatting as they stepped in and out of shops, mothers chastising their children, and couples lovingly talking while they strode arm in arm down the streets, filled Mia's ears as she continued to walk.

She particularly tried to block out the last ones.

The smells of the stores and boutiques she passed filled her nose as she walked through various areas of the city. Her nose wrinkled as she passed a sushi bar. She had never been fond of the idea of eating raw fish. She felt her mouth water as she passed a deli before it reminded her of Charlie. Varying scents of perfumes wafted out of the stores, as she walked on by the numerous clothing and cosmetics stores. And the smell of leather wafted into the street each time she passed a shoe store.

On she walked, and though she rarely looked up from the pavement in front of her feet, she knew she was entering a less inviting part of town.

The sounds of dogs barking in the distance and car doors slamming replaced the earlier sounds of shoppers and families. Still Mia walked on, ignoring the teenagers loitering on the street corners and the dubious-looking men leaning in shop doorways and alleyways.

As she rounded another corner, she heard a sound that made her stop and look up from the ever-changing pavement beneath her feet.

The sound wasn't one she was too familiar with but it was still one she recognized. She recognized it from the few occasions she had accompanied friends, particularly Dylan, to such places. She also recognized the sound because it brought back the memories that she had been walking to try and forget.

A tattooists needle vibrating away on someone's skin resonated from the store within as Mia looked through the doorway. Hunched over in his chair, the artist concentrated on the arm of his client laid on the chair arm beneath him. Though the client looked nothing like him, she automatically pictured Joel laying there with his arm extended to the burly man with the ink-filled device.

Images of the beautiful etchings that ran down his arms and across other places of his body, unknown, began to fill her mind. How long he would have sat in a place similar to where she was now standing as he had the heartaches and triumphs of his life inked across his beautiful skin, she wondered.

Normally, people with tattoos often came under prejudice, and stereotyping for the inking's they chose to have etched across their bodies, they were often labelled and branded before society even knew what kind of person they were, but for Joel, it somehow worked.

Although he wasn't covered heavily in tattoos, he still had more than the norm. And women still threw themselves at him, magazines photographed him, paparazzi chased him, and companies begged to work with him.

She shook her head as his achingly beautiful face flooded her vision once again. Wishing she could erase the afternoon and start the day again, she sighed heavily. *If only*, she thought.

Then she realised the man in the chair was frowning at her and she knew she had been staring too long. Quickly she turned from the doorway and left, heading back in the direction she had originally intended.

Since seeing the tattoo parlor, Mia couldn't get images of Joel out of her mind. His face seemed glued like one of his posters to the forefront of her mind, his nearly black eyes staring up at her from the glossy cover of a magazine. The matt pages of the morning newspaper quickly replaced the glossy magazines where he stared back at her from the center of a cluster of scantily dressed women.

Again, she furiously shook her head, as if she were trying to shake away the images stuck to the inside of her mind. Instead, she returned to focussing on the pavement—right foot, left foot, right foot, left foot…

The wind whipped down the street between the buildings and stung against her face before whirling away in another direction. Mia looked up to see that the sky had darkened incredibly and the threat of rain was imminent in the approaching dark clouds. In the usually sunny Californian air, the temperature had dropped noticeably by a few degrees as she had walked on through the afternoon and into the evening.

Her legs ached and her feet were beginning to feel sore from the miles she had walked across the city. Still she had no idea where she was. Around her, the buildings didn't look familiar and she could see no landmarks that she knew. The only thing that she could recognize was the sight of the ocean in the distance. Somehow she had walked from downtown Los Angeles to somewhere on the Californian coast, though she had no idea where.

Hugging her arms around herself, she felt the chill in the air. The traffic was quiet on the road beside her and there were few people passing by on the pavement.

Cooling of the air signaled the coming of a storm. Mia could feel that eerie calm that descended upon the land just moments before the rain began to fall. The wind had stilled, the air was cold, and there was just something that told her the storm was coming. She walked on toward the ocean and could see a road before it at the end of the street she was now walking on. As she reached the curb, she then checked the traffic before crossing the road to stand on the pathway before the beach.

The sea stared angrily back at her. Its toiling and crashing waves could be heard over the wind that returned to whip against her bare arms, now that she stood on the sea front.

Mia felt the first few drops of rain begin to fall as she stared out at the endless infinity of ocean before her. Waves were crashing loudly and appeared almost as dark as the sky in the approaching of the storm. Cool drops of water lightly tickled her skin before they began to patter against her arms as they fell more quickly from the sky. She felt the drops falling faster as the clouds began to roll over the Californian coastline, the heavy rainfall now soaking through her T-shirt and onto her skin beneath.

Hating how caught up she was with Joel, she was her angry about how one person made her feel. They didn't even have an official relationship. Mia had no idea what they were, and yet she had stormed away from the argument like a scorned lover.

In the midst of her anger, she hated how much he had gotten under her skin. She wished he hadn't heard her performing and identified with her music. Those songs were her songs, her music. No one else was meant to know them the way she did. She was happy with the world believing she was singing about an ex-boyfriend until he had shown up.

She tried to force the rising tide of emotions that was crashing toward the shore in her mind. The usual wave that she felt was now more like tsunami, headed for the shoreline. There was nothing she could do to stop it. Gazing out at the crashing ocean waves in the distance, she watched the rising rolls of water slamming angrily against one another in a furious struggle for dominance, before the water collided with the beach.

As she watched one large wave lash over the top of another before loudly rolling over and frothing out onto the sand, she felt the tsunami in her mind begin to reach its own shore. The wind whipped her hair around her face and stung against her cheeks. Her eyes began to water as she stared into the salty wind that blew angrily into the land from the ocean.

Mia began to realise she was being ridiculous. She knew she had acted too hastily. As the tempest around her thrashed and raged, she was the eye of the storm. Her anger had begun to fade as the wind and rain lashed against her on the oceanfront, and she could feel herself beginning to calm.

Perhaps she should have believed him, perhaps she should have known better than to believe a story on the front of a trashy newspaper.

She had trusted Joel enough to open up to him, to share her secrets with him. Surely, that counted for something. They had a connection strong enough for her to share those things with him. She must have seen something within him worth trusting. That something, Mia realised, should have been strong enough to overpower the initial embarrassment she felt at seeing the article.

The newspaper was a prime example of his daily life. Being so heavily in the public eye meant the media had a strong demand for Joel to fill and, if that meant fabricating the occasional story, then so be it.

Mia knew she should have realised. When the image from the

front of the newspaper entered her mind again, she could see that perhaps Joel did look slightly younger in the picture. It could even have been Josh. She hadn't looked at it closely enough without feeling scorned and hurt.

If this was how angry she felt, she needed to realise how angry the article had made Joel feel. He dealt with this day in day out and was presumably tired of denying and explaining story after story. But it was the initial shock that had hurt her most. She had been unprepared. And that was what caused her to act so rashly.

Her eyes watered furiously from the wind that now raged against the ocean and the land, at least that was what she told herself. She knew her tears were mixing with the rain that fell against her face and both ran freely down her cheeks and onto her chest. Tucking a flying strand of hair that danced around her face in the wind behind her ear, she then wrapped her arms around her body again.

And somehow, despite everything she felt, Mia wished those arms were Joel's wrapping around her body in the raging of the storm.

CHAPTER 18

Mia, just get into the taxi," Charlie demanded, her ever-elegant quiff still unmoving despite it being three a.m.

"No, I'll be fine," Mia mumbled. She was sure she was sober enough to walk home, but somehow the words that came out of her mouth didn't sound as orderly as they did in her fuddled brain.

The pounding from the beat of the music in the club resonated onto the street outside and she could feel the pavement beneath her feet shaking with the music's baseline.

Clubbers still joined the queue to get in the door, which was still winding its way around the street, despite the time of night. *Or morning,* she realised.

Charlie grabbed hold of her shoulders as she forced her to look into her eyes. "Mia, do you even know where you are?"

"LA?" she tried. She knew from Charlie's expression that she didn't buy it. Mia was sure she would be able to figure out the route back to her hotel if only Charlie would let her leave.

Charlie grinned and pushed her shoulders toward the open taxi door. "Nice try."

Forcing her head down so she could slide into the taxi seat, Charlie shouted the address of her apartment before the name of Mia's hotel to the waiting taxi driver.

"Fine," Mia mumbled and slid along the faux leather seat to allow Charlie to sit beside her.

Charlie playfully elbowed Mia in the ribs. "This is the only way I know you're going to make it back safely."

Opening the window of the taxi, Mia allowed the fresh air to fill her lungs and whip against her face as the taxi rushed along the boulevards, the passing buildings and streetlamps a blur of neon lights in the darkness.

Earlier that evening, or yesterday evening, she realised as the dawn was approaching, Charlie had knocked on her hotel door and attempted another ambush—albeit that time without her co-partner to carry Mia down the corridor. After seeing her fight with Joel and giving her the time to cool off, Charlie had arrived dressed to the nines and eagerly begging Mia to head into the Los Angeles night with her.

It hadn't taken much convincing. Mia had smiled secretly to herself at the look of disappointment on Charlie's face when Mia had so readily agreed. Then Charlie quickly began rummaging through Mia's wardrobe, compiling an outfit that was fit for the LA scene before forcing her into a chair so she could attempt her hair and make-up.

Mia knew Charlie had come prepared, expecting resistance, but Mia was secretly pleased she was finally getting a makeover by her beautifully quirky friend.

And Mia also needed to get away from the sight of the four walls that were driving her crazy. She had been fuming after her fight with Joel and, after eventually making her way back to her hotel room that night, she hadn't left the room since.

Heading into Los Angeles for a night out with Charlie had certainly taken her mind off things. Mia was starting to think she was coming down with cabin fever from being holed up in her hotel.

As the taxi sped along the quiet roads, she squinted at the blurring lights that passed by, forcing her eyes to focus on the images that blurred past her window. A night with Charlie had done more than take her mind off things. She had soon forgotten all about her hurt and anger toward Joel as she danced to the heavy beat of the music inside the crowded club.

As bodies pressed against her own in the heat of the club, Mia swayed along to the rhythm of the music and quickly forgot about why she had been so upset earlier that day. Walking alone through the pouring rain felt as though it happened years ago as she happily danced along with Charlie, who was sitting beside her still humming the tune to one of the songs they had heard earlier.

The taxi pulled to a slow stop outside an apartment block and Charlie reached forward and handed the driver a couple of bills before reminding him of the address of Mia's hotel.

"I'll see you on Monday morning, yeah?" Charlie reached across the seat and grabbed Mia in an embrace. The smell of the club mixed in with her sweet perfume and clung to her jacket.

"Yeah, see you Monday," she replied as she watched her friend climb out of the taxi.

As she watched her go, Mia wondered if Charlie and Niamh would get along. Most definitely, she realised, a possibly dangerous combination.

Charlie waved from the entrance to her apartment block. As the taxi began to speed away, Mia waved back, before leaning her face out the window. The fresh air was beginning to make her feel almost normal again.

She recognized the familiar street the taxi turned down and the hotel was visible in the middle of the block. Coming to a halt right outside the door to her hotel, she climbed out of the taxi. "Here," she said, holding out some dollars to the driver.

"Your friend already paid." He looked at her, puzzled. "Have a good night," he said and shook his head as he closed the window and pulled away from the curb.

Mia scowled. She would be having words with Charlie on Monday.

She rummaged in her bag to find her hotel key card, to let herself into the building, and tried to tiptoe her way across the empty foyer. Her heels clicked loudly in the eerie silence of the empty hotel. After little contemplation, she took off her heels to walk barefoot to her room.

The elevator dinged loudly to announce its arrival. *Why do things always sound ten times louder in the middle of the night?* Mia wondered. She could have sworn the noise was loud enough to wake up the whole first floor.

It dinged loudly again as it stopped at her floor. She tiptoed out of the noisy elevator and down the corridor to her room. Her hotel room was situated at the very end of a long corridor that zigzagged its way across the twelfth floor.

As she turned the last corner, Mia paused. Her bare feet silently came to a stop on the plush carpet.

There was a figure slumped in the doorway of her room. Hesitating, she wondered if she should turn and head back to the reception desk. Surely someone would be around.

Something about the figure seemed familiar, though, and she

found her tiptoeing feet heading toward it. During the taxi ride back to her hotel, Mia's brain was feeling a lot less alcohol-impaired and she felt almost sober as she approached the slumped figure. She knew her instincts were focussed enough to make herself run if she needed to.

Her heart began to pound loudly in her chest and she felt her blood pumping a little faster with nerves as she approached the unknown. As she drew closer down the corridor, she realised the figure wasn't slumped. It was sitting down and resting its arms on its knees, which were drawn to its chest, and its head was buried on its arms.

Mia assumed the figure was asleep.

There was definitely something familiar about it. At the end of an empty corridor in the middle of the night, it was no wonder it had gone unnoticed until now.

It was no wonder *he* had gone unnoticed until now, she realised.

The black jeans.

The boots.

The hooded sweatshirt.

He was wearing the same outfit she had seen him in on the first day she had met him. The day he had been silently standing nearby and watching her play. And now Mia was silently standing nearby and watching him sleep.

Joel Coben was fast asleep in her hotel room doorway.

Her face broke out into a soft smile at the sight of him. The beautiful, lost little boy who was an international superstar had come to her hotel room to apologise. And had fallen asleep waiting for her to return.

She knelt down in front of him and listened to the soft rising and falling of his breath. His hair was more mussed up than usual, as if he had been running his hands endlessly through it in stress. Second nature made her want to run her own hands through that hair.

Instead, she rested her hand on his forearm and said quietly, "Joel?" Nothing. "*Joel?*" she tried again and gently shook his arm.

He immediately stirred. His sleepy face looked completely adorable, Mia thought, and she had to stop herself from wrapping her arms around him.

"Mia?" His face brightened as he recognized her. He ran his hands through his hair, reached forward, and grabbed her hands. "Mia—I—" he said, his words tripping over themselves as he tried to say what he had been waiting all night to say.

His dark eyes looked haunted and troubled as he stared longingly at her.

She took hold of his forearms and began to pull him up from the floor. "Come on."

He stood and took hold of her hands again. Staring down into her eyes, he seemed to be looking for the answer he needed in her face.

Staring into those bottomless almost black eyes, she knew why Joel felt lost—she felt so lost when she gazed into them herself.

"Can I come in?" he asked in a whisper.

Mia nodded and let go of his hand to swipe her key card in the door. The green light flashed and she clicked the door open.

Stepping into the darkened room, the only light she could see came from the streetlights below and the moonlight above, casting a dark, faint glow about the room.

Behind her, she heard the door close and she could feel Joel standing close by. She turned around just as he was switching on a lamp beside the door.

The small light cast strange shadows around the room and shadows across his face.

He stared at Mia through his eyelashes. His features looked even darker with the strange light casting shadows across his already troubled face.

Taking a hesitant step toward her, he held his hands outstretched.

Lightly placing her fingertips in his open palms, she took hold of them. He wrapped his fingers around hers and pulled her closer to him so that their bodies were inches apart.

He looked down at her, his eyes full of hesitancy. "Mia—I— I'm so sorry," he whispered.

She smiled. "It's okay, Joel."

"No, it's not. I should have explained. I should have said something sooner. And I certainly shouldn't have let you walk out of there."

Blushing, she remembered her dramatic exit.

"I hated Jackson making a scene like that," he went on, "I didn't want you to see the newspaper because I knew it would freak you out. But I promise you, it's completely made up." His eyes were pleading with her again.

"I know." She nodded. "I'm sorry. I shouldn't have stormed off like I did."

He shrugged. "You had every right to be mad."

"No I didn't." She shook her head. "And I read the article once I'd calmed down." She remembered stopping to read the cover of the newspaper on her way home. Every sentence was badly written and thrown together, each quote was from a *source* and all the sentences started with *reportedly*. Immediately, Mia had known the story was a total lie. "And I realised I should have read it to begin with," she finished and glanced away, embarrassed.

Joel placed his hand along her cheekbone. "You shouldn't have to read garbage like that."

Looking back into his deep eyes, she found them staring intensely at her, their darkness almost consumed by the shadows in the room.

"I owed it to you to explain. I was scared you were going to react the way you did. I should have stepped up and explained. I owe that to you. No one has ever treated me the way you have."

Mia frowned. "What do you mean?"

"You treat me like a normal person." He shrugged again and a wry smile crept across his face as he continued. "Usually people are ass-kissing or shaking like a leaf or fluttering their eyelashes at me. You have done none of those things."

Their clasped hands in front of her made her heart race. Joel's body was within touching distance of her fingers.

"You remind me that I'm still human, that I'm still just a regular guy." She felt his head almost touching the top of hers as he whispered to her, "But yet there's something so extraordinary about you."

His eyes were locked onto hers, staring into her own soul, seeing everything within her laid bare. Yet, in that moment, Mia could see his own reflecting back at her from those seemingly endless dark eyes.

She saw the raw, vulnerable soul within that was so easily caught up in the midst of a celebrity bubble, but yet so lost among it. Joel didn't belong in the pages of gossip magazines. He thought Mia was the extraordinary one, but he couldn't see he was so extraordinary himself.

Maybe they needed each other for that same reason, she realised.

Joel paused and she sensed his hesitancy. Despite the fluttering of nerves that were crashing around in her stomach, Mia let go of his hands and slid her own onto his chest and around his neck.

Bringing his face down to hers, his lips softly came to rest there and she could feel his breath against the soft skin of her lips. She closed her eyes as Joel closed the final inch of space between them and pressed his lips against hers.

Sliding his hands around her waist, he pulled her body against his. Mia felt both the earnest and eagerness in his kiss as he brushed his tongue against hers and ran a hand up the length of her body into her hair. He pulled her body even tighter to his and she let her own hands run through that deliciously unruly mess of black hair on his head.

Her fingers entwined in his thick hair. She felt her breath catch in her throat and a small moan escaped her lips. The sound forced Joel to press himself into her and she moaned again. Before she realised it, his hands were working their way up her body and across her shoulders to the zip at the back of her dress.

His lips left hers and began softly kissing a trail across her cheek, down her neck, and along her collarbone. With nimble fingers, he unzipped her dress. Joel's hands slid back across her shoulders and worked the dress over them slowly. His eyes savored every inch of her skin as he peeled the dress down her body. With a soft thump, the dress hit the floor. He held out his hands to her. Taking hold of them, she stepped out of the dress and back into his arms.

Joel slid his hands across her bare waist, making her shiver at his touch. Seeing her tremble, he pulled her close to him again. His nose softly brushed against hers before his lips captured hers again.

Mentally thanking Charlie for giving her so much alcohol, Mia felt braver than she usually would have and slid her fingers up to the zip on Joel's sweatshirt. She pulled the zip down the length of his body, allowing herself to savor the pleasure of undressing the man. She had to force herself not to giggle as she reminded herself just who she was standing nearly naked in front of and whose arms were wrapped around her with his fingers gliding across her skin while his lips caressed her own.

Mimicking Joel's actions, she ran her hands up his chest before sliding his sweatshirt across his shoulders and onto the floor. She felt him smile against her lips as she traced her fingers across the top of the waistband of his jeans, feeling the bare skin underneath. Then taking the hem of his T-shirt in her hands, she slowly peeled it off to reveal the glorious body underneath.

It was Mia's turn to allow her lips to leave his as she unashamedly gazed open-mouthed at what she saw. Joel's body was lean and muscular and yet perfectly slender too. His tattoos worked their way up his arms, across his chest, and down his back. They were all black and white and were incredibly artistic. Some were song lyrics of his and others were of his idols. A large, shaded guitar ran up the side of his torso and appeared to move as his body did. Its design was eerily similar to the silver one that hung around her neck.

His chest was sculpted and so were his perfectly formed abs. His waist curved into a delicious V-shape at his hips. To Mia, it looked like perfection. And its owner was grinning down at her staring at his waist.

A soft chuckle escape Joel's lips and she immediately looked up at his face. Though he said nothing, his amused expression said everything his lips didn't. He was enjoying her enjoying the sight of him. Mia smirked as she ran a hand up his naked torso toward a perfectly chiselled jaw, which she pulled down to her own. Her free hand began unfastening the button on his jeans and his hands freely caressed her body. She slid the jeans over his hips and heard the denim land on the carpeted floor. Joel stepped out of them and pulled her by the waist to his body, pressing their bare skin against one another. Allowing her hands to run across his sculpted back and down his waist, she felt him exploring her body too.

Joel's hands slid down her waist and he gently grabbed hold of her thighs. "Hold on," he whispered against her lips.

Mia wound her arms tightly around his neck as he picked her up and wrapped her legs around his waist. He carried her through the semi-darkness toward the bed in the corner of the room and

gently laid her body down with his, never breaking their closeness.

And against the glowing light of the early morning Los Angeles skyline, their bodies melted into one another as they made
love.

❧❧❧

Smiling dreamily as she opened her eyes, Mia squinted in the
morning sunlight. She stared through the open curtains at the
bright light shining through the windows before remembering
what had happened last night.

She rubbed her eyes and rolled over in the sheets to see that
the bed beside her lay empty. Throwing herself back against the
pillows in frustration, she reminded herself she shouldn't be surprised.

What had she expected from one of the world's most notoriously reclusive rock stars? That they would shower and have
breakfast together before strolling hand in hand out of the hotel
and down Sunset Strip? She laughed to herself at the thought.
There was no way Joel Coben would ever allow himself to be
pictured like that.

With a heavy sigh, she turned to stare out of her window at the
Los Angeles skyline, a skyline that had seemed so different in the
early morning light. She looked at the clock on her bedside table.
11:03 a.m. *Joel could be anywhere out there in that city by now.*

For a few more minutes, she gazed out at the skyscrapers before swinging her legs out of the bed and wrapping the bed sheet
around herself. She frowned as she noticed her dress, from last
night was folded and placed on the chair nearby.

Who tidies up before they leave without a word? Mia wondered. Rolling her eyes at the mystery that was Joel Coben, she
padded barefoot into the bathroom. She turned on the shower and
allowed the bed sheet to fall by the bathtub as she stepped under
the faucet. The hot water couldn't dissipate her wandering
thoughts.

She felt as though her mind was running a million thoughts all
at the same time. Somehow she felt confused and angry, hurt and
ashamed, and yet satisfied, free, and happy all at the same time.

With a month left until she had to leave Los Angeles and go

back to Dublin, she wondered if she would see or speak to Joel again. In the space of forty-eight hours, she had gone from fighting with him, to being angry at him, to trying to forget him, to forgiving him, and making up with him, to being confused by him all over again. She wondered where he was at that moment and what he was doing. Was he even thinking of her?

The studio entered her thoughts and she realised how happy and content she was in finally feeling as though she had found her dream job, her calling in life, and yet it had a looming expiration date that was approaching all too soon.

She was beginning to feel as though she could settle in Los Angeles. She had friends at the studios and could happily picture herself living in the permanent sunshine that radiated over California.

And yet she felt confused about so many things.

Unable to help herself, she wondered what would happen in a month's time. She wondered a million things about Joel. She wondered about her friends back home in Dublin. And most of all she wondered about her brother.

As she did with Joel, she wondered where he was out there in the world, what was he doing, and if he ever thought of her. Or was he buried deep under the earth somewhere in a nameless grave?

Mia pinched the bridge of her nose at the painful thought. She rubbed her eyes in attempt to rub away the tears she could feel stinging under her eyelids.

Why, she wondered, *does life have to be so confusing?* Why couldn't there be an answer to all these things, to how Joel felt about her, to what would happen in a month, and most of all to where her brother was?

Her brother was the last remaining piece of her family that she had to cling onto and she had no idea if he was even still here at all. The not knowing, the lack of closure, was so frustrating she could have beat her fists to a pulp against the tiles on the wall. She could have screamed, shouted, and cried until everyone in the hotel beat down her door and came running into the bathroom.

But she didn't. She simply gazed up at the showerhead as the water poured over her face, taking her tears with it in the free flow, staring at the showerhead as if she expected all the answers she needed to come pouring forth from it like the water.

Eventually, when her she could no longer tell if her tears were falling and her fingertips resembled dried prunes, she switched off the water and climbed out of the shower. She rubbed her body down with a soft white towel embroidered with the hotel's logo. As she ran the towel along her arms and down her chest, she remembered Joel's hands in those places only a few hours earlier.

Mia sighed, wishing his hands were on her bare skin again, wishing his body were close to hers. Remembering falling asleep in his arms with her face buried against his chest, she wished he had been there to hold when she woke up.

She wondered if she could ever have that kind of relationship with Joel.

Would he ever truly open himself up to her? Where would they stand in a month's time if she had to leave Los Angeles? Did they even have anything to hope for?

Grabbing a handful of her damp hair at the roots in frustration, she felt like ripping it from her scalp. So many thoughts and so few answers.

With dejection, she sighed. Looking around the empty room, she decided to go for a walk in the Californian sun, hoping she could navigate her way to the coastline again and stroll along the beach to clear her head.

Embracing the warm spring weather, she threw on a pair of cut off denim shorts and a T-shirt and rubbed her damp hair with the towel. As she did, the clock on the bedside table caught her eye—11:30 a.m.

After standing in the shower for what had felt like hours, Mia realised it had only been minutes. Emotions did strange things to the passage of time, she thought.

She applied a little mascara to her eyelashes and, as she finished and put the bottle down on the counter in the bathroom, she heard a knock on her hotel room door.

Frowning as she wondered who it could be, she crossed the bedroom to the doorway. As her hand was on the latch, she realised it was probably Charlie in a hung-over state, wanting to go for coffee.

She opened the door.

Well, she got the coffee part right, anyway.

Standing in her doorway, looking clean and refreshed and wearing a dark blue T-shirt and aviator sunglasses, was Joel Coben. The tattoos that Mia had dreamily stared at last night were visible down his arms as they ran under the sleeves of his T-shirt. He lifted his glasses onto his head when she opened the door, and in his hand was a tray from Starbucks bearing two coffees in polystyrene cups.

"Coffee?" was all he said and he smiled innocently and held the tray toward her.

With a knowing smile back at him, she opened the door to let him inside.

Joel walked into her hotel room and waited by the small sofa in the center of the room for Mia to join him. He sat down and patted the seat beside him for her to sit.

"I didn't know what you drank, so I just brought lattes," he said, offering her a cup.

She grinned and sat down next to him. "That's perfect, thank you."

Sipping his coffee, he began to stare at her.

She instantly felt self-conscious in the bright morning light wear a T-shirt and denim cut offs in front of someone who always looked so effortlessly perfect.

"You look beautiful," he said with a soft smile.

Mia wondered if the man could read minds too. He seemed to have a knack for reading her like a book.

"I—I thought you left," she mumbled.

Sometimes her mouth worked in time with her thoughts, rather than allowing them to process first.

She could have mashed her palm against her forehead. Why did she say that out loud?

Joel's smile faded and he looked down at the cup in his hands. "I didn't. I just…" He shrugged and held up the cup to her, a boyish smile playing on his features.

Seeing that smile made her brighten. She felt as if it were her smile—one he only shared with her. The rest of the world was so used to seeing a brooding Joel that she delighted in seeing his perfect face the way it ought to be.

She felt her own features crack with a smile at the sight of him looking happy. It was infectious.

Then he leaned across the sofa and placed a soft kiss on her lips. Mia opened her eyes in surprise and her own were filled with animated almost-black ones.

"I wondered if we could spend the day together?" he asked against her lips.

CHAPTER 19

Walking down the street in Los Angeles, Mia had to shake her head, albeit it with discretion.

People stared.

A lot.

Whether they were fans recognising him, or simply curious, people stared at Joel. He had an aura about him that drew attention. And, of course, she realised, women in particular couldn't help but notice him.

Only in Los Angeles could a rock star walk down the streets every day and people took it in stride. It wasn't without interference, though. They were stopped numerous times on every street they turned down. She once counted fourteen people stop Joel in the space of thirty minutes and ask him for a picture or autograph.

They entered a music store after spotting a guitar in the window they both liked and by the time they left the store, a crowd of people had gathered outside, waiting for Joel.

A very nervous-looking shop assistant was standing at the door, trying his best to keep it firmly closed to the awaiting crowds outside. Mia was more amazed at having the store all to herself to browse around than at the mass of people that had gathered outside so quickly.

As soon as the shop assistants had spotted Joel walk through the door, hand in hand with Mia, they had quickly escorted all of their customers from the shop and locked the door. Some customers were more obliging than others were.

"Can I please just ask him to sign my guitar first?" a young girl, who couldn't have been any older than twelve, pleaded with the employee behind the till as her mother paid for her guitar.

"Sorry, miss, we need you to leave as soon as you've finished here," the middle-aged man behind the till said in a curt voice.

Mia frowned.

Joel had his head down looking at a rare Gibson that was locked in a glass case, but as soon as he heard the young girl's request, he snapped his head up. He smiled at Mia. "Excuse me for a second."

How could a girl refuse that look? He was adorable. The more she got to know the Joel behind the media mask, the more she could feel herself falling for him. His hardened defenses, which went up whenever he saw a reporter or photographer, were simply to protect the sensitive, deep soul underneath, who could also be incredibly sweet.

"But I..." The girl's words trailed away as she saw Joel approaching the till.

Mia also noticed the girl's mother run her eyes up and down his body before running a hand through her coiffed hair several times as he approached.

He grinned and squatted down to meet the girl's eye level. "Hey."

Her eyes were as wide as saucers and her mouth hung open even wider.

Watching in silence, Mia suppressed a giggle. She knew she had worn exactly the same look the first time she had met him.

"Did I hear you say you wanted me to sign your guitar?" he asked.

The girl nodded, her eyes and mouth still wide open. All her earlier confidence from arguing with the cashier had vanished.

The Joel Coben Effect, Mia thought as she tried not to laugh.

"Amber?" her mother prompted.

"Yes, please," the girl managed to squeak.

Joel's mouth curled up on one side in a grin. The sight made Mia's own face crease into a smile.

Joel stood up and asked the cashier, "Do you have a pen?"

"Sure, here you go." Scrambling around near the till, he handed him the nearest thing he could grab.

Joel stared down at the biro in the man's outstretched hand.

Then Mia really did let out a giggle. He turned to look over his shoulder at her and his smile crept up even farther at the corners.

He raised an eyebrow at the pen in the man's hand. She could tell he was trying not to laugh. "I don't think that's going to get us very far,"

"Here." A younger employee darted around the cash desk, shoving his superior out of the way, and grabbing a marker pen from the drawer beneath the till.

Joel nodded. "Thank you."

He went to open the case of the girl's newly purchased guitar.

"I can get that for you," the older employee darted forward again in an attempt to redeem himself.

"I can manage, thank you." Joel was trying his best not to be sarcastic. "Did you say your name was Amber?" he asked, looking back down at his admiring fan again.

She nodded, words still escaping her.

As he scrawled a brief message to her, Mia could hear the marker pen squeaking against the polished wood of the acoustic guitar. "There you go." He snapped the case shut and handed it to her. "Good luck with your playing. Keep at it, no matter how hard it gets sometimes. You're onto something amazing there."

He winked and a small squeak escaped the girl's throat again.

Her mother intervened and hastily shook Joel's hand. "Thank you so much."

From across the shop Mia could see him trying to prise his fingers from her grasp. She was holding on much longer than necessary.

"No problem." His smile was now firm and tight. He knew exactly what the woman wanted. 'Do you think you could let them out of the back door?" he asked the employees and pointed to the guitar case. "I don't want anyone out there trying to take that from her."

Mia admired his thoughtfulness. The crowd outside had been watching him sign the guitar. Someone out there would try to wrestle it from the girl, given the chance.

"Sure." The younger, more helpful employee ushered Amber and her mom out of the store via the back exit.

"That was really sweet of you," Mia said as Joel reappeared at her side and looped his arm around her waist.

He shrugged. "It's nothing."

"Not many musicians would have done that," she pointed out.

He gave her an impish grin and leaned in to her to place a brief kiss on her cheek. "You would have."

"I'm not a world-famous musician," she argued, trying to hold onto the conversation as his face still hovered centimetres away from hers.

He winked. "Not yet."

∽∾∽

After being continually mobbed by fans and paparazzi as word had gotten around that Joel Coben was strolling the streets of Los Angeles, he flagged down a passing taxi and gave the driver directions that Mia couldn't hear.

"Where are we going?" she asked, eyeing him with curiosity.

He grinned his boyish grin again that made his eyes sparkle. "Wait and see,"

Mia bathed in the light that radiated from his usually masked eyes. He was letting his guard down and it was all for her.

"Enjoy the view," he whispered in her ear as he looked out the window, sliding across the seat to sit beside her and wrapping his arm around her shoulder.

She winked up at him. "Oh, I will."

The heavy smog of Los Angeles was soon replaced by fresh, open air and a light sea breeze. Once away from the main hustle and bustle of the city, the taxi whipped along the roads in a southerly direction from LA toward the ocean.

Joel leaned over Mia's lap and wound down the window, letting the refreshing air flood into the back of the cab. Her hair began to whip around her face as the breeze came into the car. She looked up at Joel and saw his unruly hair doing the same. Somehow, she knew she didn't look half as good as he did, posing in the early afternoon sun with the wind blowing in his face.

Only half an hour after they had left LA, the taxi began slowing down as they entered a small coastal town named Hermosa Beach.

Allowing them to take in the view, the driver slowly passed the main streets and drove down onto the seafront, passing cafes and restaurants with tables and chairs all facing the beautiful ocean.

Miles of golden sand stretched out before this little coastal town, offering idyllic tranquility only miles from the hustle of LA. Mia wanted to lean out of the open widow and take in all the sights as they passed. The town also looked blissfully quiet compared to the streets of LA they had not long ago left behind them.

The taxi crawled to a stop beside the beach. Joel leant forward and handed the driver several bills. "Thanks, man." He clapped the driver's shoulder before getting out of the car.

His sunglasses were on before he had stepped out of the door and Mia knew he wasn't wearing them because of the weather. Even here, Joel was bound to be spotted.

The Mexican taxi driver hopped out of his seat as Joel opened her door. "Excuse me, sir." He looked sheepish as he passed him a folded piece of paper. "Would you mind signing something for me and my daughter? We're both huge fans of yours."

"Sure." Joel obligingly signed.

He agreed with the over enthusiastic taxi driver to collect them both later that evening. Something else that came as a perk of being famous, Mia noticed.

The driver was probably eager to come back just so he could tell his daughter and friends he had driven the megastar around all day.

They began strolling along the front toward the sand and Joel took hold of her hand. He immediately appeared to relax as they arrived in Hermosa Beach.

"So why here?" she asked, gesturing to the small town once they were walking barefoot across the sand together.

"I used to come here a lot as a child, before my mother died," he said with a heavy sigh. "I still do come here when I want some space from the city. I live in Los Angeles because it's easy. I don't want to stay there forever. I love it here, though. It's so quiet and peaceful."

"I can see why." She smiled up at him after gazing out at the expanse of nearly empty beach before them.

Mia knew his mother died when he was younger. The press had well documented that in previous years. She chose not to pry. Joel had opened up to her way beyond her expectations already.

"So Los Angeles isn't your forever?" she asked.

"No." He shook his head resolutely. "Not at all. It's too crazy. Like I said, I live there because of my work. It's easy to get to the studio, it's easy for interviews, for the tour rehearsals, but it's not forever. I can't stand the place. It's not in the real world. Everyone there lives in such a bubble. That's why I like my house." He gave her a fond smile. "It's my own little bubble within the LA bubble."

"Charlie showed it to me once. It looks fantastic, well, what I could see of it, anyway."

Joel laughed. "That's the best part. Tell me about Ireland. I've only ever been to Dublin on the tours."

It was Mia's turn to smile fondly. "Ireland is the complete opposite of here."

She was only a little homesick. While she loved being in Los Angeles, her work, and the recording studio, she did miss her friends and her country. Not so long ago, she could easily picture herself living there and working at the studios but Joel's life was beginning to give her more of an insight into the real Los Angeles. He was right. It was for the rich and the insane.

"Is it as green as they say it is?" he teased.

Mia laughed. "More than you can imagine!"

He pulled her to a stop, seated himself on the sand, before pulling her down into his lap. Gazing at her from over her shoulder, he clutched her to his chest. "Tell me all about it. I want to know."

Comfortably snuggled between his legs, staring out at the Pacific Ocean with the sun shining down on them and the sand beneath their bodies, she told Joel all she could about Ireland.

He listened with eagerness, taking in every word she said, and asked questions about everything. He really wanted to know everything about her home country, about where she came from, what made her who she was.

‹››‹›

Exhausted, Mia slumped down into the comfortable sofa that was nestled in the corner of the bar. After walking for what had felt like miles across the sand and around the quaint little town, Joel had taken her hand and led her back across the seafront to an oceanfront bar that was his favorite place in Hermosa Beach.

Gilbert's was a cosy little bar that offered a quiet place to drink, talk, and listen to music while watching the ocean waves roll in outside the window.

"They sometimes have a band on here, but I guess it's still early."

He shrugged as he placed her drink on the low table in front of them.

"Thanks," she said as she raised her glass from the table.

A few heads had turned as they entered the bar. One man got up from his seat to ask Joel for a picture, but after that the customers returned to their drinks and they were left alone.

The normalcy was bliss. After being pointed at, stared at, and photographed for most of the morning, the quiet and invisibility Hermosa Beach and Gilbert's offered Joel was heaven.

They had sat together on the sand for a few hours, talking, as they watched the ocean roll in. Mia marveled at how not once did anyone ask Joel for an autograph. Families, dog walkers, surfers, and couples walked past them, unaware they were strolling past one of the world's biggest stars.

As the tide began to draw closer, they had walked farther down the beach to the pier, where they had strolled along among the families and fishermen. They had stared out over the end railings. Joel stood with his arms protectively around Mia as they watched the ocean together.

She remembered thinking she could have stayed there forever, feeling the heat on her skin, watching the waves while nestled in his arms.

Eventually, they had walked back to the town, strolling among the quiet streets of shops and cafes before stopping at Gilbert's.

Joel clinked his glass against hers. "To you," he toasted, "may you be as successful as you deserve to be."

Her cheeks blushed at his words. "Thank you," she managed as she took a sip.

He leaned in toward her and draped his arm around her shoulder. "Hey, listen."

She stilled, listening to what he had heard.

Gilbert's was playing a radio station over its speakers but the volume was faint so their customers could talk while they drank.

Mia immediately stiffened. She heard the following bars of music of the first notes Joel had recognized.

The lead singer of Glasshearts's voice was filtering through the speakers and into the bar. And he was singing Mia's song.

"Hey, man," a punter called out from across the bar to the bartender who was refilling wine glasses in racks above his head. "Can you turn it up? It's that new Glasshearts track."

A few people around him murmured in agreement and Mia felt the corners of her lips creep up at the corners in pride.

"Did you hear that?" Joel nudged her gently and nodded in the direction of the requester, his face beaming with pride.

She could hear a few voices across the room singing along to the chorus of the song.

> "I want you to hear me,
> I need you to hear me
> Can you feel me?
> Tell me can you hear me."

Joel was also singing along to the song, his gravelly voice low and soft in her ear. Mia wasn't paying attention to the customers in the bar anymore. She wasn't listening to her song playing out over the airwaves to Los Angeles. Instead, she was listening to the liquid gold that was pouring into her ear—her own intimate Joel Coben performance.

Hearing him sing her lyrics was a strange feeling. She was used to singing along to Joel's music and hearing his voice on the airwaves. The reverse was something Mia couldn't quite wrap her head around. It was if their roles had switched.

Content, she nestled into the cushions of the sofa with Joel's arm around her shoulder, his rich, deep voice singing in her ear. *If only this could be the norm*, she thought. She wouldn't have to share this incredible man with the rest of the world. He would be hers alone. She could sing to the world and he could sing to her alone.

CHAPTER 20

The phone rang for several moments before its owner picked up.

"Hello," answered a groggy voice from the other end of the line.

Mia closed her eyes as she silently cursed herself. She had forgotten all about the huge time difference between Los Angeles and her adopted home city. "Niamh, it's me."

"Mia!" Her voice shrilled with recognition as she brightened at hearing her friend.

"Whoa, shh!" Mia calmed her. Despite it being one a.m. in Los Angeles, Mia's eardrums were never prepared for the volume that could emit from her tiny friend's lungs.

Niamh giggled before whispering back, "Sorry, hi."

Mia laughed along with her before continuing. "How are you?"

"I'm good, things are good." Niamh sighed wistfully down the phone. It had been almost two weeks since they last spoke. Between being at the studio and seeing Joel, Mia hadn't found the time to make a long distance call. Text messages weren't the same as hearing a familiar voice.

"I know that tone," Mia teased as she recognized the all-too-familiar tone in Niamh's satisfied sigh. "Who is he?"

Niamh giggled again. "No, no, no, you first. How's Los Angeles?"

It was Mia's turn to sigh. "Oh, man, where do I start?"

"Well, the last I heard you were settling in, things were going great, you were hanging out with someone named Charlie and you had met the *b-e-a-u-tiful* Joel Coben."

Mia laughed out loud at her over emphasis on the word. Niamh was right, though.

She exhaled before launching into the stories of her time in LA since they'd last spoken. She told her about her friendship with Charlie and how she was sure they would get along, like a house on fire, to which Niamh shrilled with glee at the thought.

She told her about her night in Los Angeles, shopping with Charlie in Beverly Hills, her work in the recording studio and any other detail she could think of that didn't include Joel Coben. She was saving the best until last.

"Yeah, yeah, yeah." Niamh sighed. "That all sounds wonderful. Now tell me about the good stuff. Have you met Joel again?"

Niamh knew her too well.

A grin spread across Mia's face and almost to her ears. She could feel her eyes crinkle as she smiled, thinking of Joel.

"Yeah, you could say that…" She trailed off, allowing the sentence to linger on the line.

"Whoa, what on earth does that mean?" Niamh's voice rose several octaves by the time she reached the end of her sentence.

Mia shrugged although Niamh couldn't see her. "Well, we've kind of been seeing each other, I guess."

Mia hadn't known how to label what she was beginning to have with Joel. She didn't know if she could label it at all yet, it was such early days.

"Tell me everything. *Now.*"

She knew her tiny Irish friend was serious. There would be no detail left out, no stone unturned. Niamh was ruthless in her investigations of this kind.

Mia giggled again before telling her about the last couple of weeks. She recounted how things had started out with Joel and how one thing had led to another.

"He waited outside your hotel room?" Niamh squeaked in disbelief.

"Yeah, I've no idea how long for. Like I said, he was fast asleep when I got there."

Again Niamh squealed with glee. "Well, then what happened? Have you seen him since?"

Mia felt her cheeks flame as she relayed more information than she cared for her to know.

Niamh, however, was the only person she could tell other than

Charlie. It was a relief to have a friend from home to listen to her, one she could relay her inner thoughts to. She went on to tell her how she and Joel had seen each other almost every day since that night. The things they had done together and the time they had shared. It was almost as if they had become inseparable. Joel had become a magnet for Mia. He seemed programmed to appear at her side at almost every moment.

After relating as much information as she possibly could with Niamh, she paused to take a breath.

"Wow…I mean wow…" Niamh sighed on the other end of the line. "I really can't believe it."

"I know. Me, neither. Anyway, what's your news?" Mia asked curiously.

From her tone earlier it was clear something had changed in her friend's life. She had been waiting to hear Mia's news before she divulged her own.

"Well—I—We—Umm—" Niamh stuttered, stumbling over her words as she attempted to tell her news.

"Niamh, what is it? Is everything okay?"

"Everything is more than okay," she whispered.

Then, right on cue, she heard the muffled sounds of someone mumbling as they woke up from their sleep. She also heard her friend's sharp intake of breath.

Grinning, Mia raised an eyebrow at the phone against her cheek. "Niamh, who's there with you?"

"Umm…"

She heard someone talking beside Niamh. Or rather, she heard *him* talking beside her. Mia heard the unmistakable voice of Dylan grumbling in his just-woken-up haze. "Is that *Dylan*?" her own voice was now several octaves higher.

"Sshhh," Niamh hushed down the phone as she attempted to quiet her friend.

"Hey, Mia," Dylan mumbled into the phone line and she heard Niamh giggle as she tried to push him away from the phone.

"How long has this been going on?" Mia feigned an interrogative air to her voice as she quizzed her friend, or *friends,* for the details.

"Probably around the same amount of time as you and Joel," Niamh confessed.

Despite her quietness, Mia could hear the girlie smile on

Niamh's face as she spoke. Mia could picture her looking across at Dylan lying in the bed beside her. "I'm happy for you, Niamh," she said with the smile clear in her voice.

She was pleased that Dylan had finally opened his eyes to see the beautiful woman right under his nose who had long adored him.

"Thanks, Mia," she whispered.

"You and Joel?" came a confused voice from beside Niamh, "What the—as in *Joel Coben*?"

Mia laughed out loud at the sound of Dylan's confusion. It was obvious he had been listening to their conversation. She knew Niamh was bound to tell those who worked at Glen's Tavern all the details, anyway.

"I'll speak to you later, Niamh." Mia laughed as she made her getaway, still listening to Dylan's confused questions on the other end of the line.

"We'll talk some more later." Niamh giggled. "Speak to you later, Mia."

"What? Wait a second—"

Mia caught the beginning of another of Dylan's confused sentences before the phone cut off. She knew, in a matter of seconds, Niamh would be telling him about her and the famous rock star.

Shaking her head, Mia was still laughing at her friends even though the line was gone. She marveled in how one phone call could lift her mood so much from an already high-spirited one. As she got up from the sofa to make her way to the bed, she felt as if her feet barely touched the carpet she was so happy.

She got herself ready for bed, undressing and throwing on her pyjamas. Then she plugged her mobile phone into the charger on the nightstand beside her before crawling under the covers with a contented smile on her face.

Turning her head on the pillow to face one of her favorite views, she watched the Los Angeles skyline. As the night-time lights twinkled and sparkled from the city beneath her, Mia began to close her eyes and drift toward sleep with her smile still firmly in place.

Just as she was on the brink of sleep, the room around her lit up with a glow before the ringing on the nightstand beside her pierced through her near slumbering state.

She scowled before leaning over to grab her phone. An even

bigger smile than before replaced the scowl as she recognized the caller ID.

"Hi."

With a grin wider than the skyline outside, she settled back down into her pillow with her phone and pulled the duvet up around her chin.

"Hey." The sound of Joel's deep, calming tones filled her ear and she could almost picture him lying there beside her with his beautiful features silhouetted by the Los Angeles skyline.

ℰↄℯↄ

The mobile phone's loud tone rang again on the bedside table where she had left it. Running from the other side of the room to grab the phone before it went to voicemail, Mia almost went flying over the bed.

Breathlessly she grabbed the phone and answered. "Hey."

She had already seen the caller ID and knew she would hear the deep, gentle Californian accent on the other end of the line.

"Hey," came the delicious accent she was expecting to hear. "You ready to go?"

"Yeah, just about. Are you coming up?" She had expected Joel to come to her hotel door, as he usually did.

"No, I'm downstairs waiting for you. Go to the reception desk and ask them to let you out of the back door."

Mia frowned at the phone. "Okay…" she responded.

"Just trust me, okay?"

Her puzzlement amused him. She could hear the tone in his voice. Hearing the humour in his voice was nice, a sound that he should have made more often. *It suited him*, she thought.

"Okay, okay. I'll be there in two minutes."

She hung up the phone and grabbed her hotel key before heading out of the door, down the corridor, and into the elevator.

As the elevator dinged to announce its arrival on the ground floor, Mia peered cautiously out of the doors toward the reception desk. Seeing only a young couple checking in on arrival, she joined the queue behind them and waited for her turn.

Once the suitcases were out of the way, she approached the desk.

"How can I help you?" The receptionist gave her a polite

smile. Her dark hair was pulled back in the tightest, slickest bun and her professional smile was emphasised with red lipstick. Without subtly, she eyed Mia up and down before returning to her eyes.

Self-consciously, Mia ran a hand through her hair and looked down at her dress, feeling underdressed in front of the woman who was so immaculate in her suit.

"I was wondering if I could leave through the back door?" she asked, expecting a less than friendly response.

The receptionist gave her a sceptical look. Mia knew she sounded ludicrous. The front door was only a few meters behind her.

The woman eyed her suspiciously. "You're Mia?"

"Umm, yes."

"Can I see your room card?" The woman rose from her seat and outstretched her hand. Her red lips pursed together as Mia fumbled in her bag for her card.

"Here you go," she said holding it out to her.

The receptionist swiped the room card on the side of the screen in front of her. After a moment, apparently satisfied with what she saw, she beckoned Mia with a talon-like fingernail. "Come with me." She curled her finger before looking down her nose at Mia even less subtly than before.

Mia wondered if Joel had called the hotel in advance to ask them to let her out of the back exit. She followed the receptionist through the foyer and through a door marked *Private*. They headed down a long empty corridor before arriving at an emergency exit.

The receptionist held open the door, scanning the loading bay behind it to see who was waiting. After finding what she was looking for outside, she faced Mia again. "There you are. The tip has already been provided."

Unable to resist, she sneered one final time as Mia slid past her in the doorway.

"Thank you," Mia added, as the door was slammed shut behind her.

She suddenly had a mental image of sticking her tongue out at the closed door, but realising she was twenty-three and not three years old, she decided on rolling her eyes instead before turning around to look at the loading bay.

In a gated, walled area behind the hotel was an almost empty loading bay, save for several wooden pallets and garbage cans in one corner.

But parked directly in front of the emergency exit, with its paintwork glinting in the morning sun was a large black Escalade.

Mia could hear its engine still humming, knowing the driver was patiently waiting inside for her arrival. The car's windows were all tinted black, so she couldn't see the occupant. Although she knew who one was for sure, she wasn't sure if Joel had a driver.

She took a step toward the car and the driver's door opened.

Joel hopped down from the driver's seat and strode across the tarmac toward her.

White was certainly the second-best color she had seen him wearing. In fact, Joel looked good in every color. She was sure of it. A simple white t-shirt had never looked so good.

Forgetting she was in a loading bay of a hotel in downtown Los Angeles, Mia could have easily pictured herself sitting in the front row of Milan fashion week as she watched her model stride effortlessly toward her. Joel completed his look with his trademark black jeans, tucked into his boots.

His hair was his usual mussed-up perfection, although she noticed he seemed to have styled it a little more than usual. Completing the look were his aviator sunglasses that he whipped off as he approached. She wanted to jump up and down with glee. *That man*, she thought with an appreciative smile, *has come to see me.*

"Hey, beautiful." He smiled a broader smile than usual as he stopped in front of her, immediately looped his arms around her waist, and pulled her body against his lean, muscular one.

"Hey, yourself—" Mia's sentence was cut short as a wonderfully delicious pair of lips brushed against her own. She heard her throat let out a small moan, followed by the feeling of his lips breaking into a smile as he kissed her.

Eventually, Joel parted his lips from hers, but he only broke the contact of their lips. His body and face remained glued to hers.

"So where do you want to go today?" he asked as he touched the edge of his nose to hers.

"I really don't know. Did you have anywhere in mind?" she asked as she placed a small kiss on the edge of his lips.

Joel held their kiss for a moment longer before replying, "Actually, I did." He hesitated before continuing. "I wondered if you wanted to come over and see my place?"

His eyes misted over with doubt as he waited for an answer. Mia got the impression this wasn't a regular occurrence for him. He didn't just let people into his life unwittingly. It was too much of a risk.

At the thought of visiting Joel's house, and the thought of knowing what that meant to Joel, she felt herself smile. "I'd love to," she said before he planted another kiss on her lips.

☙❧☙

Mia stepped over the threshold and tried not to stare too obviously as she entered Joel's house.

He held the door open for her and led her inside with his other hand, his fingers clasping hers in a gentle hold. The first thing she noticed in the entryway was the staircase. It was open and wide, made from white marble, and curved up the side of the hallway wall before reaching the second story. Something flickered in her memory as she noticed the staircase, but as soon as it had arrived, the thought was gone.

"Come on through." Joel threw her a smile as he guided her through into a room adjacent to the hallway.

Noticing how his lips turned up slightly at the corners, she returned his smile. *He is nervous again.*

Joel Coben, global superstar musician, was nervous at having her inside his house. She tried not to squeal in delight at the thought.

He led her into a spacious sitting room. One large leather sofa filled a great portion of the room in with its L-shaped design. Mia resisted the urge to run and jump onto the sofa and sprawl out as much as she could. She doubted he would have appreciated that.

Her footsteps echoed on the oak flooring as she walked across the room.

The room was decorated in a modern style, but she could see Joel's touches here and there.

Its walls were crisp white and a large glass coffee table sat in front of the sofa. She noticed both the hallway and living room had large pieces of artwork hanging from the walls. One in particular in the living room caught her eye and she recognized the abstract expressionist style, something she wouldn't have imagined Joel buying.

He stood watching her face as she looked around the room. "What is it?"

"Nothing."

Grinning to herself, she walked away from his side to look at the painting.

She walked around the room, taking in the furnishings and paintings, before running her finger across one of the glittering awards that was seated on the mantelpiece.

"What are you smiling about?" he asked curiously.

Mia noticed he still looked nervous and decided to put him out of his misery. "Nothing," she said again, laughing and hoping to put him at ease. "This just isn't how I imagined your house to look."

He raised an eyebrow at her. "You were expecting walls painted black and girls draped over the furniture?"

She heard the humor in his voice. He was beginning to relax.

"Something like that" She grinned again as she walked back across to where he stood watching her.

"You want something to drink?" his soft, deep accent floated out the words, "then I could show you the rest of the house?" he added with caution.

"Yeah, I would like that." Mia stepped closer and took his hand again as she spoke. She felt her confidence soar, knowing that Joel was nervous at having her in his house.

"Have a seat." He gestured to the sofa as his gentle touch led her by the hand. "I won't be a minute."

She watched his sculpted shoulders as he walked across the room, through an archway into a large kitchen. Mia could see him flicking switches on a coffee machine and opening a cupboard before setting two mugs on the counter in front of him. Knowing that it wouldn't be long before he was at her side again, she took a seat on the large leather sofa. Still resisting the urge to kick back and lay down on the L-shaped couch, she perched in the corner. It was then that she allowed her earlier reminiscence of the staircase to come flooding back to her.

The staircase, the sofa—Mia then realised why the two objects were playing on her mind.

As Joel returned and set two mugs down on the glass coffee table with a clink, he took a seat beside her on the sofa. She could tell he was wondering how close he should sit next to her. He hovered momentarily before sitting down.

Scooting over on the leather seat closer to Joel, she sat so that they were almost touching. As she did, a soft smile crept across his lips before he leaned forward to hand her a mug.

"Thank you," she said as she took the hot mug from his hands.

Joel leaned back in his seat after retrieving his own mug and stretched his arm around her shoulder. She nestled into the crook of his arm, feeling the warmth radiate from his body as his hand caressed her shoulder.

"Joel, do you have an indoor swimming pool?" Mia blurted out. She felt his body let out a small chuckle beneath her before he answered.

"No. I live in California, why would I want an indoor pool? It's out back. Why'd you ask?" Looking up into his face, she resisted grinning at his bemused expression.

Mia instantly regretted asking.

She wished she could press rewind, only for ten seconds. Then she would still be happily nestled in Joel's arm and they would carry on with their afternoon as planned, instead of her screwing it up. There went her brain to mouth filter again, she realised. "Umm—no reason, I just…" She trailed off, not knowing how to finish her sentence. She had never been any good at lying. Instead, she preferred not to say a word rather than tell a lie.

"What?" Joel frowned, looking confused. "Why'd you ask?"

Mia let out a deep sigh, knowing she would have to admit why she had asked. "I just—I read this article once—and someone said you had an indoor swimming pool—among other things."

Then it was his turn to sigh. He looked down at Mia, his arm still wrapped around her shoulders. His nearly black eyes looked saddened as they bored into hers before flicking down to look away.

She knew Joel felt defeated. She saw it in his eyes. It was the look of someone so weary of hearing the same old lies told. But in this instance, the whole world was hearing those same old lies.

Placing her hand on his thigh, she said, "I'm sorry. I didn't mean to upset you. I only saw the article by chance. I don't usually read those things. She was talking about your house and I couldn't help but wonder what it was really like." Looking back up at her, his eyes seemed to register something different. *That's not the answer Joel is used to hearing*, she thought.

He frowned, bewildered. "You read that article and that was the only thing you thought? What my house was like?"

"Well, among other things."

"Oh." His eyes returned to staring at his lap and his hand loosened on Mia's shoulder.

"No, no," she added in haste, squeezing his thigh. "I wondered why someone would make something like that up. I knew Josh wouldn't have left." Referring to the article she had seen on the newsstand, she continued, "I knew it would have been his idea to offer them a lift home. I knew you were just in the wrong place at the wrong time, with the wrong people. I knew that you and Josh would have gotten out of the taxi and the driver would have dropped her off at her house. I didn't believe a word of what she said."

Joel's hand slid back to her shoulder, he squeezed it gently as he said, "You didn't?"

"No." She shook her head and added, "I also wondered why you didn't sue her skinny ass."

He laughed as he put his other arm around Mia, embracing her. He pulled her body closer to his before tilting his head to her lips.

As he drew closer, she could feel his breath on hers and her eyes focussed on the pair of soft lips that were open ever so slightly as they came toward her. She felt a sly smile creep upon her own lips as they connected with Joel's, knowing that this beautiful man appreciated her belief in him. This gorgeous, too-perfect global superstar had allowed her into his life. He wanted her. And she wanted him. Mia knew then, that she was his.

❦❦❦

"Come on." Joel gave her an impish grin as he hauled himself from the sofa and held his hands outstretched to her. "Let me show you around."

Giggling to herself before placing her hands in Joel's, she allowed him to pull her body from the comfort of the huge leather sofa and into his even more comfortable arms.

He looped his arms around her waist and placed a soft kiss on her lips before taking her hand again and leading her back into the hallway.

Mia tried not to grin from ear to ear as she followed him into the adjacent room.

Now that she felt more comfortable in his home, she took in the impressiveness of Joel's entrance hall with more detail than before. It amazed her how nerves could shroud her perception of things. They seemed to make her see in a tunnel-like vision while she focussed on getting through the moment.

As she strolled back into the entrance hall, hand in hand with Joel, she took a moment to look around the spacious room.

The grandeur couldn't be put into words. Mia felt the room belonged in an English stately home or a castle nestled in the Irish valleys, not a mansion in Beverly Hills. But somehow, the room fitted with the rest of the house—well, the parts that she had seen so far, anyway.

A wide, white marble staircase curved up the side of the room to the second floor where her eyes drifted to the expanse of space above her. Most of the house had impressively high ceilings and the hallway only amplified that with its cathedral-like height. She gazed up at the intricate light fixture that hung from the center of the ceiling and was suspended in the middle of the room.

As she stared skyward, her neck craned back, she became aware of the sound of footsteps on the white marble. Pausing for a moment, she inhaled as she realised they were not alone in his house. She wondered who she was about to see, what mysterious part of Joel's life was about to unveil itself from within the upper rooms of the house. As she slowly tilted her head back to normal level, her expression turned puzzled.

Mia realised she wasn't hearing the sound of footsteps after all, it was the sound of padded feet and claws skittering down the marble as their owner careered toward them.

Or toward *its* owner, she corrected herself as she righted herself from her moment of indoor stargazing to see a bulldog racing down the remaining stairs and careering across the tiled floors.

Joel's fingers left her hand as he squatted down to greet the four-legged friend that was rushing to see him.

"Hey, buddy," he cooed as the dog finally skittered to a halt at his feet.

Panting with exertion, the dog's tongue lolled from one side of his mouth as he fussed around Joel for attention.

She beamed at the adorable dog. "Hey, there," she said softly as she squatted down to join Joel and greet his dog. The dog instantly left Joel's side and began sniffing around Mia, determining her scent before placing his paws on her knees, reaching up to her face, and licking it furiously.

Mia erupted into giggles as the dog smothered her with kisses. Its rough tongue licked every inch of her face and she couldn't help but laugh. She ran her hands over the dog's head, petting him in return for his generous affection.

"All right, all right." Joel tried to control his laughter but Mia could see he was desperately trying not to laugh as her new friend smothered her with doggy kisses.

"Diesel, that's enough now or I might get jealous."

Joel lifted the dog away from her so that she could regain her balance. She was still laughing as she wiped her face with the back of her hand in an attempt to remove the dog kisses.

"I'm sorry." He bit his lip as he spoke. "I think he likes you."

Exhaling a breathless laugh, she answered, "It's fine, honestly. I love dogs."

In truth, she did. Mike and Sharon had a dog when she was growing up and she loved him to pieces. Secretly, she missed him as much as she missed her adoptive parents.

Not having the time or space to keep pets in her apartment in Dublin, she missed having one around. She had always been drawn to animals. Their unwavering loyalty and inability to judge made them dedicated companions—particularly dogs.

Joel let out a relieved exhale and let go of his beloved Diesel so that Mia could return to fussing over him.

"I always worry about how people are going to react," he said as he watched her pet Diesel. "Not that I have many people over to the house, but not everyone likes dogs."

"No, I know what you mean." Mia smiled and told him about the one she had grown up with. "I love him to pieces. I miss having a dog around so much."

Joel's grin spread even wider as he realised they a shared love for animals. Admiring his smile, she resented the media so much for making this beautiful man so cautious and reclusive. He should have been able to go about his life as he pleased, without fearing being photographed and followed at his every move. That was the price he paid for his fame, Mia realised.

"As you've probably guessed, this is Diesel." Joel's grin was still firmly in place as he formally introduced her to his four-legged companion.

"Diesel, this is Mia." He held out his palm to Mia as he introduced them, to which Diesel saw as an opportunity to re-attack her with showering kisses.

They both erupted into laughter as she gently pushed Diesel down to her lap where she could resume petting him.

"He's a blue French bulldog," Joel explained. "He's a rescue dog. So many people in LA buy designer breeds and then ditch them as soon as the novelty wears off."

Mia let out a sigh. "That's so sad."

Joel nodded. "It is. The shelters here do great work, though. I help them out when I can."

Her eyebrows shot up. "Really?"

His lip curled in a smile. "Don't sound so surprised."

"I'm sorry, I just didn't expect—"

"A rock star to have time for abandoned puppies?" Joel finished her sentence for her.

"No, that's not what I meant." She scowled. She had only been impressed to hear that Joel had so much compassion for a good cause.

"Relax." His face softened as he petted Diesel's head. "I'm just teasing. I know you wouldn't think that."

Her smile returned as she realised he understood. She wasn't the press, she wasn't an industry exec, she wasn't a groupie, or a fame-hungry wannabe.

She saw Joel for who he was. She saw the caring, compassionate soul beneath the fame-hardened exterior.

"I donate money to them all the time," he continued. "I help them out as much as I can."

"That's so great of you."

"I'd hate to see them close down. That's where I got this guy from."

Joel's smile disappeared as the dark thought crossed his mind. Mia could see how much he cared.

"They won't. Not with you helping them," She placed her hand on his forearm in reassurance and his eyes brimmed with gratitude. "I had no idea you had a dog," She changed the subject to lift the mood.

His face instantly brightened again. "Dog*s*," he corrected, emphasising the plural. "I have two. There's another one upstairs somewhere but he's lazy as hell. Useless as a guard dog."

At his last words, he shot her a grin, causing her to giggle. "What's his name?" she asked.

"Sonny. He's a Boston terrier. He's a rescue too."

"I'd love to meet him."

"Come on then. Let's go find him." He stood up, grabbed her hand, and motioned to Diesel to follow them. "Ah," Joel exclaimed as he pushed open the ajar door. "Exactly where I thought you would be."

Mia could see the amused smile dancing across his face as he pushed open the door farther to allow her to see.

Sprawled out across the luxurious sheets on a comfortable looking king-sized bed was who she assumed was Sonny.

"Keeping my bed warm for me, huh?" Joel asked as they walked across the spacious room to greet the unmoving dog sprawled across the bed.

Mia's stomach fluttered with excitement as she realised she was in Joel Coben's bedroom. Pushing her inner teenage fan-girl to one side, she followed him across the room. Sonny half raised his head in a way of greeting before flopping back down on the bed again.

"Man." Joel sighed as he laid down beside his friend. "Life's so hard, huh?"

Sonny let out a deep exhale in response, before rolling over to show Joel his belly.

Amused, he raised an eyebrow at Mia as she perched on the edge of the bed. "Glad to know I have my uses," he mumbled as he began rubbing the dog's stomach.

She giggled again as she watched the pair. Diesel sat at her feet, longingly staring up at her and the comfortable bed she was sitting on.

As she watched Joel lounging on his bed with his dog, she realised he was completely at ease. The notoriously reclusive global superstar had let her into his home and his life and was at ease with her being so intimate with his personal life.

Mia found herself smiling down at him. She couldn't help but imagine waking up on a sunny morning in the ridiculously comfortable bed with the sunlight peeking through the curtains from the veranda outside. Imagining waking up in Joel's arms, she pictured his warm and reassuring smile staring down at her as she opened her eyes. She could picture them lounging in bed together as Joel was doing now, with the dogs happily sprawled out with them on the spacious mattress.

To Mia, the idea sounded like heaven. It sounded perfect— like what she had been waiting for all her life.

As her imagination furtively ran away with her, she realised Joel was staring at her.

"What?" she asked with an embarrassed smile.

He shrugged. "Nothing." He looked so relaxed as he lounged on his bed with his arm behind his head and the other rubbing Sonny's stomach. "You ready to see the rest of the house?"

"Sure," Mia answered, feeling the flush leaving her cheeks at the change in direction.

Joel stretched out before sitting up on the bed, to which Sonny gave a disgruntled sigh at losing his masseuse.

Sitting up, he placed his hands on his thighs, his nearly black eyes staring up at her from under his heavily framed eyelashes. His face creased slightly into a soft smile as he took in the picture of Mia sitting on the edge of his bed. He seemed deeply lost in thought and, despite his unwavering scrutiny, she felt comfortable under his gaze. She reflected on how, in such a short space of time, their relationship had changed so fast.

Not so long ago, she would have squirmed and been irked at the thought of Joel staring wordlessly at her, but now she felt as though she understood. She had a brief, but deeper understanding of the troubled soul sitting before her, and it had altered her perception of him entirely.

Without a word, Mia turned the tables and held out her hands to him. He glanced down at her upturned palms before his eyes met hers again and a gentle smile lit up his dark features. He placed his hands in hers and curled his fingers around hers before rising from the bed and pulling her into an embrace.

Joel rested his head in the crook of her neck and exhaled deeply. He held her body tight against him, as if fearful that she were about to disappear at any moment. Mia felt the softness of his bedhead hairbrush against her skin and the warmth of his cheek on her neck as he held her close. She nestled her face into his body, breathing in his familiar scent and cherishing the warmth of him and the tightness of his hold. Still wordless, they continued to hold one another. They both knew there was no need for words in that moment. There was no need for words or lyrics to spell or sing out how they felt. She knew they were connecting on a deeper level, a level that stirred Mia to her core. Her soul came alive within her body, as if welcoming home an old friend. Senses stirred with recognition as if she were returning to her soul the missing part of her being. And she knew that Joel was feeling the same.

ҼᴗҼᴗ

As he showed her around the rest of his home, no matter where they wandered throughout the house, they were followed by the sound of padded paws on the carpet behind them or the soft clicking of claws on the wooden flooring.

Somehow, Joel had managed to coax the incredibly lazy Sonny from his comfortable spot on his bed and the two dogs were joining them around the house as they wandered from room to room.

Mia knew that the dogs were not only being loyal by following their master, but their inquisitive nature warranted following his new-smelling companion around as she investigated their territory.

Joel wandered casually through his house. From room to room he strolled, hand-in-hand with her, and explained the things they saw. He pointed out various pieces of furniture that he had collected on his numerous world travels and numerous awards that littered the available space in each room—which Mia tried not to stare at incredulously.

With each of the varying pieces of artwork that hung from the walls of his sprawling mansion, he explained to her the themes behind each piece.

Although Mia wasn't an artist of that kind herself, like Joel, she could appreciate and admire what she was seeing.

After he finished showing her the modest sized home cinema and gym on the ground floor—to which Mia had asked why someone needed a cinema or gym in their house and Joel had replied that he couldn't exactly visit either of those places unnoticed—he led her by the hand back into the living room and into his kitchen.

Like the rest of his house, the kitchen was large and decorated in a monochrome, ultra-modern style.

Mia marveled at the unnecessarily large refrigerator in the corner of the room and the enticing coffee machine with its varying dials and levers that wouldn't look out of place in a shopping mall sized Starbucks. She admired the modern-looking island in the middle of the kitchen with its bar stools tucked in the sides before she noticed the French doors in the kitchen that opened out to the garden beyond.

As he led her by the hand to the glass doors and slid them open to allow her outside, she inhaled a quick breath at what she saw beyond the door.

Joel really was full of surprises.

Sonny and Diesel careened out of the kitchen, their claws skittering on the floor as they tried to get out as fast as possible when they realised they were being allowed into the garden.

And what a garden it was.

It pushed the boundaries to describe what she saw as a "garden."

What lay beyond the walls of Joel's house was phenomenal. An ornate formation of beige and gray flagstones made up the patio beyond the sliding doors. Outside was a table and chairs, prefect for enjoying the Californian sunshine, and a stone barbeque was tucked into the corner. As the stones petered out toward the garden, Mia's eyes became riveted on where the steps led.

An enormous, turquoise blue swimming pool lay three steps down from the patio. The flag stones ran around the edges of what Mia was sure was a larger-than-an-Olympic-sized rectangular swimming pool.

The backyard of Joel's house was beyond what she had envisioned. It was breathtaking.

Staring out at the swimming pool and the several sun loungers that lined its perimeters, Mia could have easily imagined she was standing poolside in a five-star luxury resort in Mexico or the Caribbean. This was the type of luxury people paid thousands of dollars to stay in on their vacations, not to live in. This was another world to her.

She was a million miles away from the gray skies that hovered over the city of Dublin, her little apartment, and her job at Glen's Tavern. This home and lifestyle was the type of thing she saw on television and in the movies. It just didn't happen to people like her. But there she was, standing in the glorious backyard of a multi-million-record-selling rock star's house. *It's amazing what several million dollars can buy.*

This time, Mia couldn't hide her amazement. She let out a gasp. "Wow", she breathed.

Joel turned to watch her expression of amazement as she took in the view. A curious look crossed his face as he watched her appreciate what she was seeing. When he appeared satisfied with what he saw, whatever it was he was searching for, his shy smile returned. Multi-million record selling rock stars weren't usually supposed to be shy either, Mia noted.

As she gazed open-mouthed at the lavish garden before her, Joel came to stand behind her and wrapped his arms around her waist. She leaned back into him and closed her hands over his.

He rested his head on her shoulder and let out an exhale. It was a frustrated sigh and made Mia turn in his arms to stare at him.

"What's wrong?" she asked.

Joel shook his head and a wry smile crossed his lips. Mia wasn't convinced.

She squeezed his hand, trying to convince him to open up to her.

"It's just—" He hesitated before continuing. "No one's ever appreciated the things I have like this. People are always trying to get more out of me, trying to find out what things cost or how much I earn. No one has ever been here and simply admired what I have, like you did today."

She squeezed his hand again and smiled up at him. "I'm not interested in anything like that." She gestured to the building behind them and the pool before them. "This is all just a bonus. It's you I'm interested in."

Joel reached down and kissed her. "Thank you," he whispered against her lips.

Mia's eyelashes fluttered against his cheek as she looked up and met his eyes. Eyes that were usually so guarded and walled up were overflowing with emotion.

His beautiful eyes took her breath away. Often she dreamt of eyes so dark they seemed endless, eyes that she could fall into and never return from. But at that moment, she felt as though she might drown in what she saw within. She also knew that Joel was hiding more than the way he felt about her appreciation of his lifestyle.

Their tender moment was then interrupted by a loud splash and a wave of water. Sonny and Diesel took a running leap from the poolside as they chased a tennis ball and landed in the pool.

Mia cried out as the spray of water covered their bodies and drenched their clothes. Joel let out a shout of surprise as the water covered them both, before bursting into fits of laughter. Shaking the water from her body, she laughed along with him and looked at the two dogs happily swimming about the pool as if nothing had happened.

Joel laughed as he shook the water from his arms and attempted to wipe her down. "Sorry about that."

"It's fine, honestly," she said as she ran her hands through her drenched hair, pulling it away from her face. Her skin tingled at the touch of his skin against her bare arms. Her eyes flashed up to his, as their skin prickled with the contact, and she saw Joel's fill with passion in the brief moment where their skin connected.

Joel ran his hand down the length of her arm before cradling her hand in his and leading her away from the pool and the risk of a further drenching.

"Will they be okay?" Mia looked back over her shoulder to the two dogs still paddling around the pool together.

"Yeah." He shrugged and pointed in the direction of the end of the pool. "There are steps into the water so they can just walk out when they're tired."

Satisfied the dogs would be okay in their absence, she returned her eyes to the direction Joel was taking her.

At the end of the pool, the stones beneath their feet curved to a stop before they met a lush green lawn. Wanting to feel the grass beneath her toes, Mia kicked off her shoes and padded barefoot into the garden.

As soon as she'd removed them, he took her shoes from her hands and carried them for her. With a grateful smile she said, "Thank you." *A rock star and a gentleman, what a rare combination*, she thought.

The garden beyond Joel's swimming pool area only amplified her earlier impression of a five-star luxury resort. They were extensive and beautifully manicured. Trees, plants, and hedges created beautiful little pathways in the grass that they strolled down while enjoying the afternoon sunshine as they walked hand in hand.

Mia looked up at his face as they wandered through another gap in the hedge that led to another pathway.

Joel appeared lost in thought—troubled thought. He seemed to be at war within himself, toiling between one decision and another.

Though he should have been enjoying the afternoon with her, she knew something was bothering him. He seemed to be thinking something over. Although comfortable with the silence, she wanted him to be at ease, to enjoy his rare afternoon off and her company.

"Joel?" She stopped and turned to him. Taking his face in her hands, she brought it down to look at her. His hands gently took hold of her waist as she cradled his head. "What's wrong?"

He closed his eyes for a moment before returning his gaze to hers. Their near blackness was once again shrouded in doubt and angst.

"Talk to me," she whispered.

Still he didn't say anything and Mia wondered if she had pushed the boundaries of their early days too far too soon. As she began to take her hands away from his face, Joel pulled her hips tighter to him.

"You're right." He sighed. "I should talk to you."

He closed his eyes then opened them again after a moment's pause. Reaching out to take her hand, he led her across to a nearby bench nestled among the trees.

Once they were seated side by side, their shoulders touching with their closeness, Joel took hold of both Mia's hands in his and pulled them into his lap. He stared down at their entwined fingers for a moment while he gathered his thoughts. "You opened up to me a while ago about your family." He exhaled a shaky breath. "About your brother."

She nodded.

"It's only fair that I do the same." He looked up and met her eyes, his own full of honesty. "I want to do the same."

"Okay," she whispered and allowed him to go on.

"I want to tell you about my family," Joel continued, his voice growing quieter, "about my father. You probably know already that our mom died when Josh and I were young. I was nine and he was seven."

He paused as she nodded. Mia had already read this story many times over in various articles and blogs about him. It felt surreal to sit beside the man himself, the multi-award winning, global superstar and hear the story straight from his mouth. The press had only speculated about his family, as Joel had never given an interview about his upbringing.

She had read several times that Joel's management would always instruct the interviewer not to ask questions about his family. The subject was off the agenda. The press had researched his family, his school, his friends, and anything they could to get their hands on about his past. But so far they had come up empty handed.

The only piece of newsworthy information they had been able to find on Joel Coben was his mother's death certificate.

Kate Coben had died at only thirty-five from a brain haemorrhage. That piece of information, of course, sent the press into overdrive. It was also a piece of information that Joel and his brother had remained profusely tight lipped about.

"She—" He exhaled deeply, his breath still shaky as he let it out.

Mia rubbed her thumb over the back of his hand in reassurance.

"She put Josh and me to bed one night like she always did. She read us a story and tucked us in, and in the morning she was gone. Just like that. I remember coming downstairs with Josh. He had woken me up, asking why we hadn't gotten up for school. It was half past nine. We were still in our pyjamas and we should have been at school by then. We came downstairs together and my dad was sitting at the table with his head in his hands. He was just slumped there. He didn't say anything. He didn't move. He didn't even look at us."

His eyes misted over and Mia could see he wasn't looking out at the beautiful scenery of his garden around him. Those eyes were revisiting a scene played thousands of times over in his head. He was watching his bare footsteps pad down the stairs of his old house and into the kitchen, leading his little brother in their search for their mom.

Staring into his eyes, Mia could almost picture the scene Joel was watching himself. She could see the two young Coben brothers looking lost and confused, their tousled mops of dark hair rumpled from sleep, and their eyes looking scared as they wandered together in their pyjamas, searching for a mother who would never come home.

She could see them together, wandering through the house, opening and closing doors to empty rooms, calling out for the mother—their calls always going unanswered. Mia was picturing them tiptoeing down the stairs into the quiet of the house, their little faces shrouded in confusion and panic. Despite the noises of the garden around her, she could hear their little feet come to a stop as they reached the kitchen and saw their father sitting at the table. She could almost hear a little voice asking, "Daddy?"

No answer.

"Daddy, where's Mommy?"

Still no answer.

"I remember Josh walking over to his side and tugging at his arm, trying to see his face." Joel's adult voice brought her back to the present and into the garden. "Even though I was only nine, I remember seeing his face when Josh pulled his hand away. I can still see it clearly now. I knew as soon as I saw that face there was no going back. I knew our happy family was gone. Things would never be the same again. I somehow knew."

It was Mia's turn to look down to the ground and scuff the grass with her toes.

She knew that feeling all too well.

Although she was much younger than Joel when her family was torn apart, she could still recognize the feeling. Children knew when an irreparable event had taken place.

"The police came round to the house that day. Josh and I sat together in our room, too scared to go downstairs. I now know that the police suspected foul play. My mom arrived at the hospital in the back of an ambulance. I'm told my dad placed a 911 call asking for help because his wife had fallen down the stairs and wasn't moving."

Joel exhaled again.

Mia loosened her fingers from his grasp and, in the moment

before her arm slid around his shoulders, his fingers desperately reached for her hand.

His eyes looked lost and confused—as if he wondered why she was leaving him.

Immediately, she could picture that same look on a nine-year-old Joel as he searched for his mother. When he realised Mia wasn't leaving him, he relaxed into her and carried on with his tale.

"The police think—" He paused and stared away into the farthest corner of his garden. "—the police think that my mother was pushed. They think that she died as a result of being pushed forcefully down the stairs and hitting her head on the way down. They just never found enough evidence for a conviction."

Mia closed her eyes shut as she listened to Joel's words and tightened her hand around his waist. She nestled her face against the crook of his neck as she heard him relive his painful story.

What did someone say to such a tale? She had no words that could comfort someone who had relived those twenty four hours of his life over and over again each day since. As she listened to the quickened rising and falling of his chest beneath her cheek, Mia was sure that Joel had spent the last nineteen years replaying that night over and over in his mind, wondering if there was something he could have done.

Not that a nine-year-old little boy could have done anything to prevent such a tragedy, but tragic circumstances did strange things to a person's conscience.

She also knew that feeling too well.

Despite being barely able to remember anything about her parents, not a day went by that she wouldn't wonder how different her life could have been if her parents were still alive. At least Joel had Josh in his life. They had been able to pull through the tough times together. They both had someone in the world who knew exactly how the other was feeling.

Mia didn't. She had no one.

No one understood how she felt.

She had no brother to lean on for support. She didn't even know if her brother still walked the same earth that she did. Her brother could have left this world long ago and she would be none the wiser. At least Joel had closure. He had finality. Mia had none of those things.

But he did have something she didn't—someone to blame. Joel knew who had caused his loss and suffering. He knew who was responsible and he knew there was someone out there who could have prevented every painful moment he and his brother had endured.

"Things just went from bad to worse." He shook his head as his wavering voice continued. "I remember standing with Josh at the funeral, both of us in little black suits, watching a big heavy box being lowered into the ground. We knew that our mom was in there. We just weren't old enough to understand what was going on. Everyone around us was crying, looking at us both with red, sympathetic eyes. I remember holding Josh's hand as people started looking from us to our dad, and their eyes turned angry. I guess they knew what would happen."

He ran a hand through his thick, dark hair and massaged his head in frustration as he brought back the painful memories. His eyes closed and his brows furrowed deeply as he went on. "Our dad was just standing there, far away from everyone else, with his hands in his pockets, staring at the ground. No one would go near him. No one said how sorry they were to him. I had never felt so confused. There Josh and I were, in the middle of a graveyard watching our mother being lowered into the ground, people crying everywhere, and our dad standing all on his own. I couldn't understand why. But now I do."

Mia looked up into his eyes as they opened to stare out across the garden again. They still wore the haunted, distant gaze that told her Joel was seeing things that had long since passed, but now they had turned cold. She was beginning to understand why those eyes had worn a haunted, cold stare for so many years.

Joel sighed. "Loss changes a person so much, it alters everything about them. You think you have seen every side to someone but you haven't until you've witnessed someone grieve. It changes you too. You have to find strength in yourself that you didn't know you had. You have to try and continue with the everyday things that were once so easy, with this crippling pain that feels like your chest is going to tear apart at any moment. You have to try and support those closest to you go through the same pain. You try to help them while dealing with your own grief. There's no feeling in this world that compares to it."

Then his eyes misted over as he recalled the days and weeks

following his mother's death. He spoke as a person changed by grief, as someone who had suffered years of his adult life with such pain, but she had to remind herself that Joel had experienced all of this at the age of only nine.

He took in a huge breath and exhaled before continuing. "After the funeral he gradually started disappearing. I knew he was drinking but I guess he was trying to keep it hidden from Josh and me. He started slowly—he would go out on a Friday and come home on Saturday. Then he would come home on Sunday. Then he would go out on a Thursday." He shook his head, still staring out at the grass in the distance. "You can guess how that story ends."

Mia nodded.

"Josh and I didn't want the authorities involved. We had already lost one parent, and we didn't want to lose another."

Feeling her own eyes begin to tear she nodded again. She had lost both her parents. As bad as Joel's father was, she could understand wanting to hold onto what Joel had left.

"As far as anyone knew, he was still living at home with us. But Josh and I raised ourselves. He couldn't do anything for us. He couldn't cook or clean. He didn't know how to use the washing machine. I had to learn how to do all of those things." He shrugged again. "Our next door neighbors were a wonderful old couple. They would bring us food, groceries, anything we needed. Eleanor would bake things for us, clean the house when our dad wasn't around, and make sure we went to school with clean clothes and lunch. I owe her and Edward so much," he said wistfully.

Rewinding to the words that he had said a moment ago, she asked, "Eleanor?"

"Yeah." Joel's face lit up and a grin flashed across his face.

His grin told Mia he understood her question.

"Dear Eleanor" was a famous song of his.

Though the name was old fashioned, it was still in use today and his fans had assumed Joel was singing about a lover.

The song was regretfully apologetic, about not being able to thank someone for everything they had done. The lyrics spoke of someone who had gifted his life with so much but was no longer a part of it. Naturally, Joel's fans had guessed he was singing about an unappreciated lover who was now long gone.

An understanding passed between them and she returned his smile.

They both knew too well about the hidden meanings of songs that were often misunderstood. She now knew that Joel was singing about the elderly neighbor who had taken care of him and Josh in their darkest hours of need and, from the tone of the song, Mia guessed the elderly lady was no longer with them.

"Is she..." Her voice trailed away as she saw Joel's smile quickly disappear from his face.

"Yeah." He nodded. "They both are."

"I'm so sorry." Mia squeezed her hand around his waist again. She could see the regret in his eyes, but Joel wasn't finished.

"I always said I would pay them back one day. For everything they did for Josh and me, but I never got the chance. I promised them I would buy them a nicer house and take care of them, give them the retirement they deserved. But they both passed away before my career took off."

He gazed away into the distance. Mia could see he was hurting. He was regretting he never had the chance to thank the people who had helped him when he had needed someone most.

"I'm sure they both knew you would. They'll be looking down on you with pride." She smiled and lifted her hand to gesture around at the obvious wealth. "They know they helped you to get here."

Letting out a low chuckle, he added, "It's ironic you should say that."

"Why?"

"Because *this*—" He gestured to the garden they were sitting in. "—is for them. They both loved gardening. They just didn't really have a lot of space. So I did this as a kind of thank you and a tribute to them. It's what I would have done for them if they were still here."

Inside her chest, she felt her heart melt. It was heartbreakingly romantic and generous. An eternal symbol of gratitude would forever live in the grounds of his mansion to the people who had put him on the road to where he now was.

"They know." Mia nodded. "I'm sure they know. I'll bet they stroll hand in hand around here every day."

Tears began to form in Joel's eyes as he looked around the garden and she could see him picturing the elderly couple walking hand in hand. Joel nodded as he did, before looking down at Mia watching him.

"They were incredibly old fashioned so they wouldn't dream of involving the police or social services. It's crazy when I look back now. I'm amazed we both made it through and turned out okay enough."

Joel raised an eyebrow at Mia and she giggled softly. The media had their own theories about Joel and why Josh was fun loving, crazy, and loveable.

The two were so incredibly different yet so incredibly alike. The brothers had simply found their individual way of dealing with the hand life had dealt them.

Josh's answer was to be as upbeat and charming as he could. He made the most out of his charm. Whereas Joel was the older brother who had dealt with the responsibilities and learned things the hard way. He had become introverted and reserved.

Mia could easily see how they had both adopted their own methods of dealing with things. She could also understand Joel's relationship with music, which was one of her own ways with dealing with pain and loss. Music had become her solace and her own unique method of counselling—a method Joel could also understand. Where there were often no words, music would have a song. When she couldn't say how she felt, or had no one to say it to, music was her outlet for expression. Somehow, things could be expressed so much easier through a song.

These were the things that music had allowed them both to say to the world throughout their lives. Words that were never able to form had been said through music and now, finally, they said to one another.

Mia had never told anyone about her brother, about the pain and reasoning behind her music. Joel had never opened up to any reporter, no matter how big the interview offer, about his life and his past. He hadn't sold his story to the world for anything. They had both kept the muse behind their music secret from the world, until now.

Both Mia and Joel had found another outlet for their pain and suffering. They had finally found another form of counselling other than music. A form that gave even more back than they ever put in. A form that both understood and sympathised. A form that also loved in return, despite everything.

They had found each other.

Joel's eyes darkened as he returned to telling Mia about his estranged father. "He still shows up occasionally. I heard from him for the first time in years after I released my first album. He had seen me in the press and assumed I'd already made my fortune by signing a deal. When he realised I had yet to make any profit from my album, he disappeared. The first time I had seen my dad in years and he disappears again because he found out I didn't have any money. That's all he was interested in."

"I can't imagine what that felt like," she whispered.

"You can't." He sighed. "As harsh as that sounds, you just can't. There are no words I can use to describe the feeling that came over me, after not seeing him for so long, and then for him to vanish again. All he was interested in was cash. He turned up again when I won my first Grammy. Huge milestones in my career that he should have been there for, cheering me on and supporting me in the crowd for—he turns up just to ask how much I earned."

Mia shook her head. She was saddened that someone as successful as Joel was plagued by a money hungry relative.

He was right. His father should have been his number one fan. His father should be cheering his son on from the front row, clapping from the side of the stage, or watching with pride from behind the scenes.

Instead, he could only see his son from behind the glowing dollar signs in his eyes.

"What about Josh?" she Joel cast his eyes down to the ground. "Josh has heard even less from him than I have. He has no interest in Josh. He knows that I have the career, the house, the money. That's all he's interested in."

Josh was involved with Joel's career, but from behind the scenes. Mia thought it was ironic that the more outgoing of the two brothers was the one who spent his life behind the camera while the reclusive one spent his life in front of it.

The Coben brothers had been born and raised in the city of Riverside, California. Joel had moved to Los Angeles to build his musical career and Josh had willingly followed his older brother.

Mia didn't have to ask to know that their father hadn't bothered asking for their new address when they had moved.

"He finally got the message that I wasn't going to give him

any money about two years ago. The last I heard was that he was in Mexico. He crossed the border after going broke and hasn't been seen since. I couldn't care less."

"Do you think he will turn up again?"

"Who knows?" He shrugged. "Maybe. I'd be surprised if he didn't. But it's Mexico. That's a dangerous place for a man like him to vanish."

Joel's great grandfather was Mexican. The press had also learned that from searching into his past. Joel's surname wasn't particularly common and the press had uncovered as much as they could about the notoriously private rock star in a bid to dish the dirt on his private life.

If only they knew, Mia thought.

"He must still have connections down there." His dark eyes narrowed again and she could see the faint traces of Mexican heritage in his Caucasian features. That was the only answer for his eyes being so dark they mirrored the night sky.

A silence fell upon them as they sat with their arms around one another in the cooling air of the waning afternoon. Mia could hear the faint splashes in the distance, letting her know that Sonny and Diesel were still playing in the swimming pool.

Gentle birdsong echoed around the garden from birds nestled in the trees high above them and the hedges around them. Easily, she imagined Joel wandering around the garden for hours upon end, peacefully mulling things over and enjoying moments of rare solitude in his hectic life.

She could picture his dogs obediently following at his heels or nestled in the grass beside him as he sat writing lyrics in the afternoon sun.

"Thank you," she whispered into the warmth of his neck.

Inhaling his delicious, unique scent, she closed her eyes, wishing she could stay wrapped in his arms in the quiet of the garden and the warmth of the sun for a long, long time.

"What for?" Joel asked, pulling back to meet her gaze.

"For opening up to me," Mia whispered again as his eyes searched her own.

The corners of his lips creased into a soft smile, one that was still saddened by his memories.

After opening up to him and baring her soul to a stranger, she had eventually gained his trust. Mia understood why Joel had taken longer. He had more to lose than she did. She could easily have misled him, sold his story to the world, and made herself a small fortune in doing so.

But she knew there was no price she could ever be paid to persuade her to do so. She understood Joel's pain too well. There were some things the world simply didn't need to know.

CHAPTER 21

U gh." Mia sighed after yawning loud. "I'm beat." She stretched her arms back over her head and strained against her tired limbs.

Charlie flashed a devilish grin over the rim of her coffee cup. "I'm not surprised."

After playfully kicking her underneath the coffee shop table, Mia only laughed more.

Charlie eyed Mia with suspicion. "It sounds like you had a fun weekend."

"We did." Mia shrugged her off. She had told Charlie all she needed to know about her weekend with Joel. The details about Joel's dad were not ones she was prepared to divulge. "How was yours?" She swiftly changed the subject as she lounged back in her chair and sipped the delicious, smooth latte.

Charlie's eyes sparkled with glee as she grinned up at her from across the table. "About as hectic as yours, I'd say."

Mia spluttered on her latte. "*What*?"

Charlie nodded.

"You and Josh?"

Charlie nodded again.

"You? You're *official?*"

Charlie nodded again. A little laughter escaped her tightly pressed lips. "I guess so."

Mia squealed with glee. "I'm so happy for you."

"It's taken us long enough. We've liked each other for ages."

Mia nodded. She could see how much Charlie and Joel's brother liked one another and they were so well suited. It had just taken them a little while to cement their feelings for one another.

Charlie's grin looked as though it would split her cheeks before she burst into giggles. "So how about that? We each bagged ourselves a Coben brother."

Mia winked at her. "I'd say we did pretty good."

Charlie winked again and her now neon yellow nails curled around her coffee mug. "This is gonna make for some interesting festive holidays in the future."

Almost dropping her mug, Mia waved her hands in front of her. "Whoa, slow down."

Charlie's face turned serious. "Girl, you know you and Joel have something special. Something *different*."

"It's still way too early for that."

Charlie pointed a talon away from the mug toward Mia. "You just wait."

Mia's ears pricked at the sound of whispering nearby. Charlie's eyes darted across to something in Mia's peripheral vision. She was instantly suspicious and turned in her seat to see what had caught Charlie's attention.

"Mia, don't..." Charlie trailed off as Mia turned around.

A cluster of teenage girls were gathered around the end of the coffee machine, waiting for the barista to finish preparing their drinks. One of them held in her hands the glossy pages of a gossip magazine.

They were all staring at her.

One girl looked from the magazine to Mia again. "It is, it's definitely her," she whispered to her friends.

"What's Joel doing with *her*?" another added louder.

The others erupted into giggles.

Mia turned her attention back to her table as the girls collected their drinks and filed out of the coffee shop.

"Skank," one spat over her shoulder as she stalked out of the shop.

"Bitch," called another.

"Keep your hands off him," said the last one as she tossed the folded magazine at Mia.

"Get back in your playpen, bitches," Charlie called over her shoulder. "You okay?" she asked Mia.

Mia nodded. Her head was down, looking at the magazine in her lap.

"Mia?" Charlie's small hand rested on her forearm. "Mia?"

She still didn't respond. Charlie got up from her seat and dashed around the table, squeezing her petite body into the arm-chair beside her.

Joel Coben dates unknown Irish songwriter.

Charlie sighed as she read the headline. "Well, that explains a lot."

Mia was already halfway through the article.

"'Pictured here entering a restaurant in Los Angeles earlier this month and then only this weekend leaving Joel's house in Beverly Hills…'" Charlie read out loud. "'The virtually unknown Mia Ryan is rumoured to be signed with Joel's music label, Sixth String Studios, in a lucrative six-figure recording deal. Could their romance be a fabrication to kick-start this Irish unknown into Hollywood superstardom?' Ah," Charlie said when she had finished the article. "Give it here. I'll toss it."

"No," Mia snapped and grabbed the magazine from her hands. "I want to show Joel."

"Why? You guys know the truth. And, besides, you'll be old news by tomorrow. The gossips have made this trash up for years."

"I know. I just don't want people thinking I'm using him."

"Using him? Girl, he's using you for a career boost if you've signed a six-figure deal," Charlie said, arching an eyebrow at Mia who giggled.

"Joel doesn't need a career boost," she pointed out.

Charlie waved her away with her yellow painted fingers. "Speaking of, if you've signed a six figure deal…"

Mia laughed. "You know I haven't."

"Well, come on. I want to show you this amazing bag they have in that store around the corner. You can buy it for me when you finally sign on that shiny dotted line." Charlie winked again and grabbed her arm, pulling her from the seat and out of the door in the direction of the boutique.

༺༻

Joel let out a heavy exhale. "It's fine, honestly. I just didn't want you getting caught up in this." He tapped the glossy maga-zine on the arm of the chair. "I knew it would happen soon enough, though."

Mia searched his features for signs of annoyance, but he seemed calm. He was slouching in the comfortable sofa that rested against the wall of one of the studio's many practise rooms.

When she found him, he had been jamming out the rhythms to some of his favourite songs. Alone in the quiet of the practise room, he came to strum out his favorite songs for inspiration.

Now he was lounging in the comfort of the plush leather cushions of the well-used couch with Mia curled in his lap. He had one arm around her waist and the other stretched out beside him on the sofa.

"You could always sue them. You're American, after all," she teased.

"Hey." His usually calm voice feigned insult before he tickled her under her ribcage.

"Joel!" she shrieked between fits of giggles. Seeing her reaction and realising how ticklish she was, both his arms were soon around her body, tickling every inch of her sides and making her shriek loudly.

Though she tried to wriggle out of his clutches, quick as a flash, he pinned her down on the sofa with the weight of his body keeping her in place.

She could feel Joel's chest vibrate with laughter against hers as she tried to maneuver out of his hold. It was no use. She was stuck fast.

He grinned from ear to ear, the tip of his nose touching hers. "Are you sorry?"

"No."

Mia giggled and Joel's fingers danced along the underside of her ribcage again. His tickling made her squeal out loud, but she was unable to move as his weight kept her in place. She writhed under the sculpted, muscular torso that was pressed against her own.

"Okay, okay fine!" She gave in, her breathing coming in ragged gasps.

Joel chuckled and feeling the rumbles against her chest made Mia laugh too.

Their breaths mixed together as Joel's face touched hers.

His playful grin was still in place and she tried to burn the image into her memory. Her beautiful, troubled rock star didn't often look so happy and relaxed. Joel's eyes sparkled with humor, dancing with happiness, and his full lips curled into an adorable lopsided smile. Though his hair usually looked tousled, it was even more mussed from their play fighting.

Mia wriggled her arms loose from his hold and slipped them around his waist. Joel's hand reached up and brushed a loose strand of her hair away from her face. His fingers softly trailed down her cheekbone.

The tip of his nose left hers as his lips moved forward and closed the millimeters of space that separated them from one another. Their ragged breathing became slow and heavy as their lips melded against each other's. Their tongues danced and tangled together.

As she entwined her legs around Joel's, locking his body against hers, she wished they were alone in the studio building.

Eventually, they parted, though their breathing was still heavy. Joel turned onto his side, relaxing into the back of the sofa and wrapping his arms around Mia, pulling her against him.

She laid her head on the contours of his chest, feeling to the steady rise and fall beneath her cheek. His hand slipped up the back of her top and his fingers traced light circles against her bare skin. With a contented sigh, she mumbled; "I wish we could just stay here."

Joel's lips nestled in her hair and tenderly kissed the top of her head. "Me too," he whispered into her hair.

They lay entwined together, neither of them moving from the comfort of their embrace on the well-worn sofa. There was no clock in the room to tick by their minutes of solace, no radio to announce the hour elapsed with the news, no infiltrating noise of the television and, best of all, no other people to disturb their privacy.

A quiet knocking on the practise room door suddenly reminded Mia otherwise. They were not as blissfully alone in the world as she would have liked.

She thought of the sprawling rooms of Joel's mansion in the Beverly Hills, the endless rooms of comfortable furniture, and the electronic gates keeping the two of them locked away from the rest of the world.

She suddenly longed to be back in the weekend, in the safety and privacy of Joel's house.

Maybe she would suggest going back there with him later.

"Yeah," Joel called over her head.

"Oops, I'm so sorry guys," Charlie's voice came from the doorway.

Mia turned from the comfort of his chest to look at her friend. She prepared herself to scowl at Charlie for intruding on their moment, but the instant she saw the worried expression on Charlie's face, Mia's heart sank.

"What's wrong?" she asked, trying to sit upright in the array of limbs in which she and Joel had entwined themselves.

Charlie's face dropped and she averted her eyes to the floor. "Joel, I think you need to come out here."

Mia could feel the icy chill wash over him beside her.

"Why?" Joel's happy demeanor was instantly gone. His media-ready mask was back in place and his voice was hardened.

Standing up from the sofa Mia held out her hand to Joel, who took it, entwining what little they could of themselves together again as he rose.

"I—it's—" Charlie stammered.

Hand in hand, Joel and Mia crossed the room to where Charlie stood holding onto the doorframe for support.

"What is it?" Mia asked, placing her free hand on Charlie's bare arm. Her skin felt cold beneath her hand. She could sense something bad had happen, or was about to.

"I know exactly what it is," Joel's deep said came from beside her.

Charlie looked up to meet his eyes before stepping out of his way.

"It's my dad," he spat through gritted teeth as he began to stride down the corridor.

In a rage, Joel strode down the corridor, his boots quickly pacing out the distance until they reached the foyer. Mia had to walk twice as fast to keep up with him. With a vice like grip of his fingers against her hand, he clung to her for support.

Mia wouldn't let go. After his confessions to her, she knew exactly how much this meant to him. She wouldn't leave him.

The clacking of heels behind her let her know Charlie was not far behind them.

They reached the foyer of the reception area and Mia could instantly tell from the atmosphere in the room that something was wrong.

"He's, well—He's over there." Charlie gestured toward the main doors of the building, but she needn't have.

Joel had already seen.

Clustered around the sliding doors of the entrance was a mixed group of employees, artists, and friends. They were all observing the scene behind the now closed and clearly locked sliding doors. Mia felt Joel's body tense as he strode across the expanse of the foyer.

"Joel," a familiar voice called out from a nearby corridor.

Josh came dashing out of the corridor where Joel's studio was. He saw his brother among the crowds and headed toward him.

Both brothers turned to see what the crowd was staring at behind the tinted glass.

Mia felt her heart rise into her throat. Remembering her thoughts about meeting Josh for the first time, she thought how he looked the spitting image of Joel but on a time delay. The man pounding his fists against the unmoving glass doors was the opposite. If Mia could have fast forwarded time, the two brothers beside her would resemble the man behind the glass.

As they stepped forward, she got a better image of the maniac attempting to enter the building. Then she saw that there was something different about this man from his sons. There was something deeper, something darker.

A lifetime of darkness and bitterness had hardened his soul and his face in a way that neither of his sons faces would ever see.

Joel's eyes masked his emotions. Josh played away his feelings with humor and charm. Joseph Coben simply had none—no humor, charm, or mask. His face looked wild. He was furious, raging even. His fists hammered away at the glass doors as he tried to get through.

He stopped short as soon as he saw his sons standing side by side watching him. His fury fell away and something colder washed across his features as he stared at them.

"The police are on their way." Charlie's voice sounded timid in the quiet of the room.

Josh nodded at her.

"Let me go out there," Joel said to her.

"Joel, I don't think that's a—"

He turned to faced her. "Just do it. Please."

The usually colorful, exotic bird of paradise that twirled about the studios looked tiny and afraid. Mia wanted to wrap her arms around her friend, but she held tight to Joel.

Josh turned from his brother and his girlfriend to stride across the room to the reception desk. Mia knew he spent far too much time leaning over that desk talking to Charlie. He must have known how everything in the building worked. He pressed a button somewhere behind the desk and an audible beep sounded near the doors. He jerked his head at Joel as he walked toward the doors. "Come on."

"Stay here." Joel squeezed her hand tightly before letting go and following his brother.

Josh pushed a button beside the door and the glass slid soundlessly open, allowing them both outside to confront their father.

Mia stepped toward Charlie, who instantly grabbed her hand.

Joseph Coben paused as his sons stepped through the barrier, he had been relentlessly pounding against, and confronted him.

It didn't take long to see their words were becoming heated. Joel was getting the angrier of the two brothers, his hands were raising and he was pointing at his father. Josh was getting involved, but allowing Joel to do most of the talking.

A loud gasp sounded from across the room.

"Oh God," called someone else.

Mia's eyes left Joel momentarily to see a huge swarm of paparazzi descend upon the family reunion. Somehow, they had broken through security to snap their own photos of this long awaited reunion.

"Where the hell is security?"

Mia instantly recognized Jackson's voice as he strode across the foyer, marching toward the gathering. His well-polished shoes clipped across the tiled flooring as he approached. For the first time, she noticed, he appeared a little dishevelled.

His tie was loosened and his top button was undone, his hair looked like he had run his hands through it in frustration.

"Charlie!" he snapped. "Get them here now!"

Darting from Mia's side to her desk, she grabbed a walkie-talkie and began speaking into it.

Jackson quickly snatched it out of her hands and began yelling into the device. The brothers were now inches away from their father, the yelling and gesturing was increasing. Mia knew if security or the police didn't arrive soon, there would be blows.

Paparazzi swarmed around the group. The flashbulbs were blinding as they snapped away only inches away from the commotion.

Everyone knew this would be front-page news on all the glossies and newspapers in the morning.

Four burly men dressed head to toe in black suddenly barged through the paparazzi, shoving some to the floor before tackling Joseph Coben to the ground. One of the security guards was yelling at Joel and Josh. Mia knew he was ordering them back inside.

She dashed across to the keypad where Josh had hit a button only a moment earlier. Aiming for what she hoped was the right one, she held her finger over the button and prayed.

Joseph must have damaged the usually silent door with his pounding. The sliding door hissed as it opened, allowing them back inside the safety of the building.

The confusing sounds of yelling, scuffling, flashbulbs, and police sirens pierced the doors as Joel and Josh were shoved back through by the burly security guard.

"What the hell is going on?" Jackson shouted over the noise at the brothers.

Behind the glass, Mia saw the police were arriving on the scene, shoving their way through the crowd of paparazzi to get to Joel's father.

This really is going to make the front page, she thought.

"It's not our fault," Josh yelled back.

"He just turned up, demanding to be let in," Joel explained.

"Why? What the hell is he doing here?" Jackson raved.

"Doing what he always does." Joel wiped his hand across his forehead before shoving past him toward Mia. "Asking for money."

Jackson's mouth fell open. "All this is for money?"

Joel had grabbed her hand and was about to leave the room. He stopped short. Turning on his heel, he faced Jackson. "Yes fucking money," he spat and the room went silent. "*Money.* My goddam money that I've spent a lifetime having to earn because his sorry ass fucked off and left my brother and me alone when we were kids. He wants money, royalties, a house, you fucking name it, Jackson, he wants it!"

Mia could feel the heat radiating from his anger.

Jackson was silent.

"And you tell me why the fuck I should give him any of that," Joel snapped, before turning his back on Jackson. Pulling Mia with him, he stalked from the building.

e/ɔe/ɔ

The Escalade sped too quickly through the streets of Los Angeles, zipping through yellow lights and round corners on two wheels.

Dusk was beginning to settle on the city, the heat from the day was diminishing, and the traffic was thinning for the evening. The ever-present smog hung heavy in the air over the buildings. The heat in the car was still not diminishing.

Mia kept silent as they drove, flying their way across the city toward the sprawling houses of the city's wealthy Beverly Hills.

The area was the playground of the rich and famous. It was bubble-like in its appearance, a strange fairy-tale in the otherwise typically grim and dirty city. She had never understood why the rich and famous chose to settle there. It was vibrant, exciting, and ever-changing. But it was a city nonetheless. And cities were usually dirty, busy, and sometimes dangerous. With more money than sense, the only apparent reason as to why celebrities had descended on the hotspot for musicians and actors was convenience.

They could pick anywhere in the world to live, but they chose to live in the little dream world they had created for themselves that was conveniently close to their jobs.

The familiar electronic gates of Joel's mansion appeared soon enough and, after pressing the fob on his keys, he drove silently up the driveway. His eyes were rooted to his rear-view mirror as the gates closed. Mia knew he was checking that they weren't being followed.

He pulled the car to a stop right outside the front door of his house and turned off the engine. Wordlessly, he hopped down from the driver's seat and slammed the door.

Mia sat back in her seat and stared up at the fabric-covered roof of the car. *Give him a minute*, she thought. This was a lot for him to take in. As she unclipped her seatbelt, he opened her door. Joel's eyes looked up at her apologetically from the ground below. He held his hand out to her.

Placing her hand in his, she allowed him to help her out of the car. *He truly is a gentleman*, she thought, *despite his anger.*

His other hand slammed the door shut behind her. He stood for a moment, holding her hand, his eyes roving across her features, analysing her.

Slowly, he pulled her toward him.

Stepping into his arms, she allowed his hands to slide across her body and pull her into him.

Joel buried his face in her shoulder, deeply inhaling her scent. "I'm so sorry," he whispered.

Mia slid her arms around his back, tightening him against her. "Don't be," she whispered in his ear.

"But this is so much for you to deal with," he mumbled against her neck.

"I don't care," she said, running a hand under his pronounced cheekbone, tilting his head up to face her.

He lifted his head and stared down at her. Mia gazed into his eyes, losing herself momentarily in the haunting space inside them. Her hand slid up to the back of his head and into his hair. She ran her fingers through his mussed up hair, before pulling his face down to hers. "It doesn't matter," she said firmly against his lips.

Joel said nothing. His eyes bored into hers, their eyelashes brushing against each other's, as he stared deep into her soul.

Finally, he exhaled heavily, pressing his lips against hers. Mia moulded herself into him, their lips saying to one another all the things their voices didn't. She didn't care about the trouble, the baggage. There was something about him that made her disregard everything. He was all she wanted. Nothing else mattered.

Joel was expelling all his tension and fury from earlier into his kiss. His passion was desperate and longing. His hands were soon sliding up under her T-shirt, their softness turning to eagerness as he explored every inch of her skin. Mia mirrored his actions, desperately wanting to see the defined, sculpted, and tattooed body beneath the thin fabric.

Pushing her back against the cold metal of the car, he slid his hands down her thighs before lifting them off the ground and wrapping her legs around his waist.

Desperate to be closer to him, she gripped him tight. Joel's lips left hers and trailed down her cheekbone before snaking their way across her neck. She breathed in the delicious scent of his cologne and his body as she ran her hands up the muscular contours of his upper arms. One hand slid down toward his jeans, and she fumbled inside his pocket.

Joel looked up from where his lips had been teasing the skin of her collarbone.

She held up her hand. Clutched in her outstretched fingers were Joel's front door keys.

His face cracked into his adorable lopsided grin. When he saw what she had in her hands, a promising hint seeped into his smile.

"Let's go," she mumbled against his lips.

Joel let out a soft chuckle as he lifted her body off the cool metal of the car, carefully carrying her up the steps of his house and in through his front door.

CHAPTER 22

"Mia," Jackson called out across the foyer.

About to head out of the studio building, she turned to see him holding a door open at the opposite end of the foyer to where she usually retreated. She smiled at the ever-professional Jackson. "Hey."

"Can I borrow you for a moment?"

He stole a glance at Charlie's arm looped through hers.

Mia met her eyes and saw assertion reflected back at her within them. She nodded. "Sure."

"I'll wait out here for you." Charlie motioned to her usual spot behind the desk.

With a knowing grin, Mia glanced at her. Charlie seemed permanently rooted to that desk.

Jackson held out his hand to Mia as she approached. "Wonderful to see you again, Mia." He pulled in his lips in a tight, professional smile that mirrored the tight grip he enveloped her hand in.

She nodded, equally polite. "And you."

"I hope you're still enjoying yourself here?" he asked.

"Of course," Mia said enthusiastically. "More than ever."

"So I hear." A flicker of a teasing smile crossed his face and she saw his non-professional demeanour materialise for a moment.

She also felt her cheeks turn scarlet. "N—No," she stammered. "I meant—"

"It's okay. I know what you meant," Jackson said with a shrug. "Anyway, I want you to meet someone."

He thumbed over his shoulder at the room behind the door that he was holding ajar and motioned for Mia to follow him inside.

Taking the door from him, she followed him into the room. Immediately, she wanted to slam the door and run back across the foyer, grabbing Charlie for security and heading to their original, safe destination of the deli.

She felt the familiar feeling of an insecure schoolgirl, nervous giddiness that she felt upon meeting Joel for the first time, but with less intensity.

Mia didn't deal with meeting superstars well, but she was quickly learning.

All five members of Glasshearts sat around the boardroom table and she assumed they were waiting to see her.

"Mia, these guys you probably recognize." Jackson gestured to the band. "But I want to formally introduce Glasshearts to you."

She waved to the band. "Hi."

Ironically, she heard her voice and it sounded as meek as she felt before them. They were one of the biggest bands in the world, a band who had also been performing her song for their legions of fans.

By now, everyone in LA had heard Glasshearts performing her song, "Hear Me," on the radio, and the track was getting played repeatedly by the most popular radio stations. There was great anticipation bubbling in the studio for another number one hit.

Mia had tried to diminish the rumors and whispers. She wasn't allowing herself to get her hopes up. Big breaks didn't happen very often in Los Angeles. The city was swarming with wannabe musicians, singers, artists, actors, and so on. There weren't many openings and the number of success stories versus the number of artists was a terrifyingly low ratio.

She failed to see how she could be one of the very few lucky ones.

Jackson began his introductions to the band, who all rose from the table to greet the writer behind their latest hit. And, in true Los Angeles style, the band members were all incredibly gorgeous.

As with Joel, she could see why their army of fans were so enamoured with them. They looked every inch the model rock stars, from their dark jeans and boots to leather jackets and fitted tees.

Their mussed up or spiked heads of hair were all styled, and every one of them appeared to have strolled off a recent photo shoot. The five band members simply oozed raw rock star sex appeal. Mia had even seen them live in Dublin the previous year. She remembered their energetic show, dancing, jumping up and down, and screaming along to their hits in the wild crowd.

Jackson introduced the drummer of the band. "This is Chris."

She shook the hand of an incredibly buff, tanned man. Chris got his work outs on stage, their high-energy songs gave the drummer all he needed to achieve his toned arms and torso.

"And this is Joey."

The bassist of the group was a little more reserved than his outgoing band mates were. He came forward and quickly shook her hand before moving aside. Mia still got the impression that Joey was as confident on and off stage as the others were—when he needed to be. It was interesting how being in the spotlight altered a person, she mused.

Jackson pushed forward one of the two guitarists of Glasshearts. "Mia, I'd like you to meet Rob."

Rob was very tall, had long, mussed-up brown hair and, like his Georgia-born band mates, had a rich brown tan.

"Nice to meet you, Mia." Rob's southern accent had softened from years away from home on the road.

Several leather and beaded bracelets clicked together as the second guitarist of the band shook her hand. "Amazing song, Mia, thank you so much for giving it to us." Nick's blond hair fell across his face as he leaned forward to greet her.

"Thank you, I'm glad you like it."

"And finally—" Jackson's sentence fell short as the lead singer of Glasshearts stepped forward and cut him off. "Adam."

A too-friendly set of fingers clamped around Mia's hand before their owner leaned forward and placed a lingering kiss on her cheek.

"I'm so pleased to meet you." His breath ticked against her cheek as his lips hovered close to her skin.

"Thanks." Mia tried to prise her fingers from his grip, but Adam kept a tight hold on her hand.

He turned her fingers in his hand, giving the impression to the room that he was holding it in a gentlemanly fashion. "'Hear Me' is such a beautiful song. I see now that its creator is equally as beautiful." He stared suggestively through his eyelashes at her.

Oh God, Mia thought. She tried not to retch on the spot. *So this is how rock stars get their fans into bed?* "I'm glad you like the *song* so much," she said, putting a little too much emphasis on the word song.

His chocolate brown eyes danced suggestively again. "Oh, we do."

While Mia could see what his fans saw in Adam looks-wise, there was something in his eyes that she didn't like.

Adam was ridiculously good looking. There was no doubt about that. With his tall, toned and tanned body and dark hair and features, he was almost Greek looking. His features and coloring gave him a Mediterranean allure that his teenage fans fell head over heels for.

But there was something that was lacking in those eyes that Mia immediately didn't trust. Adam had all the airs and graces of a charming, good-looking man, but one who knew all too well the allure he had on women. He had the annoying air of a man that thought of himself as God's gift to womankind. And the lacking that was in his stare was a lacking of compassion or emotion.

Something had happened to this man to make him turn off those emotions. But not in the same way Joel did. She knew that Joel had a heart full of compassion and emotions. He just masked it from the world to protect himself.

No, Adam was different. He purposely didn't want to feel.

The realisation was then obvious to Mia. Adam was a multi-million selling rock star with thousands of females throwing themselves at him. This man did not want to become attached. He was running on primal instincts and would do whatever he needed to in order to satisfy those urges before closing the door behind him.

Mia's skin suddenly felt dirty and contaminated. She wriggled her fingers free from the grasp of Adam's hand and immediately took a step back toward Jackson.

Resisting the urge to wipe the palm of her hand down the leg of her jeans, she crossed her arms over her chest.

"The guys were just in town for a meeting, I thought it would be nice if they finally got the chance to meet you," Jackson continued.

Clustered around the rock stars, Mia nodded.

"I apologise. It's only the briefest of meetings. They have to head across town for a press conference, but I'm sure you will all cross paths again soon enough." He finished his pleasantries and held open the door once again for the band to file out of the room.

Mia gave Jackson a relieved smile. "No problem."

She was glad the band was leaving. While the others seemed lovely, she didn't want to spend another minute in the close proximity of Adam.

Rob clapped her on the shoulder as he filed out of the room. "Thank you again, Mia."

Joey smiled as he left. "Yeah, thanks."

"We'll see you around, kid." Chris clasped her hand in an almost crushing grip and gave her a toothy grin before ushering his muscly frame out of the door.

"Thanks, Mia, see you again." Nick's bracelets clicked again as he shook her hand before filing out of the room.

Mia smiled after them. The band did seem like such nice guys, with the strange exception of Adam. She wondered how they got together and how they stayed together.

She knew that the frontman held the band together. This went for any group. Without the face of the band, the rest of the group would diminish into nothingness. Adam's good looks and charm on and off stage were one of the key ingredients in the band's success. Stealing her chance, she darted out of the boardroom door before Adam and into the safety of the open foyer.

Jackson then assured Mia he would speak to her soon and discuss the progress of her career. "Your three months are nearly over now. We'll have a meeting soon, Mia. I'll send you an email."

"Thanks," she called out after him as he turned and strode across the foyer after the rest of the band.

The remaining member was still lurking behind her, after pretending he had left something in the boardroom to steal an extra minute away from the group.

Stepping within the boundaries of her personal space, Adam leaned toward her, his breath flickering on her skin as he spoke. "I can't thank you enough, Mia, the song is truly amazing." His hand ran up the length of her bare arm as he continued. "Is there anything I can do to express how grateful I am to you?"

Her skin crawled at the trace of his fingers against her. "No," she snapped, taking a step backward.

"Are you sure?" He quickly mirrored her action and was within centimetres of her face again. "Wow, what a pretty necklace." He brushed his fingertips against the nape of her neck before fingering the pendant that hung around it.

As he leaned in to take a closer look at her necklace, his face was dangerously close to hers, his lips almost brushing her own.

Taking another step back, she firmly pushed her hands against his chest, forcing him away from her.

"I'm glad you like the song." She glowered before marching across the foyer, grabbing Charlie by the arm, and dragging her out of the building.

Adam remained where he was—a bemused expression creeping across his features as he watched her leave.

※※※

"What's going on?" Charlie's eyes darted from Mia to Adam who was still where she had left him.

"Nothing, let's go," Mia snapped.

Charlie sensed her mood and kept quiet until they were well away from the studio.

Once they were inside the safety of the deli and seated at their usual table by the window, Charlie broke the silence. "So, what happened back there?" She cocked an eyebrow at Mia as she leaned across the table.

"Just give me a minute," Mia mumbled, still fuming.

Charlie tapped her long acid pink nails on the table in front of her. "I already gave you a few, now spill."

Mia gave a restless sigh. Begrudgingly, she told Charlie what had happened with Adam. To Mia's surprise, Charlie's eyes narrowed before she shrugged. "Yeah, he's always been like that."

"What?" Mia asked, startled. "You knew? And you still let me go in there?"

"Whoa, hang on a second." Charlie held up a finger, "I couldn't stop you. Anyway, Jackson wanted you to meet them. They agreed to do your song, so you kinda had to meet them at some point. And you're a couple of weeks away from the end of your contract. You can't start refusing to do things until you're permanently signed. *And successful*, I might add."

Mia exhaled sharply.

"And," Charlie continued, "Adam would have been onto you at some point. You would have seen him around here sooner or later. I have a feeling the label is going to keep you. I've been around long enough to know." She winked. "Just act surprised."

Motioning for her to continue with her original topic of conversation, Mia urged her on.

"Okay, okay." Charlie rolled her eyes, which today were shadowed with neon blue. "Adam's a dick. Bottom line. Always has been, always will be. As soon as he sees a new face and a pretty one at that—" She winked at Mia again. "—he's onto them. And he won't stop until he gets what he wants."

"Excuse me?" Mia's voice rose an octave or two.

"You know what I mean." Charlie's sculpted eyebrows arched. "He's a predator when it comes to women. And since the band hit the big time, he's been even worse. Let's face it. Those guys aren't short of an offer or two. But Adam likes a challenge. And you've just provoked him."

"Oh, great." Mia remembered the look on his face as she had shoved him away.

"He won't leave you alone until he gets what he wants from you. Just be on your guard, okay?"

"Okay," Mia muttered.

ⅇⅉⅇⅉ

"I just thought you ought to know," Mia whispered quietly as she stood in the circle of Joel's arms.

He tightened his grip around her body, as if clutching his dearest possession to him against the threat of it being stolen.

The whispering was because she was cautious. She knew she ought to tell Joel. Several people had been in the foyer when Adam had gotten too close to her. Word would soon spread. And some people might not tell the story as it ought to be told. Mia knew she should tell Joel herself.

It was nothing. But being in the limelight made stories escalate quicker than they should. The press were already speculating about her and Joel. If the wrong person told the media about Adam, things could escalate pretty fast.

"It's okay," he whispered back before placing a gentle kiss on her lips.

Feeling the tension leave his body as she kissed him back, she pulled him against her. She ran her hand up the back of his neck and into his deliciously messy bedhead hair. Joel's hands slid farther down her back to her waist and he wrapped her tight against him. The desperation in his kiss was clear, the longing and need to feel what was his. Mia knew she needed to remind him she wasn't going anywhere. She was his. No boyband rock star was going to take her away from him.

They were virtually alone in the building. It was late at night and Joel was working late to avoid the waiting paparazzi outside the studio. Since his dad had sensationally reappeared in his life, and so publically, the press were having a field day over Joel. His face would be covering inches of column space over the following weeks. Mia knew her own image would be right beside his, too.

She gently tugged on his bottom lip with her teeth before breaking their kiss and untangling herself from him. Joel's eyes flashed open and a worried look covered his too beautiful features.

"One second," she breathed against his neck before placing a kiss in the crook of it, where her words had tickled his skin.

A low moan escaped Joel's throat as she let go of his hand and crossed to the other side of the room.

Turning the key, she flipped the lock to the studio door down and sealed them inside the soundproof room together. Then she turned out most of the lights before crossing the room again and sliding back into Joel's waiting arms.

A devilish grin spread across his face in the low lighting. She could feel the desire coursing through her as his inhumanly beautiful face lit up with anticipation.

His arms were quickly around her waist, pulling her body tight against his own. Mia could feel the hardness of his sculpted chest against her own and the tautness of his arms as they gripped around her body. She smiled back against his lips, wrapped her arms around his neck, and turned his body in line with hers, as she leaned back against the mixing desk behind them.

CHAPTER 23

Sunlight peeked through the long curtains that covered the large window in Joel's bedroom that looked down into the garden below.

Mia squinted as she opened her eyes and saw the bright sunlight rising in the distance between the curtains. A small terrace lay beyond those curtains and looked down on the impressive views of the swimming pool and the extensive gardens of his home.

Smiling contentedly to herself, she remembered leaning on those railings the night before staring out at the view. Joel had come up behind her, wrapped his arms around her waist, and nuzzled his face in her neck. She had been so happy, so content that everything had felt right with the world. For the first time in as long as she could remember, Mia felt at peace, and at home.

She marvelled at how, after everything life had thrown at her, she had finally found contentment in the arms of a worldwide superstar musician in his Beverly Hills mansion. It was the things dreams and movies were made of, she realised. Things like that didn't happen to small time musicians from Kinsale, Ireland. Men like Joel Coben didn't even know girls like Mia existed, let alone fell in love with them. They were the endless sea of nameless faces that stared longingly up at him from the depths of the crowds, night after night at his shows, each and every one of them admiring him, longing for him, desperate for him to even look their way.

Those girls weren't supposed to get the rock star. They were supposed to return to their routine jobs, return to being a face without a name, and return to the textbook plan life had for them.

Somehow, Mia had managed to tear up that textbook. Life had always dealt her an unusual hand and the more she explored life, the stranger her hand became. Not that she was complaining, she reminded herself, as she turned over in the all-too-comfortable silk sheets of Joel's bed.

There he was, sleeping peacefully. Her worldwide superstar musician was fast asleep beside her, his breaths coming slow and shallow with the gentle rising and falling of his chest. Her eyes drifted up the defined lines of his chest, over the scripted lines of ink that ran around his collarbone, to the light stubble on his angular jaw to the ends of his long dark eyelashes. His troubled eyes were closed tight. *He looks so peaceful.* The last few weeks of their lives had been a rollercoaster.

When boarding the flight to Los Angeles, Mia could never have envisioned this was where she would end up. She saw herself doing what she did now, writing songs in the studio, hearing them come to life in the session booths, and perhaps making a few friends in the city, maybe even being offered a permanent job.

But falling for the label's biggest star was not something she ever imagined happening.

She felt her chest swell with a mixture of emotions— excitement, happiness, contentment, anticipation. Her life had already changed so much in a matter of weeks and things could be about to change again.

In three days' time, she had a meeting scheduled with Jackson. That was when she would find out if she was to stay in Los Angeles or end her three-month contract and board the first flight out of LAX airport to Dublin.

Joel had been encouraging, promising her there was no chance the label would let someone as talented as her go. Still, she couldn't help but feel nervous. She didn't know for certain and neither did he. Where would they stand if she had to go back to Dublin? How would she continue her career?

Against the pillows, she shook her head. She would cross that bridge in three days' time. Wriggling closer to Joel under the sheets, she felt the warmth of his body against hers as she nestled closer to him.

She rested her head on his chest and listened to the sound of his breathing as she watched the sun continue rising. A firm, warm arm sleepily snaked around her waist and she knew he was stirring.

"Morning," he mumbled and she felt his lips kiss the top of her head.

"Morning," she replied, kissing his defined chest.

Joel sleepily mumbled something incoherent before the rhythmic sounds of his breathing beneath her ear told Mia he had drifted off to sleep again.

She wasn't surprised. They had been in the studio until the early hours of the morning, finishing some loose ends on his album and, once they had arrived back at his house, sleep hadn't been the first thing on their minds.

Closing her eyes again, she felt herself becoming sleepy in the warmth of the sheets and Joel's body. She soon gave way to sleep again in the comforting circle of his arms.

ꙮꙮ

Whether it was minutes or hours later, Mia had no idea, but she was startled awake. Her eyes flashed open at the strange sound. She immediately knew something was wrong.

"Joel!" She began to panic and shook the slumbering beauty beside her. If she hadn't felt a sense of urgency, she would have taken a moment to admire the beautiful, adorable sight of Joel opening his sleepy eyes. His hair was its usual tousled style, but it was rumpled from sleep and his dark eyes looked glassy as he cracked them open. "Joel, wake up!" Raising her voice, she shook his arm as she felt the panic in her rising.

"What—" he began but as soon as he came to his senses, he sat bolt upright in bed.

"What is that noise?" she asked.

Already out of bed, he began throwing on whatever clothes he could find that were strewn around the bedroom.

"It's the alarm," he said as he pulled a T-shirt over his head. "Someone's trying to, or has—" he corrected himself, "—broken into the house."

A cold chill ran through her body. Were they about to be attacked? Was it the press, or someone more sinister? They could be armed, she realised.

She began to get out of the tangled sheets but Joel quickly

leaned over her and gripped her shoulders in his hands. "Stay right here," he ordered, the urgency clear in his eyes. "I don't want you to get hurt."

Mia stared straight into the depths of his eyes. He meant every word.

She tried to wriggle out of his hold. "I can't let you go down there on your own,"

He was too strong and she was stuck tight.

"*Please*," he emphasised, "*stay here*."

He leaned down and produced a baseball bat from underneath the bed before dashing out of the door and slamming it behind him.

And then he was gone.

She could hear his footsteps running down the stairs toward the sound of the alarm. She had seen the high-tech piece of equipment beside the front door the first time she had been in Joel's house. An LCD touch screen showed various camera angles outside the house. The screens also showed almost every room of the house—thankfully, not his bedroom—and the security alarm could pick up exactly where the intruder was.

Ignoring his advice, Mia jumped out of bed and threw on her clothes. Anyone could be in the house, waiting for Joel to come downstairs alone.

Thankfully, he didn't appear to keep a gun in the house. But if his intruder had one, a baseball bat wouldn't be much of a match for one.

Mia had no idea what she would do if she came face to face with an armed intruder, but she couldn't sit in bed and wait for sounds of a struggle, or worse, to reach her.

Noticing Joel that had left his cell phone on the floor, as it had fallen out of his jeans, she grabbed it in case she needed to call 911.

Opening the bedroom door, she peered out onto the landing. She couldn't see Joel or hear anything. As she made her way down the large open staircase, her bare feet felt cold on the cool marble beneath her. Her hand firmly gripped the cell phone between her fingers, holding onto it for dear life, in case she should come face to face with the worst.

Joel had moved fast. The hallway was empty and the alarm had gone silent. Mia realised he must have looked at the screen before turning it off and heading in the direction where the alarm had triggered.

She paused in the middle of the hallway, listening for sounds of life in the large house. The stillness and silence were eerie. It made the hairs on the back of her neck stand on end. Immediately, she regretted her earlier thoughts about clichéd scenarios happening in movies.

Right at that moment, she felt as though she were in a horror movie, waiting for the killer to sneak up on her.

A clattering of wood on tiles told her that Joel had dropped the baseball bat on the kitchen floor.

Without thinking, her brain kicked into autopilot and she found herself dashing through the opening on her left, through the living room, and straight into the kitchen.

Mia had run through a million scenarios in her head in a matter of seconds.

Paparazzi, journalists, burglars, criminals, over enthusiastic fans, ex-girlfriends, all eager to invade Joel's privacy, ran through her head, but somehow she had missed out the obvious answer.

That answer was standing in front of her grappling with Joel.

His dad.

Why, Mia asked herself, *has neither of us suspected it would be his dad?* Out of all the people in the world, only a scorned relative would be stupid enough to break into an alarm-protected Beverly Hills mansion. Anyone else would, or should, know they would be immediately arrested.

And after seeing Joseph arrive unannounced at Sixth String Studios recently, they both should have guessed he would be back for round two sometime soon.

Hindsight is a wonderful thing, she thought as she dashed across the kitchen tiles to where Joseph was attempting to hurl his fists at his son, who was pinning him down against the island in the center of the kitchen.

"You owe me some of this fucking money!" His father's face was turning bright red as he yelled at Joel in fury.

"I owe you nothing!" Joel hurled back and shook his father's arms. "Just like you left us with! *Nothing!*"

"I never left you two! How dare you!" Joseph wrestled against the vice-like grip on his arms and attempted to throw a punch in Joel's direction.

"You were never there! We were nine and seven. How the hell were we supposed to take care of ourselves?"

"You had a roof over your heads. What more did you want? You ungrateful little bastards!"

"Ungrateful?" Joel screamed in disbelief, furiously shaking his head, "Mom died and you left your kids to cope on their own. How the hell does that make us ungrateful?"

"You've abandoned me all these years," his father sneered up at him, "since you hit the big time, you've wanted nothing to do with me!"

"I've wanted nothing to do with you for years!" Joel yelled, "I saw the real you when Mom died. You left your kids to fend for themselves. Josh and I wouldn't even be here if it wasn't for Eleanor!"

"Ah, that nosy bitch didn't give a damn about you two. She only thought there might be something of your mom's in it for her!"

Hearing his father insult the elderly lady who had rescued him and his brother in their darkest hours, pushed Joel over the edge. He let go of his father's arm and swung a heavy blow straight into his face.

Mia heard the sickening crunch as Joel's fist collided with his father's cheekbone.

"You bastard!" Joel screamed as his father regained his balance and came toward him, eager for a fight. "She did everything for us! Where the hell were you all those years? Throwing your life away, that's where!"

Joseph lunged toward him with his fists in the air. Joel didn't care, he was still yelling. He deftly moved out of the way of his father's blows.

"And you still are! You tell me why I should give you anything. I've earned everything, EVERYTHING!"

"I brought you up you little bastard," Joseph continued.

"You couldn't give a shit about us when Mom died!" Joel screamed in his father's face as they locked arms. Both had their hands pinned against each other, trying to lunge for one another. "You're dead to me! As far as I care, you died the same night Mom did!"

Joseph let out an almighty yell before pushing him to the floor.

Both bodies crashed onto the tiles together. Joseph was still firmly holding on to Joel, determined to beat his anger into his son. He reached over his head, his body pinning Joel in place, and fumbled for the baseball bat that had skittered to one side.

Hearing the crash of the bodies and seeing Joseph finally having the upper hand, Mia ran toward them.

"Mia, no! Get out of here!" Joel called out as she ran toward them.

Joseph hadn't seen her enter the room. He had been to focussed on getting what he wanted from his son.

She grabbed the baseball bat from Joseph's hands, threw it as far as she could across the room, and pulled him away from Joel. Her hands dug into the flesh of his upper arms, making him scream out in pain. Forcing all her weight into him, she tackled him to the floor, throwing him off Joel. He landed heavily on the kitchen floor.

Joseph was no match for his son. Joel worked hard on his body. He was muscular and lean, his well-defined body was toned and ready. Joseph was thin and weak. Years of wasting away his life, drinking himself to death in sleazy bars, had worn away at his aging frame. He had easily aged himself by ten or twenty years. His body had crashed into the floor as she threw him off Joel, who was quickly on his feet again.

"Call the police." She grabbed the phone out of her pocket and thrust it toward him as they both stood over his father, lying in the corner of the room.

"They're on their way." Joel stared at the phone in her hand. "The alarm has already done it."

Mia shook her head. It had only been a matter of minutes, or even seconds since she had come down the stairs. Adrenaline coursed through her veins and she could feel her heart pounding in her chest as she gathered her breath.

"You okay?" Joel asked, his dark eyes full of worry as he looked down at her. His gaze roved over her body, scanning for any signs that she was injured.

"I'm fine." She shrugged. "You?"

Joel nodded, his lips set in a firm, hard line.

The front door of the house crashed open loudly making them both jump.

"*Police*," someone shouted from the hallway.

"In here," Joel called over his shoulder as if it were the most natural thing in the world.

"Intruder, sir?" a police officer asked as his colleagues ran into the room and immediately hauled Joseph off the floor, holding him tight in their grip.

"Yeah, he broke in through here this morning." Joel pointed to the broken French doors in the kitchen.

"Do you know this man?" the officer asked as Joseph was locked into handcuffs.

"Sadly, yes." Joel shook his head. The officer cocked an eyebrow at him. Joel sighed. "He's my father."

The officer nodded.

"You're under arrest, Mr Coben," the officer announced to Joseph. He then looked to and from Joel. "Mr. Coben, Senior," he corrected himself.

Mia forced away the little smile that crept across her face.

The officer looked at her and a slight flush crept across his cheeks as he realised his mistake.

"I see you've done well for yourself once again," Joseph sneered as he looked Mia up and down and spat at Joel.

She tried not to squirm as his eyes roved up and down her body.

Joel simply shook his head in disgust and dismay as his father was lead out of the room.

☙❧☙❧

"Are you sure?" Mia asked.

Joel nodded.

His lips were clamped in a hard-set line again and his head was resting on his hands. He looked deep in thought.

Those almost black eyes were gazing down at the floor across the room, but she knew he was looking somewhere darker. They had that glassed-over effect she had seen when he had opened up to her about his past. She knew he was looking back in his mind to another time.

In silence, she sat beside him. She placed one hand on his shoulder in reassurance, just enough to let him know she was there.

Joel sighed heavily and his eyes snapped out of his past to the present. He raised his head off his hands and allowed them to fall weakly into his lap.

He was mentally exhausted, that was clearly evident.

A lifetime of battling his father and his father's demons was catching up with him. The brothers had spent years building their lives, away from their father, only to have him begin to swim in and out of their lives, once he knew the extent of their success.

"I don't want to add fuel to the fire," Joel mumbled. Despite his low tone, she heard the firm, seriousness in his voice.

It was her turn to simply nod.

"If I press charges, it gives him another chance to come looking for me, or for Josh," he added. "Josh's home isn't as secure as mine. I wonder why he didn't try there first."

"I do," Mia whispered with irony clear in her voice.

He lifted his eyebrows and nodded, as he understood. His father had gone straight for the big money. Why waste his time chasing Josh, when he could go straight for the millionaire?

It was no secret that Joel was incredibly successful, and with success came wealth—something, which Joel had aplenty.

Josh was successful and independent in his own right, but had caught the Joel Coben train in order to get where he was today. Joel had worked for years, building his reputation and climbing the industry ladder. And, once he had made it, he ensured his brother did too. Josh was a musician for Joel's backing band, a personal assistant, and roadie of-sorts, when Joel was on the road and on promotional tours.

Joseph Coben knew where to go if he wanted money. He had also wanted to take down the big shot first. Going straight to the top was clearly his aim.

"You shouldn't have seen any of that," he shook his head firmly.

"It's okay."

"No, it's not." His voice hardened and she could feel the panic rising in her stomach. "You shouldn't be getting caught up in any of this."

Mia fell silent. The panic was now rapidly turning to fear. She remembered how content she had felt that morning, lying beside Joel in bed before the alarm had sounded. She was realising how quickly things could change again.

"You could have been seriously hurt, or worse. I dread to

think what he would have done to you." Joel clenched his fists in frustration. "I was stupid not to think he would come here." He turned to face her fully on the sofa and took her hands in his, his long fingers running over the palm of her hand as he caressed her skin. "I'm so sorry."

The rising lump in her throat didn't leave when she swallowed. She tried to meet Joel's dark eyes but could feel her own beginning to mist. Looking down at their clasped hands in her lap, she wished she could hold them there forever. She didn't want to hear what was coming next.

Then she felt his skin brush against her cheek as he leaned his face toward hers. He paused for a moment as if savouring the sensation. His lips came down to hers and slowly placed a soft, lingering kiss on them. Mia closed her eyes and allowed the tear that was welling in each eye to fall down her cheeks.

"I love you," he whispered.

Her eyes flew open. "Huh?"

Joel's expression dropped. His eyes widened and his mouth fell open in surprise. He looked hurt, embarrassed almost. "I'm sorry. I guess it's too soon."

"No, no, no," Mia stumbled over her words and tried to pull him back to her. "I thought you were…"

He eyed her. "You thought I was what?"

"I thought you were—c—calling things off." Embarrassed, she scrunched her face up as she forced the sentence out.

Joel let out a soft chuckle in relief. "You *what*?"

Mia saw the humor finally back in his eyes. The hurt was gone and amusement was sparkling there. She wanted to reach over and swipe him across the side of the head for laughing at her. "I thought you were ending this. After what happened today, I thought you were ending it, that you didn't want me around anymore." She couldn't look him in the eyes. Instead, she stared across the room at Sonny who was snoring loudly on the opposite sofa.

Joel's hands were quickly around her body, pulling her into his lap. He wrapped his arms around her and buried his face in her neck before he whispered in her ear. "I've never met anyone like you, Mia." He softly kissed her cheek and she finally looked up into his eyes. "You amaze me, you intrigue me, you have me doing things I wouldn't usually do. You're smart, you're funny, you're incredibly talented, you're down to earth, and unlike like anyone else who I've ever met. You seem to want to know me— rather than the guy in the media. I'm serious, Mia, I love you. I know that this sounds a bit crazy and I know we haven't known each other that long, but somehow I know this feels right." He paused, looking through long dark eyelashes, waiting for her response.

"Okay, you can keep talking," she teased before cupping his face with her hand. Bringing him to her, she kissed his lips with all the passion and sincerity she could muster. "I love you too," she breathed.

His lips quickly sought hers again, both of them finding relief that the other felt the same. As she sat in his lap with his arms around her body, she felt the same feeling she had earlier that morning coming back to her. She knew that she and Joel felt the same, that despite their coming from different worlds, despite only knowing each other a short time, despite the world watching their every move, they knew they loved each other.

Mia knew that he had opened up to her in ways he had to no one else, as had she to him. They had confided their deepest secrets in one another and, in return, they had found a kindred spirit feeling a similar pain.

And in that pain, they had found each other.

Joel was her tranquillity, her calm. She found in him something she had been searching for—silence. When she was with him, she felt all the emotions, which had been toiling forever away under the surface, calm and still. All the hurt, the confusion, the pain of losing her parents and her missing brother, all silenced when she was in Joel's presence.

It was obvious he felt the same. With her, he found an escape from the media and celebrity-fueled world he was forced to live in for his art. The anger toward his father, the anger toward the media, and the pain of losing his mother, all stilled when he was with Mia. By finding each other, they had both found the missing pieces in their own jigsaws.

CHAPTER 24

Her shoulders gave a loud creak as she stretched her arms above her head with lethargy. The afternoon had been long and tiresome. Mia had found herself growing weary in the sunlight-deprived room full of buzzing electronic equipment and fluorescent lights as the afternoon had worn on.

Her ears were ringing from hearing the same beat over and over again. Although she admired the thoroughness of her producers, their need for repeatedly checking the same song bordered on obsessive-compulsive disorder.

Mia wondered how she would feel if this were her own album that she was working on. Would she feel tired of hearing her own song played repeatedly through the studio speakers?

However wonderful a song could sound—and she knew the adrenaline-fueled feeling that rose whenever she heard an incredible song—even the most patient of souls could grow tired of hearing that same song forty or fifty times in one afternoon.

Chad yawned loudly in the seat next to her and TJ rubbed his weary eyes with the back of his hand. His eyes were still riveted on the laptop screen in front of him and his head bobbed along to the beat he was hearing through his oversized headphones.

Mia was sure those headphones cost several hundred dollars. She gingerly lifted them over her head whenever she was required to use them, paranoid they were about to snap in half on the headband.

"Man, we done yet?" Chad groaned.

Suppressing a chuckle, she realised that even the experts had long days.

The news was a relief. She was beginning to wonder if she

was cut out for the job, even though she knew in her heart of hearts she loved the place. Some days were more testing than others were. Today had been one of those days.

"Yeah, dude, almost." TJ yanked one headphone away from his ear to reply before snapping then back into place. His eyes never left the screen.

Chad leaned back in his chair and began to gently spin it from side to side with his foot. "You coming to the show tonight?" he asked with his head lolled back.

"What show?" Mia asked curiously.

"Joel's show. He's performing on that TV show and a bunch of us are going along to watch."

She frowned. Joel hadn't mentioned anything about a TV show appearance. She wondered why he had invited others from the studio and not her.

"Dude," Chad reached across to TJ and yanked the sleeve of his T-shirt to get his attention.

TJ scowled as he turned in his seat and lifted his headphone again. "What?"

"What's that TV show that Joel's playing on tonight?"

"Chad!" TJ exclaimed and thrust his hands in the air before pointing at Mia.

"What?" Chad's face furrowed as he clearly struggled to understand what TJ was suddenly so wound up about.

TJ thrust his thumb towards her again. "You weren't supposed to say anything!" he snapped before landing a heavy punch on Chad's bicep.

Chad yelped loudly the moment TJ's fist connected with his arm, making Mia wince. Her pity for him dissipated as soon as she realised what TJ had said.

They weren't supposed to say anything. To her.

She wondered why Joel wouldn't want her to know. If he were appearing on a national television show, he would be hard to miss. He hadn't mentioned anything to her either.

Although the situation with his dad had been playing on his mind a lot recently, Mia was sure that wasn't the explanation for him not telling her.

TJ was shaking his head in frustration as he continued with his work at the computer while Chad was rubbing his arm with a sullen look on his face.

Suddenly hurt that the colleagues she had grown to befriend and trust had kept secrets from her on Joel's behalf, Mia had a sudden need to be out of the room. And out of the studio. She wondered if Charlie and Josh were going to the performance tonight.

Angrily slamming her things into her bag, she jumped up from her seat. "See you later," she muttered before heading out of the room and giving the door a loud slam behind her.

Thankfully, Charlie wasn't at her desk as she stomped across the foyer.

Unnoticed, she slipped out of the studio and marched across the car park and over the crossing before disappearing into the pedestrian traffic of downtown Los Angeles.

ΩΩΩ

The television irritated her.

Only ten minutes of TV had played before she hit the standby button and tossed the remote across the room. It hit the wall with a loud clatter as the back fell off on impact and the batteries scattered across the floor.

Mia shrugged. She would pick it up when she was in a better mood.

Her guitar stared longingly at her from beside the door where she had dumped it upon entering her hotel room. It called out to her, it longed for her. She longed to hold the instrument in her hands and run her fingers across the strings, to extract the rhythms from within which she commanded.

Feeling the familiar ache in her soul and the twitching of her fingers, she got up from her haphazardly jumbled pillows and duvet to retrieve her instrument.

As her fingers curled around the neck of her guitar, a knocking sounded at her door. There was no need to look through the peephole, as she knew who would be standing on the other side.

Joel's voice sounded from the other side of the door. "Mia, open up."

She scowled and folded her arms across her chest. Although she knew he couldn't see her, she felt the action was necessary.

"Mia, I know you can hear me." Joel continued knocking. "Mia, open the door."

Hearing his beautiful voice calling out to her made her heart stir and she hesitated. Her heart immediately disregarded the need for her guitar. A greater need was standing inches away from her behind the door.

Traitorous heart, she thought as her fingers loosened on the guitar's neck and reached out for the door handle.

"Mia?" Joel's hand rapped against the wood.

Her fingers curled around the cool metal and she unlocked the door. As she knew he would be, Joel was standing with one arm propped above his head against the doorframe. His other hand was raised and curled into a fist, ready to knock again on the door. He lowered it as he saw the door move open a fraction. She peered around the corner of the door, but refused to open it farther.

His face contorted into a mixture of puzzlement and sadness. "Mia, what's going on?"

"Don't you have a TV show to be at?" she asked.

The show started soon. He really should have been at the studio.

"Yeah." He frowned at the ringing phone that was illuminated in his pocket.

Mia could see the faint glow of the screen shining through the denim of his jeans, reminding him that he had somewhere else to be.

Joel held out his hand to her. "Listen, I need you to let me explain."

Mia knew he was being honest, sincere even. She could see it in his features. A man tired of having to prove himself to the world was, once again, having to prove himself.

Letting go of the door she took his hand. His long, soft fingers curled around hers and he brought her hand to his chest. She felt the warmth of his body and the tautness of his muscles under the fabric beneath her fingers.

He let out a relieved exhale. "Mia, tonight was meant to be a surprise."

Her own exhale sounded just as shaky as his did. She had overreacted—again—she knew she had.

But she had gone on her gut instinct. A lifetime spent trying to trust people, and failing, had her instincts honed to the automatic negative in any situation.

Instead of asking Joel, she had done what she always did—run. She had left the situation. Mia had wrongly assumed her friends had deceived her and Joel also, when all she had to do was ask. If she had asked, she would have found out.

Though she hadn't known Joel long, she still felt a deep, soulful connection with him. A connection she didn't feel with anyone else. They were two kindred spirits. They understood one another. They both felt and thought the same. If she could rewind time, she would have left the studio, gone to the one beside hers, and simply asked.

"Tonight was meant to be a surprise for you. Chad messed up."

Joel's face cracked a wry smile and she couldn't help let out the giggle within as she pictured his goofy face.

"I'm sorry," she whispered and stepped toward him.

He let go of her hand, slid his own around her waist, and pulled her body against his. She felt his lips in her hair as he kissed her head before pulling back to look at her.

He brought his lips down to hers and she felt her lips mold against the softness of his mouth. Joel tightened his embrace around her body as he kissed her deeper.

Mia's arms ran up his chest and around his neck. Her hands teased through the deliciously thick hair on his head, the hair that always looked so good. That beautiful rock star, bedhead black hair was tousling between her fingers as she kissed her beautiful rock star boyfriend.

His lips lingered on hers lip for a second before he pulled away from her and she could hear his breathing was fast and heavy. It tickled against her face as he rested his forehead on hers.

In those familiar eyes, she saw a calming serenity in the endless black depths that stared back at her.

Joel eyed her with a loving smile before speaking. "I was going to ask you to come tonight, but it was a surprise. The song I'm playing is new. I've never played it before."

Mia closed her eyes and inhaled deeply. "I'm sorry. I overreacted." The familiar scent of Joel filled her lungs and nose. The smell of his aftershave made her want to bury her face in his neck and breathe him in. Reluctantly she opened her eyes.

"It's fine," he said, smiling down at her. "I don't blame you. I know how it must have looked."

She wryly smiled before staring at the floor. Her socked feet were nestled between Joel's distressed boots. His black jeans were tucked into the tops and she realised then that he was wearing a different outfit from when she had seen him earlier that day.

The crisp, white T-shirt that covered his sculpted body was worn with a denim shirt thrown over the top and the sleeves rolled up to the elbows. Mia cast a swift glance over the tattooed forearms that bulged from underneath the sleeves of the denim shirt.

A low chuckle escaped Joel's chest and her eyes flitted up to see that he was watching her eyeing his body again. She gave an embarrassed laugh and then buried her face in his chest. Joel wrapped his arms around her back and pulled her body tight against his. Mia felt comfortable in his arms. Nestled against him, she felt content.

She had no desire to be anywhere else on earth other than in the arms of this beautiful man. As she inhaled his intoxicating scent, she slid her hands underneath his denim shirt to the fitted cotton of his T-shirt.

Joel's chest rumbled with a soft chuckle again before he kissed the top of her head and brought his lips to her ear. "So do you want to come and see me perform tonight?" he whispered.

She heard the hesitancy in his voice again. A man like Joel Coben had no reason on earth to be nervous, but Mia seemed to make him act that way.

"I'd love to," she said into his chest.

He began to laugh. "You sure?"

"Mmm-hmm," she mumbled before prising herself away from him.

"Come on then." Joel motioned to leave and went to grab her hand.

"Whoa, hang on." Mia jumped back. "At least let me get changed."

After giving a dramatic roll of his eye, he laughed at her.

౭ఌ౭ఌ

Despite Joel being adamant that she didn't need to change, Mia still swapped the clothes she had been wearing at the studio all day for a different pair of jeans and a prettier top. He had to admit that she was the fastest girl ever to get ready as she had ran around her hotel room changing her clothes, spraying perfume, and adjusting her makeup.

Soon she was nestled in the crook of his arm in the back of a large, blacked-out limo with his driver and manager in the front.

Joel's manager, Lyle, reminded her of a dressed-down Jackson. The label definitely had a prototype for their employee bigshots.

Lyle had a slightly friendlier appeal than Jackson, though. She got the impression he could break the professional boundaries when he wanted to. Mia would have loved to have seen Joel and Lyle backstage together on his tour.

"Guys, we're here," he called over his shoulder to them.

Swarms of fans began to press around the slowing vehicle. Mia tensed and sat upright as the fans pressed their faces against the glass to get a glimpse of their idol.

"Relax." Joel's hand pushed her back down into her seat. "The windows are fully tinted. They can't see a thing."

Joel sat back in his seat, looking completely at ease. No one would have guessed he was about to perform on national television to an audience of millions. As a performer, the thought made Mia's stomach begin to twist. She had played to a few hundred people before, not millions.

"How do you do it?" she asked, looking up to see him watching her.

Joel also wasn't paying a blind bit of notice to the swarms of people outside the car. He frowned. "Do what?"

"Perform on TV, knowing millions of people are watching you?"

He gave her a comical roll of his eyes, "Well, miss reporter, since you asked—"

Mia playfully elbowed him in the ribs. She knew Joel must have tired of hearing the same questions, but she was curious.

Joel squirmed at the ribbing and laughed before continuing. "I don't see it any differently. Millions of people can come and watch my shows, they can watch my videos on the music channels or the internet, and I don't see how this should be any different."

Mia pursed her lips and raised her eyebrows as she mused over his answer.

"Think of it like a music video." He cocked an eyebrow at her and she fixed on his exquisite dark eyes and the lashes that framed them. He grinned. "There's a camera, a bit of an audience, and you're just standing there playing your guitar and singing. It's no different."

She laughed at how simple he made the performance sound. "Okay, if you say so."

Joel grinned in triumph and pulled her body against his, pressing his lips to hers in the comfort of their embrace.

"Um...guys?" The voice in the front of the car sounded far and distant as they melded their lips together, blissfully ignoring the hundreds of people outside their window.

"Joel, time to go!" Lyle called out and she felt Joel's hand leave her body.

She cracked open an eye to see Joel holding a finger up to him, indicating one minute.

She let out a giggle and reluctantly broke apart from Joel.

Lyle sighed and rolled his eyes. Mia giggled again as Joel trailed kisses along her cheek and down her neck.

Lyle sighed and she noticed he was trying to suppress a smile himself. "Whenever you're ready, Joel."

Untangling himself from Mia, Joel took tight hold of her hand as he prepared to step out of the car and into the swarms of people waiting outside the television studios.

"Umm...Joel." Lyle hesitated. "Are you sure you want to..." He motioned to Joel clasping her hand tightly in his lap.

Mia knew what he meant. He was asking Joel if he wanted to be publically photographed with her, if he wanted his fans to see him with her. There were hundreds of girls waiting outside the car for their heartthrob idol to appear and they were about to see him emerge with a woman on his arm.

Though he was frequently thrown together with women in the press, rarely did they photograph him with anyone. Joel would be declaring to the world that he had a girlfriend.

The press would go crazy. Mia's face would be front-page news the next day and all over the gossip magazines for the next few weeks. Paparazzi would begin following her, they would start looking into her past and trying to find out who she was.

She swallowed a lump in her throat, hard.

Joel was not the only one about to take a huge leap of faith.

He was staring back at Lyle, his gaze fixed and determined. Mia knew that gaze was unrelenting. It was fierce and unmoving. From the look on Lyle's face, he knew the expression as well.

"Yes." The word sounded firm and clear. His eyes spoke dozens of things that his lips didn't. His hand tightened around hers and both she and Lyle understood.

It was time. The world was about to see Mia as Joel Coben's girlfriend.

He took one final, firm, reassuring glance at her before the door opened. She knew what his eyes were saying—*Let's do this*. Together, they would face the world. Together they would take that huge leap of faith.

The security guard slid open the car door and the noise outside of their little cocoon was deafening. As soon as the door was open, the crowd of waiting fans began to scream and cheer for Joel.

Mia wanted to slam the door shut, turn the car around, and head back to the quiet of her hotel room with him.

Joel's head went down as he ducked out of the car. He stood with his back to the crowd, his hand still gripped around hers, as he helped her climb out of the large car.

His free hand went protectively on the small of Mia's back as she climbed out. She knew he was protecting her from the crowd they were about to face together.

"JOEL!" was all she could hear from every direction.

Hundreds of girls, teenagers and women, cried out his name as they saw their idol emerge from the car.

Mia felt dizzy in the swarm of people who all called out his name. Others called out anything they could to get his attention. She saw Joel's mask was still in place. He was ready to defend against anything that came their way.

Dozens of hands reached out between the security guards and the small metal barriers that formed their way toward the studio's rear entrance. All were desperate to grab hold of the man holding Mia's hand. She felt her own fingers tighten on Joel's hand.

She hadn't been ready for this. This was one side of fame she hadn't been prepared for.

The screams and calls intensified, women cried out and wailed. Hands flung out and snatched wildly in a bid to grab a piece of their idol. Camera's flashed and cell phones reached into the air. She could hear the incessant clicking noise as hundreds of phones and cameras caught their every move.

"Joel, I love you!"

"Joel Coben! Oh my God!"

"It's him! He's here!"

"I think I'm going to faint!"

"Joel, marry me!"

Though she tried to take in as many of the shouts as she could, they began to merge in the deafening noise of the crowd. Mia understood why Joel spent so much of his time away from the press and the crowds that came with fame. The noise and the intensity was overwhelming.

Paparazzi were nestled among the waiting fans and their large flashbulbs went off in every direction she looked. They had their shot. Mia knew her face would be paraded on every magazine as the mysterious girl arriving with Joel Coben.

Joel began to sign a few autographs along the way politely smiling and greeting his waiting fans. His hand never let go of Mia's. He took the pen and scrawled on whatever his fans thrust in front of him.

"Who's she?"

"Who are you?"

"What are you doing with Joel?"

"You can't have him!"

The fans calls began to get more invasive, as more and more of them registered that Mia was standing hand in hand with Joel.

Each time she gave as a polite smile as she could manage before turning away. She didn't want to say anything. This was Joel's moment. It was not her place to say why she was with him. That was down to Joel and his management. She didn't want to jeopardise her position at Sixth String Studios by lashing out at some over jealous fan just to admit she was Joel's girlfriend.

Besides, she thought, as one overly enthusiastic fan reached over and planted a kiss on his cheek, *we haven't confirmed with each other what we are, let alone to the press.*

Mia didn't know if that was a conversation they needed to have, or was that something that just happened. Did you just casually ask your globally successful rock star if you were his girlfriend?

A cluster of paparazzi were waiting by the studio door behind several more security guards as Mia and Joel approached the end of the queues of waiting fans.

They furiously began snapping away on their cameras as she and Joel reached the doors. A crewmember wearing a headset was waiting by the studio door, ready to take them to the set.

Surprising Mia, Joel stopped in his tracks and pulled her into his side to pose for the gathered paparazzi. She tried to look relaxed as he held her, showing the world they were together. The paparazzi called out and shouted as they snapped away, the dollars were clearly glinting in their eyes as they photographed the new couple before them.

Joel wasn't the type to profess to the media about his relationships. He kept as much as he could under lock and key. For him to openly pose with Mia by his side was a huge statement. There was too much happening in such a short space of time. She tried to take everything in as her eyes were blinded by flashbulbs.

After a few seconds in the spotlight, Joel took her hand again and started to pull her with him into the waiting studio door.

"Joel!" paparazzi called out as they went to leave.

"Joel, who's this hottie? Is she your girlfriend?"

His face smirked into a knowing smile, he turned and quipped to the paparazzi, "Yeah, she is," before disappearing into the open doorway.

The door slammed shut behind them as the noise of calls, shouts, and flashbulbs intensified at Joel's admission.

Mia stared open-mouthed after him as he followed the crewmember down a corridor to his dressing room.

People were milling around all over the studio. There was a hub of noise and energy in the air as the busy studio went about its routine.

Several people stopped and stared as Joel passed by them down the corridor. She still felt like her mouth was hanging agape as she followed behind him. Joel chatted politely to the young man, who looked no older than eighteen, as he led them to his dressing room.

"Here's your dressing room. You're on in thirty minutes. I'll call back for you in twenty." He glanced down at the clipboard in his hand before scooting away again.

Over her shoulder, she saw Lyle deep in conversation with another production assistant farther along the corridor.

Joel, however, was already tugging her into the dressing room and closing the door behind her.

As soon as the door clicked into place behind them, he pulled her by the hand until she gently bumped into his body, and he wrapped his arms around her.

Mia still felt dazed as she stared up at the now gleaming dark eyes above her.

Joel brought his face down within millimeters of hers.

"I can't believe you just did that," she said, shaking her head.

Joel chuckled as he placed a kiss on her lips. "Why?"

Mia's eyes were instantly filled with nearly black ones as his were level with hers. "Because…" she started, unsure how to finish her sentence.

"Because I just told the world you're my girlfriend?" He raised an eyebrow at her and she could see the humor dancing in his usually still eyes.

She swallowed. "Yes."

"Well." He closed his eyes for a second before he looked back into hers. "You are—aren't you?"

The hesitancy was there again. He was still playful, which was also unusual for Joel, but there was a trace of hesitation as he awaited her answer.

Knowing what she needed to do, she brought her hands to his cheeks and cupped them with her palms. His eyes flitted to her hands before returning to her gaze. Mia reached up and, closing her eyes, brought her hands toward her and kissed Joel's lips. Throwing every ounce of her passion and belief into her kiss, she held him in place. She could feel his body weaken against hers, his hands around her waist and his hard chest against her own. She felt his lips against hers and the softness of his breath as their lips parted. Heat radiated from his body against her skin. She felt the movement of his jaw against her palms and the urgency in his kiss.

Mia pulled away from Joel and he let out a gasp.

"Yes," she breathed.

His face creased into the most heartfelt, relieved smile she could imagine. Her own heart swelled as she realised she was the reason for the cracking of the hard shell on his exterior. She was the reason he was breaking out his show-stopping smile for the world again.

Joel closed his sparkling eyes. His lips were on her mouth again, his hands tightly holding her body to him, as if he were afraid she would leave at any moment.

"Knock, knock," a chirpy voice called out before swinging the door wide open.

They parted for only a second before Josh swaggered into the room, his eyes gleaming with mischievousness.

"*Heyyyy*," he called out and winked when he saw them still in each other's arms. "How's it going, bro?"

A lean, tanned arm shoved him out of the way as Charlie bounded into the room.

"Mia!" she squealed before dashing over and prising her away from Joel and into her own arms. "How excited are you for the show?"

"Erm…yeah, it should be great." Mia realised she hadn't given the show much thought after they had left the comfort of their car.

"Everyone's here to see it." Charlie stepped back so she could see TJ, Chad, Ruben, Lyle, and even Jackson step into the room.

"Hey, Mia," TJ called out and lifted his hand in a wave.

Chad sheepishly waved before ducking out of the way, making her giggle.

Ruben slipped into the room, smiled at her, and nodded before making his way over to Joel.

Jackson was typing away on his cell phone as he followed the group into the room. He looked up from his Blackberry as he nearly walked into her.

"Mia, how are you?" Holding out a hand, he then gripped hers in his firm, familiar handshake before clapping her on the back in addition to his professional greeting.

She returned his warm, friendly smile. "Great, thanks. You?"

"Fantastic. Well done again with the Glasshearts' track. 'Hear Me' went down in an absolute storm." His face lit up as he spoke about the track.

It had recently shot to number one in the charts. After meeting the band, Mia wasn't as elated about the news as she should have been.

"Yeah, I'm really pleased with that. I'm so glad they liked it."

"You have a very special gift, Mia." Jackson turned serious. "And you're a very beautiful girl, too. It's a shame to have you locked away working as a songwriter. We need to talk. I've been meaning to discuss things with you for a while now. We'll talk on Monday at the studios."

She stared wide-eyed at him as he pointed to the space in his calendar on his phone.

"Sure—of course," was all she managed.

This evening really was full of surprises. That little piece of information was more than Mia had bargained for. She had already been scheduled for a meeting with Jackson, but that little extra bit of information made her thoughts run wild. Was he really talking about extending her future at Sixth String Studios? Could she be about to be signed to the label?

Her head swam at the thought. She really needed to talk to Joel. Or Charlie. Or Niamh. She needed to share her excitement with someone.

At that moment, someone scooped her up by her knees, threw her over a shoulder, and twirled her around in circles. She let out a scream as she was grabbed, being completely caught off guard.

Straight away, she knew who had picked her up. No one else in the room would be so brazen. Well, apart from Joel, but only if they were alone.

"Josh!" she squealed, "put me down!"

He laughed as he spun her even faster and she heard Charlie cackle loudly.

As the room turned, Mia caught a glimpse of Joel who was laughing, along with Ruben at his side.

"Josh!" Mia wriggled in his firm hold and, eventually, the room slowed its spinning and gradually came to a stop.

He lifted Mia from his shoulder, plonked her down in front of him, and clapped his hand on her shoulder. "How ya doin?"

"Fine," she mumbled as she clutched her still-spinning head.

Josh laughed loudly with the rest of the room before pulling her in for a hug.

Glad for something stable to hold onto, she hugged him back. As unpredictable as he could be, Josh was harmless. He was also a lot of fun. And very cute.

"Joel," a voice called out from the doorway and the room turned to look at who was standing there. "It's time to go." The young assistant had returned, as promised, to collect Joel for his performance.

Stealing her away from his brother, Joel grabbed her hand and pulled her with him as they left the room. Mia heard numerous footsteps behind them and knew the rest of their group was following them.

She could also hear Charlie's laughter echo down the corridor from behind them and knew Josh was up to his usual tricks.

"Through here, Joel." The assistant motioned through a doorway to a backstage area where yet more people were milling around.

A makeup artist appeared in front of them at the assistant's cue and motioned for Joel to follow her to a table waiting nearby.

"My name's Kayley and I'll be getting you ready for your performance," the bubbly blonde said, introducing herself, and held out a manicured hand to Joel.

He politely shook her hand. Mia noticed the girl's hand was trembling slightly as she introduced herself and forced herself not to roll her eyes. Joel obviously had that effect on women.

"I don't think we need to do that much to you," Kayley hinted as she assessed his face.

"Thanks." Joel cocked a lopsided grin at her, making her giggle shrilly.

Mia knew he was being sarcastic but Kayley had mistaken it for flirting. She turned away while Kayley applied a few touches to his already perfect face.

Charlie was brimming with excitement as she grabbed Mia's arm. "Are you coming to the after party?"

Tonight her hair was styled in its usual quiff, but somehow it appeared more flicked out. Her eyes were highlighted with sparkling, electric blue shadow and her eyelashes were so long they appeared to touch her eyebrows.

Mia wondered why she couldn't look more like her super-confident friend. Charlie could pull off anything. She just had a knack for throwing together an outfit and looking like she had strolled off the runway.

She was wearing a tight, white, vest like dress that highlighted her mixed ethnic skin coloring and her toned body, with sky-scraper heels. Josh's eyes were roving over her as if she were a four-course meal.

"What after party?" Mia asked, while giving Josh a scowl for unashamedly eyeing up her friend.

Charlie danced up and down on the spot at the anticipation of the night ahead. "It's at this house in the Hills. The studio has laid it on. They own the place."

"I had no idea." Mia shrugged. "Sounds great."

As Charlie squealed with glee, Mia laughed at her excitement. Lyle was standing nearby and rolled his eyes. Mia caught his eye and threw him a smile.

Another assistant appeared beside Joel and was motioning for him to head to the stage. "Okay, we're ready to go." he scowled at Joel's assembled entourage. "You guys need to stay quite at the sides, if you're watching, okay?"

Everyone around Mia nodded and mumbled their assurances before he was led away toward the stage.

They all heard the noise from the studio as they entered another room. The large, black backdrop announced they were behind the live set and were to be silent at all times.

Lights and cameras were rigged everywhere they turned and Mia could hear the show's host announce that after the break. Joel would be performing his new single. The crowd went wild with applause before the studio lights returned to normal, signaling they were no longer on air.

Joel was ushered to the side of the stage where the host was having her makeup tweaked by an assistant.

Kelly held out her hand to him. "Joel, nice to see you again."

He nodded. "Pleased to be here."

"We're so thrilled to have you. We can't wait to hear the new song. I know it's going to be great." She gave him the thumbs up, before clacking her heels across her studio to be back in place after the commercial break.

"Time to get into place Joel." The assistant gestured at the stage where a lone microphone stand and a stool were set up.

"Sure. One minute." Joel held up a finger again and Mia suppressed a giggle at her earlier memories of him doing the same.

He took her hands and pulled her toward him, sliding his hands around her waist, he then stooped to meet her eyes.

"This—" Joel glanced around the room. "—isn't the surprise I was talking about."

"The after party?" she asked.

He cocked an eyebrow at Mia and she laughed, knowing that wasn't his style.

"*This*—" He nodded to the stage. "—is your surprise."

She frowned at the stage and back at Joel.

"The song I'm about to sing is for you. I wrote this song for you. It's about you, about us." He closed his dark eyes and kissed her lips.

Still in shock, Mia quickly closed her eyes and kissed him back before their moment was gone. The countdown to the return to air had started and Joel was being beckoned away from her.

"I hope you like it." He squeezed her hand before letting go and walking across to the stage where an assistant was waiting with his guitar.

Mia was ushered back to where Charlie, Josh, and the rest of their party were waiting in the shadows of the stage for Joel's performance to start.

Nervously, she fidgeted with the silver guitar pendant around her neck, running it from side to side on its chain as the host, Kelly, chatted to her final guest before Joel performed.

Joel was sitting on his stool, checking the tuning of his guitar while he waited.

Every few moments, he would cast his eyes over to where Mia was standing, as if checking that she was still there.

Coffee with Kelly had been a popular daytime television chat show until recently, when the show had grown so much in popularity that Kelly had been given a prime time evening spot.

Mia could see why.

Kelly was chatty, friendly, and down to earth. She also gossiped like the best of them. It was easy to see how the celebrities just opened up to her. It really was like having a cup of coffee with your friends and gossiping about the latest news.

The audience and their group laughed together when Kelly asked her final guest, a well-known kooky female artist, if she was dating at the moment. It was magazine gossip that the artist's sexuality was questionable.

But Kelly had a way of asking that was so unobtrusive, it was as if you were gossiping over coffee with your girlfriends, not being interviewed in front of the nation. Hence the show's title, *Coffee with Kelly*.

Mia wondered idly if they could persuade Kelly to join their after party. She seemed like she would be a lot of fun. And, for once, Kelly didn't bat her eyelashes or quiver her manicured nails at Joel whenever she was near him. She treated him like a regular person.

"Now, ladies." Kelly turned to the audience, who had already begun the hysterical screams. "We have a special performance for you tonight…"

She let the words hang suggestively in the air, which made the women in the audience shriek louder.

"To play us out tonight with his brand new single *Chasing Shadows*, please give a warm, estrogen-fueled welcome back to the stage for Joel Coben!"

The crowd went into overdrive as the lights went down and a spotlight appeared on Joel. Mia giggled along with them at Kelly's introduction before realising what the title of the song was.

"Chasing Shadows."

Joel had said the song was about her, about them. Those were the words he had used when describing how Mia felt when she had told him about the memories of her brother.

She wondered if her worst nightmare was about to come true.

Was he about to publically display her turbulent, disturbed family history to the world through his new single? He had just announced to the paparazzi that Mia was his girlfriend. It wouldn't take a genius to put the two together.

But Joel had begun to play and Mia had to turn off her thoughts and listen to the song that was beginning for a multi-million viewer audience.

He was seated on a stool in the middle of an empty stage. A single spotlight lit up his face and his guitar, where a quiet, soulful sound emitted. The delicate sound of a few simple bars of music sounded before the song began. Joel had his head down and was focussing on his guitar. As he raised his head to the microphone, his eyes appeared to be anywhere but on that stage.

The image was haunting.

> "You'll never know how many times
> I've stayed awake each long night…"

His deep, gravelly voice echoed hauntingly around the studio. Mia was enraptured. Her eyes were riveted to the stage.

Joel began to reach the chorus of the song and she felt her

nails dig into her palms, she was about to find out if the song was about her, one way or the other.

> "I'm only chasing shadows,
> Still picturing you near.
> I'm just chasing shadows,
> Just wishing you were here."

Mia felt her body relax as the chorus faded into the second verse. The song was about her. But not in a way that the rest of the world would understand.

To anyone listening, the song sounded like it was about a lost lover. But like always, she heard the song the way it was meant to be heard, for her. The song was about her brother, Luke. It was about how much she was hurting over not knowing what had become of him. It was also Joel's way of telling her he understood and that he was going to be there for her.

A tear escaped down her cheek, quickly followed by another, as she listened to the rest of the song.

When Joel reached the final verse, she felt her tears running freely down her face and landing on her chest. Charlie stepped closer to her side and wrapped her arm around Mia's shoulders. Mia leaned into her as she watched Joel play out the final lines of the song.

> "What kills me deep inside
> Is not knowing if we'll survive.
> I need to know where we stand,
> If we're gonna make it through.
> How can I live without you?
>
> "I'm only chasing shadows,
> Still picturing you near.
> I'm just chasing shadows,
> Just wishing you were here.
>
> "Just wishing you were here..."

The final note faded away into the studio and the crowd erupted into applause and carried on cheering after the *On Air* sign had been turned off. Mia kept her eyes focussed on Joel. He stood up from his stool, his eyes cast down as he shook hands again with Kelly and she walked with him to the edge of the stage.

"...incredible. Just beautiful, thank you so much for performing," Kelly added before walking away.

Feeling the slight dampness in her hair, Mia knew Charlie had been crying too. Charlie's arm dropped from Mia's shoulder as Joel approached and she tiptoed away toward Josh to allow them some privacy.

Joel's shoulders were hunched and his head was bowed as he approached her.

Doubt again, Mia thought.

He cast a nervous glance at the people lingering nearby before stopping just out of her reach. As he looked through his long eyelashes at her, he shoved his hands in the pockets of his jeans. "So, what did you think?" His lip was curled in his lopsided smile again but Mia noticed it didn't quite reach his eyes the way it usually did.

She stepped forward, closing the distance between them, and, as before, she reiterated her point by taking Joel's cheeks in her hands and pulling his face down to hers. He exhaled heavily against her lips in relief as he clasped her body against him. Mia giggled beneath his mouth, astounded that a worldwide rock star could be so nervous about such an incredible song. "It truly was beautiful."

"You liked it then?" he whispered against her lips.

A loud wolf whistle echoed from somewhere in the audience as they broke apart.

"I can see another Grammy glistening away on your mantelpiece," she teased and Joel shook his head, his smile finally reaching the corners of his eyes for a moment before they closed and his lips molded against Mia's.

CHAPTER 25

L isten." Joel looped his arm around her waist and whispered in her ear. "I've got an interview to do after the show. Do you want to head on over to the party with Josh and Char-lie and I'll meet you there?"

"I don't mind waiting," Mia answered.

"It's okay. I don't want you hanging around while the press is here. They'll bombard you with questions after what I said to-night."

Laughing as she remembered Joel's admittance in front of a swarm of paparazzi, she replied, "Okay, fair enough. I'll go with them and meet you there."

They walked to the end of the corridor where his dressing room door was open and Mia could see Lyle talking to a young man wearing a suit and carrying a tape recorder—a journalist.

"I'll be as quick as I can." Joel pulled her into him for one last, lingering kiss before reluctantly letting her go.

Over Joel's shoulder, she saw a journalist eyeing them togeth-er. He was missing a prime photo opportunity. The snap he could be getting could snare him thousands and he had to let it go since Lyle stared him down as he watched them.

She giggled against Joel's lips. "We have an audience."

He sighed and turned to look at the journalist with his media ready eyes back in place. She knew the journalist wouldn't be getting the scoop he was hoping for tonight. Though he was wit-nessing front-page news, he was made to stand by and watch as Lyle instructed "off the record," at him several times.

Mia could sense Lyle was getting irate. She knew it was time to go. She had to let Joel face the media. *One of the very few downsides to having a rock star boyfriend*, she thought.

"Joel," another voice shouted from down the corridor.

Still in his arms, she turned to see Josh standing with the exit door wide open and Charlie peering through at his side.

"Come on, man," he teased, "you'll see her in an hour."

"Mia, come on, you have got to come and see this house. It sounds amazing!" Charlie called.

"All right." Joel sighed and she could see in his eyes he really wanted to close the dressing room door and walk out of the exit door with her and his friends.

He winked as he finally let her go. "You'll have to do this one day."

She laughed. "We'll see."

It was Saturday night. Monday was the day of her meeting with Jackson, and Mia was terrified. She was glad she had the house party with her Los Angeles friends and Joel to enjoy tonight before she had to face reality on Monday.

The events of yesterday morning had quickly reached the press and were splashed all over the morning newspapers. Undoubtedly, the journalist in Joel's dressing room was waiting with a few questions to ask about his father.

Mia hoped Lyle had given him a list of off-the-agenda subjects.

"I'll see you soon." He squeezed her hand one final time before heading into the dressing room and closing the door.

With reluctance at leaving him, she turned to her friends who were still waiting by the exit door.

"How are you doing?" she asked Josh once they were out of the building.

Josh had arrived at the house shortly after the police had left that night. He was furious and wanted to press charges, but Joel wouldn't let him. His father had been free to go, something which Mia and Josh weren't happy about.

Josh was naturally angry with his father and frustrated he wasn't there to help Joel.

"I'm good." Josh grinned down at her, his infectious smile lighting up his face.

Mia knew he was shrugging off the drama, which was his way of coping. She loved his cheeky, outgoing personality.

It was like watching a younger version of Joel permanently

acting out the side that only she got to see. Mia let it go. She knew Josh would still be mad and stewing over the event in his own way, but for now she was happy to be heading out for one final night of celebration with her friends before having to face reality on Monday morning.

If only Joel were coming with us straight away, she thought.

"The cars are just round here." Charlie pointed around the corner of the building in the direction TJ and Chad were heading with a group of people.

As they rounded the corner, Mia immediately heard the clicking of flashbulbs and shutter lenses.

"Joel! Joel!" they began calling out.

"Not quite." Josh admired the reception that was intended for his brother. Some of the paparazzi looked forlorn and dropped their cameras when they realised it was not him, while others continued to snap away.

Mia and Charlie looked at one another before rolling their eyes and giggling.

"Mia, how long have you and Joel been dating?"

"Is it true you fought with his dad?"

"Mia, what's it like being with Joel Coben?"

"Did you enjoy his performance tonight?"

Josh put his arms around both girls and ushered them through the swarming crowds of waiting paparazzi and toward the open door of the waiting limo.

Mia clambered inside after Charlie and, once Josh was inside, the car door was firmly slammed shut, sealing out the sounds of the ever-hounding paparazzi.

Josh winked as he clambered over the seat to sit beside Charlie. "Man, that never gets old."

"Yes, it does," Charlie elbowed him. "You're just showing off."

The car slowly tried to ease its way out of the assembled crowd of paparazzi and gathering fans and did a repetition of gas and break hopping, until it was clear of the studio grounds.

Neither the driver nor the passengers noticed the battered, old Hyundai pull out of the studio and follow the limo.

"This is going to be so good, I can't wait," Charlie was almost bouncing up and down in her seat beside Josh.

Mia was sitting on his other side and leaned forward to see her friend. "Where is it we're going?" she asked.

Charlie's blue, glitter-laden eyes sparkled under the passing streetlights as they fluttered up and down. "A house in the hills. It belongs to the studio and they've laid on an after party for everyone. It's huge. It's got fourteen bedrooms..."

She launched into a full explanation of every detail of the house as the car sped through the streets of Los Angeles toward the Hollywood Hills.

Every now and then Josh would throw a wicked smile in Mia's direction as Charlie nattered away about the house they were going to. Mia felt as though she didn't even need to visit the house. Charlie had practically described the entire property to her in the space of ten minutes. If ever Charlie was in need of a career change, Mia made a note to suggest being a real estate agent to her.

She wondered who else would be at the house party and secretly hoped that Glasshearts wouldn't be there.

Though she hadn't seen the band again since Adam had invaded her personal space in the studio foyer, she had no urge to see him again anytime soon, let alone at a house party. Mia doubted that being glued to Joel's side would deter a sleazebag like him.

"Who else is going to be there?" She tried to sound casual as she asked Charlie.

Josh groaned loudly as Charlie launched into a full rundown of the guest list for the party.

"Sometimes dating the girl, who knows everything about the studio, isn't such a good thing." Josh winked at Mia right before Charlie nudged him in the ribs again.

"Oww," he complained louder than necessary.

Mia could see the glint in his eyes as he complained in order to get some sympathy from Charlie. She laughed and shook her head as she turned to stare out of the window at the passing streets of Los Angeles.

"You all right, man?" Chad's voice suddenly quieted the car as he leaned forward to ask the driver.

"I think so." The driver frowned as he looked in his rear-view mirror at the traffic behind them.

"What's up?" Chad asked again.

Mia realised he had noticed the driver watching something in his mirror.

He scowled again at a car only he could see. "I think we're being followed by the press."

Chad turned around to look over his shoulder through the tinted glass to see the traffic behind them. He shrugged. "Nothing new there then."

"But Joel isn't with us," TJ pointed out.

"They might think he is," Charlie added, "or they know Mia's with us and they're hoping to beat him there."

"Guess so." Chad shrugged again and went back to flicking through the internet on his phone.

Mia resumed staring out of the window and watched as the limo zipped through a changing yellow light toward the other side of the road where she could see a bridge on the corner in the distance.

The sound of breaks screeching and several car horns blaring behind them made everyone in the car jump in their seats and turn around.

"Damn paparazzi in that old Hyundai again," the driver chuntered from the front seat.

Josh immediately froze beside her.

His eyes went wide and panic flooded his face. "Did you just say it's an old Hyundai that's been following us?" he asked leaning forward.

Mia pulled him back down by his shirt into his seat and into the safety of his seatbelt.

"Yeah, it's a real old one. Dark color, maybe blue or green I think." The driver frowned and the creases on his forehead multiplied as he did. "Why?"

"Shit," Josh turned to Mia, "Call Joel, right now. That's my dad—"

His sentence was cut short as a deafening bang rang through the car and it was slammed sideways off the road.

Everyone in the car screamed or yelled out in surprise as the car was jolted from the road and another vehicle crushed into the driver's side. Mia saw bodies slide from one side of the car straight into the other like dominoes as the car began to sway onto its side from the force of the impact.

"What the hell?"

"What's going on?"

"What the hell was that?"

"We've been hit by a car!"

Multiple voices all called out at the same time as they all slammed into one another with the jolt of the vehicle.

Then Mia heard the piercing sound of Charlie beginning to scream as the car began to list to one side and she realised the car was about to roll onto its roof.

Within seconds, everyone screamed as the car was flipped onto its roof and was suddenly rolling and bouncing across the road.

Metal crashed and banged as the car dented with every bounce across the road. Glass shattered and flew in every direction. She closed her eyes tightly and pulled her arm across her face in a shield as the window beside her shattered and exploded. Limbs flailed wildly and bodies slammed into each other as the car was tossed across the road like a tin can.

Mia felt the jolt of her seatbelt cut into her shoulder as she was forced forward and upward and Josh's body slammed into her side.

Bodies were quickly thrown in the opposite direction in a blurring mass of flailing limbs and shards of metal and glass as the car began to bounce back upright. Another loud crash from the side of the car suggested it had been slammed into again. Caught in the mid-motion of flying back onto its wheels, the car was quickly slammed again and began turning upside down once more. The jolt sent the car rolling back onto its roof and skittering farther across the road.

"*The bridge!*" she heard someone scream out from somewhere in the car.

But it was too late.

As the screaming increased tenfold and the crashing of metal and glass sounded deafeningly all around, the car was slammed into again and bounced once more before free falling over the edge of the bridge and into the darkness.

To be continued...

Read on for an exciting extract from
the conclusion in the Chasing Shadows series…

CHASING THE DREAM

CHAPTER 1

Beep.
Beep.
Beep.

That noise played on a never-ending loop in her mind. She was sure this was how supermarket checkout assistants felt when they tried to sleep at night.

Beep.

Beep.

Beep.

An infuriating light overhead flickered as she tried to open her eyes. Why was everything in this room so irritating? There was a sharp pain in her left hand, as if a splinter had been jarred there for days.

Beep.

Beep.

Beep.

What on earth was that infernal noise?

Someone really needed to change that light bulb, she thought as she squinted. All she was trying to do was get some sleep. There were parts of her body that ached, some more than others. Some parts she couldn't feel, which was disturbing. She tried to twitch her fingers, to wriggle her toes. But nothing. Maybe it was because she was so tired.

Days and nights had no significance in this place. Time was a never-ending entity. There was no concept of hours elapsing, minutes passing or seconds ticking. She thought back to another time in her life recently where she wished time could have stood still. She remembered being alone in a room, feeling very comfortable on a leather sofa, and also feeling very content. But that was all she remembered. She was getting sleepy again and the flickering light blurred out of focus as her eyelids closed.

છ∕◌∕৩

Beep.
Beep.
Beep.
She tried to open her eyes but they felt heavier than lead. She tried to move a hand to rub against her eyelids but that felt worse. A searing pain in her ribcage had forced her from her blissful slumber. Why was she feeling that sharp pang in her side? She wanted to cry out in agony but nothing would come from her throat. The pain forced her eyes open a fraction.

A face hovered over her. She couldn't tell who it was. They blurred in and out of focus. They turned and said something to someone else nearby, but she couldn't hear what they said. Their words were muffled as if someone were holding their hands over her ears.

Sleep reclaimed her soon enough and the mumbling disappeared.

છ∕◌∕৩

Beep.
Beep.
Beep.
She awoke sharply with the pain in her side. Her head felt dizzy and confused. She wanted to sit bolt upright and cry out but her body failed her. Still the light flickered on overhead. Didn't anyone ever turn that thing off? A face appeared over her own again. No features came into view. They spoke but their words were still muffled. Something told her there was feeling in her hand—someone was holding hers. Maybe it was the face she couldn't see. Exhausted, she closed her eyes again.

છ∕◌∕৩

Mumbling. Why was everyone always mumbling in this

place? Why couldn't she hear them properly? Their hushed voices saying words she couldn't understand kept rousing her from her sleep. It was happening more and more often. She knew that soon enough she would have to wake up and face the world.

Beep.

Beep.

Beep.

Faces. Another one was peering over her as she opened her eyes. She recognized this one. But she didn't know how. She knew it from somewhere but her sleep- addled memory failed her. She wanted to reach up and touch the features that were so close, but her body failed her again.

Who was that?

ფფ

Again. The face was there again.

There was something so familiar about it, but she just couldn't put her finger on it. Darkness.

That's what was recalling in her memory.

Darkness of the person's hair and features.

The hair was so very dark. And the eyes too.

Who was that?

ფფ

She was hearing things better. Finally, words were turning in-to sentences. She could hear them without having to open her eyes and struggle to make sense of what was happening.

"He's here?" a voice asked. Female, she decided.

"Yes," answered a male.

"Does she know?" asked the woman.

A sigh came from the man. "I don't think so."

ფფ

The face was there again. Why wouldn't it leave her alone? Every time she opened her eyes, it was there, peering over her.

Words were no problem to her now, but faces were still an is-sue. This one still wouldn't come.

So dark.

But so familiar.

ℰⱭℰⱭ

She smiled as she opened her eyes. Things were finally beginning to make sense now. She could hear clearly and the blurry outlines that were once people were beginning to become clearer.

"Mia?" a voice asked. "Can you hear me?"

She smiled as she recognized the voice. She opened her eyes and the outline steadily focussed into a familiar female face. The quiff of hair that was usually so quirkily styled looked ruffled. She smiled and the woman laughed.

"She knows!" she cried out.

Mia closed her eyes again to the sound of a low, male voice in the corner of the room.

"Hey, sweetie," a soft, familiar accent cooed in her ear.

The accent sounded different from all the others.

The sound of this voice made her think of green fields and gentle music.

Ireland. That's what the voice reminded her of.

"Niamh," she croaked. Her voice sounded horse and alien, as if unused for a long time.

"I'm right here, sweetie." Niamh's soft accent sounded close in her ear and a familiar hand curled around her own. "There's people waiting to see you," she whispered. "You can't sleep forever, you know?"

Mia felt her face crease into an unfamiliar smile. That was a sensation that felt alien too.

"There's my girl," Niamh's voice sang, "come on, sweetie, wake up. We all want to see you."

"I'm trying," Mia croaked.

Niamh sat with Mia for a long time, patiently talking to her as she tried to open her eyes. They closed again and she would try to open them again.

Eventually, she could hold them open and focus on the room around her. She was propped slightly upright in a hospital bed. The beeping noise was coming from the numerous machines that whirred beside her. The damned fluorescent bulb overhead was still flickering.

There was a long needle inserted deep into her left hand with a tube that ran to an IV drip beside her.

"How are you feeling?" Niamh asked as she handed her the paper cup of water from the nightstand.

"Like death," Mia croaked.

At those words, Niamh's eyes misted over and a tear quickly ran down her pale face.

Mia managed to squeeze her hand. *What had happened? It must have been bad.*

The door to the tiny hospital room cracked open and a figure stepped through it.

"No, no, no," Niamh called out. "Not yet!"

Darkness.

He was here.

The darkness she had been seeing. He was there, standing before her.

His dark hair, his dark eyes.

Everything about him seemed dark. And strange.

Who was he?

About the Author

Melissa Speight lives close to the historic city of York, in the United Kingdom, with her family. After studying for an honors degree in Journalism, she has since written three romance novels. Besides writing, Speight's main passions are travelling, adventure, running, yoga, and live music.

She is also an active supporter of cancer charities in the UK and, after conquering Mt. Kilimanjaro in Tanzania, she is planning her next fundraising challenges for charity.

Speight dedicates her literary career to the memory of her mum.